Donald

A Carpet
of
Purple Flowers

A Carpet
of
Purple Flowers

Tracey-anne McCartney

URBANE
Publications

urbanepublications.com

First published in Great Britain in 2015 by Urbane Publications Ltd
Suite 3, Brown Europe House, 33/34 Gleamingwood Drive, Chatham, Kent ME5 8RZ
Copyright © Tracey-anne McCartney, 2015

The moral right of Tracey-anne McCartney to be identified as the author of this work
has been asserted in accordance with the Copyright, Designs and Patents Act of 1988.

A CIP catalogue record for this book is available from the British Library.

ISBN 978-1-910692-21-9
EPUB 978-1-910692-22-6
KINDLE 978-1-910692-23-3

Design and Typeset by Julie Martin
Cover by Julie Martin
Printed and bound by CPI Group (UK) Ltd, Croydon, CR0 4YY

urbanepublications.com

The publisher supports the Forest Stewardship Council® (FSC®), the leading international forest-certification organisation.
This book is made from acid-free paper from an FSC®-certified provider. FSC is the only
forest-certification scheme supported by the leading environmental organisations, including Greenpeace.

Acknowledgements

Heartfelt gratitude to the world's storytellers and creatives.
Thank you for inspiring us with your magic.

Dedicated to the people that I love most in the universe ~ my family, fur babies, and friends.

My family:

Dad, you're an absolute star! How many times have you read this book? ;o)

Mum, thank you for supplying all the caffeine and for the late night chats.

Charlotte, for making me giggle through the tough times.

Travis, for keeping it real as always.

Lewis, for being my little ray of sunshine.

David, for putting up with me and my crazy nocturnal muse.

Thank you, I couldn't have made this journey without you. xoxo

Super-duper, mega appreciation for these early beta readers:

Vicki Sables ~ YOU have been totally amazing, thank you. Yes, you will get that signed book, and no, Danny Dyer will not be playing the part of Brandon. *Giggles* :o)

Lizzy Layden ~ Wow! You have been awesome, from trekking in Scotland, to film casting! We've covered it all. Thank you for your loving support.

Silvia Curry ~ Hugs for the incredible support and much appreciated feedback.

Cate Hogan ~ From the very first draft (bones) you lifted my spirits and gave me hope, thank you.

Collaboration at its best!

Matthew Smith ~ A BRIGHT STAR in the world of publishing. A tremendous thank you for believing in *'A Carpet of Purple Flowers'*. I'm extremely proud and humble to be a part of the talented and supportive 'Urbane Family'. Woohoo! To new beginnings!

'Keep your light bright'

~ Brother Paul, Grandad Tom, Nanny Ellen, Aunty Mary, Uncle Peter, and beautiful friend Anna.

Lifprasira

SIDHE SYMBOLS

A𝓮 B𝓲 C𝓭 D𝓾 E𝓮 F𝓵 G𝓸 H𝓿 I𝓹

J𝓸 K𝓼 L𝓲 M𝓿 N𝓸 O𝓯 P𝓲 Q𝓿

R≈ S𝓿 T: U𝓼 V𝓵 W𝓏 X𝓲 Y𝓵 Z⊙

0 ⊚ 1 ◠ 2 ↝ 3 𝓯 4 𝓼 5 𝓼 6 𝓮 7 ✶ 8 𝓯 9 𝓏

NOTE: Glyphs are designed to be written vertically from right to left

CHAPTER 1

Leave the Past Where It Belongs

*W*alls and shutters were scrawled with neon graffiti that blinded every time a car sped past. Bea averted her eyes from the glare, and heard a cab driver screaming at a drunk for throwing a beer can too close to his car. She watched it roll, rattling across the road, until disappearing into a pile of litter that lay by an over-turned bin. She rested her head against the frame of a bare window above the Victorian bookshop. Here, nothing surprised her, it was to be expected living in one of the worst parts of South London. Perhaps that's why she never truly felt like it was home. She wanted nothing more than to go to bed, crawl under the covers and settle down for the night with a mug of sweet tea and a good book, consolation for being stupid, too ready to please, as usual.

All day she'd mentally tormented herself for agreeing to attend Leanne's party, and now it was too late to cancel. She didn't want to see Brandon, her ex. The man she had successfully avoided for six months. *Damn him! Of course he'll show up. After all, he's the birthday girl's brother.* Bea sighed, and the closeness of her warm breath on the cold glass caused an area of the window to mist up. She ran her slender finger over the damp blur of condensation, producing a squeaking sound as she casually drew a large question mark. Bea stared at it for a moment, before rubbing it away with the palm of her hand. Her feet then slowly carried her down the hall, to her bedroom, where she sat down on the bed, deflated. She looked down at her clothes with a raised brow, unimpressed. As always, she found herself in a familiar safe zone, old River Island jeans, a gold jumper and flats. *Comfort every time.* Bea couldn't help but laugh at herself, *predictable me.* She shrugged, and reached for her cup, ready to gulp down the last dregs of remaining tea, when the mobile phone rang. The sound caused a rise of silent panic, which had originated from the bad feeling that'd stirred in the pit of her stomach all day. *The feeling could be wrong though, couldn't it?* She tried to logically rationalize the sick churning inside, convincing herself it was just dread. Dread of him showing up, dread of yet another argument, dread of the past pain hitting her all at once. The words of her uncle sounded out in her mind, 'leave the past where it belongs, in the past'. She took a deep breath and answered the call. "Hi, Liza."

"You ready? I'm outside. Oh, and the girls are with me."

"Ready as I'll ever be...Coming." Bea gave herself a quick squirt of Issey Miyake on the way out the room, but paused before running down the stairs. *When was the last time I wore perfume?*

She closed the bookshop door, pulling it hard, ensuring the cranky lock was secure before turning away. The cold chill outside made Bea rush her steps down the alley by the side of the shop, where Liza was waiting in her stylish, new, black Mini Cooper. Not that you could really see it in the dark, except for the flecks of silver in the paintwork, gleaming proudly in the yellow street lights.

"Well you look…comfortable," Liza remarked, half hanging out of driver window.

Bea threw her a warning glare.

"I won't say another word." Liza popped her head back through the window and started up the car.

"Bea!" A double screech of high-pitched voices came from the back seat.

"Hi, Clare, Roxy." Bea did her best to look happy at seeing them again, but wondered if her voice sounded strained under the weight of the lie.

"Oh, we've been so worried about you, where've you been? Why've you stayed away?" asked Roxy.

Bea took a deep breath, and gritted her teeth. Roxy knew exactly why. "Busy working, you know how it is."

Roxy pouted, nodding in agreement.

Bea stared out of the passenger window, vexed, bored and already feeling out of place. She twiddled with a loose strand of her dark auburn hair that'd escaped the simple bun on top of her head. Everyone looked quite glamorous. Liza's long blonde hair was gracefully swept to one side, showing off her beautiful face. Bea had always wondered how Liza got her make-up looking so perfect. Her own technique was quite the opposite, a slap of foundation, a quick swipe of mascara and a touch of blusher, nothing fancy requiring any skill. Roxy and Claire never seized to amaze with thick layers of foundation stopping right at the chin, and eyes that displayed the biggest lashes ever, which caused them to blink a lot.

"Tell Bea what you got Leanne for her birthday." Liza egged the girls on.

Clare and Roxy giggled.

"You tell." Clare nudged Roxy.

"No, you tell her," replied Clare.

"You're not going to believe it, Bea. Is she, Clare?"

"You won't guess." Clare continued the grinding conversation.

"Tell her." Roxy nudged Clare again.

"A stripper," Clare blurted.

Bea's mouth dropped open.

Clare and Roxy burst out laughing.

"What do you think, Bea?" asked Clare.

"I think she'll most certainly be surprised." Bea's eyes briefly met Liza's.

"She'll love it!" cried an excited Roxy.

Bea was relieved the car journey wasn't long. Liza parked up, and went to get the ticket leaving Bea with Roxy and Clare, who were applying yet another thick layer of make-up. Bea excused herself from the confinement of the car before the perfume came out and choked her to death.

Liza returned, giggling at the expression upon Bea's face. "Gasping for air?"

Bea's eyes widened. "Something like that."

Liza tapped on the back window. "Ready ladies?"

Roxy and Clare threw their beauty kit back into their bags, climbed out the car, and started readjusting their clothing. "Give us a minute!" they screeched.

Bea rolled her eyes. "I'm going to the shop."

Liza gave her that look. "Nicorette…and *please*, don't be long," she begged, before Bea scurried off.

Once out the shop, Bea's hand frantically rummaged around in her bag trying to grab the lighter, but it refused to be found. *It has to be in here somewhere.* The girls called out, but she ignored them, too engrossed delving into the darkest depths of her bag, not looking where she was going, and suddenly came to an abrupt halt. She'd bumped into someone. Flustered, she looked up and encountered a pair of piercing, bright blue eyes staring back at her. "Oh…Oh, I'm so sorry," she apologised, but the stranger's gaze did not leave her. He looked familiar. *Where have I seen him before? The shop? Elly's Bistro?* Various places swept through her mind, until she realized that he seemed to actually enjoy her unreserved observation. Her cheeks became warm and she averted her eyes, aware of the blush, but felt drawn back to his face. Why? Was it the way one corner of his mouth turned into a beautifully, hypnotic grin? Or perhaps due to the depth of his eyes and how she became lost as they searched hers. Whatever it was, the silent 'hello' sent shivers down her spine, making her whole body aware of his presence.

"Bea!" Liza cried, instantly breaking the connection with the stranger. Bea lowered her eyes, quietly apologised and hurried away. After deeply exhaling, finally composing herself from the encounter, her hand returned to search for the elusive lighter.

The girls were holding up the traffic. "Come on!" they cried, waving her to hurry. Bea ran across the road to join them.

"Why did you stop like that, before crossing?" squeaked

Roxy, while clinging onto Clare's arm.

"Yeah, you looked all flustered," said Clare.

Bea ignored the comments, turning back for a second look at the stranger, but saw nothing through the heavy traffic.

"Karian, what's wrong?" asked Pia.

"*She* saw him," said Soren, his eyes suspicious.

"How's that possible?" Pia replied.

Karian finally managed to speak, his eyes in search of the female that had bumped into him. "Pia, Asta...Follow her."

"And do what?" asked Pia, looking bewildered.

"Observe...Go!" Karian's voice became urgent. "Do not lose her."

Without further question, Pia and Asta rushed over to join the humans.

"Why did she only see you? If she has the gift, wouldn't she have seen us all?" Soren asked.

"She has more than a gift, Soren." Karian replied, his eyes focused on Pia and Asta as they hovered outside the pub beside Bea and Liza, unseen.

Soren squinted across the road to get a better look at the female human.

Pia and Asta followed Bea and Liza through the doors, still invisible to all.

After Bea and Liza greeted Leanne with hugs, cards and presents, they found a reasonably quiet spot by the side of the bar, near the entrance of the pub.

Bea could feel Liza's eyes on her. "Stop worrying, all is good. He isn't here... I'm totally relaxed." She noticed the relief on her friend's face and smiled.

"Right, my round. What yah having?" asked Liza.

"Hmm, Pimms, please."

After a few drinks, Bea felt the button of her jeans digging into her stomach, and her fingers discreetly relieved the pressure, undoing the button. She discreetly pulled her jumper over the little gap that exposed her skin, unconsciously sighing. *Great, five foot one and a size twelve, definitely time to exercise.* She knew her little bulge was due to late night snacking, a setback while trying to give up smoking. *You just can't win,* she thought.

The party began to liven up as more people arrived. Without Brandon, Bea was having fun watching Liza trying to catch the eye of a guy in the crowd, but it wasn't long before Roxy found her hiding place.

"*Oh, Bea.* Why are you sitting all alone?" Her voice an annoying whine.

Choice, thought Bea, but before she could answer, Roxy got comfortable in Liza's empty seat.

Pia and Asta were hovering around Bea's table, listening in on the conversation. Pia started to stress about the crowded pub. "It's hard to remain invisible when humans are treading on your toes."

"Trip them up, I do." Asta grinned, before returning her attention back to Bea after hearing her speak.

"Seriously, Roxy, go… have some fun." Bea tried her best to be tactful, other words could've slipped out, all too easily.

"Are you sure? I just didn't want you sitting alone now that Brandon's here," she replied, with a slight smirk. Bea's heart raced. *God no.* Her eyes immediately scanned the pub. Sure enough, there he was, in his usual drunken state, greeting everyone, loudly.

Pia and Asta's eyes followed Bea's with interest.

Bea continued to try and get rid of Roxy. "It's okay, Roxy. Honestly, go." She knew that with Roxy by her side, Clare would soon follow, which meant it would only be a matter of time before the pair gained Brandon's unwanted attention with some silliness.

Roxy patted her hand. "You're so strong."

Bea forced a smile, ignoring the sarcastic tone, but her mood fell dramatically.

As Roxy left, Bea's eyes met Brandon's and she felt very alone. She shifted uncomfortably in her seat. *Damn it, where is Liza.* She did another quick scan of the pub, but Liza was nowhere in sight.

"What was that all about?" Pia turned to Asta.

"Human ex." Asta's eyes drifted over to Brandon.

"How do you know that?" Pia asked.

"Too much time spent around this kind. Right, it's time I took off my glamour and introduced myself."

"No, Asta." Pia tried to stop her, but it was too late. Asta strolled off into the ladies and returned quick as a flash, visible. She then proceeded to the bar and brought two drinks. The barman drooled. She was used to human men behaving this way in her presence, and gave him her most charming smile. She loved to play, and watching the opposite sex melt right before her eyes was one of her favourite games.

"Irresistible isn't it, sister?" Pia laughed from across the room, though no one heard or saw her, as she was still using glamour.

Pia and Asta, being sisters, looked so alike that they would often play tricks on unsuspecting men, swapping roles for fun. Both had the deepest, midnight-blue eyes, framed with long, thick black hair that enhanced their tall, slim physiques.

Asta approached Bea. "Excuse me, do you mind if I sit here?" She pointed to the vacant chair.

Bea felt relieved someone other than Roxy offered to keep the seat occupied. "No, help yourself."

"Thanks." Asta got comfortable, and leant towards Bea. "I just had to escape that guy at the bar." She tilted her head in his direction.

Bea looked over and saw the barman still melting, and laughed.

Asta placed her hand over her mouth and yawned. "I am *soooo* bored with that kind of attention from men. I hope you don't mind, I used the excuse that I was getting you a drink to plan my escape. You're the only person I noticed through the crowd that was alone." Asta pulled a face. "Sorry." Quickly passing Bea the drink.

"Erm, no, thank you. Pimms?" Bea stated, surprised that the woman had guessed her drink correctly.

"I have good eyesight." Asta laughed, her eyes gestured to the glass. "I noticed the fruit."

"Oh, of course." It made sense to Bea.

Pia still hovering, smiled at her sister. "Oh, you are good."

Asta raised her glass. "Cheers…I'm Asta."

Their glasses clinked.

"I'm Bea…How do you know Leanne?"

"Oh, my sister knows her. I tagged along, you know how it is. I feel rather like a spare part," Asta replied.

"Yes, I was feeling…" Bea's attention drifted, drawn by Brandon's impending arrival.

"Are you alright?" asked Asta.

Bea forced a smile. "I'm fine." She noticed Asta's stare drift to the man now standing in front of them.

"Bea," Brandon slurred, looking surprised at seeing her.

He hadn't changed at all in the last six months, same stocky build, same short brown hair, and, not surprisingly, still reeking of drink. Bea had to turn her face away.

"Bea, *please* don't ignore me." He bent down closer, meeting her face. "It's been a long time, babe."

Not long enough, thought Bea.

Asta introduced herself. "Hi. I'm Asta."

Brandon started to drool.

While Brandon was conveniently distracted, Bea grabbed her coat, and escaped through the nearby doors.

Pia quickly followed, knocking a man to the floor as she pushed him out of the way. Everyone in the pub laughed, not able to see invisible Pia, and blamed his fall on drink. Karian had said to follow Bea, and she was not about to lose sight of her.

Asta changed out of glamour, becoming visible in front of Brandon. He blinked and stepped back. "What the...?" He turned to Bea, but she'd gone, and Asta slipped off to find Pia. Brandon shook his head, and realising that Bea must've left, and ran outside in search of her.

"Why are yah running away? Bea. Fuck's sake, hold on!" he yelled at the top of his voice.

"Leave me alone, Brandon!" she yelled back.

"Bea, I only wanna talk with yah, darling. Don't walk away from me, come on...Babe?"

She heard him running up behind her and stopped to face him. "You've been drinking, I'm tired. Go back to the party. It's your sister's birthday, for god's sake; just this once, think of someone other than yourself."

"You can be so cold, d'yah know that? Fucking cold."

Bea noticed passers-by turn their heads at his unstable stagger. Their six months apart hadn't changed his odious charm. She knew this side of him all too well. There would be no reasoning when he was intoxicated on god knows what, and she turned away.

"Bea, fuck's sake. I didn't mean it. I'm a bit pissed," he stated, jogging to catch up with her, but invisible Pia stuck her foot out and he tripped, stumbling to the floor.

On hearing a thud, Bea spun around and saw Brandon sprawled out over the pavement. *Typical,* she thought.

"Are you alright?" a delectably smooth voice asked, making her jump.

Bea turned and saw that a familiar pair of striking blue eyes staring back at her. It was the stranger she'd bumped into earlier. Her stomach fluttered at his closeness again.

"Get away from her!" Brandon yelled, struggling up from the floor.

"Do you want me to stay?" The stranger's voice remained silky calm, his eyes sincere in the asking.

"I…" She didn't have time to reply.

Brandon swayed beside her. "Fuck off, mate. I know your game."

"Brandon don't do this, *please*, just go back to the party." Bea pleaded, wanting to avoid further confrontation, but it was too late. Brandon stepped up to the stranger and poked him hard in the chest with his stubby index finger. "Yah fucking looking for trouble, mate?"

The stranger didn't reply.

Bea hid her face in her hands.

Asta and Pia stood either side of Brandon. Soren joined them, all invisible.

"Why has Karian taken his glamour off?" asked Pia.

"Duh, it would look rather strange Bea talking to herself don't you think?" replied Asta, rolling her eyes.

"Now that would be funny," Pia replied, quickly followed by a big grin.

"Brandon *please* ...Go." Bea turned to the stranger. "I think its best that you go too." The tone in her voice changed between the two.

"Yeah, hear that? Fuck off, yah mug!" Brandon warned, pointing his finger in the stranger's face.

Pia was about to retaliate on Karian's behalf, but Asta grabbed her arm just in time and pulled her away.

Karian's eyes remained fixed on Bea. "His manner is rather...unsavoury."

That's one way to put it, thought Bea, though taken aback by the stranger's unperturbed attitude. He treated Brandon with the same contempt as an annoying fly.

"Fucking what?" Brandon pushed the stranger with all his strength, but he hardly moved.

"*Please*, go home." Karian's eyes said more than his words, and she found it hard to pull away from his mesmerizing stare.

Brandon suddenly yanked her arm, pulling her away from the stranger. "Don't fucking listen to this cunt, he's polishing his newly-found bollocks."

Bea couldn't believe Brandon's foul mouth and shook her head in disgust, pulling her arm from his drunken grip. "This ends now! Do you hear me? Enough is enough, Brandon. I'm gone." She gave the stranger a quick, mimed thank you, and walked away. Brandon cried out to her as she turned the corner, but she refused to look back.

The two men now eyed each other.

"I'll have you later, mate," Brandon spoke through gritted teeth, and saliva foamed from his mouth, trickling down a section of his lip.

"Why wait until later? *Mate*," Karian jeered, taking a step closer, until he stood directly in front of him, blocking his path. Brandon threw a punch at Karian's face, but he moved quickly, avoiding the blow. The momentum from the missed attack almost forced Brandon to the floor, but he quickly straightened himself back up. "Oh, you wanna play? Let's fucking play, come on!"

Karian smiled as the frothing mass came towards him.

Brandon's advance stopped abruptly when Karian punched him, hard, on the temple. Dazed, his legs wobbled, but somehow, he managed to remain standing.

"I'm still waiting," Karian taunted. His composure, as it was before, calm and controlled.

Brandon refocused and threw another punch. Again, Karian moved unbelievably fast, avoided it and laughed.

"Yeah, fucking funny innit, you wanker!"

Suddenly, lots of laughter erupted around them. Brandon spun around, eyes searching, until a punch arrived to his jaw, knocking him to the ground, where he lashed out into empty space.

Karian used his glamour and re-materialized in front of him. Brandon shook his head, eyes wide in disbelief. Soren advanced, but Karian ordered him to stop. "No. He's had enough."

Pia mischievously jumped in, explaining she'd overheard in the pub that Brandon had previously hit the female human. From that moment, everything changed. Karian's fist connected with Brandon's thigh, a deliberate move to immobilize him. Brandon, crippled from the excruciating blow, mumbled obscenities. Karian nodded over to Soren, who grabbed Brandon by his neck, lifting him completely off the ground. Soren grinned as he dangled him like a limp doll in front of his Lord. They all knew Soren hated humans, ever since they'd tried hunting him down centuries ago, and no doubt the grudge would last a couple more.

"You struck her?" Karian asked. His face filled with rage and disgust before releasing a clenched fist, full force, into Brandon's stomach. "Under such circumstances you deserve no gentlemanly conduct. Never strike a woman." He finished Brandon off with several, swift movements of his hand, which connected with Brandon's neck and head, leaving him lying flat out on the pavement. Blood streamed down his face and started to form a red puddle on the ground.

"Would you like me to finish him off, My Lord?" asked Soren.

Karian paused in thought. "Tempting, but no, we don't want to attract any further attention."

Soren nodded, and once instructed, dragged Brandon's body into a nearby alley.

Asta stared at Karian, while whispering thoughts in Pia's ear. "A little slap is one thing, but why would our Lord lose his temper with someone so detached from him? A human? It's out of character. Did you really hear someone say he hit her?"

Pia gulped, as she always did when her sister caught her out on a lie. "I didn't know he was going to beat him to a pulp."

Asta rolled her eyes.

CHAPTER 2

A New Friendship

$\mathcal{B}$ea's mobile continued to buzz and her hand idly fumbled around on the wooden bedside cabinet in readiness to press the snooze button, until she heard a thud. She sat up and groaned. *Really?* looking down at the spilt tea forming a dark stain on the cream carpet. The phone continued to scream and she scrambled out of bed, huffing, skipping over the mess on the floor, and grabbed the phone from the dresser. "Hiya."

"Oh, thank god. I have been ringing you all night. Where've you been?" Liza's voice seemed higher pitched than normal.

"Umm, asleep." Bea rubbed her eyes, kicking the bed sheet out of the way.

"*Asleep?* I've been ringing all night. Where did you go after leaving the pub?"

"I ...I came home, why?"

"Brandon's been beaten up, found in the alley by the pub."

"What?"

"He's been beaten up. Where were you? Did you see anything?"

The desperation in Liza's voice woke her up. "No, I...I left the pub, Brandon followed me, this guy stepped in and-"

"What guy?"

"I don't know. He told me to go home."

"He confronted Brandon?" asked Liza.

"I don't think so." Bea felt a slight thudding sensation; a headache was brewing.

"Were there other people with this man?"

"No...no. He was alone," Bea replied.

"God, Bea, you freaked me right out. I thought you might've been with Brandon and...well, I'm just relieved you're okay."

Bea struggled to put her dressing gown on, while holding the phone to her ear. "I'm fine. How's Brandon?"

"The Doctors said he'll be okay. Tommy told me the hospital's keeping him in for observation. What sort of person would do that?"

Bea rubbed her temple. "To be honest, Brandon has been so lost in drugs and drink, it could be a number of people. Most of the characters he calls friends now, are not my scene at all." She made her way into the kitchen and switched on the kettle. "Poor Leanne, she's always left to pick up the pieces."

"She's okay. Well, now that Brandon has stopped going crazy at the hospital. He wanted to know you were safe. Apparently, they had to give him something to calm him down."

"Oh." Bea didn't wish to go further into the Brandon conversation.

"Do you remember how you got home? I looked for you."

"I think Asta gave me a lift," replied Bea.

"You think? Asta? Who's Asta?"

"A girl I met in the pub. Her sister knows Leanne."

"Oh, okay, well, I'm just glad you're alright. Don't disappear on me again, ever." Liza sounded more her normal self.

"Hello? Ahem, who disappeared?" Bea corrected, placing the tea bag in her cup.

"I was in the pub. I wouldn't just leave without a word. Make sure you find me next time."

"Oh, there won't be a next time." Bea would make certain of that.

"Right. I gotta go to work. Just call if you need me, okay?"

"You know I will, but first I have to delete around thirty missed calls."

They both burst out laughing.

Liza always made her smile. They'd met at primary school. Bea was now twenty-two, and the bond they developed as children remained strong. Bea decided to leave the shop closed, and collapsed on the sofa, trying to remember the evening, but apart from walking away from Brandon, and getting in a car, everything else, like getting into bed, remained a blur. She checked her phone to see if she had taken Asta's number, nothing.

What happened to the stranger? Was he all right? Could he have anything to do with Brandon getting beaten up?

Bea spent the next morning giving her customers a lame excuse with polite apologies for being closed the previous day and felt grateful for lunchtime. The new Bistro next door was a godsend. She'd never been great in the kitchen and Elly's gave her the perfect excuse to avoid any unnecessary cooking.

On entering the Bistro, Bea found herself greeted by Elly in her usual pleasant manner. The world had become normal again. She made her way to the large, white counter, which filled the far end of the small space. The red walls made the place feel tiny, but cosy, "Your usual, Bea darling?" Elly asked, with a slight accent that Bea could never place.

A familiar word echoed through her mind, *predictable*. "Erm, no, I fancy a change."

"No cheese and onion toasty?" She stared back at Bea in disbelief.

"No." Bea smiled, as she eyed the dishes roughly scribbled on a chalk board behind the counter. "The pasta salad, dish 'b', please."

"I'll bring it out…as usual?" Elly tilted her head, obviously unsure of another possible change. Bea laughed. "Yes please, *as usual.*"

Elly appeared relieved, which kept a smile on Bea's face as she made herself comfortable in her usual spot outside. She hooked her bag straps under the chair leg, just in case. One never knew if a passing opportunist might take fancy, despite the camera signs displayed. She felt good, strangely good in spite of everything. The street was hectic, and as expected, the young trainee butchers were hanging around outside on a cigarette break a few shops down, gaping at females in their near vicinity. The traffic continued to expel choking fumes, but Bea was well used to the congested city and its smell.

"May I join you?" a slightly familiar voice asked.

Startled, Bea looked up and saw the stranger that had come to her aid.

He quickly apologised and slightly bowed his head. "I'm sorry. I have surprised you…I didn't mean to disturb."

"No, I… I just didn't expect to see you again. Please, take a seat." Her heart rate soared behind the casual reply.

"I wasn't sure whether I should stop to say hello, but, I admit, curiosity got the better of me."

She smiled, extending her hand. "I'm Bea, but you already know that." *With Brandon screaming my name the whole of London must know it*, she thought.

He took her hand in his and gently kissed it. "My name is Karian, but I prefer Kari."

Her body shivered at his touch. She felt a little uncomfortable with the outdated act, but his warm blue eyes and confident smile removed any uneasiness.

He was about to sit down when Elly came out delivering lunch, asking the stranger if he wanted anything. As he and Elly talked, Bea seized the moment to look at him more closely. His tall, lean figure was handsomely framed in a fitted black suit and matching dark shirt. His style of dress would make anyone else look like they were attending a funeral, or at the very least, appear ghostly, but somehow it complemented his opal complexion. She couldn't help notice that the fabric clung more tightly to the more muscular areas of his body, and admitted he had a certain charm. Maybe the attraction she felt was due more to his self-assured poise than his looks; his hair a casual, short mass of dark chocolate waves. If it wasn't for the sunlight gleaming on his locks, it would appear more black than brown. On first impression, he seemed a business type, perhaps, due to the well-mannered persona and clear confident speech. However, he also had a fun element about him, not stiff or boring. Bea had apparently missed something as she noticed both Elly and Karian staring at her.

"I'm sorry, did you say something?" She tried to hide her embarrassment at being detached from the conversation by casually resting her chin in her hands, fingers spread, covering her flushed cheeks.

"He said you are beautiful... I agreed." Elly grinned, with a slight twinkle in her eye.

Bea felt a fresh wave of heat spread across her cheeks as Karian's eyes playfully glinted her way. *What was the word Asta had used? Oh yes, having the ability to melt.*

Elly wandered off giggling and Karian sat opposite Bea. "I was quite concerned the other evening. Did you get home without any further trouble?"

Bea cleared her throat. "I did...thank you. You were kind, offering to help." This was her opening. "What happened after I left?"

His brow furrowed and his eyes drifted away from hers. "Verbal abuse, called a varying manner of things, but, surprisingly, no violence."

Bea felt relieved. "I'm sorry. He has a tendency to act that way when he's had a drink." On reflection, apologising on Brandon's behalf made her feel stupid – another bad habit she needed to break.

"Please, don't apologise. A former boyfriend, I presume?" His eyes met hers.

Bea nodded, shying away from his inquisitive stare.

"I'm sorry, it's none of my business, forget I asked."

Bea gave him a weak smile. "I'm pleased you're okay. Did you see any other people around?"

"Other people?" He looked confused.

"Brandon was being quite loud and has drawn quite a crowd in the past," she replied.

"There were...some people. That's when I decided to

make my departure, a rather rowdy bunch. This seems to be a bit of a rough area after dark."

It was strange, she found it hard to concentrate, yet all the hustle and bustle of the street seemed to disappear with him being present. "Well, it's obvious that you are not from the *Dirty South*."

"The Dirty South? Interesting term. That easy to tell, is it?"

There was that smile again, and she looked away to hide her enjoyment at seeing it. "Oh, just a little, getting involved in arguments when most would turn a blind eye, that sort of thing."

His eyes looked straight into hers and without any form of inhibition, he replied, "I would do it again... *for you.*"

Bea looked down at the table, breaking away from the intensity, an awkward silence followed. She didn't understand the feeling of light-headedness starting to grip her. *Am I coming down with something?* She fidgeted in her seat, trying to clear her head.

"I keep doing that, I apologise," Karian said.

The sincerity in his voice made Bea lift her eyes. "Smooth talk, I've heard too much of it in the past."

"Then, no more smooth talk, I promise."

"So, we've established that you're not from around here. Where are you from?"

"Fundamentally...I'm a country lad." The pale, slender fingers of his hand ran slowly up and down the lower arm of his chair, distracting Bea for a moment.

"A country lad?"

His fingers paused. "You don't believe me?"

"I'm just trying to picture you in wellies." She couldn't keep the smile from reaching her lips and they both laughed. She enjoyed the sound.

"I moved around a lot as a child and sort of ended up in West London."

"So, why are you here, in the South?"

"Forward, aren't you?" he teased. "No, I understand, you're quite rightly checking my background, making sure that I am not a crazed, stalker type." He raised one eyebrow. "Or anything worse."

Bea laughed, missing the doting in his eyes. "One can never be too careful, *especially* of anything worse. You still didn't answer my question, why are you here?"

He leant forward, resting his arms on the table. "I'll let you in on a little secret. I'm actually negotiating to purchase a theatre."

"Really?" She didn't expect that answer.

He nodded, his eyes danced with excitement as he spoke. "I'm pursuing a dream."

"Owning a theatre?"

"It was drummed into me by my father to take my career seriously. That chasing one's dreams is nothing but pure folly, that my heart will get broken in the process. Now I'm older, I can finally choose what I wish to pursue… So, here I am, ready to get my heart broken."

"Well, you're almost there and your heart isn't broken, yet. Looks promising," she replied.

He nodded, seeming a little distant. "Yes, it does look promising, now that everything is so *very* close. I have to remind myself to take time, not to rush."

"Do you have any experience?"

A smile quickly presented itself in his eyes, and he discreetly placed his hand over his mouth to hide it forming on his lips.

"In *theatre* production?" Bea quickly added, shaking her head.

"Enough…I hope."

His attempt at hiding a laugh was attractive, but Bea was determined not to let it show. "So, what theatre do you have in mind?"

"I shouldn't speak about it too soon."

"Waiting on that deal, huh?" she asked.

"Something like that. May I ask why you're in the *dirty South*?"

"Oh, I run a second-hand bookshop."

"How's business?"

Bea tilted her head from side to side. "It's…steady."

"Steady?" He sat back in his chair, silent, obviously waiting for a better explanation.

"The internet, e-books, hit smaller businesses like mine. Luckily, I don't do it for the money."

"Why do it, if not for the money?"

She shrugged. "I love books, people. It makes me happy… like you following your dream."

"As long as it brings you happiness. What about your dreams, Bea?"

She gulped. The way he said her name made her want to hear him say it again. "No dreams, but lots of hopes and maybes."

"I'm intrigued." He sat forward.

She laughed, unsure if she wanted to expose her thoughts further, but he sat waiting attentively. "Okay, *well*...I would change certain things."

"Such as?"

"*Such as*...manufacturers using hemp as a substitute for paper. It can be replenished more easily than trees, doesn't use bleaching chemicals, lasts hundreds of year's longer, and reduces deforestation as well as toxins in our waterways. Oh, and also aids family farms." She laughed at the expression on his face. "Bet you wished you hadn't asked?"

"No, on the contrary, I agree with you."

"You do?" Bea wasn't sure if he was mocking.

"Definitely, humans tend to be a destructive race. Anything that could improve the environment has to be commended."

"Exactly." She smiled. "*Humans* are a very destructive race."

Engrossed in conversation, they didn't notice that Elly had brought Karian's drink to the table, until he almost knocked the glass of water over.

"Isn't intrusive at all, is she?" he stated, repositioning the glass. "So, you're a local?"

"Great guess." Bea playfully applauded, feeling more relaxed. "My shop's next door." She gestured behind her.

He looked surprised. "So close." His fingers played with the edge of the paper napkin on the table.

"Handy for lunch."

"Tomorrow then?" came his quick reply.

Bea almost choked. "I didn't mean-"

"I know. I took advantage." He gave her that charming grin. "Lunch tomorrow?"

How could she resist, especially when accompanied with such a beautiful smile. "Why not?"

Karian's eyes lit up. "It's a date." His phone bleeped. "Excuse me." He looked perplexed after reading the message. "I am sorry. I have to leave, business."

"Of course," Bea replied, as he got up from the chair.

"I'll see you tomorrow, around one?" The way he bit his lower lip waiting for a reply made her feel giddy and she found herself replying with only a nod.

Karian walked over and held out his hand. Bea instinctively gave him hers. He placed his soft lips against her skin, but this time, the gesture didn't feel uncomfortable, quite the opposite. It was as if the whole movement were playing out in slow motion. Karian gave her one last melting smile, and left.

After paying Elly and leaving the bistro, Bea saw Jenny, the bookshop volunteer, waiting outside. She looked more petite today, somehow. Maybe, it was due to the extra-long skirt and cropped top that wrapped round her tiny, short torso, worn with flat sandals. Nonetheless, she looked amazing as ever, with her long, strawberry-blonde hair tied up neatly into a ponytail and bearing a perfect white grin. Jenny was nothing short of a miracle, an adult student offering her services in the shop, reading to the children twice per week- for free. Bea glanced down at her phone. "Oh, Jen, I didn't realise the time, sorry."

"No problem, I saw that you were busy with that *gentleman*. You looked quite engrossed."

"A little." Bea grinned, opening the shop door and turning the closed sign around.

Jenny disappeared to prepare the children's reading area, while Bea tucked her bag away under the counter. Picturing Karian's smile, she sighed, and stared down the aisle. The little tinkle of the shop's bell broke her away from the image. The first of the parents had arrived.

Jenny's idea of advertising in the local paper for the children's reading nook had paid off. The shop became busy, something Bea hadn't experienced in a long time, and she was grateful.

She watched Jenny read to the children by the front of the shop, but became distracted when a new customer entered. A young man walked straight past her without so much as a word or a glance. Curiosity got the better of her, and she went in search of him. As she strolled down the central aisle, her eyes glanced down each of the ten, narrow book sections, standing proudly, opposite the long, mahogany counter, but he wasn't in any. She finally found him at the other end of the bookshop, tucked away in the dark, little coffee nook. He'd taken a seat in her uncle's favourite place of solitude, a tatty, brown, leather-winged armchair. She'd stopped in her tracks, for a brief second, she'd imagined her uncle sitting there. She took a deep breath and forced herself forward. The man appeared bewildered by her approach.

"Hi." She extended her hand. "I'm Bea."

He looked speechless, staring at her like she was crazy.

Bea immediately lowered her hand. "Sorry, I normally greet people straight away but you walked-"

"I'm Chance," he interrupted, jumping to his feet and looking awkward in his eagerness to extend his hand. Bea wondered what was wrong with him. *Maybe, he's just shy?* "Nice to meet you, *Chance.*" She thought his name unusual, but didn't mention it. "Please, help yourself to refreshment, and if you can, leave a small donation in the pot. Call me if you need any help."

"Thank you." His eyes looked everywhere but at her.

Once Bea had gone, he turned to a blonde woman standing beside him. "Explain how she saw me?"

"I...I don't know, and more to the point, why she didn't see me beside you?"

He paced the nook, peering down the long aisle. "You've never come across this before?"

Her brows rose. "No."

Chance frowned. "Something's not right here."

"Hence, your presence being required...Don't worry, I'm sure there's a simple explanation."

"Don't worry? We're not meant to make contact with humans. Don't you find that she saw me...*beyond a simple explanation?*"

"Well, it's too late to worry about that now." She shrugged. "Did you see the sign of the Sindria around her neck?"

"It doesn't mean anything." He wasn't impressed by her nonchalant attitude.

"Maybe it does, maybe it doesn't. Though, not many humans wear the seven-pointed star." The woman sighed. "I see no point in us both being here. I could be making enquiries."

"And what exactly am I supposed to do?"

"Exactly, what you were meant to do, observe."

He shook his head. "That was fine before she saw me

…but I …I haven't interacted with *humans* in such close proximity before." Chance thought he saw the slight hint of a smile creep onto her lips.

"They didn't cover this in warrior training?" She raised her brows.

He glared at her.

"Okay, no need for hostility. Look, it's easy, if she asks your profession tell her …you're a professor of mythology."

"Of mythology?"

"Yes."

He saw her lips fight another grin.

"Tell her that you're looking for books on the Sidhe," she replied.

"Very funny, Kitty."

"I'm serious, it's a subject she won't catch you out on. Meanwhile, I'll make a few enquiries about her being able to see you. It actually does rather un-nerve me too. Keep your phone on. I'll send a text when I'm outside. I'll pick you up at closing, at six."

"You know what time the shop closes?"

"How long have I been watching this place?" She laughed. "It's on the door. I'll see you soon." She gave him a teasing wave, quickly followed by another grin before departing.

Chance hated admitting Kitty was right. He hadn't been in this realm long, and she had all the contacts. He wasn't happy about being sent here and hanging around, simply observing, felt like a complete waste of his skills and time. His social skills with humans were non-existent. Most of his life he'd spent training for his Order, far away from his own society, let alone any other beings. He didn't know why he'd been chosen for this mission, but an order had to be obeyed, no matter how he felt. He was stuck here and had better get used to it — fast. Still, observing a human female in a bookshop wasn't his idea of being a warrior. Chance wondered why Bea looked so uncomfortable at seeing him. Did she know what he was? One thing was for sure, he had to adapt and quickly, look normal, like one of them, so not to arouse any further suspicion.

He strolled over to a row of books by a small window and ran his hand across the spines. Everything felt old, and the smell reminded him of the libraries back home. As he continued his solitary tour of the shop, he felt more and more restricted by the clothes he was given to wear by Kitty, after his arrival. They were too tight, stuffy, compared to his usual attire: loose, natural fabrics that moved when he did — more useful, fluid for combat. He pulled at the collar of his shirt and two buttons pinged off in different directions. He gritted his teeth and quietly grunted. His normal self-control was going to be tested in this realm for sure.

Bea watched him with interest from one end of the counter. He seemed uncomfortable, quite child-like in his ways, restless and bored. Her observations of customers were usually that of expressions when the customer read something. She'd watch their amusement or shock, but this time, she found herself observing due to a strange kind of allurement.

He removed a book from a shelf and his head tilted slightly as he browsed its pages. Her eyes took in the sinewy curve of his neck that his short, fair hair exposed. Bea's stare then drifted down his arms to his hands. They looked strong, firm, not coarse or callused as you might expect from some men of his build. His nails were short and tidy, she liked that. From his hands, her eyes followed his not overly muscular form, and strength came to mind. She couldn't help but notice that the white shirt he wore appeared a little too tight under his well-fitting blue jumper. She sensed a boyish charm, adding warmth to his countenance. Her eyes followed his well-defined physique, eventually pausing at his bottom. Feeling intrusive, she swiftly averted her eyes back to his face. Her stare soon dropped as his eyes caught hers. *Oh, god, does he know I was staring at his body? At his bum?* Embarrassed, she tried to look busy at the counter.

After a few minutes she found the courage to look back up, he glanced over, smiled and returned his attention to the book. Bea remembered to exhale. Something about his manner intrigued, and her gaze soon found its way back to his face. It was round, with a prominent brow, *a perfect hiding place for his shy eyes,* she thought. His skin was flawless, *a soft peach.*

"What are you staring at?" a voice bellowed, echoing throughout the shop.

Bea froze, only slowly regaining her composure after realising it was Mr. Brough. "You startled me."

"Sorry love, you seemed far away. Mary asked me to check if the Andrew Lang books were in yet?"

"No, I did ring to explain one should be in at the end of the week," replied Bea, trying not to sound snappy.

"Oh love, she was hoping that it might have come early. I'll check tomorrow."

"It's best to check at the end of week." Bea insisted.

"End of the week? That's a long time, init?" He wiped his

perspiring head with the back of his hand.

"I'll ring if it arrives early. It'll save you the journey."

"Okay, I'll pop in tomorrow, just to check. Bye love." He tapped the counter and left.

Bea's eyes wandered back to Chance who started to make his way over to the counter. A crazy panic rushed through her. *Did he hear Mr.Brough's comment about staring?*

Chance stood in front of her and gave her a slight smile, but didn't speak.

"Did you find anything interesting?" Bea prompted.

He looked confused.

"To read?" she replied. *Is he on something? Why does he appear so distant?*

"Not really." He glanced down the aisle towards the entrance.

"What type of books do you like?" She wanted to find out more about him, and the type of books someone read was always a good place to start. That's if she could hold his attention long enough.

He recited Kitty's words. "Mythology."

"Oh…what area?" *Did his jaw tense a little?*

"Sidhe lore."

"Oh, that's Folklore isn't it? I'm not sure I have anything along that line. I could help you go through some of the books on the top shelves. My uncle placed the less popular reading there. I haven't climbed up there in a while, but there may be something of interest." *I'm actually blabbering.* It was the first time that his eyes became fixed on hers. They were beautiful, secretive, dark blue pools of enticing mystery. Bea forced herself to blink.

"Your Uncle?"

"Yes. He's gone now." Bea tried to pull herself away from the gravity of his eyes.

"Gone?"

"Passed over, died…dead." *Did I really just say that?* Bea forced herself to regain some form of sanity.

He looked uncomfortable at the revelation. "I'm sorry."

"What got you interested in folklore?" She saw a faint smile appear upon his lips.

"I drifted into it."

"And the Sidhe?" Bea wondered if she had pronounced it correctly.

"The *Shee* is a relatively unknown area. The unusual always catches my eye."

Bea was pretty sure that she appeared unusual. "What is a Sidhe exactly?"

She watched as he tried to slip his hands into his pockets, but only the tips of his fingers fitted, he still left them there. "It's a word for a mound, where otherworldly beings supposedly once lived. The race became known as the people of the Sidhe, long forgotten by modern society."

"I'm sure I've heard my uncle talk of them. I'd love to hear more." Bea propped her elbows on the counter and rested her head in her palms, waiting.

He seemed more relaxed and a warm smile reached his eyes. "The Sidhe are of Irish and Scottish legend. They're known by other names elsewhere."

She found his voice soothing, until the sound of a phone rang out and he delved into his back pocket, excusing himself, but her eyes refused to leave him. He was fascinating. Liza would be so proud. She'd finally started to find men attractive again. This was quite a leap in the life of Bea. She prized herself away to check up on Jenny while Chance took his call.

She watched as the children remained captivated by Jenny's different tones and funny expressions while reading aloud.

A few moments later, Chance tried to quietly gain her attention. "I'll have to leave the book search until tomorrow. I hope you don't mind?"

"You're going?" Her heart sank a little.

He nodded, walking away before she had time to say another word.

CHAPTER 3

Shimmers of Purple

The following day, Bea expected Karian to join her for lunch, as arranged, but he didn't show up, but the slight pang to her ego soon passed as Chance's visits to the shop became more frequent over the month. She enjoyed their conversations, but he seemed reserved at times, still, it was a refreshing change from the likes of Brandon. The more she got to know him, she realised that he expressed himself with his eyes, but would hide them, when uncomfortable, by lowering his brow. He never spoke unnecessarily, and he'd place his hands in his pockets when unsure of himself. Chance intrigued her and today she decided to be brave and ask him to join her upstairs in the flat for something to eat. It was quite a big deal, as the only other male she had invited into her home was Brandon, and she quickly shook that thought off.

Bea had it all planned with the help of mastermind Elly, who offered to make a stew for two that she would drop off in Chance's presence, thus enabling her the opportunity to ask him to stay. She had not yet informed Liza of the new friendship. She didn't want to face any form of embarrassment later, if he declined. Bea wanted to keep him her little secret for a little while longer.

Her tiny flat had a slight bohemian feel and Bea hoped it felt normal enough for a professor to feel comfortable. The colours in the rooms were calming, a mix of pastels and white, with a few bright stencils on the walls adding a shabby charm. Large mirrors were used everywhere in an attempt to make the flat feel bigger. Fairy lights adorned nearly every window and lace the rest. The grey linen sofa could hardly be seen through the vast array of silk throws and velvet cushions. Bea lit a couple of vanilla candles, either side of her iPod station. She now felt prepared, thanks to Jenny offering to watch the shop. They'd said their goodbyes and Jenny suspected nothing. It felt good having a secret.

He would normally be here by now, Bea thought, as she continuously scribbled loops in her already full notepad at the counter. Her eyes darted over to the shop door as the little bell rang. Her heart sank as Mr. Brough thudded in.

"Hello, love!" he bellowed.

"Hello, Mr.Brough. Yes, one's arrived. I'll go and get it for you."

"You're a good girl. Mary told me to say sorry for nagging you all week."

"It's okay," she replied, going through to the small office just behind the counter to get the book. When she returned, she didn't notice Chance standing to one side.

"Here you go. I think Mary will find it worth the wait." She handed him the book wrapped brown paper.

"She'll not speak to me for days now, as I was just telling your bloke here."

Bea's eyes, guided by Mr. Brough's, met Chance's. Both smiled, neither bothering to correct him.

"Well, love, I'm off or I'll get an ear-ache from the Missus." Mr. Brough nudged Chance. "You know what I mean?" He roared with laughter as he left, making Bea's whole body tense.

Once Mr. Brough was out of earshot, Chance spoke. "I didn't correct him, as I've noticed from your previous conversations, he tends not to listen."

He'd obviously been paying more attention than he'd let on. "I wasn't sure you were going to show up." Her palms started to feel damp with nerves, and she discreetly ran them down her jeans.

"I went home and...got changed." He slipped his hands into his pockets.

Granted, he looked more stylish, modern, but she missed the quirky professor chap in tight-fitting jumpers, tweed jacket, and Brogues. Bea couldn't help but tease a little. "Into a suit?"

That boyish grin appeared that made her heart skip. "How are you getting on with the book?" she asked, trying to regulate her pulse.

"I've read it," he casually replied.

"All of it?"

"Isn't that what you normally do?" Chance's dark blue eyes glinted her way.

"Well, yes, but not normally in one night. You must have flown through uni, huh?" She dismissed the confused expression on his face as they made their way the coffee nook.

Earlier that day, Bea sorted out various books from the cellar that she thought might be of interest to Chance, all mythology. As he browsed through them, she gave the occasional quick glance towards the door. She knew the bell would chime to announce Elly's arrival, but still couldn't help check and willed even harder for Elly to come. Her lack of normal babbling didn't go un-noticed. "You seem distant. Are you alright?" Chance's blue eyes searched hers, and in the dim light of the nook, Bea felt mesmerised by their shine. "Yes, sorry, drifted a little. I do that sometimes." *God, why did I say that...Where are you Elly?*

"Are you comfortable with me being here?" He leant forward in her uncle's old chair, closer to Bea. Her anxiousness had been misconstrued and she quickly reassured him. "I'm *very* comfortable with you being here," she replied, maybe a little too quickly. His eyes didn't look away this time, and her heart started beating faster as they sat looking at each other. Neither speaking a word, and at that moment, the shop bell rang. *Really? She arrives now?*

"Hello?" Elly's voice echoed through the aisle, breaking the silence.

"Elly." Bea tried her best to act surprised.

"Hello, darling. Oh, *hello* there." Elly was playing her part well.

"Hello." Chance replied, getting up from the chair.

Elly turned to Bea. "This is for you darling, a beautiful hot stew. Maybe, your friend would like some? There's enough for two." She winked.

Chance smiled at Elly who beamed his way.

"Wow, that's so kind of you. Chance, would you like to stay for dinner?" Her nerves started to fade away as she took the pot.

"If you're sure you don't mind?" He took the opportunity to shake Elly's hand, now it was empty. "Thank you, very considerate."

"My pleasure, darling, do you live nearby?"

Hold on, thought Bea, *the plan was that you leave now, Elly.*

"I'm staying with my sister in North London."

"North London. That is so far to travel, you must *really* like the books here."

Bea's mouth dropped open.

"I do," he replied, looking over at Bea.

"Where do you live in North London?" Elly continued her questioning.

"Muswell Hill. Do you know it?"

"No, I don't know it *personally*. I've heard of it, on some programme once. You're looking very handsome in that suit, isn't he, Bea?" Elly waited for an answer.

Chance smiled in Bea's direction.

"He does… you do." She felt silly still holding the pot and placed it on the table by the old chair.

"I'm sure there's enough stew for three. Won't you join us Elly?" asked Chance.

"Oh darling, you're so *charming*."

No way! Bea silently screamed, noticing that Elly appeared to be enchanted, her eyes twinkling at the invite, obviously, now thinking of staying, that was until Bea threw her a death look breaking Elly from his spell.

"Oh, I can't. I'm busy, busy. It's closing time for me and Bea. Nice meeting you, Chance."

"Pleasure meeting you too, Elly. Thank you again for the food."

Elly patted his hand. "You're welcome, darling. I will see you tomorrow morning, no?"

Bea had to stop her from saying anything further. "Thank you, Elly. Let me walk you out."

"No need, go get food and nice wine, darling."

Bea forced a smile in Chance's direction as she guided, pushed Elly to the door.

"How was I?"

"Elly, shhh."

Elly giggled and winked. "I'll see you tomorrow."

"See you tomorrow." Bea wondered if Chance saw her exhale once she'd finally got Elly out of the door, or maybe in her haste to ensure that the door was now locked.

Right, now to invite him upstairs...I can do this. Her nervousness slowly started to creep back with every step closer towards him.

"Elly's friendly." He slid his hands back into his pockets and Bea wondered if it was a sign that he was as nervous as her.

"Yes, she's lovely."

There was a brief silence.

"Does she usually bring you food?" he asked.

Good grief, he thinks I need a mother figure. "She worries that I don't eat enough. Shall we go up?" *I did it, I asked him,* she silently applauded.

"Here, permit me." He took the pot and followed her up the stairs into the kitchen, placing the pot on the table. "I have a bottle in the car, would you mind if I brought it up?"

He has a bottle of wine. Did he have it in the car already? Did he plan to stay longer tonight? Act cool, act cool. "Course not... just buzz and I'll let you back in." She heard the door downstairs close and paused for a second at the worktop. *Deep breaths,* she felt all jittery. Her mind raced as fast as her heart. *Is it just nerves or am I just scared of where this might lead? Am I ready for something else?*

Calm down, it's only wine and dinner, she reminded herself, trying to curb her sudden rush of adrenaline.

An enormous smile appeared on her face when the buzzer rang. She hadn't felt this excited in a long time. She ran and buzzed him in. By the time he was up the stairs, she'd already served up on the table.

"I hope you don't mind." Chance apologised. "This isn't wine, but tastes similar. It's actually mead." He tilted his head in a way that was positively charming and her stare lingered a little bit longer than it should have done. She loved the way his eyes had a smile of their own, and she imagined the feel of his soft cheek against hers.

She forced herself to speak before sighing aloud. "I've never drunk mead. May I?" Bea extended her hand, and as he passed her the bottle, their fingers brushed against each other, and their eyes instantly met. He smiled, but averted his gaze. Bea found his bashful retreat endearing. It was such a refreshing change from Brandon who had to feel in control for fear of appearing weak.

Bea looked down at the bottle; it was unusual, dark purple with a shimmery label. "I can't make out the writing. What is it?"

He moved closer behind Bea, and instinctively she wanted to turn her face to meet his. It took all her strength to resist the urge. His voice sounded soft and inviting by her ear. "Hieroglyphs created by the brewer. Distinctive to his brand." He returned his hand to the bottle, slightly overlapping hers. "It's a vintage mead made from purple flowers. I believe that it is no longer produced, now."

"Really?" Bea's face finally turned to meet his. "Oh, you

mustn't open it. Please, save it for a special occasion."

"This *is* a special occasion." His eyes confirmed his words.

Bea bit her lip to hide a smile and handed him her glass. As he poured, a strong, sweet aroma filled the room.

"Wow. This smells amazing, and it's actually purple. I thought it was just the bottle."

He held his glass up to toast. "To special occasions and precious moments in time." His eyes never left hers as she repeated the words. Their glasses clinked and Bea took a sip of the aromatic liquid. It was unlike anything she'd ever tasted before. From the first sip, her senses began to tingle. *Was the light-headedness caused by the mead or him?* She took another sip and then held the glass up in front of her. "This is incredible."

"I'm pleased you like it." The adoring glint in his eyes spoke more than his words.

"I love it…thank you." She took a deep breath. "Okay, shall we try Elly's stew?" Bea felt giddy and needed to sit down.

He nodded, and pulled a chair out for her, before sitting down himself.

As they sat opposite each other, Bea felt his leg against hers under the table. *Was it un-intentional or deliberate?* She hoped the later. Tingles went up and down her spine, it felt good being so close and she fought hard to resist the urge of moving her leg even closer still.

After his first mouthful of stew, Chance nodded in appreciation. "This is good."

"Elly will be happy that you like it." Bea felt grateful that she wasn't reduced to serving up her own cooking. What a disaster that would've been.

After the meal and several glasses of mead later, Bea invited him into the living room. The smell of vanilla still lingered in the air. "My humble abode, make yourself comfortable. Do you like music?" She laughed, rolling her eyes. "Well, of course you like music. I meant, what type of music do you like?"

He stood in the doorway smiling. "My sister insisted that I listen to someone called Ed Sheeran."

"Oh, he's great. She's got good taste. Do you have a favourite track?" Bea hovered by the iPod station.

He answered immediately. "Give me love."

Bea fumbled around nervously with the buttons on the station, not seeing Chance take out his phone, dismiss a call, and switch it off before going to sit on the sofa.

"Here goes." She sat down next to him, throwing some cushions behind the sofa as he topped up their glasses. The music began to play. "Do you dance?" Bea asked, but wondered if it was too soon and bit her lip.

Chance placed his glass on the table, stood up and held out his hand.

Bea smiled, *nope*. She wondered if he noticed her nervous trembling as she placed her hand in his. Her heart started to race even faster as he, rather cautiously, placed his hands gently upon her waist. He was taller than her and his broad chest felt as if it were inviting her in. She wrapped her arms loosely around his neck, and slowly they began to move.

Bea could smell his cologne, and recognised the scents, a sensual blend of Bergamot and Jasmine, her favourite. Was she still in her little flat or in a dream? She found it difficult to concentrate, being so close.

A little more into the song, she felt his muscles relax and he gently rested his head against hers. Bea's body automatically responded to his touch by moving closer, and she placed her head on his chest. She could hear his heart beating fast and her own breathing deepened to its rhythm. He felt warm as her body melted against his. The quiet, seductive, yet innocent, language of movement, passed between them. Chance's face nestled further into her neck. She could feel his breath on her skin, sending a shiver through her entire body, causing her to want more of him.

As she became more confident in their closeness, her hands travelled slowly from his neck down to his lower back. He quivered at her touch and it excited her. He felt like home and all of her senses became alive with him. His breathing deepened in time with hers. She felt dizzy, dizzy good.

Bea felt his lips begin to move against her skin, followed by words sung softly by her ear.

She smiled, apprehensively, joining in.

The room filled with a sensual intensity, both wholly intoxicated by the other.

Bea knew that this was her new beginning.
Chance knew that he was crossing a boundary.

The song began to fade and she felt him begin to pull away, but she held his hand, not prepared to let him go. Unknown to Bea, an invisible Kitty was now standing beside him, hands on hips, fuming.

"No, by all means, keep looking into her precious human eyes." Kitty moved closer. "By the way, I've turned your phone back on. Please answer it when it rings. I've also placed my keys in your jacket pocket, giving you an excuse to leave. I'll be waiting in the car." She turned and marched out of the flat.

"Are you alright?" Bea sensed a change in his mood. "I didn't step on your toe or anything did I?

He shook his head. "Thirsty."

The next track started to play and Chance sat back down on the settee.

Bea joined him, and his eyes lowered at her gaze. *He must be more nervous than me,* she thought, at his hesitancy. She moved in a little closer, placing her hand on his. Without him realising, his shyness was pulling her in deeper with every denied look. He briefly closed his eyes before placing a hand softly on her face. She knew he was resisting, but why? She buried her cheek against his warm palm and his thumb began to stroke her skin. Electrifying tingles ran through her body at his touch. Readily, her eyes met his stirring pools of deeply mysterious blue, where she waited at the edge, about to fall in, as his luscious lips, moved steadily towards her. His phone started to ring but neither of them moved. She felt his mouth's warmth hesitate over hers, and waited for the promise of his kiss. She longed for a taste of the new, but the infernal phone refused to stop its screaming and Chance jumped up, answering its untimely cry.

"... You're sure?" Chance said, running a hand over his head.

Bea sat bewildered as she watched him go through his jacket pockets.

Chance pulled out two sets of keys. "Yes they're here. I must have picked them up by mistake. Okay...yes Kitty. I'm on my way." He looked over at Bea. "I have to go. I've got my sister's keys. She's waiting outside the house, not happy... I'm sorry."

No way! she screamed. Her heart sank. "Oh...of course, you can't leave her outside." She waited for him to say something, but only an awkward silence followed. Bea got up, about to walk over to him, when he grabbed his coat, gave his apologies and hurried off downstairs. Baffled by the sudden change, she followed him. As he was about to step outside the shop, she called out his name and he paused. "Have I...Have I done something wrong?" She didn't understand why he was in such a hurry? Surely his sister could wait a few minutes?

"No... I..." He glanced down the street and then back at her. "I really, *really* had a great time tonight." He shook his head and sighed. "I can't believe I took my sister's keys. I feel...foolish."

Something didn't feel right, but Bea shook it off. "Hey, it's alright. I'll tell Elly that you enjoyed her stew and if you don't mind, I shall polish off that wonderful bottle of mead."

They both laughed and the freeze in temperature vanished.

"Thank you." His voice became a faint whisper but his gaze lingered. "I meant what I said."

"What?" she asked.

"That time is precious...and today was a special occasion. I just needed you to know-"

Bea quickly leant forward, planting a kiss on his lips. "Yes, it was," she whispered by his ear. "See you tomorrow." She gave him a big smile before running inside.

Chance stood staring at the shop door. He ran his hands over his head, confused by the feelings her closeness awakened. What made him lose himself in those few moments? How could a human possibly affect him this way? He never expected to be seen by a human and his guard was down. What was it about this human that moved him? Why did everything fade away when he was with her? He wasn't used to feeling vulnerable. It was a weakness he didn't want, which caused an inner ache that he didn't understand. Although, he'd tried to fight the earlier overwhelming compulsion to kiss her, he knew that if Kitty hadn't saved him from the disaster, he would still be in the flat now. With that thought, his fingers touched the spot where Bea had kissed, and he closed his eyes, picturing her face. The phone in his pocket rang and the imagery faded.

Kitty was in her pink Mercedes, parked around the corner. She rolled the window down as he approached and glared at him. "Not funny. Really, what were you doing?"

"Nothing happened," he retorted.

"Thanks to me…It's all too easy to get attached to them. This place affects some of us that way, take comfort that you're not the first… The longer we stay, the more intense our emotions become, but it does pass. It's a good thing you're going back today. I'll meet you at the flat." She sped off.

Chance took one last look back down the street where Bea lived. Why did he feel such an insatiable desire?

Meanwhile, Bea had a smile on her face, ear to ear. She ran up the stairs like an excited teenager who had just experienced her first kiss. She entered the living room, pressed the replay on the iPod and snuggled up on the sofa with the mead. She couldn't wait for tomorrow to begin and wondered where the courage had come from to place a kiss on his lips. It was an unplanned moment, a spilt second of impulse that filled her with joy.

Chance found the traffic maddening on the way back to Kitty's flat in Muswell Hill and screeched up by the kerb, slamming the car door.

Kitty heard his arrival from the flat, and braced herself for a confrontation. She moved away from the window and sat poised, waiting. The door of the flat opened and closed, he marched straight past the living room without a word. Kitty waited for a few minutes, but nothing. She strolled down the hall and saw him sitting at the end of his bed, just staring at the wall.

"I know it doesn't feel like it now, but the attachment passes. Humans are strange beings… part of their attraction to us, I suppose. We're *Sidhe*, we can't get involved. I'm sorry, I had no idea you liked her in that way."

Chance didn't answer.

Kitty joined him at the end of the bed. "Once you're home, this'll all become a distant dream, well, actually more like a nightmare." She laughed, but noticed that he didn't find it funny. "Look, I'll keep an eye on her a bit longer if it makes you feel better about leaving?"

"Why do you think the Unseelie were at the shop in the first place?"

She shook her head. "I don't know. They were obviously intending to cause some mischief until they felt our Seelie presence." She shrugged. "We can speculate all we want, but they've moved on now, as must we. You've done your job and luckily no damage has been done."

"I appreciate you offering to watch over her." It was obvious that he found the words difficult to say.

"Hello, she's my responsibility, too. Anyway, I thought you *warriors* of the Heaven Stone were meant to be tough nuts to crack? Spirituality trained to overcome that *emotional* side?" she teased.

"As you say... it will pass," he muttered, looking down at the floor.

"Spoken like a true warrior...Come, let me take you home. Keep in mind however, I still haven't quite forgiven you for wasting the Court's mead on a mere human."

He lifted his head. "I'll try and get some sent to you."

"I'll keep you to that... Did they warn you of the drawbacks of being in this realm?"

"Attachment?" he replied.

Kitty shook her head. "No. What was the very first thing that you noticed on your arrival?"

Chance's frown disappeared. "The smell."

"Well, I have it on good authority that when you return, it feels like you can't remove the *Earth* stench, no matter how much you bathe in the floral temple waters. Every Sidhe will avoid you and if there are any humans left in our realm, they'll get homesick and hover around you like flies, now that's something to look forward to, huh?"

They both laughed.

Kitty led the way through Coldfall Woods. It was late and

the gates had been left open for them by the gatekeeper, who never stayed. The trees rustled in the night breeze and crickets were out in abundance as they walked deeper into the woods. They didn't follow the man-made path, but instead walked a lesser-used route, taking them to a small glade in which the invisible rings, the portals, waited. The only light off the beaten track was the moonlight dancing on patches of damp grass, but it was enough for their sharp eyes. Kitty scanned the area for any possible humans, no-one was around. It was safe.

Chance stepped into an open area that started to emit sparks. The small flickers of light became faster, expanding outward until they transformed into seven, neon blue rings which danced around him.

Kitty stood back. "Remember to send the mead!" she yelled, just before the rings burst into blue flames, fully engulfing him.

Once the flames died down, Chance had gone. There were no signs in the small clearance of anything unusual ever happening. The glade was just as it was before – empty.

Kitty had longed to return home but the Order of their Court always reminded her that duty came first, in the realm of humankind.

"Home, sweet home," she grumbled, hoping that she didn't have to wait too long for Chance's promise to materialise – the sending of Courtly mead.

CHAPTER 4

Out with the Old in with the New

*B*ea's every thought, throughout the next day was consumed by Chance. She felt different, more alive somehow. He'd affected her in a way she dared not think possible after Brandon. Her stomach performed somersaults whenever he was due to arrive. When his eyes met hers, they spoke without words, a silent agreement of mutual attraction. She adored the way he would try and hide his eyes with a slight lowering of his heavy brow, but the smile on his lips would always betray him in the slow, quiet withdraw.

Medicine for my soul, she smiled to herself. What a month it had been, trying to keep Chance a secret had been tough, but now she could tell Liza all about the young professor.

When Elly saw her earlier that day, she was all grins, quite content that her cooking brought Bea a big glow of happiness. Elly always said that there was a special magic in the preparation of food. Bea laughed, *not with my cooking.*

When Jenny arrived for the children's reading session, her eyes scrutinised Bea. "Okay, there's something different about you... oh." Her eyes lit up. "You went on a date with that gentleman, the one from lunch?"

"Nope." Bea shook her head, smiling.

"He's asked you on a date?" Jenny probed.

"Nope."

"Come on, tell?"

"Not yet." Bea grinned.

"Well, whatever it is, it suits you."

The later part of the day dragged in anticipation of Chance's arrival. It reminded Bea of years ago, waiting for the last lesson in school to end, clock watching when every minute felt like a second.

Finally, six o'clock came, Jenny had left and Bea shut the shop, but there was still no sign of him. She hung around downstairs, re-arranging books and filing papers, until she could stand it no longer, and went upstairs to check her make-up and hair before sitting down in the kitchen, still no sign of him.

Liza rang. "Yep, so Leanne said that she spoke with Brandon, but he sounded distant, not his usual self. She thinks he might have taken himself off to rehab. Sorry, you don't want to hear about all that."

"No, it's good to know he's okay. Maybe, he has, I hope so." Even after everything, she never wished him any ill will. To her, Brandon was a broken child that never learned to give, unable to sustain any kind of love. He once told Bea that his mother used to hit him with a belt, shouting that he was a mistake and would always be unwanted, just like his father. On telling Bea, he broke down, that was the first and last time she'd ever seen him cry.

Liza changed the subject. "So, all's good your end?"

"Yep, I'm good." Bea's conversation was cut short when the

intercom buzzed. "Liza, I gotta go." She abruptly ended the call, not getting the time to tell of her professor. Bea rushed to the intercom. "Hello?" Her heart sunk, it was Jenny.

"I had some books given to me. Is it okay to drop them off? They're in the car."

"Sure."

Once Jenny left, and the evening went on, her mood became more solemn .*Did I scare him? Was I too full on? I shouldn't have kissed him, why did I do that?* The doubts of the old insecurities started rising to the surface. Most of her life, Bea tried to hide from disappointment by remaining alone, especially after Brandon. It felt as if every time she grew an attachment to someone, something would happen, and at the blink of an eye, they were gone. The only person who'd remained constant in her life was Liza, and the thought made her feel a little better.

It was now eleven o'clock and all hope had gone. Bea reminded herself to think more positively, after all his absence could be due to a number of things.

After a soak, she climbed into her bed and glanced over at the clock, it was nearly twelve.

She closed her eyes and tried to sleep. Instead, her thoughts went back to Chance.

When the morning arrived, she felt tired, her eyes were heavy, the alarm a distant annoyance. "Okay, okay, I'm up," she griped, climbing out of bed. She pondered on how she'd resisted the urge to ring him. Her pride wouldn't allow it. After all, he had her number.

The day dragged, and come the afternoon even her usual

conversations with Liza didn't cast off the bland mood of grey. The little bell above the shop door would ring as a customer entered and she would eagerly check to see if it was him and each time she would sigh, more deflated than the last.

The evening came, nothing.

The next day, nothing.

The following morning Bea glanced in the mirror. "Come on, you've been through worse. He was an acquaintance, that's all."

Nothing was broken, but her self-esteem had been dented...again.

Three weeks passed and she'd given up all hope of ever seeing Chance again. *The past remains in the past,* she reminded herself.

Jenny asked if she could come in more often to participate in the children's nook and Bea readily agreed. It always cheered her up to hear the sound of children's laughter. She was relieved that she didn't blurt out anything about Chance. She'd spared herself that embarrassment at least.

"Good morning, Bea," cried a cheery voice. "I wondered if you had any luck with the other Andrew Lang book?"

"No, I'm sorry, Mary."

"Oh, not to worry, it's just that it's the last one I need to complete the collection. James asked after you." Her eyes exhibited a little twinkle as she spoke.

"Did he?" Bea couldn't muster the strength to pretend she was the least bit interested.

"Yes, we keep wondering when he'll get the courage to ask

you to on a date. He's our only son but, even so, I don't sing his praises for nothing."

God, I really don't need this right now. "I'm right off men, Mary." She didn't mean to sound so blunt and felt guilty at seeing the affect it had on Mary's elderly face.

"Oh, well, erm, I'd best be off. I can't leave Mr. Brough for too long, you know how these men are when they're ill, big babies."

"Give my regards to Mr. Brough." Bea cried out after her. It was the fastest she'd seen Mary leave the shop. She sighed and flopped over the counter. *Why am I so tetchy?* Suddenly, an envelope slid in front of her on the counter. Bea looked up, and her mouth gaped open.

"Miss me?" Karian grinned, his sky-blue eyes dancing her way.

Bea peeled herself back from the counter and straightened her posture. "Deal sealed?"

"Yes, and I *deeply* apologise for not attending our arranged lunch date. I had to fly out on business. I felt terrible. I still do, a complete fiend."

"Hmm, well, I'm not sure I should forgive anyone that considers himself *a fiend.*"

"I'm hurt, crushed." Karian placed his hands over his heart and stumbled back.

Bea dismissed his childish antics and waved the mystery envelope in the air. "What's this?"

He looked more serious. "That is my other apology."

Beas eyes narrowed as she began to open the envelope, breaking the elaborate wax seal and pulling out an invitation. The calligraphy was beautifully hand-written on white card.

"Your play."

"I wanted you to be the first person to see the dress rehearsal."

Bea could see that he was much happier that his second apology had a much better effect than the first. She looked down at the invitation then back at him. "Then, I accept."

"So, I'm forgiven?" His head tilted slightly.

His presence warmed her like the sun enticing her out to play. "You're forgiven."

"May I pick you up on Friday… at seven?"

"Friday at seven," she agreed with a slight nod.

"*Thank you.* Oh, by the way… you look *amazing*." Karian tilted his head, smiled that cheeky grin and left.

She still wasn't sure what to make of him, but this was an opportunity to have some fun and she was going to grab it with both hands.

CHAPTER 5

The Alptraum of Alithia

Friday arrived, and Bea felt intermittent waves of nervousness and excitement as it drew closer to seven. She was aware that going to the theatre with a man that she hardly knew would definitely be classed as out of character, but the thought rather excited her.

Bea slipped into her little black dress and kitten heels, making that extra effort. The dress code was more formal than she usually felt comfortable with, but it was the theatre, after all. She reminded herself that she wasn't looking for any attachment, just a little something different from her normal routine. Karian seemed nice enough and besides, she'd been cooped up far too long. She needed some excitement in her life and although it wasn't going to be a wild night out, for Bea the theatre with pleasant company was quite enough.

Karian arrived dead on seven and waited patiently by the shop door with an umbrella ready to shelter her from English weather, an onslaught of rain.

"You look ...incredible." he admired, while covering her with the umbrella.

"Thank you," she mumbled, avoiding any prolonged eye contact.

He escorted her to the car, a silver Bugatti, and opened the passenger door. "You do."

"I do what?" She nervously laughed, feeling most of her earlier bravery diminishing.

"Look incredible."

His intenseness caused her to look away as she climbed in.

Karian shut her door and made his way round to the driver's side. "You don't like compliments very much do you?"

"They tend to borderline smooth talk too often." She still avoided his eyes looking out at the puddles on the pavement.

"I'm sorry that you've been hurt, Bea." He started up the car, and before she could react to the statement, he asked her another question. "Have you been to the theatre before?"

"Once…a very long time ago." He made her nervous and she knew why, it was difficult to hide from him. Unconsciously, she twiddled her thumbs as nerves got the better of her.

"What did you see?"

Bea's eyes drifted to his hand sifting gear. "Madam Butterfly."

"I have a lot to live up to then?"

"Yes, you do." When he looked at her, she always wanted to shy away. Maybe, it was noticing how often his penetrating eyes searched a little too deeply into hers. She shrugged it off, putting it down to being alone with someone she hardly knew. Bea was more used to shy men, or rather; men that didn't know how to easily express their emotions and Karian certainly didn't come across as that type.

The rain stopped prior to their arrival at the theatre and she could see the building clearly. It's bold, round façade was shabby but unique and stood proud for its years.

Karian escorted her up the huge stone steps, inside. She hadn't noticed the grace with which he moved before, but her attention quickly diverted as her eyes took in the splendour of the 1920's interior décor. Her eyes were everywhere. Tall streamlined columns welcomed them in colours of teal and gold. As she entered further, her feet felt the softness of the short-tufted carpet in a deeper teal. Bold, dark Bakelite adorned every surface, so highly polished it gleamed in the light. It was then that she noticed the murals on the ceiling, half-naked men and women, their white gowns floating in a purple haze. "Wow...It's incredible."

"Wait until you see the play," he whispered near her ear.

The hair on the back of her neck stood on end. He was close, too close, and she moved away. "I can smell popcorn."

She didn't see the smile that crept on his lips at her running away.

Bea followed the aroma leading into a smaller foyer, which was just as breath-taking, with murals spread over every wall. She strolled over to an old fashioned, popcorn machine. "That's fantastic. I'm impressed. Does it still work?"

"Yes. Would you like some?"

She nodded and Karian handed her a carton, filled to the brim. "Thank you." As she took the box, her hand touched his, and in her haste to pull away, some of the popcorn fell to the floor. Her eyes darted around the foyer, like a guilty child and Karian laughed. "Shhh." She muffled a giggle with her finger pressed to her lips, still looking to see if anyone else was around.

"Why?" He moved closer, whispering. "I own the theatre, remember?"

Bea's stomach fluttered at him being so close again. She only noticed her mouth had become dry as she tried to speak. "I know. I ...I just-" She stopped in mid-sentence as he gently moved a strand of hair from her eyes, and tucked it behind her ear. "No-one will ever know. I'll take the blame." His gesture was meant to make her feel at ease, but instead created goose bumps.

They continued their stroll down a wide corridor. Bea remained silent, nibbling on her popcorn.

As they entered the auditorium, Bea noticed that all of the seats were empty. "Are we early?"

"No, I wanted you to *literally* be the first...the *only* person to see the play."

Bea's eyes filled with astonishment. "For me?"

"For you."

"Oh."

A young man with long dark hair, and the purest blue eyes approached, and kindly escorted them to their seats in the dress circle on the first floor, providing central viewing of the stage. Everything gold glistened in the array of glass droplet lighting suspended from the high ceiling, including the glided carving on the many rows of seats, covered with teal velour.

Once they'd got comfortable she asked, "Who was that?"

"A friend of mine, pretending to be an usher. I know he's a little unusual, don't hold it against me. He's quite harmless. Would you like a drink?" He waved his hand and another man, dressed in a rather ill-fitted butler's uniform, poured them a drink and then went on his way.

Bea thought he looked bizarrely comical and muffled another giggle.

Karian laughed too. "My pretend staff have quite the sense of humour don't they?"

"They do." She continued to giggle.

Karian held up his glass. "To Bea, who will no doubt be my most severe critic."

"I promise to be gentle." She smiled and raised her glass. It was then, that a familiar smell hit her. The floral aroma was still very fresh in her mind, but she took a sip just to be sure, confirming that it was the same mead that Chance had brought on the night of their meal.

"You look puzzled?" Karian said.

"Oh, I…it's just that I have tasted this before."

"You're mistaken," he coolly replied. "*This* is a very rare vintage."

"Really?" She laughed, holding her glass up trying to get a better look. "It's mead made from flowers and the label on the bottle has some crazy symbols on it."

Karian's face dropped.

"It's alright. You don't need to impress me. I'm already overwhelmed, but it would seem that the mead is not as rare as it claims." She smiled, taking another sip and observed Karian's jaw tense. *Maybe, I've embarrassed him*, she thought. "This quiet Kari, I'm not used to."

"I'm sorry… I…I'm disappointed. I wanted to surprise you." His eyes hid from hers for the first time, staring out into the auditorium. "When did you try the mead?"

Bea wished that she hadn't said anything. She really didn't need reminding of Chance, or mean to deflate Karian's mood. "A while ago."

Karian nodded, remaining quiet.

"And by the way, you have surprised me. I *adore* the mead and the company is *very* charming."

The Karian grin returned and she felt relieved, sitting back further in her chair.

A sombre melody started to travel throughout the auditorium and he leant closer. "The play is about to begin."

Bea eyes met his in excitement. "This is going to be wonderful." Her attention went back to the stage as the luxurious, red velvet curtains started to part exposing the stage. Bea quickly became mesmerised by the scenery. First a night forest setting, trees glittering via moonbeams, changing to daylight for the next scene where the props of trees had leaves that moved in a warm breeze which spread throughout the theatre, and dangling white-silver birds gracefully floated across the stage. "*It's beautiful,*" Bea muttered, under her breath.

Karian's eyes never once left her.

Bea had forgotten to ask what type of play it was, but once a couple entered the stage her question was answered – ballet. Through the first part of the play, Karian watched her every expression as the story unfolded, his reaction, accentuated by hers.

A young woman with long golden hair, dressed in a white tutu graced with lengths of flowing blue fabric, danced across the glade into the arms of her waiting lover. He swept her up in a loving embrace and swung her around, ecstatic that she'd managed to escape home and come to meet him.

They swirled and twirled with elegant bounds and lifts. The woman's laughter filled the room as the young man danced a proud peacock strut. The male lover then took her hand and they sat on a nearby ruins wall. He cried out, "I care not what they say, for I love my Alithia, and I swear by the light that burns bright within me that I shall *never* love another."

"Karian, *please* don't tempt Vororbla." The woman, Alithia, pleaded, before placing a kiss on his lips. The sun began to fade behind layers of purple hues, an otherworldly sunset casting the shadow of night, blanketing every part of the stage. A twinkling of tiny lights, imitating stars, started to flicker as the sombre music of interlude started to play and the rich red curtains closed.

During the interval, more mead was poured by the odd-looking butler. Bea observed that he too, had long silky black hair, pale skin and the most incredible blue eyes. "Are they brothers?" She kept her voice low.

Karian shook his head and smiled. "No, though I think they could be related somehow… Would it be unfair to ask what you thought of the play so far?"

Bea placed her hand on her chest. "It's breath-taking, and so romantic, though I'm a little confused on one thing."

"What's that?"

"Where it's set?"

"In another realm." His stare drifted to the stage.

"What realm?"

Karian looked at her, his mouth turned to form a gentle smile. "Wherever you wish it to be."

"Oh, great answer…Did you actually write the play?"

He nodded.

"Quite an accomplishment. Where did you get the idea from?" Bea sipped more of the mead.

His eyes lowered. "I've carried the story in my heart for many years. I've yearned for so long to get to this point. It has forever been a part of me."

For the first time, Bea thought she saw a glimpse of vulnerability. "I imagine it feels quite surreal, finally fulfilling your dream?"

Karian's eyes fixed on Bea's. "More than you know."

She placed her hand on his. "Well done." But she didn't see him close his eyes at the contact, her attention had returned to the stage as the melody began to play once more. On removing her hand, she also failed to see the impact it had.

The curtains opened and she quickly leant over and whispered, "I forgot to say…the name of the main character *Karian*, is a clever way to incorporate your own signature. Was that in case you forgot?"

A big grin swept over his face.

Bea quietly chuckled, before returning her attention to the stage.

During the last part of the play, Bea was aware that her eyes were glistening, but it didn't matter. She was too engrossed to care.

The scenery had changed to dense, green woodlands, where sat a stone well. The male lover was now on his knees, blooded and bruised sobbing his love's name. Several men surrounded him, clubs and whips in hand.

Bea's breathing became shallow, more pronounced, as the

devastated cry of the male lead filled the auditorium which, once faded, left an eerie silence.

Bea wiped her eyes as the melody filled the room for the last time, and the curtains closed. She immediately got up from her seat and started to applaud but quickly, sat back down again.

"Are you alright?" Karian asked, as his hand steadied her.

Bea rested her head in her hands. "I must've got up too fast."

Karian started clapping in her stead. The curtains re-opened as the dancing actors took their bow. Bea forced herself to get back up and resume her show of appreciation, until the curtains made their final closure. Suddenly, she started to sway.

Karian stabilized her in his arms. "What's wrong?"

"My head, it feels... too much mead." She forced a laugh but the dizziness violently returned. "I need to stretch my legs. I'm sorry, Kari."

"No, please don't apologise, here. Lean on me." He gently placed his arm around her waist and escorted her to the end of the aisle. "Do you feel any better?"

Bea couldn't seem to shake the odd sensation fogging her concentration, but didn't want Karian to worry. "Slightly." He looked unconvinced and held her closer and she reluctantly rested her head on his chest.

Bea's heart started to race as she felt his breathing deepen against her cheek. She moved away, confused by the new feelings of wanting stirring inside her. "Wow. No more mead for me." She exhaled to try and clear her head managing a smile. "The play was fantastic, by the way, sad, but *really*, quite touching."

Karian edged closer. "I never intended for there to be any sadness."

Bea frowned. "So, why did you choose that way of death for her? And hearing her lover's cry, it was so...devastating."

"Don't you remember?" His eyes became fixed on hers and looked bluer somehow.

"Remember?" She repeated, confused. Her head still felt foggy. "Kari I think... I might need some fresh air."

"Try to remember?" His voice was gentle, yet demanding.

Her head pounded. "What are you talking about?" The room was starting to blur.

"I did all this for you... *to remember.*"

Suddenly, an image of blurred trees flashed before her eyes. Her head started to spin and she became more disorientated as another unexplainable image flashed before her. She tried to pull away, but Karian held her even closer, tighter.

"My Alithia," he whispered, tenderly placing his cheek upon hers.

What's happening? Bea tried to move but couldn't. She felt scared, unsure of what she heard.

"I have waited too long to hold you in my arms again. *Feel me.*"

She was shocked at her body responding to his words and found herself in an embrace that she had no control over. She tried to pull away, but his hold was fast.

"*Remember.*" His eyes begged, before his mouth suddenly met hers.

Her head was spinning, her body accepting. She used all her will to pull back and slapped his face. "Let go!"

His mouth released its temporary claim on her, but his

hold remained firm. His eyes searched hers. "*Please*, don't turn me away, not now, now, I've found you."

Bea instinctively kicked out at him and the tip of her shoe connected with his shin. He groaned and relinquished his hold and she started to run, but it felt as though her feet were making no ground. Her head was pounding, spinning. She could hear Karian crying out behind her but it was not her name that he was calling, it was Alithia's. The haunting echo of his voice became more distant once she managed to find the theatre's emergency side exit and she scrambled out into the cold damp air of the night.

CHAPTER 6

The Return

A loud buzzing made Bea stir. Her head began to thud as she sat up, and she quickly laid back down, but the continual noise drove her crazy. She opened her eyes trying to focus on where the sound was coming from, but she still felt disorientated from her dream. The buzzing eventually stopped and Bea tried to rest, at least until her head settled.

The images of her dream kept playing over in her mind of running, someone calling her, but she couldn't see who it was. It was no use, she couldn't get back to sleep. Bea got up, went to the bathroom and splashed cold water over her face, which helped with the grogginess, once the internal pounding passed.

She was optimistic that tea would help and the kettle was on. She reached for the teabags but the box fell to the ground. It was then she noticed that her hair was damp. *I must've wet it when I splashed my face*, she thought and finished off making tea. She strolled into the living room and was about to sit down until, out the corner of her eye, she noticed that her kitten-heel shoes were left the landing. She went to investigate. By the stairs also lay her little black dress. She walked over and picked it up, it too, like her hair, was damp. A flashback of her running out of the theatre appeared in her mind. She instantly dropped the dress and went in search for her bag. She found it with half the contents sprawled down the stairs.

After scooping everything up, she placed the bag on the kitchen table, and noticed the invitation announcing itself from the front flap. She pulled it out and placed it in front of her on the table. "Shit!" she exclaimed, in realisation that it was not a dream at all.

The memory of the night's events vividly returned. Her eyes filled with angry tears as she recalled Karian's mouth on hers, calling out the name, Alithia. Bea rested her head in her hands, and jumped when the buzzing returned. This time she knew it was the intercom. Her heart quickened at the thought of it being Karian. She paced the small kitchen as the buzzing persisted, then sat back down on the chair, wondering what to do. Bea pleaded to the void for the noise to stop and in that moment, it did. She exhaled with relief, slumping on the table. The thought of seeing Karian again scared her. Having to kick him to let her go had pushed her to a point that she hadn't been to before, using aggression. She waited a few more minutes before creeping downstairs to check he'd gone.

Bea hovered by the side of the shop door. She'd never bitten her nails ever, until now. It was hard to stay still. Should she risk a peek? If he saw her what would she do? She briefly closed her eyes and took a deep breath, bracing herself before slowly moving the blind aside. She saw a dark figure standing in the rain and quickly released the blind. "Shit!" Her heart skipped. *He didn't see me,* she reassured herself, taking more deep breaths. Luckily, the figure's back was turned. After a few more seconds, Bea plucked up the courage to take another peep, this time from a different angle. Once again, she slowly pulled the blind to one side and a face suddenly appeared. She jumped back, holding her chest, making sure that her heart was still intact. *It can't be?* Once Bea regulated her breathing a little, her trembling hands unlocked the door.

Chance was soaked through. Water droplets tippled down from his short, fair hair down onto his rounded face, where his cool, blue eyes were quietly pleading.

Bea was speechless, not knowing whether to laugh or cry with relief. She cut her eyes and walked away, but left the door ajar as she made her way back upstairs. The mix of emotion left her confused, but with every step, her earlier fears of it being Karian became replaced with anger. As she entered the kitchen, her hands began to shake, trying to contain the feelings of hurt and relief at seeing Chance's face again.

Chance glanced down at the wet dress and shoes left on the landing before he entered the kitchen.

Bea's eyes flashed with flickers of accusal as she silently waited to hear the excuse of his disappearance. Maybe, the two hurts were blending, she wasn't sure.

He stood by the door and stared uneasily in her direction. "I wasn't sure you'd let me in…thank you."

Bea's foot tapping was the only response she gave to his words, a habit only exposed when annoyed.

"I didn't think you would talk to me after…" He corrected himself. "Well, you're not talking to me." His hands rested either side of the doorframe, his head lowered.

Bea didn't reply, still trying to rationalise the raw emotions stirring within her.

"I…I shouldn't have left like that. No words can express how sorry I am."

She still didn't answer, knowing he felt her angry stare as his eyes met with hers. She was in turmoil, but refused to let the tears, welling in her eyes, to fall. Finally, she broke her silence. "Just out of curiosity, why? Why did you leave without a word…Nothing? Then, all of a sudden…look, you're here." The events at the theatre had reminded her of how safe she felt with Chance. All she wanted to do was feel the warmth of that secureness again, for him to hold her tightly in his arms. She needed him, but her pride refused to let him know.

He stepped closer, letting his arms fall to his side. "I will *never* walk away like that again."

She shook her head, turning away, discreetly wiping one of the tears that had managed to escape.

Chance backed off, his eyes stared down at the invitation lying on the table. He picked it up, and his eyes narrowed.

She felt vulnerable in that moment. Her strong barrier began to crumble.

"Who is he?" Chance calmly enquired, throwing the invite back on the table.

How dare he even ask? Bea thought, slowly shaking her head.

He walked over and placed a hand on hers. "Who is he?"

She pulled away, and stormed out of the kitchen. "I think it's time you left."

He marched after her. "Who invited you to *that* theatre?"

"What right have you got to even ask?" They were face to face. Her whole body was in conflict, she wanted to grab him, kiss him, but also scream at his audacity.

"It matters. Tell me!"

Bea resisted his demand, but a tear escaped and rolled down her cheek. Her defence was falling. He lowered his eyes, and his voice softened. "I know I disappeared but …*I need to* know who invited you to *this* theatre?" He went to wipe the tear, but Bea pushed his hand away.

"Why? You weren't here. You just left," she replied.

"I still…I care, Bea. *Please,* tell me who he is?"

In pure frustration she shouted his name. "Kari… his name is Kari. Satisfied?"

He stepped back, not saying a word.

To Bea, it was a visual acknowledgement that her words stung. She stared at him confused. "Why did you disappear? You say you care…but where were you?" The pain caused by his absence, she knew, was evident with every new, glistening tear.

He winced.

"Why did you leave without a word?" she asked, but actually meaning I need you.

He didn't reply.

"You never rang, you never -" Without warning his mouth met hers, but he quickly pulled away. They stood staring at one another, each waiting for the other to confirm what they both wanted. The atmosphere grew more intense with every breath of jumbled emotion.

"I get *lost* in you." His voice strained, eyes damp with a strange confession that she didn't understand. She was trying so hard to resist the man that she hadn't seen for so long. Who had left her, with no word of his return, yet, through his eyes, had promised everything. She wanted to remain angry, strong, but she couldn't bear another moment without his touch, his mouth on hers. She'd been starved and now she knew that he'd been the source of her starvation. Bea stepped closer to him. "I don't want to get hurt, not again.

I'm scared. Say that you won't hurt me. Tell me that you'll stay."

Chance grimaced as he wiped away another of her tears. "I never meant to cause you any pain." His eyes stared into hers. "Believe me, not one day passed that I didn't think about you...the way your mouth moves when you smile. The way you hide your cheeks when you're embarrassed, tap your foot when you're annoyed. Don't ever think that I don't see you."

She was about to say something, but only mumbled as his mouth passionately embraced hers. Bea gasped, not realising how much she'd missed the feel of someone in her arms, and her body expressed her rising need by pressing against his.

Chance lifted her with ease from her feet, keeping his tight embrace as he carried her through to the bedroom, laying her gently on the bed. He hesitated, his arms abreast of her. She could see that he was fighting with his usual restraint and so pulled him closer. "Don't stop."

Their lips met with a consuming need as she encouraged his hand to explore her for the first time. She pulled Chance's shirt up over his head, throwing it in the air. Hers eyes took in every exposed muscle as her hand ran slowly down his smooth, strong, inviting chest. Her fingertips caressed a faint scar, then another. "What happened to-" She was cut short as his lips overpowered hers and the question fled from her mind.

After the detour of every curve, Bea's hand reached the band of his trousers. Her fingers artfully made entry and slid down further. He groaned her name, as if asking his weakness for mercy. Bea's senses heightened with the sound but she had no intentions of releasing him, he was finally hers.

Side by side, they caressed and explored one another's bodies. He mirrored Bea's movements, her flesh now fully exposed. His mouth tenderly slid over her breast and she gasped at the sensuous, playful touch of his tongue. Her mouth opened slightly, exhaling a groan as he gently lowered and pressed between her thighs. He was gentle, slow and considerate in his giving.

Bea turned him over and sat astride his burly body and as she gyrated, his eyes stared up at her, until she paused in movement, due to the deftness of his fingers. She moaned, jittered and flexed in ecstasy with every one of his carefully placed caresses.

Chance gently flipped her over, taking control. Bea knew he'd waited before fulfilling his own needs. The faster his body moved, the more she began to pull at the sheets as her body screamed out in readiness for his completion. He tensed and shuddered and with this tremor, she reached a new state of satisfying bliss.

When Bea woke, Chance was leaning on the pillow; head tilted, staring down at her, which made her smile. He tenderly kissed her lips and slowly ran his hand down her side, his fingers again, tracing every curve.

"Is it really morning already?" she asked, as her hand met his, entwined.

"We have a few more hours before the light officially announces the morning." He spoke softly and then kissed her shoulder, moving down to her breasts. His tongue tantalized and sent shivers through her whole body. Bea wrapped her legs around him, bringing her closer still to what was ready and waiting.

Their pleasures continued deep into the early hours.

Bea's alarm screamed for attention as it did every morning, but this time, another pair of hands made the noise disappear. Chance kissed her nose and smiled. "It's officially morning." He didn't want her to wake. He enjoyed watching her sleep, but he knew with her warm naked body next to his, he would never get out of bed.

"Last night, you called me your weakness? What did you mean? Did you make a vow of chastity?" She giggled, caressing his smooth chest.

"Something like that." He ran his fingers over the inside of her left arm and read aloud the words of her tattoo. "What you seek is seeking you?"

She looked down at the text. "A quote by Rumi, my uncle introduced me to him. When he died, my friend Liza and I got so very drunk, somehow we ended up at a tattooist." She laughed. "I don't actually remember most of that evening, but I like to think this was done in memory of him."

"He must've been very special." His fingertips traced the writing.

"He was…How did you get those scars?" Her eyes drifted to the silvery-white lines on the top of his right shoulder.

"Can we talk about it another time?" His eyes remained on her tattoo in the brief silence that followed.

"I missed you."

She surprised him with the revelation, but it felt good and his eyes met hers. "I missed you, too… *very* much." He leant forward, placing a kiss between her brows, and decided that he would try to approach the subject of Karian. "What was the play at the theatre about?" He felt a slight tension in the air, and was about to change the subject, until she said, "Some woman fell in love and died."

Chance couldn't help but smile at her attempt at flippancy. "I know the play."

Bea looked up at him in astonishment. "Really?"

He slid down the bed, closer to Bea, to try and engage her further. "I'm a professor of folklore remember? It's a folk tale."

"Oh."

"The woman's name is Alithia."

Bea remained silent.

"She falls in love with a…a man that her family does not approve of. If I remember correctly, she drowns at the end of the play?"

"Yes." Bea quietly replied.

Chance saw no fun in her eyes of the stories re-telling. His heart, his senses told him to stop, but his job, his role as a warrior, pushed a little further. He placed his hand on Bea's. "What did he do to upset you?"

Her eyes met his in an instant. "What makes you ask that?"

"I feel it." He gently stroked her nose.

Bea got up from the bed, slipped on his shirt and strolled over to the window.

Chance followed her. "You can talk to me."

"About an evening spent with someone else?" she replied.

Bea's words hit him harder than they should have, and he wrapped his arms around her waist, pulling her closer. She buried her face in his chest, and he whispered by her ear. "If you don't want to tell me, it's okay. I'll wait."

Bea's voice became a mumble, as she re-told the night's events. "So, really the moral of the story is that mead should only be drunk in small quantities."

Chance cupped her face in his hands. "Thank you. *Please,* don't ever feel that you can't speak to me. You can tell me anything."

Bea smiled as he tenderly rubbed his nose against hers. "I feel better airing it. It really freaked me out at the time. I've never experienced anything like that before. I've tried so hard to put it to the back of my mind, but-"

"I shouldn't have left." He knew that he failed to protect her.

"No, no you shouldn't have." She tenderly kissed his mouth. "But that's in the past. *Hold me.*" Chance held her even tighter, but it took all his strength to contain the new emotion stirring inside as her words echoed in his mind, *Karian wouldn't release his hold until I kicked him.* Jealousy twisted his gut, even picturing her kicking him didn't ease the rising of anger. It confirmed what he already knew, Karian was pursuing Bea, trying to recapture the soul of his past love, Alithia, but there was one thing Karian did not know, the next time he came calling...he would be waiting. Chance sighed, and needed to lighten the mood. "Ready for breakfast?"

"Wow, erm, sure...Toast please, with just a touch of jam." She gestured the size with her thumb and index finger.

He laughed, and picked up his crumpled trousers from floor by the bed, and slipped then on. Before leaving the room, he blew her a kiss.

Bea lay back down with a big, fat, contented grin spreading across her face. *How quickly life can change,* she thought. But his quietness concerning his scars bothered her, and she wondered what awful thing had caused them.

After breakfast Bea looked at the clock and pouted. "I have to get ready to open the shop."

He wrapped her up in his arms and sighed. "I have work too, but I don't want to ask for my shirt back." He stood back a little, admiring her figure.

"I can take it off if you like?" she asked, as her hand reached for the band of his trousers.

He backed further away and laughed. "No, I won't have the strength to go. Leave me with the image of you wearing it." He looked down at his naked chest. "I'll just have to pop home and grab another shirt. May I come over tonight?"

"Are you kidding, you'd better be here tonight." She pressed her body up against his, and placed her mouth within an inch of his. "If you're not here, the shirt will get it, and be warned, I'll show no mercy."

His lips met hers, mumbling, "I'm definitely returning."

CHAPTER 7

No Way Home

From the street, Chance stared up at the sash windows of Kitty's flat in Muswell Hill, bracing himself for an interrogation. As he approached the front door, the downstairs neighbour exited, greeting him with a broad smile as she brushed past. "See you later." Chance nodded, he'd only seen her twice before, and her over-friendliness made him feel uneasy. He never understood why Kitty would want to live in a converted Edwardian house, surely it would've been safer, more private, to own a house. Once upstairs, he took a deep breath before unlocking the door and entering.

"You didn't come back?" Kitty bellowed from the kitchen.

He wasn't going to be fazed by the pre-lecture mode, and walked straight into the lounge.

It wasn't long until she appeared, arms crossed in front of her. "Well?"

"I found out something."

"Really? Enough to justify your absence last night?"

He walked over to the window, moved the curtain aside, and stared down to the street below. "Bea met someone while I was away."

"Who?" Kitty's tone changed.

He took a deep breath. "Karian." The name left a bitter taste in his mouth.

"Karian?" She looked baffled. "*Unseelie* Karian?"

"Is there another?" He muttered, hardly believing it himself.

"No need for flippancy…No, that's not possible. I made sure the shop was watched."

"For how long?" He turned to face her.

"Two weeks after you left. There wasn't any Unseelie presence, let alone the Prince. How-"

"Bea first met him outside a pub. He apparently came to her aid when her ex showed up and then she bumped into him again, outside Elly's."

"Elly's?"

"The bistro next to the shop…When we came on the scene, Bea didn't see him again. It was only when…when I left that he showed up." He looked away and Kitty joined him at the window. "You're saying they… *Karian* was present because of Bea?"

"Yes." He closed his eyes. Hearing her say the words somehow made it more real.

"I don't understand. Why? Why would Karian risk getting found, for a *human*? No. It doesn't make sense. Why Bea?"

"Karian invited her to a play…The Alptraum, nightmare of *Alithia*, at the Dorcha Crùn theatre." Chance passed her the invitation.

Kitty's eyes widened. "No, it can't be…*Alithia*." She gasped, and promptly sat down. Her hands then covered her mouth, saying something in their own language. Chance couldn't figure out the muffled noise, but could tell that her mind was racing. "We have to report this straight away," she blurted. "So, she told you it was actually *Karian* that invited her?"

"She called him…*Kari*…His search is finally over."

She leaned forward. "You have to stay close to her now. We'll have to take it slow, but we need to know if he's told her anything. You said she looked upset, do you think Bea is aware of our presence here? Or even the reason for her own presence?"

Chance ran his hands over his head trying to figure out the best plan of action. "I'll talk with the Queen. It's best that we don't inform the Order yet. Let me find out what she knows and what Karian wants."

"He wants Bea," blurted Kitty.

Chance glared at her. "That's not going to happen."

"Why wouldn't you want to inform the Order? It's protocol."

"Just give me more time to assess the situation." He didn't want the Order of the Court, or rather, Saras, knowing anything.

"We might not have time. Queen Eliseis will want her daughter back. The form that Alithia's soul has taken will not matter." She reminded, pacing the room.

"If that's what Bea chooses. Free will *is* her right, and how can she make a choice if she doesn't know who she is? Give me more time."

"You're implying the Order will not give her a choice."

"They would advance her knowledge too soon," he replied.

"I'll delay in notifying the Order, if Queen Eliseis agrees. Be careful how you tread, Anathon. The Order will not take kindly to a guard of the Court breaking any ancient rulings, not even for one of The Heaven Stone…I mean it. Be *very* careful. For some unfathomable reason, I have grown quite attached to you."

He nodded in acknowledgement, knowing Kitty used his true name to emphasize her friendly warning. "Have there been any developments with the Unseelie hunt?"

"No, we can't get near the theatre. His Deisi, witch girlfriend has placed some sort of protective shield around the building."

"Cynthia?"

"That's the one." Kitty slumped back in the chair.

"Eliseis previously informed me that a *Seelie* Deisi was sent here."

"Yup, I heard that too, but we haven't heard anything more."

"Odd...How many Unseelie reside in the theatre?"

"It's difficult to say...Our reports estimate between twenty and forty at a time. We track any Unseelie that leave, even captured a few and sent them back home, but until they've all returned, my stay here is a prolonged agony," she groaned.

"Cynthia's the problem."

Kitty nodded. "It's just too difficult to track most of them, we're no match for her magic, and Karian knows it."

"I will ask Eliseis where this Seelie Deisi can be found."

"Did she give you a name?" asked Kitty.

"She said it isn't important we know right now."

"Well, I hope it's soon, Karian won't stay away from Alithia long."

"Bea. Her name is Bea." he corrected.

"Bea to you, Alithia to him...Remember that important difference."

He glared at Kitty, but thought better of retaliating. "We still have one advantage."

"What's that?"

"Karian isn't aware that we know he's found Bea." Kitty seemed distant. "Has something happened that you're not telling me?"

She rolled her eyes. "I've been removed from our realm for so long, that I sometimes forget I'm even a Sidhe...I asked if I could go home."

"They refused?"

"I'm too valuable. No-one has my amount of experience with the human kind," she mimicked. "You know, sometimes, I really have to concentrate when I want to picture the fields of home, even the inside of the Court."

"I can make some enquiries. Maybe, another voice will help get you home sooner."

"Would you?"

He smiled seeing the hope in her eyes and nodded. "I would really appreciate you agreeing to do a favour for me, too."

"What?"

"I want Bea to meet my sister."

"Oh. The human bonding thing. We talked about that boundary."

"It's only dinner. You don't have to meet with her again."

"How long are you going to play at a pretend relationship?"

"That hurt."

"*That* is fact. We're here to investigate, no more, no less."

"I didn't want this, she saw through my glamour, remember? I returned home and they sent me back. Someone else could've been sent in...Why me?"

"I don't know." She shrugged.

"I'm doing what is asked of me, that's all." He was fed up with being reminded to draw the line.

"At least be honest with yourself...that is not all." Kitty raised her brow.

"I take full responsibility for my actions here. Now, will you please join us for dinner?"

"Where?" She looked bored.

Chance smiled, he knew she wouldn't be able to resist. It was the crème de la crème of Sidhe hangouts, reserved for the more elite of Seelies. "The Bluebell Manor."

Her eyes lit up. "How did you? Never mind...Well, of course I must assist in your observations of the human."

He had her. "Thank you."

Kitty eyes twinkled with excitement. "When are we going?"

"Tomorrow."

"Tomorrow! That's *extremely* short notice."

"It's twenty-four human hours."

"*Yes*, and I need to shop. Here, female humans shop for every occasion. I'll need a new outfit...Hello, the illustrious Bluebell."

He dismissed her whining. "I'll pick you up tomorrow."

"Time?" She blankly asked.

"Two."

"I'll be ready" Her grin reappeared.

When Chance met Bea, he explained that he had planned a surprise. She hounded him so much that he finally admitted it was to meet Kitty. He would never forget the broad smile that appeared on her face. All night Kitty's warning tormented him, but he had no intentions of re-building broken boundaries. He would just have to be more careful.

CHAPTER 8

Bluebell Manor

$\mathcal{T}$he big day arrived, and Bea was perfecting her make up when Chance beeped the horn. She grabbed her bag and met him outside.

Standing beside him was Kitty in her best, retro, Camden Town garb.

"Bea, this is Kitty. Kitty, Bea." Surprisingly, he was enjoying the charade.

Kitty gave Bea a double kiss greeting on each cheek. "It's wonderful to meet you, Bea." She turned to Chance. "She's adorable."

Don't overdo it, thought Chance, forcing a smile her way.

"I've been looking forward to meeting you, Kitty. I see you both have the same incredible blue eyes."

Kitty chuckled, climbing into the rear seat of the car.

"So, where are we going?" Bea asked.

"Yes, Chance, do tell." Kitty grinned at him.

"This is the one part I'm keeping a surprise," he replied, his eyes narrowed in Kitty's direction, silently warning her to behave.

The women chatted away for most of the journey. He was pleased that they seemed to be getting along, and he secretly hoped that Kitty would think twice of informing the Court and Saras.

"We're here." Kitty smiled as they approached two massive, steel gates.

"You knew where we were going?" Bea looked at her surprised.

"Chance had to tell, I nagged him terribly. He made me swear to utmost secrecy...sorry." Kitty winced.

Chance spoke into the intercom and the gates began to open. They drove along a wide, winding, cobbled driveway, and as the car swept around a second bend, Bea gasped at the imposing manor house before them. It was huge. Once the car got closer, she saw a mass of purple wisteria on the house's exterior, beautiful.

Chance pulled up in front of the Manor's steps, and the doors of the car were opened for them by two ushers. Chance offered his hand, as Bea and Kitty climbed out.

The surroundings, combined with the aroma of the flowers, made Bea's senses soar.

"What do you think?" whispered Kitty.

"I'm speechless."

Chance threw his car keys to the valet. "Ladies." He extended his arms. Both Bea & Kitty looped their arms through his, and were escorted up the stairs to the entrance.

Bea had made a special effort in her apparel to meet Kitty, but on entering the manor, felt a little under dressed for the occasion, it screamed pure luxury. She stood in awe at her surroundings as Chance talked with Kitty. The entrance hall boasted the most spectacular, largest chandelier that she had ever seen. One word sprung to mind, exquisite. Out the corner of her eye, she saw Kitty wandering off, up a huge staircase to the side of the main entrance hall.

"Where's Kitty going?"

"To powder her nose." He smiled, escorting Bea further inside.

He gave the maître d' their names and they were shown to their table.

Bea's eyes were everywhere. She'd never seen such splendour in one place before. Everything glimmered, sparkled and looked new. Chance ordered some champagne, while she sat in awe taking everything in.

"Do you like it?"

"I love it…and by the way, your sister's great too."

Chance swapped seats with Kitty's empty chair and held Bea's hand. His other hand crept into the fold of her neck and he gently pulled her closer, placing a slow kiss upon her lips. Bea felt dizzy with happiness. Everything but him faded, and all that mattered was his touch. *Am I living inside a dream*, she wondered, hoping the magic would never end.

When Kitty returned, they ordered their meal.

Bea found her funny, especially as she tormented Chance at any given opportunity, and he, to his credit, tolerated her playfulness. It was just what she imagined having a sibling would be like.

After their meal, everyone applauded as a pianist entered the large hall. He sat down at the grand piano and nimbly played I Giorni by Ludovico Einaudi. Goosebumps covered her entire body. She'd never heard anyone other than her mother play the tune, and it felt as if she were giving her approval. Tears formed in Bea's eyes.

"Is something wrong?" Chance asked.

"No." She shook her head and gave him a reassuring smile. "Everything's perfect."

He was about to kiss her cheek, when his attention suddenly drifted, as did his grip of her hand. She followed Chance's eyes and saw two men standing in front of their table.

They slightly tilted their heads as a manner of greeting.

"Chance, Kitty." The slimmer one, with collar-length blond hair spoke first. "And who is this charming lady?"

Bea noticed Chance's body tense, and her eyes reverted back to the men.

Kitty answered their question. "This is Bethany, but she prefers to be called Bea."

The taller, dark-suited man, offered his hand and Bea met it out of courtesy. "I am Saras, and this is my acquaintance, Valu. It is our pleasure, Bea."

She forced a smile, tilting her head in return.

Valu politely asked Bea to dance.

"Oh, no I…" She was about to decline when Kitty's eyes gestured that she accept, so she did… reluctantly.

Valu was not as tall as Saras, and only slightly broader. His blond hair shone under the light of the huge chandeliers in the hall. She felt his stare and looked away. As they danced, her feet clumsily followed his lead, struggling to keep up. Valu moved gracefully, it was Bea fumbling her way through. At every opportunity, her eyes glanced over at the table in Chance's direction. He appeared unhappy since they had announced themselves. *Who were these unusual men?*

Valu tried to converse with Bea, but she kept her answers

to swift yes and no's, which he seemed to find amusing.

Making their way back to the table after the awkward dance, they found that Chance had gone.

Valu graciously dismissed himself.

"Where's Chance?" Bea's tone alerted Kitty to her concerns.

"It's alright, look, he's at the bar talking with Saras." Kitty's head gestured behind her.

Bea sat down. "Why did you want me to dance with Valu?"

"Was he that awful? I've never danced with him." Kitty pulled a face. "I'm sorry. Saras and Chance needed to catch up, and Valu seemed to really want to dance with you. I've known him many years and he's never asked me to dance. It's quite a compliment."

Bea looked over at the bar then back at Kitty. "Chance isn't happy about them joining us, is he?" She had second thoughts at seeing Kitty's raised brow. "Maybe, it was the element of surprise I saw? I don't know."

"You really like Chance, don't you?" Kitty ran her finger around the rim of the glass, and a note softly rang out.

"I do." Bea took a deep breath and leant closer. "I think I'm falling in love with him." She couldn't believe her revelation, or the look that it brought to Kitty's face.

"You haven't been together long. Can you be sure it's love, maybe you're just infatuated?" Kitty replied.

"It's not infatuation." Bea gently protested. "As you're his sister, I wanted you to know that I do have strong feelings for him." *Maybe, it was too soon to be so open.*

Bea sat in silence as Kitty glanced over at Chance, and gulped down the rest of her champagne. "No... No, I'm glad you feel that you can trust me enough to reveal your heart's secrets. I think Chance…" Kitty looked uncomfortable. "I *know* that he has a strong attachment to you, too."

"Really?" It made Bea felt better about her confession.

Kitty answered with a nod. "Here, have some more champers." She shooed the waiter away, and poured herself.

"What do you think they're talking about?" Bea glanced over at the bar.

"Who knows? Men and business means boring." Kitty rolled her eyes.

"They're business associates?"

Kitty gulped down more of the champers. "Oh, look, he's returning."

Chance joined them back at the table. He seemed different. There was no warmth in his face, and his eyes made no contact with hers.

"We're leaving, I'll meet you both outside." he said.

"What happened?" Bea asked, confused by his abruptness.

"Business didn't work out as planned," he mumbled, before marching off.

"Have you seen him like this before?" Bea asked.

"No." Kitty answered, truthfully.

Outside, Chance was already in the car, engine running, and passenger doors open. Bea and Kitty climbed in. He didn't speak a word, and once the women were in, he sped off.

Bea was in shock at his lack of acknowledgement and brash manner, but still decided to reach for his hand. To her surprise, he moved it away. Her embarrassment at his rejection began to build up in the form of tears. She turned her head towards the window. The atmosphere in the car became tense.

Bea did not see the glare that Kitty gave him, but she heard the snarl that he gave in return.

How could such a perfect day end like this, who was this man? Bea silently asked the blurring world outside her window.

The return journey was nothing like the arrival. Bea couldn't wait to get out of the car. She remembered feeling like this before with Brandon, on several occasions. An excruciating need to escape the confinement of silent aggression. Bea hated conflict, after an argument it would take her hours, perhaps days, to become fully relaxed again. Every part of her body became anxious, not entirely brought on by Chance's coldness, but the adding of old hurts, and the way her body would instinctively react to them. It wasn't a feeling that she wanted to experience with someone new, of whom she'd told his sister only a short time ago that she was falling in love with.

A last, the uncomfortable journey of internal torture ended, as the car pulled up in front of the bookshop. The silence in the car was like a crushing weight at stress point, until Kitty spoke. "It was really nice meeting you, Bea." Kitty gave her a warm, but uncomfortable smile.

"You, too, Kitty, take care." Bea's gaze paused at Chance, but he still wouldn't look at her. She took a deep breath, rising above it. "I had a great time...I'm only sorry that you didn't."

He turned his face away and her heart sank.

"Bye," she whispered, before getting out of the car. It was horrible, everything good turning so sour, and the worst of it – she didn't know why.

Bea refused to turn around on hearing the car screech off. Instead, she fumbled frantically in her bag for the keys to the shop. Her hands began to shake as she opened the door. Her emotions were all over the place. She slammed the door behind her, and began to make her way through the shop, but paused on reaching the stairway, glancing over at her uncle's winged chair. In that spilt second, she pictured him asking what was wrong. She sat on one of the steps, placed her hand over her mouth to muffle a sob.

Back in the car Kitty reproached Chance. "And what *exactly* was all that about?"

The car came to a sudden halt, nearly sending her flying.

"*Anathon,* what is wrong with you? What did they say?" Kitty climbed into the front seat, and saw tears welling in his eyes, and sighed.

He rested his head on the steering wheel. "What have I done?"

Kitty didn't know what to do, *what would a human do?* She placed her arm around him. "What did they say?"

Chance's voice changed as he lifted his head. "Remove your arm, Kitty."

She did so immediately.

"You told Saras, didn't you?" His eyes stared blankly out of the window.

"I've told Saras nothing."

"Don't lie to me, Kitty." His voice became stern, angry.

"I told you I would wait. Why would I tell Saras, now?"

His eyes met with hers. "I don't know, you tell me."

"I never said anything. Did Saras say that I did?"

Chance didn't reply.

"Did Saras tell you that I said something?"

"No!" he snapped.

"So, why do you think I have?" She looked confused.

"No one else knew," he mumbled.

"Knew what?"

Chance glared her way.

"What? Knew of you and Bea? Knew of Alithia? What? What did Saras say?"

"He knows, Kitty. He knows who Bea is."

Kitty's eyes opened wide. "I swear, I never told him. Does he know about you and Bea?"

"I think he has an idea, he didn't say."

"And that's why you treated her like that? They were watching. Go to her. Tell her that you're sorry. Go to her now, before it's too late."

"I can't. I shouldn't have taken her to the Bluebell. It was stupid of me. Why didn't I think?" He hit the steering wheel.

"You weren't to know he'd be there."

"Come on Kitty. At least let me wallow in my stupidity."

"It's done now. I should've known better, too...You can't leave things like this...Go."

"No!" he snapped.

"*Why*?"

"I've hurt her... again. I said that I wouldn't." He got out the car.

Kitty leant on the empty seat and called after him. "Where are you going?"

"I don't know."

Kitty scrambled out of the car and ran after him. "Anathon,

listen to me, Bea told me something…while you were talking with Saras…she told me… she told me that she was falling in love with you."

He paused, rubbing his hands over his head.

"You *still* have time. If Saras knew about your feelings for Bea, you wouldn't be walking around. Think about it. By cutting off this way, you give Karian the opportunity he's waiting for. How can you protect her if you're not around?"

"I don't know what to do. Everything's out of control." He leant against a wall. The conflict between head and heart, evident with every twist of pain on his face.

"What do you feel?"

"Fear." His answer was quick.

"I'm not going to lie to you, I would too." She leant on the brick wall next to him.

"Not helping," he groaned, staring out into thin air.

"Sorry."

"How can I protect her like this? Nothing makes sense anymore. Have you ever loved someone, Kitty?"

"Have I ever loved? Once, guess you can tell with me being single it never worked out."

Chance closed his eyes. "I love her."

"Well, that'd explain why nothing makes sense. Come on, get in the car. I'll drive you."

Chance shook his head. "I'll see you later." He began to walk off.

"Where are you going? *Please*, let me give you a lift?"

"No. I need space to think. I'll see you later."

"Anathon, remember what you were sent here to do, *protect* Bea, That's what's important, above everything." Kitty grumbled as she got back in the car, "This human emotional stuff I can do without, way too complicated."

Bea lifted her head when she heard frantic banging on the door of the shop. She knew it was him, and the tears began to fall. She wasn't angry anymore, she was hurt.

"*Please*, open the door." Chance pleaded, his head resting on the backs of his hands, palms against the glass.

She closed her eyes and dragged her hands down her face while her mind tried to block him out, but his voice kept tugging at her heart.

"Bea, *please*, shout, scream …anything, but please, *please* don't shut me out." He pulled back as the door slowly opened. Her dampened face stared back at him. "What did *they* say to you?"

He grimaced before speaking, "They have a hold over me…and I can't tell you what it is. You can tell me to go, that you never want to see me again, but I couldn't leave things the way they were. Not this time."

"What trouble are you in?" She was used to Brandon's escapades, but this felt different. He looked torn, like he wanted to tell her.

"I thought… I want to protect you…I was wrong to cut off like that…I feel…"

She watched as he struggled to find the words, her eyes searched his hoping to see what he refused to tell. He looked vulnerable and some part of her knew that deep down, Saras had played a part in their argument. "Protect me from what?"

"From me." He recoiled. "I don't want to hurt you anymore."

"Then don't."

Their eyes met and in the following silence, she leant forward, and softly placed a kiss on his lips.

"You should be angry with me."

"I know," she muttered, before her lips met with his again.

King of the Castle

Kitty greeted Chance at the door of the Muswell Hill flat.

"You were forgiven then?"

Chance nodded with a slight smile.

"You realise that I've now confirmed with Saras that Bea is Alithia? You have a matter of days before he'll contact you. This is no game, Anathon, be careful."

"Was that what you called me here for? To lecture? I know the penalties for getting close to her." He needed no reminding, the thought haunted him.

"No. I called you because recently there's been a surprising amount of interest from a particular human." She slumped down on the sofa, arms crossed.

"Interest in what?"

"The Sidhe. The Unseelie. This particular human was beaten up by Karian."

"Brandon."

Kitty nodded. "He's been snooping around. I've informed everyone to leave him alone, but we have a problem… someone saw him by the theatre."

"Who?" He knew this was potentially dangerous.

"Roel, he keeps an eye on things for me. Karian must have put on quite a show that night to evoke such an interest. Brandon might have told others, more of his kind."

Chance was quick to speak, "Don't touch him."

"We can't have a human running around, talking about the Sidhe."

"I'll talk with him."

Kitty's eyes widened. "And say what?"

"I don't want him touched, Kitty."

"Are you aware that he's been to the bookshop? Hovering outside when you're not there. He doesn't stay long, but he watches the shop from an alley. The first time he was alone. The second, with…his so called right-hand man, Tommy."

"He's seen me with Bea."

"Yes, he's keeping a close eye on you. Maybe. more so than Bea."

He realised that Brandon must have followed Bea to the theatre.

"What do you think he knows?" asked Kitty.

"I'm going to find out," he muttered, thoughts distant.

"I'll come with you." Kitty was about to get off her chair until Chance held up his hand.

"No, it's better if I go alone. It's about Bea, not us. He's looking out for her, trying to figure out what he's up against. He might even be an asset."

"Not if he knows about you and Bea." Kitty raised her eyebrows.

"If he knows I'm not a threat to her, we might be able to talk. There's only one way to find out." If they knew about Brandon, then it meant Karian did too. "Ask this Roel to keep an eye on Brandon and the pub." He sighed when she protested. "Kitty, it's one Seelie." He knew she didn't like the idea when she launched into a full assault of how his plan was crazy. Stating that Saras would never approve, and even if did, why would Brandon help? Chance listened to her babbling on about the danger of exposing themselves to humans, and asked him what he was thinking.

"Alithia's soul has never been located, until now," he replied.

"Saras will not permit it." She was being stubborn, and he was getting tired of the battle. "Then we won't tell Saras, will we?"

"I can't keep the Order in the dark. Saras knows about Bea and they want Alithia back."

"They can't force her, Kitty."

"No, but they're not going to let time age the body she's in either, think about that."

"Are you going to get someone to follow Brandon or not?"

She glared at him. "Yes."

Chance asked her about Brandon. If he was to confront him, he needed some background information. Kitty explained that he was a minor criminal, and listed all of his petty crimes, "That's probably why Bea got rid of him. Or maybe she liked that kind of thing at one time." Chance's unimpressed glare forced her on. "He's been attending a rehabilitation unit for drug and alcohol addiction. He hangs out at a pub in Mitcham, imaginatively called the Mitcham Castle." She rolled her eyes. "A haunt for those with less creativity than the proprietor...if that's possible. Luckily, it's out of the way and doesn't attract any undue police attention."

"His friends?"

"They're basically the same, in desperate need of an overhaul in etiquette."

Chance noticed that whenever he asked something about

Tommy, Kitty appeared antsy. "Is there something I should know?"

She shook her head, staring down at her nails.

"I know that you don't want to spare anyone to watch Brandon or his men, but you're here to protect them, too."

"Don't play that card, Anathon. These are not what I would call *vulnerable* humans."

"Maybe not where other humans are concerned, but up against a Sidhe? And if Saras did hear of you wasting Sidhe to watch them, you could air your concerns of a possible Unseelie involvement. I'm sure that would catch his attention."

"A week of observation, that's all you're getting."

A smile pursed itself on his lips. "That's all I need."

Kitty scribbled down the address of the pub and handed it to him. "Are you sure you want to do this? These particular humans are not gentle, their manner is…degenerate to say the least."

"I can look after myself."

Chance stood across the street from the Castle pub, a small, insignificant building situated on the corner of a bland, residential street. It looked as uninviting as it intended to, suitably dowdy and rundown.

He crossed the street and noticed that the windows were dark, a little too dark. Once he got closer, he realised it was because the curtains were drawn. Not one window could he see through as he walked past. This place obviously avoided any possibility of prying eyes, which put Chance's senses more on edge.

He approached the entrance, where two men stood, as if

on guard, reminding him of two knights, all dressed in black, but bearing huge cigars not shields. Chance casually strolled straight past them, waiting for them to make their move, but instead, they only silently eyed him as he brushed past, straight through the pub's double doors.

More like two pawns. Now, let the game commence as I meet the King of this castle, he mused as the two men followed him in.

The screeching of the hinges, announced his arrival, and all heads turned in his direction. The pub became silent as he continued making his way towards the bar at the other end of the room.

"Can I 'elp yah, mate?" A scruffy man stepped forward, his eyes as unfriendly as his tone.

Chance paused to scan all the faces in the room, finally stopping at one.

"It's alright, Bob, he's come to see me, ain't yah, mate." A deep, coarse, South London accent came from the corner of the room.

Chance knew at least three men were behind him waiting for an order, a simple nod from their King to finish him off.

Brandon got up from his seat and casually strolled past Chance, to the bar. He was thickset, his stroll more a swagger. Tattoos adorned his thick, muscular arms. He propped himself up against the bar, and stared his way. "Well, well, what brings you to my manor...Chance?" His cold, brown eyes readily confessed that the grin on his face was false.

"We need to talk."

"Talk then, mate." Brandon continued his cocky stare.

"In private." Chance was forceful, but not aggressive.

"*This* is private, or do yah mean, you 'ave somethin' to

say that you don't want my mates 'ere to know? I wonder what that could be?" He gestured to his the men and they all laughed. "Bob, any idea what could be so secret?"

Bob, behind the bar shook his head, and continued to put away some glasses.

"This thing you gotta talk to me about, exactly 'ow secret is it?"

"I think you know what it's about." Chance's senses were on high alert, and he didn't bother to act surprised when Brandon pulled out a gun and placed it against his temple. "You could be right, mate. I don't want your fucking kind in my manor. You fucking cheeky cunt." He pushed Chance with the gun still at his head, to the back of the pub, into a small yard outside. The same two men from the doors, the pawns, accompanied him.

"You got some fucking front coming 'ere, mate, I'll give yah that."

"I only want to talk." Chance remained calm. His hands were held out in front to him, trying to diffuse the situation.

"Do yah, now? And what would we need to talk about, 'uh?" He pressed the gun harder against Chance's temple.

"Remove the gun," replied Chance.

"Nah, I like it just where it is." Brandon's face met his. The grin was sincere this time.

Chance moved with such incredible speed, that Brandon didn't have time to react. Disarming Brandon, taking his gun in a moment and forcing him into submission.

Once the other two men realised what happened, they pulled out their guns and pointed them in Chance's direction. Too late. Their eyes darted from Brandon to Chance.

"Now, let us talk without the play? Tell them, they can go." Chance demanded, gesturing his eyes towards the two armed men.

With a nod from Brandon, they lowered their guns and disappeared, re-entering the pub.

Chance slowly removed the gun from Brandon's temple, and handed the weapon back to him. "As I said…I only want to talk."

Brandon slid the gun into the back of his pants and grinned. "I'll 'ave to remember not to get so close next time. Better still, shoot on sight."

Chance wasted no more time. "Why are you watching the shop?"

"You fucking know why!" Brandon leaned against a brick wall. "Amuse me."

"She doesn't know what you are, does she?" Brandon eyed him.

"What do you think I am?"

Brandon moved his face closer. "Well you're not fucking one of us, are yah? What d'yah want with Bea?"

"I don't *want* anything from Bea."

"Don't fucking play with me. I could've blown your fucking head off in the pub, mate."

"So why didn't you?" Chances eyes locked on Brandon's, and they stared at each other until

Brandon let out a deep groan. "I'll try again. What d'yah want with Bea?"

Chance played the honesty card. "To protect her from the kind of introduction *you* encountered, that night outside the Red Lion."

Brandon nodded his head. "Who is he?"

"His name is Karian."

"What's he doin', sniffin' 'round Bea?"

"She reminds him of someone he used to know."

"Someone he used to know, 'uh? And you?"

"I'm here to protect her."

Brandon burst out laughing, and moved closer to Chance's face. "By fucking her?"

Chance didn't say anything. He was trying to keep his cool.

"Yeah, that's what I thought." Brandon moved away.

"You still love her, don't you?"

"She's my fucking world, mate, and no cunt's gonna fucking 'urt 'er. D'yah understand?"

"I don't want to hurt her." Chance realised that he wasn't the only one that Bea had caused a weakness in.

"Who is this Karian?"

Chance knew that by telling Brandon, he would be crossing another boundary, but it might go in his favour if Brandon knew that Karian was an enemy to them both. He explained that Karian was an Unseelie, a Sidhe.

"A what?"

"A Sidhe, we're not from here."

"No shit."

Chance didn't care for Brandon's brash manner, but reminded himself that it wasn't important, and continued to explain that the Sidhe has been divided into two courts, the Unseelie and the Seelie. Brandon had sneered when he explained that the Seelie were actually the good guys. Brandon confessed that they had been watching the Sidhe, both sects. He even mentioned Kitty. Chance didn't realise how much Brandon had seen, or knew, until now. Of course, the Sidhe could decide when they wanted to appear in front of humans, apart from in Bea's case. He would let Kitty know they should use glamour more. Something felt off as far as Kitty was concerned, but he shrugged it off when Brandon asked how long the Sidhe had been present.

"A long time." *He doesn't know that much* thought Chance.

"How long?"

"Pick up any book on folklore and you'll find us in there somewhere." He held in his compulsion to laugh, imagining Brandon behind a book of mythology. "Our kind used to help your kind. Most of us left a long time ago. Some Unseelie hid out here. The Seelie go in search of the Unseelie, and send them home." *Keep it simple,* he thought.

Brandon lit up a cigar. "Why did they stay 'ere?"

"We're at war. It's been a very long war."

Brandon asked, "So when yah get this Karian, you're all going back home?"

Chance nodded.

"Then, I think we might be able to give a 'elping 'and to get rid of Karian, as long as *you* go home too."

"Keep away from the theatre." Chance was offering a deal.

"Why?"

"Because you don't know what you're dealing with." Warned Chance. "You want us... *me* gone? Leave it alone."

"I'm not gonna just sit watching shit 'appen on my doorstep."

"I'll let you know if we need your help."

"Yah want me to just-"

"Leave everything to us."

Brandon took another pull on his cigar and nodded. "We'll be watching you, mate. Remember, the Seelie are on temporary grace."

"Something tells me, you knew some of what I told you already." *Brandon acts dumb, but his mind is sharp,* observed Chance.

"You got your secrets, I 'ave mine." Brandon winked before bellowing, "Let 'im through."

Chance extended his hand. "To temporary grace."

Brandon grinned and shook his hand. "Very fucking temporary."

Chance walked back through the pub, and just before he exited the main door, the tension eased, the stony silence ended, as the men inside started talking.

CHAPTER 10

Strange Delivery

$\mathcal{B}$ack at the shop, Chance let himself in and found Bea asleep on the sofa. As he walked over, he saw what appeared to be journals spread all around her. He sat down and gently removed the open journal from her hand, but on turning it over, he froze, quickly discarding it and picked up another, then another. His heart raced as his eyes roamed over more pages. He jumped when Bea spoke.

She laughed, placing a quick kiss on lips. "You look like a schoolboy that's just been caught doing something he shouldn't."

He tried to act casual in light of what he knew. "Where are these from?" He desperately tried to hide any strain in his voice.

She sat up. "Oh, I found them earlier. Someone left them in a case by the door with a note, all very mysterious." She stretched.

"A note?"

Bea reached down beside her and handed it to him. It simply read:

Bethany Wolstenholme
A gift for you.

As he examined the note, his thoughts drifted to what Kitty

had said about Brandon being near the shop. A Sidhe wouldn't have written all their history down for a human to find, and it was a far stretch of the imagination to equate the journals to Brandon. *But how would another human know so much, and why would they involve Bea?* His mind was running overtime. "Do you recognise the handwriting?" He forced himself to ask.

"No, but what's really odd is this…" She pointed to the journal in his hand. "They all have the same symbols as the mead's label. See?"

Chance remained quiet.

Bea nudged him and smiled. "Hey, my professor lover, aren't you the least bit curious? Surely, we can figure out the text between us?" She proceeded to open up a journal that she had bookmarked. "Look at this drawing… I wonder who she is?"

As Chance looked at the sketch, he slumped back on the sofa.

She turned to face him. "You don't look very excited."

"I'm sorry. Tired…it's been a long day." He was still in shock, and couldn't muster a better reply.

Bea put the journal down, snuggled into him, and ran her hand down his shirt. "Then, let me tuck you into bed early."

He saw the glint in her eyes and a smile crept over his lips. Her timing couldn't have been more perfect. He placed his mouth to her neck, and started to gently nibble. Then, without any hesitation, he picked her up and carried her into the bedroom, as far away from the journals as possible.

Chance closed his eyes as he felt her hand run down his back, and waited in anticipation for more of her caress as they lay on the bed.

"I love you." Her voice was a low whisper.

Chance's whole body trembled at hearing her say the words, and she buried her head into the nape of his neck. Her warm breath against his skin sent a shiver down his spine. He wanted to tell her that he loved her too, but knew it was too soon, too risky. He was scared, uncertain of revealing how he felt, especially now that these journals had mysteriously appeared. "Bea... I..." He broke off, at hearing her breathe more deeply and opened his eyes. "Bea?" She seemed deep in sleep. "Bea?"

"Karian."

Chance's stomach turned and every muscle in his body contracted at his enemy's name released from her lips. At first, he was unsure whether he heard correctly, until she spoke *his* name again. Chance sat up, horrified as she started to groan. "Bea." He gently shook her. "Bea, Bea!" His voice grew louder each time he called her name.

She stirred, opening her eyes. "*Why* are you staring like that?" She quickly sat up and looked behind her, then realised it was actually her that he was looking at. "What's wrong? You're freaking me out... Chance?"

He cleared the lump in his throat. "You drifted off."

"I did?" She looked confused.

Chance didn't want to ask her what happened. It might mean hearing more of Karian. Besides he was still trying to wrap his head around her saying the name aloud, and buried his face in her chest to hide his relief that she was back with him again.

Bea wrapped her arms around him and giggled. "I seriously thought someone was behind me by the look on your face."

He didn't reply.

"Are you okay?" She lowered her head to meet his eyes, but he'd closed them. "Something's wrong? What is it?"

He held her tighter, too scared to let go. "I never want to lose you."

She smiled, not realising how much her unconscious words had affected him. "You're not going to lose me. Look at me."

He couldn't, he didn't want her to see the pain in his eyes that would instantly betray him.

She wiggled her body down his, and gently kissed each of his eyelids. "There's no getting rid of me now."

Chance held her tighter, still hiding his face. His wasn't used to feeling fear. The word didn't exist, until meeting Bea. As she lay in his arms, the sickness in the pit of his stomach, still stirred with the tinge of jealousy, creating a vile taste of dread.

"I won't be able to breathe if you squeeze anymore." Bea pulled away, kissing the tip of his nose. His eyes immediately met hers. Selfishly, he wanted to hear her say, 'I love you' again, even though he knew that he couldn't say it back. He needed confirmation that it was *him* that she spoke the words to, not Karian. Chance could see that she didn't understand his silent torture. So he moved closer, placing his mouth on hers to try and block out her cry of 'Karian' repeating over and over in his mind. His lips started to press harder, more uncontrollably against her skin, and she gasped at his sudden intensity with no knowledge that, in his mind, he was reclaiming her.

CHAPTER 11

Deciphered

$\mathcal{B}$ea's phone rang. "Liza. Wow stranger, where have you been?"

"Oh, I've missed your voice. Sorry, I feel like I haven't stopped in this new job. Anyway forget me, how are you?"

"I'm good, well...actually great." Bea replied.

"You and Chance are still going strong?"

"Yep."

"Good...you sound happy, which of course makes me feel less guilty about not being there. I've been asked something ...are you ready for this?"

"I'm ready." Bea giggled at hearing Liza's excitement.

"Work has asked me to go and run their offices in the U.S!" Liza screeched.

"Noooo. Oh my god...Wow. That's brilliant. When?"

"They want me to start in two weeks."

"Two weeks?" Bea's heart sank, *so soon.*

"I know its short notice, but apparently the previous person ran off with the secretary, and there isn't anyone they trust to run things. Crazy stuff, anyway, I had to ask you if it was okay. I didn't want to accept without your blessing."

Bea knew Liza meant, if you need me, I'll stay. "Oh, I love you. Of course you have my blessing. I'll miss you like crazy. Just don't forget to call me, you know, the little woman in the bookshop, on a small island, the United Kingdom."

After the conversation, Bea blankly stared out down the

aisle. The idea of her best friend leaving the country, she admitted, frightened her a little. Liza was the one person that knew her inside and out, who she trusted without question. Bea had never been without her for any length of time, and felt a slight pang in her heart. She'd miss the simple things, their chats, girlie laughter and cuddles. She wondered if Chance would notice those little things that her friend could feel without seeing, and would he step in and wrap his arms around her, promising a better tomorrow. The memory of his previous absence brought with it a wave of doubt, which she quickly pushed to the back of her mind. *It's different now*, she reminded herself.

Later that evening, returning to the shop, Chance thought that he heard Kitty's laughter as he walked up the stairs. The sound led him into the living room, where, sure enough, Kitty and Bea were sitting on the floor with the journals scattered about them.

"Ladies." He forced a smile in Bea's direction.

Bea jumped up and ran into his arms, placing a brief kiss on his lips. "Look who's come to visit."

His sly blast of a glare made Kitty gulp. "Hope you don't mind. I was in the area and thought it'd be nice to pop in and say hi."

Bea joined Kitty on the floor. "Don't be silly. Why would he mind? We're happy you did, aren't we?" She looked over at Chance standing by the doorway.

He nodded and Bea's attention went back to the journals. He was angry, especially as he and Kitty had spoken only a few hours earlier, declaring that everything was under control, now that Queen Eliseis had told him to find a discreet way of deciphering the symbols.

"Kitty kindly brought some mead over, and we compared the hieroglyphs, they're the same." Bea announced, placing one of the journals texts up against the label of the bottle.

"Isn't this exciting?" Kitty remarked, getting comfortable on the sofa. "So, who knows the background on the mead?"

Chance sat down, seething. His fingers rubbed over the arm of the chair to stop from clenching. Meanwhile, Bea went on to explain that she had looked up all the meads of Europe, but nothing came close. She turned to him. "You'd think something would come up?"

He felt squeezed into the tightest corner. Taking a deep breath, he started the slippery descent of deceit. "I bumped into a linguistic professor at work. I showed him one of the journals."

"Really?" Bea eagerly waited to hear more.

He pulled out the journal that he had borrowed to show Kitty, and removed a slip of paper from the inside, handing it to Bea. "He thinks that the writing stems from an early, unknown form of Gaelic. He's only seen it once before, via a facsimile sent to him many years ago by another linguist. The writing was scribbled throughout an old book, discovered in a monastery in Ireland. The mainstream authorities that he approached put the writing down to a medieval hoax. That copy of the fax shows the symbols, deciphered into letters, in English… Right, I'm thirsty." He went to get up, but Bea pushed him back down.

"No, stay there, I'll get the mead." She disappeared to the kitchen.

"What do you think you're doing?" He spoke to Kitty in their own tongue, at frequency that humans couldn't hear.

"I could ask you the same thing. Why didn't you let me in on the plot to introduce the text? Very clever by the way."

"It would've spoiled the element of surprise if I told you, and as for showing up behind my back…"

"As you said earlier, Queen Eliseis said it's time that Bea should know. You would've just kept putting it off," replied Kitty.

"Oh, so you alone decided when the appropriate time would be?" His patience was wearing thin.

Kitty shoved a piece of paper and a pen in his hand. "Stop putting off the inevitable and decipher the missing pieces. It'll be fully translated then, and, Anathon, don't look so glum, she's not stupid, you're meant to be excited."

"Don't test me, Kitty." He warned, throwing the pen and paper to the floor, marching off into the kitchen. He removed the bottle of mead from Bea's hands, placed it on the side, and embraced her. "You're sure you want to go through all this tonight?" His nose rubbed against hers.

"Bored already?"

He pulled a face.

"Well, Kitty's not." She poked him. "Come on. It's fun."

His mouth was about to reach for hers, when Kitty's annoying voice carried through to the kitchen. "I think I found something!"

Chance tried hard not to let the look of aggravation spread over his face, as Bea placed a quick kiss on his lips, grabbed the mead, and hurried out of the kitchen. He leaned against the sink, head lowered, arms outstretched and fingers tapping. *If only she knew what finding out will mean for us, and I'm powerless to stop it.*

Bea sat next to Kitty, excitedly. "What've you found?"

"That sketch that you showed me, look, I think that could be a name." She pointed to some symbols. Bea picked up the pen and paper and started to decipher the symbols in the journal using the translation of the fax. On discovering a name, she ecstatically shouted out to Chance.

His jaw tensed, but, before leaving the kitchen, he managed to replace agitation with a slight look of interest on his face, and entered the living room.

Bea held up the translation. "Look, it says 'Eliseis'." As she got to her feet, she swayed.

Chance grabbed hold of her. "Are you alright?"

She placed the palm of her hand on her head. "I think… the mead…it…I should've remembered it doesn't agree with me."

Kitty watched as he guided Bea to the sofa.

"Maybe we should stop for a while?" he suggested, stroking away the hair that had fallen over her eyes.

"No." Both women answered at the same time, and then laughed.

"I thought you tasted mead before? With Chance?" asked Kitty.

"I did, but soon after, it lost its appeal… it makes me dizzy. I'm better off sticking with my normal fix of tea."

"I'll make you a cup." Chance threw Kitty a warning glare before leaving the room.

"I found this sketch of a woman in water, have you seen it?" Kitty handed her another journal.

"No." Bea took a closer look. "It's some kind of plant around her."

"I think you're right." Kitty replied, peering over her shoulder.

"What does it say?" Bea squinted at the symbols.

"One minute." Kitty scribbled down the letters that corresponded with the hieroglyphic writing.

Chance returned, and Bea moved over to make room for him, taking the cup and sipping the tea. "Hmm. Thanks. Kitty found a picture of a woman in some water. She's working out what it says now." His silence puzzled her. "Maybe mead doesn't agree with you either." She teased, stroking his cheek.

"I have it." Kitty blurted, turning around, pausing on noticing the look of dread on Chance's face.

"Well, what does it say?" Bea egged her on.

Kitty placed the journal and the deciphered text into Bea's hands, and she began to read aloud. "It was in the darkest depths of the cold that Alith-" She broke off, her face turned deathly white.

"What is it?" Kitty asked.

Chance placed his hand on Bea's. "You don't have to read it."

"Why? Is there something wrong?" Kitty replied.

"No, honestly, it's nothing. It reminded me of a play, an old folk tale. The name just threw me for a minute." She continued reading. "The daughter of Eliseis, departed from their world, passing through a carpet of purple flowers." She looked around at Chance, as he suddenly started laughing.

"The linguist was right. It's a story someone's made up, a medieval hoax. Old writers used to code their work. These are just plays, pure fable. Pretty clever, stops anyone from stealing the idea, unless they have the code." He hugged Bea, still smiling. "There, the mystery is solved."

"We should still decipher the rest of it." Kitty urged.

He closed the journal. "Enough for tonight, I think."

"I fear we've bored Chance." Bea smiled, tenderly running her hand down his nose.

Kitty resigned. "I guess I should be making a move. We all have work in the morning, huh?" Chance knew that it had been the perfect opportunity for Bea to discover more, and that Kitty wasn't impressed that he nipped it in the bud. The thought of Kitty being disgruntled made him keep the smile on his face.

"What do you work as, Kitty?" Bea asked.

"I'm a buyer for a department store, ladies fashion. I wish I could say working there saved me money, but it just encourages me to spend more."

Chance admired Kitty's ability to lie with such ease, before trying to hurry her out the door. "Do you want my car keys?"

"It's okay, I can get a cab. I've been drinking, remember." Kitty poked her tongue out at him while Bea ordered the cab.

"He said, ten minutes." As Bea was about to sit down, she knocked one of the journals to the floor. The pages spread open, and as she bent down to pick it up an image flashed before her eyes. She froze, as a strange feeling of deja vu began to reappear. Chance and Kitty's voices became more distant as another, sudden, image of her running and laughing, wearing a long, blue, silk dress. It felt like her, even sounded like her, but Bea looked completely different. She was slimmer, taller, with long, blonde, wavy hair which bounced as she ran on a cobbled pathway, surrounded by tall evergreens. Someone was chasing her, but every time she turned to see who it was, another flash would blind her. The vision started to fade and Chance's voice become clearer. Bea found herself wrapped in his arms. Her head felt heavy, and she had to close her eyes.

"Bea, what did you see?" Kitty asked holding her hand.

Chance snapped at Kitty to be quiet in the Sidhe tongue,

"Don't be angry at Kitty." Bea mumbled, opening her eyes.

Kitty and Chance stared at each other. Then, Kitty asked, again, in her own tongue if Bea wanted some water.

Bea didn't reply, but instead groaned. "Chance, I feel sick."

As Kitty ran to the kitchen to get a bowl, the intercom screamed out. She didn't know what to do first.

"Kitty, we need that bowl." Chance called out.

"Hold on, the intercom."

"Now!" he demanded.

Kitty quickly rushed into the living room, Sidhe speed, dropped the bowl next to Chance's feet, and rushed to answer the intercom. "I am sorry we don't actually require your services now…excuse me? Look, I haven't got time to listen to your foul rendition of wasting time." She slammed the receiver down, and ran back into the living room. "Eww. Is she actually going to be sick?"

Chance's glare shut her up.

"Oh…I feel it again." All colour left Bea's already pale face. Unknown to them, another image appeared before her, and she scrambled to the floor.

Chance lowered himself to the ground, and held her face in his hands. "Tell me what's happening?"

"He's ...he's behind me." She jolted back.

Chance caught her in his arms. "Bea, look at me." He wanted to bring her back to reality, to him.

"Where are you?" asked Kitty, also kneeling on the floor.

Chance rested her head on his lap. "Bea."

Kitty and Chance watched helpless, as Bea's eyes rolled back. Her body violently jerked, and she started coughing. Chance sat her up, not knowing what to do, as she gasped for air.

"Lay her on the bed." Kitty urged, following him as he carried Bea into the bedroom.

Once he laid her down, the coughing stopped. He turned to Kitty. "Why did you start this if you didn't know how to snap her out of it?"

"I thought she would remember bits more slowly. I had no idea it would come on so sudden. I should contact Saras."

He stopped her reaching for her phone. "No...I'll get her back."

"How?"

"I don't know...let me think." He sat on the bed, resting his head in the palm of his hands.

About an hour passed, but nothing he tried seemed to remove Bea from her comatose state. In the end, Chance could do nothing but lay beside her. He kissed her face, and she groaned.

Kitty sat up in the chair, suddenly alert. "Do that again."

"What?" He stared at her, wondering what she talking about.

"Kiss her. You got a reaction. Do it again," she insisted, flapping her hands.

"No." Chance was scared, supposing his touch became mistaken for someone else in Bea's mind.

Kitty's eyes narrowed. "She's done this before hasn't she? The dream thing?"

He didn't reply, but he knew Kitty saw straight through him.

"Why didn't you tell me?"

"Would it have made a difference?" he replied.

"Maybe, when did it happen?"

Chance remained silent, the memory of it still hurt.

"Tell me."

"Yesterday," he spat.

"And?"

"She…she called out his name." He closed his eyes at recalling, but it didn't blot out the heart wrenching agony or calm the sick feeling that violently returned in the pit of his stomach.

"You need to kiss her again." Kitty insisted, gesturing with her eyes.

"I told you …No."

"This isn't about you, *Anathon*. Kiss her, now."

His eyes sent out a piercing signal to leave well alone.

"Okay, in your own time." She immediately backed off.

He needed to bring her out of the dream state and fast. He leant forward and kissed her lips… nothing. His heart sank, that hurt too.

"You need to be more passionate." Kitty pushed.

He glared at her again, this time his eyes flashed with a

more severe warning, and Kitty gestured her mouth shut with her hand. After a few moments silence, he asked her to turn around.

"What do you mean turn around? Why should I turn around?"

"I can't have you looking at me," he mumbled, uncomfortable at having to explain.

Kitty stopped the creeping smile from appearing on her face, before turning away. "You know you have-"

"Shut up!" Chance blurted, lying down next to Bea, gently placing his hand on the side of her face. He slowly ran his thumb over her mouth, and her lips responded by searching for more his touch. He cautiously placed his mouth upon hers, hoping that she would wake for him, not Karian. Her mouth responded, caressing his in return. Suddenly, her body arched, then lowered, she started mumbling.

Kitty spun around. "What's she saying?"

"I don't know." He tilted his head trying to make out her mutterings. "Bea?"

"Call her by the other name," advised an eager Kitty.

He didn't want the name to pass his lips, but he had to try something. His mouth tightened before speaking. "Alithia?"

Bea groaned, "Please don't."

"Wake up...*for me*," he asked, his voice a whisper, not wanting Kitty to hear.

Bea suddenly screamed, making Chance and Kitty jump. Water started to tipple from her mouth, her body began to tremble and convulse.

Kitty pushed Chance out of the way. He watched horrified

as Bea started choking again and started gasping for air. Kitty leant over her and started to recite some words in Seior, the tongue of spell working, a language normally only used for magic by the Deisi.

The convulsions stopped and Bea slumped back on the bed, restful.

Chance grabbed Kitty by her arms. "How do you know the words of Seior?" His eyes burned into hers.

"I'm sorry, Anathon. I was only to use the words if she entered a re-enactment of Alithia's death."

"*What* have you kept from me?" He couldn't believe what he was hearing. *Did he really know Kitty at all?*

"Come into the other room, I'll tell you everything."

He looked over at Bea, and released his hold of Kitty.

"She'll be alright now," Kitty reassured, rubbing her arm, gesturing for him to follow her into the kitchen.

Chance stood by the sink, his eyes filled with rage as he waited for Kitty's story to unfold.

"The Seelie Deisi is already here. I told her everything. I…I was instructed to…to *enhance* Bea's memory. I wanted to tell you, they said you were taking too long. Just the journals were not enough to trigger all of her memories. Everything is as it should be."

"Did the Deisi or Saras tell you that?" he scorned.

"It was an order and I followed it."

"Who gave the order?" He didn't get a reply and marched up to her. "Who gave the order?"

"Saras…it was Saras."

He shook his head in disbelief. "Enhance her memory…

you put something in her drink didn't you?" She didn't answer until he shouted. "*What* did you put in her drink?"

"The flower of Vororbla," she confessed, looking sorry for herself.

"Poison." Chance gasped, incredulous at her deceit.

"Not in the quantity that I gave her."

He began to see things clearer. "It was you who left the journals...wasn't it?"

"I had no choice. Your attachment to her has blinded you to what needs to be done. I'm under the service of the Order, as are you," she snapped.

"My loyalties are to the queen and The Heaven Stone. Their instructions are above Saras's, and the so-called Order. Saras works independently from the queen, not for her." He couldn't believe how blind she was.

"*Anathon,* you know as well as I do, that Saras has the full backing of the Seelie Court, and that's where the true power lies, not with the queen. You're only here because they agreed to it. The Heaven Stone do not speak here. Bea is not their concern. Whether you like it or not Saras has full control in this realm. Eliseis permits him to govern the Order, because she trusts him."

"Why does Saras want Bea to remember so badly? Have you asked yourself that? What's the urgency?"

"The queen wants her daughter back."

"Not like this!" he yelled, banging his fist on the cupboard.

"Look, right now, all that matters is that we *both* follow orders. Saras is still the commander, is he not?"

Chance had to look away. He knew that while he was here, in the realm of humans, he would have to abide by Saras's rules, but he didn't have to like it. "You *deceived* me, and you risked Bea's life."

"I was doing my duty. Just as you are, or rather should be. I wouldn't have let any harm come to her. I was given the words of Seior if...if things went too far."

"Too far? She was reliving drowning in water. Protect...do you remember that vow, Kitty? What about loyalty?"

"I was given an order and I followed it!" she snapped. "Open your eyes, Anathon. The queen knew it would come to this. Saras told me."

"Another lie to get you to do his bidding. She would not approve of Bea remembering by force. Freewill is something you've forgotten in following Saras's orders, as has he."

"Anathon, you protect the human, Bea, I protect her soul, Alithia. We're *all* here to put things right again, to return balance, and send the Sidhe home. *All* Sidhe, including Alithia."

"Is that what Saras offered you?" He turned to face her.
"What?"

"A quick way *home*?" He emphasized the word.

Kitty's face dropped and she averted her eyes.

"You *knew* all along what was wrong with Bea, and you acted as if you knew nothing. I thought we were on the same side?" He walked over and stopped within inches of her face. "You're right, you've been in this realm too long." He brushed past her, and went back into the bedroom.

Kitty gingerly followed and stood in the doorway. "We're on the same side. Deep down, you know that this needed to happen...it'll all be alright, you'll see."

He threw her a look of disgust. All he saw was a betrayal

of trust; knowing about the Seelie Deisi; leaving the journals; turning up at the flat without his knowledge; using the flower of Vororbla with Seior magic; and prematurely bringing forth Alithia's memory against Bea's freewill. It was too much to forgive. "GO...Tell Saras that you followed orders."

"No. Bea needs me here, too!"

CHAPTER 12

The Awakening

There were no more outbursts or visions through the rest of the night. Chance never left Bea's side and Kitty hadn't spoken another word. The atmosphere was thick with animosity.

Slowly, Bea's eyes opened and they met Chance's. "Hello? Good to have you back."

She sat up. "Back? Oh, my head, did I drink too much last night?"

"You don't remember?"

"Past Kitty arriving, no. I didn't do anything stupid in front of your sister, did I?"

Chance shook his head. "Stupid? No."

"What's the time?"

"Eleven."

She gasped. "Eleven! I must open the shop." Bea was about to get up, when Chance stopped her. "It's okay, Kitty found Jenny's number. She opened up for you."

"Jenny?"

He nodded. "Now relax…I'll go make tea."

Kitty was already in the kitchen, and approached him about Bea's condition.

"Who are you speaking to?" Bea called out.

Stunned, his eyes automatically met Kitty's.

Bea strolled into the kitchen. "Kitty, you stayed?"

Kitty smiled and answered her in the Sidhe tongue. "I hope you don't mind?"

"Course not, I'm sorry. I must've conked out last night. My head is killing me." She pulled out a chair and sat down.

Kitty sat on a chair next to her. "We had a great time last night, but I agree, we drank too much. I'm not surprised you have a headache. I'm still waiting for mine to catch up with me." She grinned, obviously excited by Bea understanding every word.

Bea laughed, but quickly regretted doing so.

Their conversation continued in the Sidhe tongue, Lifprasira, and Chance sat opposite them, silent. Bea's mobile began to scream out from the bedroom. "Excuse me." She went off to answer it.

"Morning." Liza sounded extraordinarily loud and Bea held the phone away from her ear. "I'm coming back next Tuesday."

"That's brilliant," replied Bea, still holding the phone at some distance from her ear.

"What? I can't hear you?" Liza burst out laughing. "What are you doing, I can hear a strange screeching noise? Is it interference?"

Bea didn't have a clue what she was talking about. "Liza, can you hear me?"

Kitty stood in the doorway watching her, still talking in Lifprasira. "She can't hear you."

The line went dead, Bea looked over at Kitty. "What did you say?"

"You need to use the common tongue with humans."

Bea's heart started to race. "The common tongue? What

are you talking about?" She looked at Kitty as if she had found an escapee from mental hospital.

Chance joined them in the hall and glared at Kitty.

"Your sister said…what's-" Bea broke off, starting to feel dizzy again and made her way into the living room. Once she caught sight of the journals, the images started to race off the page, expanding before her eyes. She ran straight past Chance, into the bathroom, locking the door behind her.

He ran after her. "Bea?" There was no reply. "Open the door."

Bea wiped away some water that started to trickle from her mouth with the back of her hand, and looked in the mirror. Alithia's round face, blonde hair and startling blue eyes stared deep into hers, and Bea quickly moved aside, heart pounding.

She heard Kitty say. "It's okay, Bea. We're here."

Bea wiped her perspiring forehead. She started to tremble, felt sick and rushed over to the toilet, lifted the pan, ready, but nothing came.

"Please, open the door. Let me help you," Chance pleaded.

"What's wrong with me?" Bea rested her head back against the bath.

"You're remembering," Kitty replied, as her eyes briefly glanced at Chance.

"Kitty, shut up, you're freaking me out," Bea blurted, rubbing her temple in the palms of her hand.

Chance paced the hall. "Did Saras talk you through this part?" he snapped.

"Shhh… she'll hear you."

He walked over and knocked on the door. "Bea, please, let me help."

"No. Give me a minute." She got up and walked over to the basin, keeping her eyes closed, not wanting to see Alithia's reflection again, and splashed her face with water.

Kitty walked off into the living room and picked up a journal.

"What are you doing with that?" Chance was ready to snatch the troublesome thing from her hands.

"She can speak in Lifprasira, maybe she can read it, too?"

Chance ran his hands down his face as Kitty sat down by the bathroom door.

Bea's voice was shaky. "I'm freaking out right now."

"What's happening?" asked Kitty.

"I'm seeing things, images." Bea rubbed her eyes in an attempt to get rid of the visions.

"You'll be alright, I promise."

"No, Kitty, I won't be alright. I'm sitting on the bathroom floor, with images of myself that are not really me. I'm far from alright! Did I take anything else last night? I'm hallucinating!"

"No, it was just mead."

Chance's eyes burned into Kitty's back, giving their disapproval, the Vororbla flower still fresh in his mind.

"God, this is so embarrassing. I need a cigarette," Bea mumbled.

Kitty looked at Chance. "She smokes?"

"At stressful times, I think." He'd kept his voice low.

"Please can you get my cigarettes, they're under the sink, in an empty plant pot."

Chance retrieved Bea's tea and cigarettes. "I have them here, but you need to open the door."

Bea unlocked the door, on her knees as it made her feel sick to stand. She only opened it slightly, enough for Chance to pass the tea and cigarettes through.

"May I come in?" Chance softly requested.

"No, I need some time alone." She shut the door and shakily lit a cigarette. "I'm going crazy," she mumbled to herself, scanning the bathroom, relieved that the images had stopped. Just when she was beginning to feel a bit calmer, another image flashed before her. Bea backed up against a wall, her breathing deepening as she saw herself running. She blinked and rubbed her eyes to try to stop it. The flashes stopped, but the imagery remained. It was a clear, sunny day. She heard birds singing in the trees around the path on which she ran.

"Bea, talk to me, what do you see?" Kitty asked, in a calm soothing tone.

Bea took another drag of her cigarette, her hand still shaking. "You'll think I'm crazy...I think I'm crazy."

"If we go through it together, it might help." Kitty suggested.

Tears started to flow from Bea's eyes. "I'm scared. I can't see anything but..." she broke off.

"It's just an image Bea...it can't hurt you. Share it with us. We will be there with you." Kitty promised.

Bea took one last drag of her cigarette and threw it down the toilet, as the vision became clearer, not so bright. "I'm in a blue dress."

"What kind of blue is it?" Kitty replied.

"What?" Bea asked, thrown by the question.

"We want to visualize it, too."

Chance shook his head, and resumed pacing.

"It's a...a cyan blue," replied Bea, closing her eyes again.

Kitty looked over at Chance and spoke in a low voice. "The colour of the Seelie Court."

Bea continued, "The fabric feels so light. I'm wearing it..." she broke off again, opening her eyes.

"I'm still here." Kitty's voice remained soft.

Bea bit her lip. "I am wearing it for someone."

Kitty sheepishly looked in Chance's direction, his anxiousness becoming more transparent. They heard Bea moving about, and Kitty continued. "Bea, stay with us. You have a blue dress on."

Bea permitted herself to drift back into the vision. "It's so beautiful here. The air smells sweet. I think, I'm in a labyrinth, but I know the way...I'm with someone."

"Who are you with?" Kitty asked, her eyes evading Chance's.

"He's chasing me," Bea replied.

Chance gripped the banister.

"Who's chasing you?" Kitty sat up straighter.

"Karian." Bea gasped at his name escaping so easily from her mouth, and opened her eyes, but his face was still laughing back at her.

"Bea, it's okay. Stay calm."

"Stay calm! Why am I seeing him?" she squealed.

"You're remembering. It's who you used to be."

Bea sat down by the side of the bath. She didn't bother to ask Kitty what she was talking about, getting rid of the images was her only concern. She lit another cigarette.

"Bea. The only way out of seeing the images is to face them."

"Okay, okay, give me a minute." Bea was still trying to make sense of the imagery. "I'm looking for him. He's hiding." She couldn't help but smile at feeling the same happiness that Alithia did in that moment. "I keep looking over my shoulder."

"What do you see?"

"He has our horses ready."

"Where are you going?" Kitty kept the questions going.

"Riding, as we always do, but no one knows. I told him that I would beat him in a race." Bea dropped her cigarette and it lay smouldering on the ceramic tiles as she drifted further into her vision. "I feel it…I feel the wind of home in my hair. I forgot how much I loved riding over the hills of our beautiful land." Suddenly, the imagery changed to a different place. "Where am I? I…I'm somewhere else. It's our special place. No one will find us here. There are ruins nearby, somewhere between his Court and mine. We're laughing so much and…" Bea's eyes suddenly opened. "Where's Chance?"

"He's gone to see if Jenny's okay. Do you want to wait until he returns?" Kitty placed her finger upon her lips, gesturing to Chance to remain quiet.

He wasn't happy.

"No I…I don't want him to hear."

Kitty gestured for Chance to go, but he adamantly shook his head. "I don't trust you alone with her, not after last night's revelations." He braced himself as Bea continued.

"We meet here as often as we can, but it's never enough. I miss him so much. I wanted to be open with my family about seeing him, but Karian is the son of King Farlyn, it would never be permitted. He begged me not to speak a word to anyone."

"I bet he did," Chance mumbled, under his breath.

Kitty tapped his leg. "What happened next?" She wanted to get Bea past this stage of the vision, as quickly as possible.

Bea's eyes rolled back as an overpowering image played over in her mind. Her head rubbed against the rim of the bath and she groaned. Karian was lying naked beside her, caressing every inch of her body with his tongue. Bea jumped up, nearly knocking herself out on the bathroom cabinet. She was trembling, not with fear, but with wanton desire, and it made her feel as if she were betraying Chance. Her mouth became dry and she gulped down some tea.

"Are you okay?" asked Kitty, hearing movement.

"No!" Bea raised her voice. "I feel violated."

"Did Karian make you do something?"

"No," she muttered.

"I don't understand?" replied Kitty.

"Karian is...touching *her*, but I'm feeling, seeing everything."

Chance stormed off down the stairs, he couldn't listen anymore.

Bea heard his footsteps and began panicking, wondering if he'd heard what she had said about Karian.

Kitty pretended he'd just returned. "Thank you, no Bea's okay, you were quick."

Bea sat back down in silence.

"What happened next?" Kitty pushed her on.

Chance quietly came back up the stairs, and sat on the top step, head in his hands.

Bea took another gulp of tea, sat back and closed her eyes. "It's night, we're asleep in a glade, near the forest, but I heard something and woke up. There's a noise in the bush behind us. The horses were becoming uneasy." Bea screamed, "They've found us. Nooooo!"

Chance jumped up, and ran to the bathroom door. "Out the way! I'm breaking the door down."

Kitty stood in front of him and spoke in a low voice, "Wait…just a few more minutes."

Chance gritted his teeth, but stood back.

"They hit him, while he was sleeping." Bea wailed, "He's bleeding!"

"Where are you Bea? Who's with you?"

Bea opened her eyes and looked around the bathroom, but all she could see was the trees blurring, as she ran past. Branches brushed her face and clawed at her blue dress. "They're chasing me. I'm scared. I don't know where to run."

"Where are you now? Bea concentrate, Alithia knows the woods." Kitty was now on her knees, palms against the door.

"Ouch! I've been hit with something, everything is… Noooo!" she cried. "Let him go! Please don't hurt him! … Don't hurt him." She continued to cry. "He's hurt, he's trying to talk to me, but they keep hitting him." Bea started to sob.

"Who's there?" Chance asked.

"I can't see. Someone's shouting," she replied, not distinguishing between Kitty and Chance's voice. "King Farlyn looks so angry."

Chance nodded. "Who else is there?" His head rested on

the bathroom door, as if it somehow brought him closer to Bea.

"I can't hear what the King's saying. Where's he going? No please…wait, please help us. What are you doing?"

They could hear Bea banging about in the bathroom.

"Bea, what's happening?" Kitty took over the questions.

"They're placing me in the well. I don't want to go in there… stop."

"I have to get her out." Chance was about to push Kitty aside.

"Wait, please, just one more question." Kitty pleaded with him. "Bea… who placed you in the well?"

Bea was still sobbing. "Don't hurt him."

Chance was growing impatient with Kitty refusing to move from the door.

"He…he's holding me down." Bea started choking, gurgling.

Chance heard a thud. He pushed Kitty aside, kicked the door open, and ran in, sliding on water surrounding Bea, who was lying on the floor. He checked her pulse and started to push down on her chest. Water streamed from her mouth, and it continued to flow with every push on her chest.

"Bea, don't leave. Kitty, repeat the words of the Seior, now."

"I can't!" He heard the panic in her voice.

"Kitty, just repeat the words!" He demanded, still trying to get a response from Bea, pushing down on her chest and breathing in her mouth.

"It only works once," Kitty replied, horrified.

He couldn't believe what he was hearing, and desperately

continued to try and resuscitate Bea. "Don't leave. Don't you leave me…Wake up," he begged.

She violently shuddered, becoming limp in his arms.

Chance yelled, "Nooo!"

Kitty knelt down on the floor, aghast. She watched as Chance pounded Bea's chest and pleaded for her to return to him.

"Anathon, look!" Kitty pointed to Bea's hands.

He looked down and saw her fingers twitching, and within seconds, Bea sat up gasping for air. Chance embraced her in his arms. His head rested against hers in relief, but he was angry with himself for listening to Kitty and for waiting so long to enter the bathroom.

Kitty leant back on the door until she heard Jenny's voice, and rushed out onto the landing to intercept her.

"What's going on?" asked Jenny, trying to look over to the bathroom door.

"Oh, Chance stubbed his toe. He's been running around like a madman…men. Bea's nursing him in the bathroom. She told me that you read to the children." Kitty redirected Jenny back down the stairs, while Chance carried Bea into the lounge, and laid her on the sofa.

Bea's voice was shaky. "What's happening to me?"

He knew the pain of telling her the truth would be evident in his eyes. "You have the soul of a Sidhe."

"Alithia?"

Chance nodded, cupping her hands in his.

Her eyes searched his. "Are you a Sidhe?"

He nodded again.

"I have no recollection of you in any of the images."

He gave her a weak smile. "You have a very old soul."

Her tears started to fall at the realisation of having a past life, and the fact that Chance was also a Sidhe, an otherworldly being. Slowly, it all began to sink in. "I died…didn't I? In the well?"

Chance held her closer. "It's over now."

Once Bea was asleep, Kitty entered the room and placed the shop keys on the side. "How is she?"

"Better, no thanks to you," he snapped, staring over at Bea.

"Anathon, please."

"I don't want to hear it. Haven't you got something to report back? Somewhere to go?"

"I've already told you. I'm not going anywhere." Kitty stubbornly folded her arms and sat down, nose in the air.

A few hours later, Bea whispered to Chance. "Thank you. For not leaving me. You know, the crazy woman in the bathroom."

Kitty interrupted with her best smile. "It was time for you to know the truth. I'm sorry that you had to go through all that."

Chance felt exasperated by Kitty, it was her fault Bea had gone through it all so violently, but he remained silent, for Bea.

"I'm still not sure what it all means. I remember Alithia, who admittedly looks a little like me, but everything else about her seems just the opposite… I remember…*him*, but everything else is a jumbled mess." She sat up and looking over at Kitty. "So, you're a Sidhe, too?"

"Yes."

Chance saw the excitement reach Kitty's eyes and he mumbled something, but neither Bea nor Kitty heard.

"The water I brought up...was from the well that Alithia drowned in?"

This time Chance nodded.

"How's that possible?" she asked.

Kitty couldn't help herself, and replied before Chance, "You're at a transitional stage. Your soul is still sort of connected to our realm. Your recollection just removed the veil of obscurity, enabling you to see into both realms for a short period of time." She was about to hand a journal to Bea when Chance stopped her.

"It's alright," Bea assured.

He moved his hand, and sat back down next to Bea. She looked down at the journal and started turning the pages.

Kitty eagerly waited. "You can read it now, can't you?"

Bea nodded. "As well as I can read English."

"I knew it." Kitty grew more excited.

Chance got up and stormed out the room.

"I think I really upset him." Kitty announced.

Bea placed her hand on Kitty's. "He won't stay angry long."

Bea found Chance in the kitchen. His face solemn, "You're upset?"

He gently caressed her cheek with his. "How are you feeling?"

"It was so frightening when Alithia was being held under the water... she felt this lifeless, silence surrounding her. It was awful. She was terrified, so alone. When she tried to scream out for help, in that moment, it wasn't Alithia in the water …it was me." Bea's eyes welled. "I felt myself sinking deeper into this cold, bottomless void, imprisoned by walls of stone that my fists frantically beat themselves against… but in those last moments of breath I saw-"

He pulled her closer. "What did you see?"

She remained in quiet turmoil. How could she tell him that she saw him, but then his face blurred and changed into Karian's. She avoided the question. "Will I have more dizziness, visions?"

"They should stop now…the ones of *him* too." Chance's eyes gave away the pain of his knowledge that there was more to her story, left unsaid. She felt his anguish as he tried to hide his eyes, but she refused to let him turn away. Bea swept her hand over his hair. "I don't love him."

Chance lifted his eyes to meet hers. "But Alithia did."

CHAPTER 13

Sides

*C*hance mentally prepared himself to meet Kitty at an establishment frequented by Seelies. A small place, tucked away in Mayfair's side streets, far away from prying eyes. A simple sign hung above the door from two chains displaying a large stylised 'S' in metallic purple with a silver-flourished line running down the centre, declaring to all that knew, it was a Sidhe club. Chance spoke into the intercom and entered.

Kitty was sitting near the back, furthest from the bar. Chance sat opposite her. "What did you need to tell me?" His cold tone removed the smile on her face.

"Anathon, you can't still be angry with me. Can't we just start over?"

He didn't reply, but heavily sighed, hoping to exhale his agitation. *Does she really think I'd just let everything slide that easily.*

"It's your human side that enhances your stubbornness. You realise that, don't you?" She stated, arrogantly.

"So I've heard." His eyes scoured the room for anyone that looked like they could be working for Saras. The club was dark, but his keen eyes would still notice anything out of the ordinary.

"It's alright. It's safe here. Look, I think Saras is planning something."

"With or without the backing of the Court and the Queen?"

"This is serious, Anathon." She kept her voice low. "He wants Karian and all the Unseelie gone."

"About time. Isn't that what you're here for?" His eyes still refused to meet hers.

"But now we know that Karian did not kill Alithia. You heard it from Bea's mouth yourself."

"Farlyn must have given the order."

"I don't think he did."

"Why? Because he rode off? Get to the point, Kitty."

Kitty slid back in her chair, tapping her fingers on the table. "Ask Bea who held her under the water."

"No."

Her fingers stopped tapping and she leant forward. "We need to know."

"Why don't you ask her? You talk with her often enough."

"I haven't asked her because I don't want to go behind your back."

"A bit late for that now...and Saras? Maybe, you'll warn me of his arrival...maybe you won't."

"I'm warning you now, aren't I?" She rolled her eyes.

"When will he arrive?"

"He doesn't always give me the details. He probably knows I'll tell you."

"What has Saras requested?" Chance asked.

"Updates."

"What have you updated him on?" He sat back, giving Kitty his full attention.

"What we discussed," she replied.

"Remind me, what exactly?"

Kitty shrugged. "That Bea only remembers that she was

Alithia, nothing else."

"Saras's plan? His next move?"

"To persuade Bea to return home. I don't know…I'm assuming." Kitty shook her head.

"Have you heard anything of Brandon?"

"He's disappeared. His sister, Leanne, thinks he's back in rehab."

"His sister?"

A big grin appeared on her face. "I befriended her."

"Brandon's going to love that. Does Saras know of Brandon?"

"Are you just going to fire questions at me?"

"You wanted to talk, isn't that what we're doing?"

Kitty huffed. "Look, I haven't said anything to Saras. Have you heard from Queen Eliseis?"

Chance shook his head. "Nothing. Where's the Deisi?"

"I can't tell you."

More secrets. He turned his face away.

"Anathon, please."

He leant across the table. "I thought we were on the same side?"

"We are." Kitty protested as he got up.

"Once, maybe," he muttered, before leaving.

CHAPTER 14

Questions and Answers

Over the next few days, Bea tried to resume her normal daily routine as much as possible. She thanked Jenny for being there to open the shop, and talked with Liza. Chance seemed overly protective concerning any contact that she had with Kitty, and she observed a certain sadness about him, not present before the visions. She had offered to listen if he wanted to talk, but he always insisted that he was okay.

Bea had taken to reading the journals during quiet periods in the shop, but it was still difficult to make sense of all the information that they contained. Yes, she could now read their language, Lifprasira, but much of the spiritual content went over her head. She wanted to ask Chance to explain further, but knew that he'd just worry about her trying to take in too much. He always appeared disapproving and distant whenever she opened a journal, and Bea thought, perhaps, it was because he missed his homeland. So here she sat, going over what she had read in her mind, trying to rationalise everything, his world, her previous life. It fascinated, excited and scared her.

Bea yawned, placing the journals underneath the counter. Chance was right, a break would do her the world of good, and she decided to arrange for a tasty meal to be delivered. It would be a great opportunity to talk with Chance about his life in the other realm. No journals, just freely conversing, and hopefully, find out more about his identity as a Sidhe. A big grin stretched across her face. She couldn't wait to hear more about a world, his world, so far away and very different to her own, it was going to beat any movie she'd seen, this was real.

Bea heard the bell of the shop's chime and started dishing up the Thai meal.

Two glasses and a bottle of J.P. Chenet Rosé sat waiting on the living room table. Aromatic candles flickered from each corner, and the scent of vanilla and lilies filled the room.

"I'll be there in a minute," Bea shouted out from the kitchen.

Chance hung his jacket on the door, opened the bottle, and was pouring their drinks when she entered. He put the bottle down, as her lips met his. "Nice surprise. What's the occasion?"

"Remember this?" She excitedly pressed the play button on the iPod station, and he smiled.

As the Ed Sheeran track played, her lips brushed against his cheeks, and her hands found their way to his waist, up through the back of his shirt. She sighed feeling his bare skin, and Chance softly pressed against her. "I remember," he whispered.

Their feet slowly began to move to the music. Chance slid his hands from her waist to her bum, and pulled her closer. Bea whispered the lyrics in his ear, as she slowly led him to the sofa and climbed on top of him. She seductively teased his lips with her own. His tongue was waiting and devoured hers.

Bea moved from his mouth down his neck, onto his chest. Her tongue caressed his nipple while she hurriedly unfastened the buttons on his shirt. Chance eagerly moved his hands to the band of her skirt, and within seconds, all fabric slid away from her skin. His hands gently eased her body to where he wanted, and he groaned as she embraced all of him, where she needed. They both quivered at the intimate meeting.

"Great starter!" Bea giggled as Chance got up to go and warm up the food.

He eventually reappeared quite pleased with himself. "I used the contraption and amazingly, the food is hot." He kissed her on the nose and passed her a plate before sitting down.

Bea laughed. "It only took you twenty minutes. Don't you have microwaves back home? Advanced race and all that?"

He shook his head and smiled. "At home everything is fresh." He gently bit her neck. "We eat while it's still hot, and there's no *distractions* there…I'm not sure that I should even be consuming this." He moved the food around the plate with his fork, as if ready to attack anything that might move. "I eat this because I trust you, you do know that?" His smile made her stomach flutter and she changed the subject before he could distract her further. "What do you normally eat?"

"I guess…the equivalent of vegetables."

"You're a vegetarian?" She was astonished. "But you've eaten meat."

"I tried to discreetly remove the meat. You didn't notice? However, I admit that I accidently swallowed a few of pieces from Elly's stew. The meat tastes like some of our vegetables…strange."

"You should've said you were a vegetarian."

"I didn't want to appear ungrateful." He grinned, tucking in.

"So, the animals back home just keep multiplying?"

He laughed. "No. It's…It's like the perfect balance. It wasn't always like that. It's a form of our evolution. We just realised that harming another living being caused bad Vororbla."

"Karma?"

He nodded.

"Do you have pets?"

He shook his head. "We don't keep pets as you do. Our connection to animals is more, free… The Cu Sith is our equivalent of your dog, but not domesticated. There's also a type of cat. They share time with you, if it suits them."

"Have you spent much time with any *Cu Sith*?"

"In the past, but I spend a lot of time away from home."

"To be here?" She had never thought to ask how often he'd been to this realm.

"No. Now eat up or I won't tell you anymore. I'm not heating *this* up again."

Once they'd finished eating, Bea made herself more comfortable by placing her legs across his as he lay back on the sofa.

"Go on, ask away." He smiled, making himself comfortable against a pillow.

"Why do you visit other worlds?"

"I oversee. Make sure that everything is as it should be."

"Tell me more." Bea snuggled into him.

Chance's eyes started to glaze over as he told her of his homeland. Of streams that blended into various shades of purple and blue when they met, forming a large estuary at the edge of their land. He boasted that their sky displayed two moons and one sun. Emerias, his realm, was a place that was neither too hot, nor too cold. The sweetness in the air was due to the scent of the Vororbla flower called Voror, carried by gentle breezes from Calageata, the home of Sidhe elementals, known as the Sindria. The gateway leading from Emerias to Calageata was actually a portal for the Sidhe to visit the elemental realm, where the well of souls dwelt.

He spoke of unusual plants that grew in abundance, telling her that some retreated back into the soil at a mere touch of a fingertip on its leaves. Chance also explained that the war had started with King Farlyn, when he was still a Prince. She learned that once a Sidhe's deepest emotions were stirred, they could last many years, especially those of anger, loss and revenge. King Farlyn's unharnessed emotions had caused the divide of the Sidhe into two sects, the Seelie and the Unseelie, and that there was a sort of peace for a time, but it ended with Alithia's passing.

"She was a Seelie and they blamed the Unseelie?" The fun from the storytelling had disappeared from her eyes. "The Sidhe...Idorus, he was Unseelie?"

Chance slowly sat up straighter. "You remember Idorus?"

"Yes," she replied, but the memory of his face was one she would rather forget. Bea could tell Chance's mind was ticking over in thought before he asked, "Is that who held Alithia under the water?"

She nodded, staring down at her hands. "I couldn't hear their voices properly in the visions, so I kept replaying the memory over in my head and finally recognised him as a guard of the King, that's when his name came to me."

"Did King Farlyn give him the order to hurt Alithia?"

She shook her head. "I don't think he knew."

Chance lent closer, his voice calm, but carrying a wary tone. "Are you sure that King Farlyn didn't give the order, or knew of her murder?"

Bea bit her lip while retracing the memory before answering. "I'm sure."

He leant back on the sofa. "This complicates things."

"Why? Can't you just tell everyone what happened, bring peace again?"

"It's not as simple as that. Queen Eliseis needs to know." He became distant.

"Who are you, *really*?"

He lowered his gaze. "My Sidhe name is Anathon."

Bea's eyes widened, and her mouth gaped open. "Your name isn't Chance?"

"No. We're taught from a very young age that revealing our true name to a human means they could hold power over us."

"How?"

"Your history speaks of wise women, witches? Well, the Sidhe were permitted for a time to teach humans some of our arts, but later, the names of the ones that taught them were called out, summoned and slaughtered."

"By whom?"

"The men of cloth…Eventually, they succeeded in diminishing the memory of our race. Humans believed that we retreated to the hills. Remember when we first met, I told you that Sidhe means people of the mound. In truth, we're not even called Sidhe, *again,* a human term. Symbolism is used greatly here to disguise the truth."

"How? I mean, why would anyone want to stop the Sidhe presence here? Do people still know?"

"A few still remember. Let's just say, we follow different paths." Chance gently kissed her cheek. "I told you, it's complicated."

"And your scars? Can you tell me about them, now?"

"Training, others…battles."

"Battles? Have you been in many?"

He shook his head. "Not many, but enough."

Bea wanted to lighten the mood and changed the subject. "So what *is* your race actually called?"

"I think in the present era we would be classed as *aliens?*" He teased.

"You look pretty human to me. What are the main differences? I know there's not many." She ran her hand down his chest, where his hand met hers, stopping it from going any further.

"For one, our language, humans can't normally hear us when we use it. It's too fast, a higher frequency. Some animals pick up on it and we have to be more careful around them." He spoke Lifprasira. She replied in the same dialect. "It is strange. I feel a slight tingling on my tongue, but the transition from one to the other doesn't seem any different, apart from my knowledge of it." Her eyes narrowed. "Did you speak Lifprasira with Kitty in my company, before I understood?"

Chance smiled, raising one brow.

"You did." She gasped, then playfully tapped him on the arm. "Okay, if you're not the Sidhe, what are you? Don't say aliens," she asked, back in the human tongue.

He explained that the Sidhe are the later physical forms of the Aos Si and the Sindria. That they're all connected, but different stages in evolution. The Sindria are the elementals, non-physical beings, caretakers of the well of souls. Every Sidhe would eventually become Sindria, but it took many lifetimes. She saw that distant look in his eyes again. "So, the Sindria tend the well of souls in Calageata, sounds like another name for heaven."

"It could be." He wrapped his arms around her.

"What do normal Sidhe do? You know, everyday stuff?"

He explained that many tended The Gardens, the main food sources, or dedicated themselves to a craft for the benefit of all.

Bea asked about the Courts.

"The Unseelie live in one of the ancient forests to the East of our lands. I've heard that many of the original castle structures are in ruins now. It used to be a place our elders resided, the Aos Si, before ascending to become Sindria. The Seelie Court is far from King Farlyn's, to the West. It's more…modern." He laughed.

"What's so funny?"

"It's just difficult to describe. The main buildings are made from a type of stone unknown here. Similar to Obsidian, yet like Labradorite. Do you know these stones?"

"Yes, my mother loved crystals, she'd sit and tell me about the properties, but I can't remember most of what she told me."

Chance briefly explained that the stone used to construct the Seelie Court was chosen for its protective and repelling properties, because of the war.

"When you told me the story of your parents, what part was true? Kitty isn't your sister, is she?"

Again, he shook his head. "No. I don't know my real family, only that my mother's name was Kaelen. The armourer of the Seelie Court and his wife brought me up from a baby. Then, at the age of seven, I joined the Order of The Heaven Stone. There's nothing more to tell."

"What about Queen Eliseis? Alithia's mother, tell me more about her."

He started to explain that her husband, the Seelie King, fell during battle in the last big war, and after losing Alithia, the Queen became withdrawn, only attending Court when needed. Saras now governed the Seelie Court, like a Prime Minister would in the Earth realm.

"How many know about *me, Bea*, not Alithia, in your realm?"

"Not many, only those I've mentioned."

"What's going to happen now?"

"Eventually, they will ask if you want to return home."

She looked at him and smiled. "You'll be there?"

He nodded, lowering his eyes.

"You're hiding."

His eyes met hers in an instant. "I'm not hiding."

"What is it?"

"You would be returning to my world as Alithia, not Bea."

"If I'm with you, then I'll remain me." She smiled, the idea filled her with a mix of excitement and wonder.

"What about Liza, the shop?" he replied.

Her wondrous thoughts came crashing down in an instant. She nodded. "I'd miss them."

"It's a big decision, something to think about nearer the time."

"When will that be?"

Chance stroked her face. "Not yet."

"Okay, so what are Sidhe women like?"

He laughed, sitting up a little, as if on guard. "You've met Kitty."

"Yes, but she seems...more human."

"What do you want to know?"

"Have you ever loved a Sidhe woman?"

"I'm not going to answer that."

"*You said*, I can ask you anything?"

He bit his lip. "Loved...no."

"Have you loved anyone...in any realm?"

"My heart's taken and it will stay loyal to her forever."

"And who is this lucky lady?" she asked, mouth hovering over his.

He tried to kiss her, but she pulled away. "Oh no, you're not escaping my question's that easily...Are they beautiful?"

"Who?"

Bea rolled her eyes. "Sidhe women."

"Some."

"How many of *some*, did you find attractive?"

He shook his head. "No."

"No, what?"

She was quickly made quiet, as he kissed his finger, gently placing it upon her lips. "The only woman that I want, that I see...*is you.*"

"Then come *see* me, Anathon of the Heaven Stone," she teased, pulling him closer.

His eyes glinted at her words. "Say my name again."

Bea couldn't contain her smile on feeling the goose bumps appearing over his skin and laid further back on the sofa, pulling him closer by his shirt. "Come see me...*Anathon.*"

A huge grin appeared on his face as he leant over, arms now abreast of her.

"Take me on a journey to the place of souls," she whispered. "Kitty said, you're able to take me via a sort of visual thing, a meditation. I want to close my eyes and feel a little piece of heaven...*with you.*"

"You're not relaxed enough." He moved her top revealing her tummy and gently placed his moist, warm lips upon her skin.

"I'm quite relaxed, but if you keep that up, my heart rate will go through the roof."

He laughed and then whispered by her ear. "Kitty well knows, what she's talking about is a part of a special ritual. It would be the first time I have practiced this form of... training."

"Oh, it's a sex thing?" she replied, on seeing him blush.

Without warning, he suddenly got up.

"What are you doing?" Bea sat baffled at his sudden departure.

"You want me to take you on a journey?"

She nodded, still bewildered.

"Then let me get a few things ready."

Her mouth dropped as he ran out the door.

CHAPTER 15

Calageata

"What are you doing?" Bea asked Chance after hearing him frantically pottering about in the bathroom. His hands turned on the taps. "Running a bath." He gave her a cheeky smile.

"Why? What has this got..."

Chance shook his head. "No questions." He then instructed her to get in, with a promise that he would join her very soon. After planting a kiss on her forehead, he was gone.

Bea stood baffled by the door, not knowing what to make of the madness, but went along with it, especially if it meant she got to go on a journey, with him.

As she lay soaking in the bubbles, the shop's bell jingle rang out, and she submerged herself, hiding in the bubbles. Within minutes, she felt Chance's body against hers and was about to slide on top of him, but he pulled away, stating they were only to wash each other. She pouted, but ruefully agreed.

Once out the bath, Bea walked into the bedroom and gasped. There were fresh, purple petals artfully spread over the bed in the shape of a seven petal flower. Scented candles were alight everywhere around the room, releasing an aroma of Jasmine, possibly Neroli – she wasn't sure which, possibly both, but they instantly brought a sense of calm. She turned and saw Chance staring at her. The light against the rose-tinted walls gave a soft, sunset tone to their skin. Bea smiled, noticing that he'd brought the laptop in and turned the music player on.

Chance held her hand and asked her to join him, guiding her towards the bed. With a slight tug, the towel around his waist slumped to the floor. Bea couldn't help but blush seeing him sit on the bed, gloriously naked, waiting for her to do the same. She gulped, feeling a little uncomfortable at permitting her body to be entirely exposed, nowhere to hide. However, his sweet, gentle smile gave her a sense of security, and she, too, let her towel fall to the floor. Slowly, she climbed onto the bed to join him, trying to discreetly pull the bed sheet up in front of her. He shook his head while pulling the sheet from her hands. "Who's hiding now?"

She placed her arms and hands strategically over the areas of her body that she felt uncomfortable with. He moved closer, his hands gently pulled them away, too. "There's no need to hide from me, you're beautiful." His lips then softly kissed the places that she'd tried to conceal. At first, she felt self-conscious, but after taking several deep breaths, she focused purely on him, and forgot the fear of not being enough.

She felt open, a little too exposed, strangely, more naked inside than out. She knew that her old inhibitions were causing her nervousness, and tried harder to relax. It was difficult having someone looking deeper, further than just her body. It wasn't something she was used to. The only other man that she had slept with was Brandon, and he became so cold. She knew he had loved her, and his touch was always gentle, but she never felt connected with him the way she did with Chance. The last time they had slept together, she had quietly cried when Brandon fell asleep, because it felt as if she could have been any woman, as long his physical need was fulfilled – their love had become too remote, too distant. Her nakedness now seemed trivial in light of her new lover. Here was a wonderfully caring man, wanting to share his love in every way, mentally and physically. The thought made her smile at the happiness she already felt in his presence.

"Close your eyes," he softly requested.

Bea did as he asked. Her heart pounded as her stomach became a place of colliding acrobats, and she nervously laughed.

"No laughing."

"Why no laughing?" She immediately opened her eyes.

"Close your eyes."

"Okay, okay, they're closed." She waited a moment, but heard nothing. "I'm not laughing, you can begin." She just wanted something to happen to hide her embarrassment, maybe, then she could slide under the sheet.

He chuckled, gently stroking the top of her arm with his fingers. "Are you ready?"

"Yes." She waited, patiently.

"You need to immerse yourself visually and emotionally in every word I speak." His voice faded out, followed by a brief moment of silence.

Her breathing deepened even more, knowing that his eyes were still taking all of her in. She could feel their presence moving over her skin. After a few seconds, Bea giggled. "Are you there without me?" She felt the bed move with his laughter, but still kept her eyes closed.

"Bea, *please. . .*relax." She felt his breath close to her ear.

"And stop interrupting." He softly kissed her neck then spoke again. "The Heaven Stone does not concentrate on the physical, but instead focuses on energy. Feelings are our senses and we need to practice on one area of our bodies at a time to make a connection. First, you will be the receiver and I the giver, do not be constrained by the emotions that you feel, be guided by them. There's to be no direct contact to obvious areas that bring pleasure, agreed?"

She nodded and he moved closer, sliding his legs under hers and around her body. Then, she gently placed her legs around him. They now sat, with their knees slightly bending, in a close embrace. She could feel his warm breath on her face and opened her eyes. She gazed at his strong, beautiful, body, half-hidden in the shade of the dimmed room. The flickering light from the candles delicately accentuated his smooth, firm skin. His eyes secretly gave away a smile as they stared into hers and he cupped her face in his hands. "Now, let me take you on a journey to the place of souls, to your little piece of heaven." His fingers glided from her face down her neck to her arm, and then gently grasped her hand. "With your hand in mine, permit me show you something magical, a place where we will always be able to join with each other, no matter where we are, together or alone. There is no measure of time or distance where we are going …and we will stay grounded to this realm by our physical touch." He continued to guide her further. "Together we begin to walk through the most serene waterfall. Your face is gently caressed by the flowing waters, and a wave of blissful tranquillity passes through your entire body…We continue to walk hand in hand, and arrive at the other side of the waterfall, for the waterfall is a veiled door. A secret path reveals itself and we are both embraced by a wonderful feeling of calm...we're totally relaxed. Hand in hand we enter a beautiful new world, and with our first step... I inhale and you exhale. Repeat this breathing three times...We're content because we're filled with so much love. We will look into each other's eyes, and truly see, this is called Soul-gazing." The music continued to play unobtrusively in the background, and after three deep breaths they opened their eyes and stared at one another. Both still breathing as one, and as her breath deepened, so did his. She continued to gaze deeper into his eyes, they appeared to dance in the light and shadows of the candles' flames in the room, and her stomach fluttered at knowing that he was hers. It was strange, for a spilt second, she thought that she saw a fear in his eyes, but as he continued to look back at her, they filled with overwhelming love. It felt like the most pure, honest experience that two people could share, there was no hiding, no embarrassment, just silent revelation without touch or words.

He moved closer and kissed each of her eyelids. "The second step...close your eyes."

She closed her eyes and waited to be guided further.

"As we walk, you smell a familiar floral aroma, and it reminds you of being in this world before. The thought makes you smile, for you know it is the flower of Vororbla. The sweetness is intoxicating and all of your senses tingle. We walk further into the cloudlike, purple mists of Calageata... Remember, I am the giver, and you are the receiver."

Bea nodded, *easy*, she thought, until she felt his breath drifting over her skin again and visualised the mist being the essence of him encapsulating her very being. The fine hair all over her body stood on end as his mouth lingered at her shoulders, then over her breasts, but still not touching.

Slowly, his breath, his mist, travelled up her neck, and then his mouth hovered over hers, where very gently, he caressed each lip in turn. His kiss, mingled with other sensations of gentle biting and sensuous strokes of his tongue, made Bea ache for more him, and her lips opened to invite him in, but, instead, he teased her with more words. "Come and take the third step with me, before I taste…let me lead you to a carpet of purple flowers that blanket rolling hills…You look up at the two moons of Emerias. You sense it is a sacred place, which we both know in our hearts is home, and will always be our special place of meeting."

She felt his warm, moist tongue lovingly glide over each lip. Was he savouring her taste before accepting the invitation inside? Bea found it hard to resist his touch and was about to kiss him, when he mumbled, "No, you're to receive, not give." She felt a smile stretch across his mouth, which still remained against hers. "You can open your eyes, but only to soul-gaze." In an instant, she opened them, and they met his, mirroring her need. It was proving more and more difficult to not show him, give him, what his body and hers both craved. She smiled now, understanding that the steps were separating their souls from the needs of the body, to the entirety of being whole. She'd never experienced such a surge of energy travel through every part of her, as his mouth began to caress hers. First, slow, hardly moving, but still managing to tantalise every nerve, deep within her. Each stroke of his tongue enticed a dance with hers, each sudden plunge giving the promise of more. She looked into his blue pools of cosmic sky and as they mingled with flickers of light in the room, they became like stars gazing back at her. He whispered softly by her ear. "We truly start to see each other for the first time as I see your inner light, and you see mine. We are free to feel, to love, to give, and to receive." He cupped her breasts in his hands and moved his tongue's dance to her nipples. Bea gasped at his complete touch. Her hands reached out for him, but he gently moved them away. "Step four, we lay amongst a carpet of purple flowers and you guide my hand to bring you pleasure." He ran his fingers over one of her hands and she guided it along the inside of her thigh, until his fingers were at a place where he could bring her more pleasure. With each proficient movement that he made, every part of her yearned for much more. She needed to touch him. She'd never wanted someone so much in all her life.

"Step five…my turn." She forcefully pushed him down on the bed and felt so aroused by his submissive withdraw, that she wasted no time in becoming the giver to his ready and waiting body. His previous tantalising of her body, she now applied to him. Moving from his mouth, the tip of her tongue travelled down his chest, teasingly played over his nipples, mixed with gentle bites as she moved down his side. She paused, looking up at him. "Step six."

He groaned, as she travelled lower still, but pulled her back up. "Not yet." His eyes were burning with need and she knew he wanted her, but desperately, so desperately, trying to hold out just a few minutes longer.

"But I *need* you…now," she urged, and seeing the weakness in his eyes at her confession, she placed her body on top of his and closed her thighs around what he still tried to deny her. The sound of her name from his mouth was more a moan, as she pressed her body closer, allowing all of him in. He tried to fight his body's plea, but his hands betrayed him as they found their way to her hips, encouraging every movement she gave. "The seventh step...together." Chance's voice became a whimper as his eyes found hers. They climaxed with a mix of passion and ecstasy as bodies and souls met...as one. He quivered as she flexed, and he flexed and she quivered, uniting both worlds with a soaring vibrational song of pleasure, the purest form of energy – their love.

As they lay embraced in each other's arms, her hand in his, Chance whispered in her ear, "Now we are one...no matter where you are...you'll be able to *see* me and I...I'll be able to *see* you." He saw her eyes softly flutter beneath the lids, but instead of opening, he watched as a single tear escaped. He brushed it away with his thumb and her eyes finally met his.

Her hand reached out, placing the palm on his face, and she whispered, "I *see* you...You were holding back before... *why?*"

"I didn't want you to see past me being human...Remember something for me." He rested his head on her breast, away from where her eyes could easily see his fear. "You may not always feel my hand in yours...but it *is* there...please promise you'll remember...know that I would search the cosmos for you...just reach for my hand in the void." The dread panged at his heart more than ever at the possibility of losing her, but had to let her know that she could always find him.

She softly kissed his shoulder. "Anathon, *I love you*, and

promise to always hold your hand in mine."

At her confession of loving him, Chance snuggled further into her. "Even when you can't see it?"

"Especially then," she replied, running her hand over his damp hair.

He closed his eyes and gently squeezed her in his arms, scared to let go. *Why could he not conquer this fear?* Every part of him yearned to tell her that he loved her too. She was more precious to him than she knew, but by admitting his love aloud, he felt it would weaken his strength to protect her somehow. He hoped that by sharing with her, that little piece of heaven, that she would know how much he loved her. The Heaven Stone warriors only performed this rite once they met their twin flame. Not many did. The spiritual training weighed heavily on his mind, as feelings of guilt raged inside him. *Was he wrong for performing the ritual on someone that holds another's flame within? Would there be any repercussions?* Surely, his feelings of connection were not wrong. *Was it possible?* he wondered, *to have two souls residing in one body?* He'd never heard of such a thing, but he felt everything a twin flame should. *But if it were possible, would they not have been told?* In the silence, he stared down at Bea, who now lay asleep in his arms, totally oblivious of his inner torment. He closed his eyes and prayed to the Sindria elementals, pleading for a spark of light to reside within her that was not a part of Alithia's, and for it to stay bright... for him.

CHAPTER 16

The House Guest

$\mathcal{W}$hile Bea and Chance slept, an uninvited visitor entered the flat. Chance stirred hearing a chant in Seior, and suddenly sat up. He briefly froze as the bedroom door swung open, and saw Saras standing in the doorway. Resignedly, Chance climbed out of bed, he'd been caught red handed. "My Lord Saras," he uttered, daring to glance back at Bea, who was still sleeping.

Saras casually stepped towards her, and his crisp blue eyes narrowed as he hovered over her. "Ah…the Seior chant of sleep. She will not wake for a while yet, Anathon."

The muscles in Chance's jaw tensed as Saras removed his glove and ran his fingers gently over Bea's cheek. "Humans are weak…you're half-human, are you not, Anathon?" Saras placed his glove back on his hand, and stared down at Chance's clothes on the floor.

"Yes." Chance muttered, lowering his head. He couldn't believe he'd been stupid to not take more caution, but it was too late, now. His eyes followed Saras's back to the doorway, where Kitty was standing with two other Sidhe. She was about to say something, but Chance looked away in disgust.

Saras continued. "Would that human weakness in you explain why, upon my arrival, I find *you*, her protector, a Sidhe of The Heaven Stone, naked in bed with the queen's daughter?"

It sounded worse coming from Saras's mouth and he dreaded the thought of Eliseis hearing of his betrayal via Saras. "She's not Alithia," he retorted.

Saras's face hardened, like steel cooling. "Kindly explain further, Anathon. You must forgive me. I am a little bewildered. Alithia was our queen's daughter. Her soul accidently came to earth, caused by a rather premature death. Her soul then resurfaces in a human form. Am I correct thus far?"

"Yes," Chance replied, through gritted teeth.

"Good, permit me to continue. The Order receives a rather unusual request to permit a member of The Heaven Stone to investigate as to why there is an Unseelie presence around this human. Alas, the truth is finally revealed; Alithia's soul entered the body of a human, named Bethany, correct?" He waited for an answer.

"Yes." Chance briefly closed his eyes to try and escape the humiliation.

"Therefore, Bea *is* Alithia, Alithia *is* Bea." Saras sped across the room, his face met Chance's. "*You*, Anathon, have bedded the purest form of a Sidhe before its rebirth. Your human bloodline is degenerate. The queen will know of this betrayal, and your gracious Sidhe parents will carry your shame as a weeping wound. Now, get dressed."

Saras glided back towards Kitty, Valu and Ulric. "Do not keep me waiting," he stated before exiting the room. Kitty blinked away tears, and followed her Lord into the kitchen.

Chance could hardly lift his head, imagining the disgrace he'd bring upon his family and The Heaven Stone if word got back to the Court. In their eyes, loving a human was disgusting enough, but for a half-human to dare fall in love with the daughter of the queen, would get him banished from the realm. Rightly or wrongly, he felt no regret in his love for Bea, nor for his actions. He slipped into his clothes, and before leaving the room gently placed a kiss on the tip of Bea's nose and whispered in Lifprasira. "I love you." It took all his strength to finally leave the room, knowing that he may never see her again. He wanted to stay in this realm to protect her from Karian. The thought of *him* anywhere near her caused every muscle in his body to contract. Chance knew that if Saras sent him home now, he'd never be permitted to return, he'd be disgraced, shunned, possibly worse.

Valu, Ulric and Kitty stood in the kitchen while Saras sat at the table. When Chance entered, Saras greeted him, coolly. "*Please*, do take a seat, Anathon."

Chance was about to sit down when Valu slapped his face so hard with the back of his hand it caused him to stumble.

"She is of the highest Sindria!" Valu spat with the same distaste as Saras.

The room went silent, all eyes burned into Chance, who now leant, with clenched fists, on the table in front of Saras. He lowered his stare to hide his anger, but rage surged through his veins and he charged at Valu, pinning him up against a wall. "Saras is a Lord of the Court, YOU are not!"

Valu tried to remove Chance's grip, but it was too tight and his face started to turn blue.

Saras stared at his down at his fingertips, seemingly bored. "Your work is done here, Valu. Remove your hold, Anathon."

Chance glared into Valu's eyes, a silent warning, as he

applied even more pressure. Valu's eyes widened and were about to roll when Saras spoke again. "Release your hold… Now!"

Chance begrudgingly released him. Valu choked and after getting his breath back, stepped up to Chance, eyes ablaze. Both stood ready.

"Are you losing control, Anathon? Perhaps I should send you home, immediately."

The words hit him harder than the slap in the face. "Bea needs protection." His eyes never once left Valu.

"Hmm, and who, I wonder, will protect her from you?" Saras's eyes became pondering slits.

"I…" Chance tightened his lips, stopping a rash answer, now very aware, he had to choose his words more carefully.

Saras tilted his head, waiting for him to continue.

Chance broke his stare from Valu, lowering his brow. "I love her." He'd never felt so exposed, weak, but hoped that the truth would somehow convince Saras to let him stay.

"Insolence! You're not only a Heaven Stone, but a member of the Royal Guard at Court. How dare you presume that declaring your love will gain you grace or the freedom to win Alithia's heart?"

"I speak of Bea's heart, not Alithia's," Chance calmly corrected.

Saras banged his fist on the table, making Kitty jump. "You are vexing me. Hold your tongue. She *is* Alithia."

"Her name is Bethany." He dared to correct once more.

Saras casually got up from the chair and strolled over to Chance. His eyes appeared to regard him as a minuscule insect that his hand was about to crush. "You forget your place too often, *Anathon*, an unbecoming habit of yours…It is time that you returned home. Valu."

Chance held up the palm of his hand, on guard in front of Valu, as he addressed Saras. "No, please, not yet…*not yet*…I made a promise."

"Really?" Saras looked intrigued. "And what would that be? You appear to have broken many oaths of late, would one more really make a difference?"

Chance didn't want to plead, but what choice did he have? The words felt difficult to release from his lips. "Please, My Lord. I need to stay."

Saras waved Valu away. "There may be a way of avoiding placing shame on your family and The Order, enabling you to stay in this realm. Though, this generous offer will only be given once, do you understand? "

Chance nodded.

"Very well. You will speak three words to Alithia, thus ending this charade. I will say to Bethany that I have a message to give you." He smirked. "From someone back home."

Chance's senses tingled at the words not said. "Three words from whom?"

Saras shook his head and smiled. "That is not how my leniency works. Do you agree to these terms? If not, you can leave with Valu this very moment, before she awakes. The choice is yours."

Every fibre of Chance's being warned him to be cautious. He looked over at Valu, and for a spilt second, he wondered if he was capable of taking them both on in a fight. He sighed, pushing the insane thought from his mind. What was he thinking? In truth, he had no choice but to agree, and everyone in the room knew it. "I can stay in this realm, if I agree?"

"Correct." Saras replied.

Chance's eyes briefly met with Kitty's, she looked away. "Then, I give my word."

Saras smiled. "Good…The words that you will say to Bethany are, I…am…married."

Chance looked confused.

"Oh, of course, the term is unfamiliar to you. Let me enlighten you. It is a name for a special pact that humans make to their loved ones. A life oath to one another. Am I correct?" He glanced over at Kitty, who nodded. "You will speak the words with conviction, in front of me. Understood?" It was obvious that he revelled in the power over a subordinate.

Chance's whole body filled with agonising pain. The thought of telling Bea that he swore an oath with another female, for life, made him feel sick. "Ask something else of me…*anything*."

"You have swor-" Saras paused, listening. "Ah, she stirs. Do I need to remind you of the punishment if you do not abide by your oath?"

Chance shook his head and closed his eyes. "She'll despise me." His voice faded out.

"*Yes*, but at least you *will* get to stay in this realm, as promised. You need to be aware that the bonded human couple are known as husband and wife. Much like our oaths of Agnaya and Aniya, though not as elaborate."

Chance glared at Saras, aware that his eyes were filling with hate. The Agnaya and Aniya ceremonies were a declaration of bonding for life. He knew exactly what the words meant.

"What are we going to do about Karian?"

"Do not concern yourself with *Karian.* He is my problem alone. His father and I have-" He glanced towards the kitchen door. "She is up...Kitty, beverage please?" He waved his hand in her direction. Kitty scowled at Saras with the same contempt as Chance, who desperately struggled to control the insatiable hatred building up inside of him for the lie Saras was forcing him to make. He also felt anger at himself for breaking the boundary, but most of all, anger for being so stupid and not telling Eliseis, his Queen, Alithia's mother, of his love. He could've tried to appeal to her kind nature, but the real reason he'd remained quiet was through fear of her reacting the same way as Saras.

"Valu, Ulric, disappear," Saras ordered. Within seconds, they were gone.

Saras's voice brought Chance back from his thoughts. "You have been married for seven years, an easy number to remember, wouldn't you agree?"

"Who am I to say is my wife?" Chance bitterly asked.

A smile crept on Saras's lips. "Perhaps, *Parian*...Yes, she suits you well. And Anathon..."

Chance stared into his scheming eyes with a reserved stubbornness.

"...Be convincing."

The smell of the percolated coffee filled the room, and, Chance knew, Bea would be expecting to see him happily preparing breakfast. So, when she strolled into the kitchen with a beaming smile that quickly disappeared, he lowered his head – hiding.

"Bethany, so delightful to meet you again. I do apologise for turning up unannounced, but I had to deliver a message of utmost importance for Chance." He gestured to the third and last seat around the table, and Bea sat down, remaining quiet. "Kitty, would you be so kind?" Saras handed her his cup.

Kitty took his cup and asked Bea if she wanted a drink.

"Please," she replied.

An awkward silence followed, and Chance forced himself to look up. "Did you sleep well?" he tried desperately to hide the mix of dread and anger from his eyes, but wondered if she heard the strain in his voice.

"Yes…You got up early," she replied.

"Saras arrived early." He hoped that she would gather by the tone, the visit wasn't welcome.

Saras interrupted. "Yes, I was extremely lucky that Chance was awake. Normally, I would *never* be so bold."

Bea acknowledged with a slight nod of her head. She was obviously getting used to Sidhe customs. Kitty handed out the coffees and then retreated to a corner of the kitchen, just behind Bea.

"I hear that you are not so fond of Sidhe mead, Bethany?" Saras calmly sipped his coffee.

Her eyes widened.

"We are *all* friends here." He smiled her way.

Chance stared down at the table, but could feel her eyes burning into him.

"He is a little sad to be leaving, I think," said Saras.

"Leaving?" She turned to Chance. "What's he talking about?" She didn't see Saras scowl at Chance, but Kitty did.

Chance looked directly at him. "You've delivered your message, is there anything more?" Bea placed her hand on his under the table, away from prying eyes. The supportive gesture would make it more difficult for him to say the three words. Chance sensed every emotion in the room, Saras's demand of total submission, Bea's confusion, Kitty's withdrawal, and of course, his own despair. He couldn't look at Bea as he spoke. "I have to return home."

She squeezed his hand. "Why?"

"I...I am married." Those three small words condemned him. They spoke the most ultimate of all betrayals – adultery.

Bea's mouth dropped open, and he immediately felt loss as she removed her hand. "What did you say?" Her eyes searched for validation.

"My wife needs me home." The sentence burned in his throat.

Shock filled her face, and she sat speechless.

Chance lifted his eyes to meet hers, and saw a reflection of his own pain.

"Your wife!" She stared at him with disbelief. The astonishment in her voice was heard by all, but Saras still didn't appear satisfied. "I am to meet with Parian, Chance's wife, on leaving." He then directed his words to Chance. "No doubt you will be delayed in accompanying her. Do you have any words for me to say in your stead?"

Chance cringed at what Saras was suggesting. *Did he really need to hear a declaration out loud, of love, for Parian, his supposed wife?* His gut twisted violently into knots. He couldn't speak, how could he hurt Bea more?

"Oh, how forgetful of me." Saras reached into his pocket

and placed a ring, made from blue crystal, in front of Chance. "Parian said it is safe to wear now that you are returning home."

Chance's hands curled into fists under the table, fighting the urge to force the ring down Saras's manipulating, lying throat. He had obviously come prepared, knowing exactly what he was doing. A well-planned trap, and this was a warning that he had to say the other three words, not 'I am married', but the words that he didn't even permit himself to say directly to the human he loved. These words were to be the final breath, slaying their love.

"Tell her-" Chance broke off, fighting back tears of distaste, sickening deceit, building up in his eyes. His stare at Saras, he wanted him to see the agonising pain behind his eyes, and know it would be remembered. "Tell Parian that... I love her."

Saras seemed positively delighted at the deliverance. "The true words of any marriage, and sadly, I must now take my leave. Thank you, Bethany, for such wonderful hospitality."

She dismissed him, eyes smouldering. Chance knew it was the silence before the storm.

"Kitty, thank you for the coffee. Chance, would you kindly see me out?"

Chance dared to glance at Bea, but she turned away, eyes like cold stone. He was wary of walking with Saras. What if he changed his mind now that he had done everything he asked...that would be punishment indeed.

Once downstairs, Saras began to speak more freely. "Try harder to be convincing. I shall say no more."

Chance gave a slight nod, it was enough, and Saras joined

Valu and Ulric, who were waiting outside. Chance slammed the door and rested his head upon its frame. *What have I done?*

Upstairs Kitty remained silent as tears tippled down Bea's cheeks, still sat frozen. "Did you know?" Her voice was croaky. "Tell me it's not true."

"I -" Kitty broke off as Chance entered the kitchen. His eyes met hers, and she quickly excused herself from the room.

Bea grabbed the ring from the table and stared straight at him. "Is this *really* yours?

His eyes lowered as thoughts of telling her the truth and the different outcomes raced over in his mind.

"Tell me it's a lie, that Saras has some hold over you... Anything, but not that you...not that it's true...Tell me."

His eyes pleaded for her not to ask.

"IS IT TRUE?" she yelled.

He had to convince her of the lie so that he could stay. Every part of him ached knowing that this would be the point of no return. He forced himself to resign and slowly held out his hand to accept the ring. He struggled to keep his hand steady, hoping that she wouldn't see past the façade. Bea's mouth flew open, aghast, and her hand grasped her chest, as if trying to save the heart from breaking its way out to the surface. Her eyes welled as she gulped, slowly nodding. "Here. You can fucking have it!" She threw the ring at him with such force that it rebounded off his chest onto the wooden floor. The tinny sound continued as she yelled. "Why? I thought that you were *real*, that what we had was real?" She struggled to speak between sobs that came through with every word.

Chance placed the palms of his hands over his eyes, his

face twisted with pain. He wanted to tell her his love was real. That it was the most real thing he'd ever felt, but instead he remained quiet, trying to stamp out his instinctive need to grab her and confess everything.

"*You* used me." She condemned him with one look.

He shook his head. "No." He went to reach out, but she slapped his hand away.

"Don't touch me."

With her refusal, the tears he'd tried to hold back started to escape. "I never wanted to hurt you."

"Then, why did you?" Her voice was a strangled cry.

The accusation hurt more than his own words of betrayal. "Bea, *please.*"

"If Saras hadn't have said anything, how long were you going to keep lying to me?"

His eyes silently pleaded with her to forgive the lie as he sank deeper into the grave Saras had created.

Bea marched over to him, staring him full in the face. "I loved you." She took a deep breath, but the tears still became a sob. "I gave you *my soul.*"

The statement crushed him and he recoiled.

She turned her back on him, leaning against the worktop, staring out of the kitchen window. "Just go."

Chance's hands began to tremble, wanting to smash down the unseen wall that she had started building. He briefly closed his eyes, and then dared himself to take one last look at the destruction that three simple, but devastating, words had caused. He made a mistake in agreeing to Saras's demand, but it was too late, the damage was done. She would not look at him, or allow him anywhere near her. He blinked to stop more tears, too late, he could taste the salt on his lips. "*My soul* is still yours."

She spun around, her eyes bitter winds, blasting their way through every layer of his skin. "I DON'T WANT IT!" she yelled. "GET OUT! Return to your wife." She turned away, and her voice became an audible whimper. "It wasn't a piece of heaven that you showed me…but hell."

He staggered, backed out of the kitchen, into the hall, destroyed by her words. His palms rested on the doorframe, and he pressed his forehead hard against them. Hoping that if he tried hard enough, he could push the words from his mind? They'd sunk far deeper than that. Her chill enter the places in his heart that he never knew existed. He thought his heart impenetrable to loss, but he was wrong.

Kitty heard the ominous silence from downstairs, and decided to go up and investigate. She saw Chance's dampened face staring towards the kitchen door. Her feet refused to carry her any further and she stood like a statue on the landing, wondering what to do. The atmosphere weighed down on her, like a ton of lead, pressing down, squeezing every inch of air from her lungs. She glanced towards the kitchen, then back at Chance, feeling torn by the emotional parting of the two people she'd grown close to.

"I'll put my trust in you with one request." Chance's croaky voice echoed in the silence, and made Kitty quiver. He looked lost and empty as his eyes met hers. "Protect her."

Kitty gulped at seeing his distress, nodded, and placed her hand on his arm, but he turned and walked down the stairs. She wanted to say something, but fell back against the wall.

Taking a deep breath, she entered the kitchen. Bea looked

a mess, her eyes ready to burst.

"Has he gone?" she asked, in a withered murmur.

Kitty nodded.

Bea broke down, slowly sliding down the cupboard onto the floor. She drew her knees up against her chest, and Kitty heard the sobs of heartbreak spilling out into the stillness of the room. With every excruciating sound that escaped her friend, Kitty's helplessness intensified. She'd never seen two people so distressed over matters of the heart, and stood staring at the disintegration before her eyes. After a few minutes, she plucked up the courage to kneel down next to Bea. "I'm so sorry." Without warning, Bea was in her arms, a sobbing, quivering mess. Kitty tried not to gasp aloud, and hesitantly, placed her arms around Bea. She knew there was nothing that she could do but let her cry, and Kitty wept too.

After the fit of crying, Bea sat on the floor leaning against the cupboard, staring out into nothingness. "I can't believe it's true." She wiped her face dry with the back of her hand.

Kitty lowered her eyes. "I honestly didn't know any of this, until today." It was a half-truth.

"We...I felt so-" Bea sighed, wrapping her arms around her legs, which were still curled up in front of her. "I really believed that he loved me."

Kitty bit her lip for fear for exposing the truth.

"I should've known better. He never once told me that he loved me, and the crazy thing is, I didn't mind...I thought that..." She laughed hollowly. "What does it matter now?"

Kitty tried to gulp, but her mouth felt dry, in desperate need of a drink, preferably mead.

"You know, last night, I asked him if he'd ever loved someone." The welling in her eyes returned, and Kitty could see she was fighting them falling. "He said that his heart was already taken...I thought stupidly, by me." Bea suddenly got up from the kitchen floor and strolled off to the living room. Kitty followed in silence, watching on, as Bea's hands searched the sofa, finding an iPod under the cushions. She put on the earphones, pressed play, and curled up with a cushion on the sofa, closing her eyes.

The only thing comparable to this type of grief is death, thought Kitty, staring at the fragile human bundle, but then realised, it was a death...dying love.

CHAPTER 17

Every Unknown is a Beginning

The following days were hard for Bea to cope with, but the nights, were impossible. She wondered whether a secret remedy for a broken heart existed in another place and time. It was difficult to come to terms with the fact that Chance was married. Was she such a bad judge of character? Was something in her lacking? *How do you stop loving someone that you should hate?* At least with Brandon she'd seen the inevitable coming, but this, this was just too much. Bea's head ached permanently from the pressure of over-thinking, but the hardest part was pretending to the world that everything was okay. Not everyone was easily fooled, Liza knew something was wrong. Bea had tried so hard to hide any hurt in her voice over the phone. Maybe it was the way she answered, or avoided certain questions that gave her away, she wasn't sure, but when Liza threatened to break her visit to Scotland to come and visit, Bea came clean. Well, partly. She admitted that her and Chance had spilt up, but she couldn't find the words to say why, without breaking down, so she said that the spilt was over him being too needy. Bea almost managed to laugh at the lie; it couldn't have been further from the truth. Even though Liza was like a sister, Bea didn't want to re-live the embarrassment of admitting that she fell for another liar and cheat. The wound was still too fresh. Every day she forced herself out of bed. It was tough, but she still managed to run the shop, functioning enough to keep the pennies coming in. Jenny must've noticed that she needed some space, for she never once asked any awkward questions, always keeping conversations to a minimum. Bea was grateful for her discretion. Music had become her only solace, and the solitary act of escape, through lyrics, became her form of trying to heal. Trying to understand the purpose of love in her crazy life. *Why do the people I love always leave?* No matter how many times she reminded herself that it was their choice, deep down, she couldn't help but wonder if it was her fault. *Too naïve? Too trusting? Too wanting?* But she didn't want to change, to become someone else, someone stone cold to love, but how else could she protect herself? Surely, it must be easier to turn the heart off to any feeling? But how? And more importantly, would she be able to turn it back on again?

Bea sat half-dressed on her unmade bed. "I can't do this," she mumbled into the void, gazing out of the window as the ache from the starvation of him continued. The mood in the flat had changed from one of lightness to dull stagnancy, as she still felt Chance's presence everywhere she turned, even in the shop – their meeting. *When Brandon left, it never felt like this,* she remembered feeling relief, but here, alone without Chance, an inner, silent emptiness filled her. It was similar to how she felt after her mother had left the bookshop, never to return. The only difference this time was that she had the opportunity to hear goodbye. Her mind drifted to the previous day's conversation. Kitty had suggested going away for a while, and after some thought, Bea agreed, until Kitty added. "I would prefer not to drive, and I thought that we could accept an offer of a lift…in a luxurious Space Cruiser."

Bea asked who would be giving them a lift in the car, and she explained, in a roundabout way, that it would be Saras and couple of his men.

Bea shut her up with a firm – No. She was fuming, Kitty wasn't exactly the most empathetic Sidhe, not that she knew many, but the tears had barely dried on her cheeks when she'd asked. For the rest of that day, Bea had found it hard to function and Jenny, being observant, offered to take care of shop.

That same night she couldn't sleep as various scenarios played over and over in her mind. She felt bitter, hurt, but still very much in love. *He's married. He deceived me,* she reminded herself slumping her head back down on the pillow, but it was no use, she still couldn't sleep. More and more questions ran through in her mind – *was I too angry, or confused, to get any real answers as to why he lied to me, pretending to love me? Did he ever have feelings for me? Why do I still care?* she groaned. It was time to make some changes, and staying in the shop, stuck in a rut, wasn't going to help her change anything. She needed to clear her head, get a fresh perspective. She was tired of feeling that situations were beyond her control, and after much deliberation, decided for the first time to be brave enough to face the world head on.

It was the break of daylight, when she texted Kitty and committed herself to the trip, but no lifts. Kitty whinged about public transport, stating that she'd prefer the long drive in her own car. Arrangements were made to travel the next day. When Bea informed Jenny of the holiday, she wouldn't hear of the shop closing, and offered to run things. It was an enormous relief and Bea accepted her kind offer, at least she wouldn't have to starve when she returned home.

Bea had her suitcase packed, which rested against the bed. *Stay strong, you need this*, she assured herself, sliding from the bed in the attempt to raise some enthusiasm.

Kitty met her at the top of the stairs. "Ready?"

Bea nodded. "Just us, right?"

"Of course. Here, let me help you." Kitty grabbed the holdall and took off down the stairs.

Bea lifted her case and exhaled, aware that the façade could crumble at any time.

Once they hit the motorway, with London far behind them, Bea unwound the window. The rush of wind on her face felt as if it was washing away all the dust of the past few days, she had made the right choice.

Kitty turned up the music and started singing, breaking Bea from her thoughts. Her voice sounded amazing. "I didn't know that you could sing."

"You never asked."

Bea laughed. "No, I guess I didn't. It's better than my screeching."

"Now that sounds like a dare to me."

"Oh no."

"Double dare." Kitty turned up the music.

Bea shook her head. The vibration of the base pumped

through her chest, as Kitty continued coaxing. "Come on, I'll sing along with you." She suddenly burst into full swing.

Bea burst out laughing and couldn't help but join in.

Kitty pulled a face. "Yeah, I see what you mean."

They'd been on the motorway for around five hours and Bea remained hypnotised by the blurred green fields rushing past her window. Her heavy eyelids fighting to stay open, but in the rhythmic motion, she nodded off.

Bea stirred, lifting her head from its resting place, on the window. She slowly moved side to side, flexing her shoulders in an attempt to ease the stiffness in her neck. How long had she been asleep? "We've stopped."

Kitty nodded, as her lips formed a crooked pout.

Bea sat up, rubbing her eyes. "Is something wrong?"

Kitty threw her hands in the air. "We've broken down. I should've hired a car."

"What?" Bea looked out of the window. It was starting to get dark. "Where are we?"

"I'm not exactly sure. I took a short cut off the motorway. Then, the car started to make this awful noise, and now I haven't got a clue where we are. I'm surprised you didn't wake up with all the racket."

"Have you called the services?"

Kitty threw her a look.

Bea nodded. "Of course you have. What did they say?"

"They asked the same thing as you, where am I...Don't ask." Her hand wafted through the air.

Typical, thought Bea, *as if anything in my life was simple.*

An hour passed, which felt like an eternity. Everything had turned pitch black. "Ring them again, Kitty."

"My phone's dead."

Bea dug around in her bag. "Here, use mine."

Kitty didn't take it. "All the details are in my phone."

"You're kidding?" Bea's heart sank and she slumped back in the seat. *Why don't I own a newer phone, one that could go on the net?* She stared blankly out the window, *Oh yes, I can't afford it.*

Another car's lights flashed behind them and Bea's mood lifted a little. "Oh, thank god." She turned to get a better look out of the back window. "Hold on…That's-" She glared at Kitty.

"What?"

Bea shook her head. "It's Saras." She replied, through gritted teeth.

"Saras?" Kitty climbed out of the car, but leant back through the window. "I'll be right back."

Bea sat tapping her foot, still shaking her head. *I've been set up, this isn't a coincidence.*

When Kitty returned to the car, Bea refused to look at her.

"Bea?" Kitty leant back through the window. "You okay?"

"I'm far from okay, and you know why."

Kitty gulped. "I did tell you that they were going away, too…Remember?"

"Do you take me for a fool, Kitty?"

"We have a lif-"

"You go." Bea snapped, turning away before she said something more offensive.

"We can't stay here all night. Saras says the farmhouse isn't far, he knows the way. They'll take us there."

"Why did you do this? Why lie?"

Kitty lowered her guilty eyes. "Saras is my boss. He asked me to...he wants to keep an eye on you."

"Does he now?" Bea went to get out of the car but Kitty leant through the window and grabbed her arm. "No, please ...don't, for my sake. It's one night that's all. He-" She lowered her voice. "There's been talk of Unseelie troubles, he didn't want you anywhere near it. Honestly, it was only going to be me and you, well until all of this Unseelie talk."

Bea rubbed her temple. "Is Chance in the car?"

"Yes."

She hated that her stomach fluttered at hearing the confirmation. "Why is he not with his wife?"

Kitty shook her head. "I'm not sure. Saras probably asked him to stay a while longer. Just in case of any trouble, I think he's going home tomorrow."

Bea remained silent.

"*Please* Bea, one night, for me?" Kitty begged.

What choice did she have? Did she really want to spend a night in the car in the middle of nowhere with no kettle or a bed? It'd already been a very long day.

She glared at Kitty and snapped. "One night! You should've been honest with me and, just for the record, friends don't do this to each other."

Bea jumped out the car and marched to the back of it. She refused to look in the direction of the car while taking her case out of the boot. She needed this precious little time, to brace herself. *Am I strong enough to confront him? To go through with this?* She turned and froze. Her otherworldly nemesis stood a few feet away, directly in front of her. She reminded herself to breathe before bravely meeting the silent confrontation, willing her feet to move. It felt like dragging lead weights, getting heavier with each step. Only days ago she would have been running into his arms and now, he felt like an enemy. *How can I still love the enemy?* Her heart soared in prominent thuds, becoming as weighty as her feet. He stood quite still as she approached. Bea heard her name spoken aloud, the sound pierced her heart like a blasting gun, on target, but the rhythm of the war drum within kept her feet walking without any form of acknowledgement. *I did it,* she silently applauded herself.

Kitty was already waiting by the large space cruiser. "Well done," she said, in a low voice.

Brief introductions were made. Bea observed they had the same features she'd come to expect from a Seelie. Long, fine, blond hair, the bluest of eyes, and lithe build. Saras greeted Bea in his usual polite, superior tone. She dismissed the welcome, detesting him, but reminded herself that he had actually revealed Chance's deceit.

The two Seelie and Chance sat in the three seats in the middle of the car. Bea made her way to the back. Kitty was about to climb into the seat next to her, but Bea give off such a vibe that she retraced her steps, and sat in the front with Saras. *Punishment,* thought Bea.

The engine revved and the car started to move. Bea couldn't help but occasionally glance through the gap between the seats to get a look at Chance. His head low, as usual, eyes hidden. *Can he feel me?* she wondered, but he appeared oblivious to her presence. A sudden rush of anger flowed through her, and she turned away, focusing on anything but him.

An uncomfortable silence filled the space inside the car. It felt as if everyone avoided talking, while she sat brewing. Chance wouldn't look her way, nor did one word pass his lips...silence. She had to learn to endure the coldness, which always followed the dimmed ray of hope, the realisation that there would be no reconciliation. Those three words had changed their relationship forever. *I have to let him go*, she reminded herself, aware that bitterness would soon engulf her. She fiddled about with her iPod and hit the play button, closing her eyes, allowing the music to carry her away.

Kitty pulled the headphones from Bea's ear, making her jump. "We're here."

Bea just glared at her.

"You coming?" Kitty weakly smiled her way.

Bea huffed, but followed her out. The car's headlights lit up a cobbled pathway, which led to a huge farmhouse. "Beautiful," she muttered. *Secluded, lonely,* she also thought. Kitty, Ulric and Aulis started making their way towards the house and Chance briskly marched past her, his arms laden with luggage. Again, no words, not even a quick glance in her direction.

"May I?" Saras gestured towards her suitcase.

Bea snubbed him, and made her way to the path. She'd no desire to remain in his company, even for the few minutes it took to get to the door.

Once inside, she asked Kitty where her room was, and was gingerly led the way.

Chance stood in the hall. His eyes finally met hers, but this time, it was her turn to look away as she brushed past him up the stairs.

"I have sharp eyes, Anathon. Tread *very* carefully," Saras warned.

"I've followed your orders precisely."

"Yes…thus far. Now we have arrived, don't disappoint me."

Kitty guided Bea to the second landing, to a small wooden door. "I thought you'd like this room. It's out of the way from any…distractions."

"From Chance, you mean?" Bea rolled her eyes, before bending down slightly to enter. The door creaked a little from being pushed wide open. "Straight out of a storybook. That bed looks as old as the house." Bea tested it's stability by throwing her case onto the mattress.

"I'm told it's quite comfortable," replied Kitty.

"By whom?" Kitty's face said it all.

She winced. "He thought-"

"I don't want to know." Bea cut her short, shaking her head, *the usual lack of Sidhe empathy*.

"I'm sorry, I…I didn't think. Look, the window has these sweet, lace curtains." She waved the cloth around.

"Lace curtains don't interest me, Kitty."

"*Please*, don't be angry. Let's just get this night over with and everything can be normal again as we planned. What do you say?"

Bea knew things wouldn't be normal again, all she wanted was to go home, but that wasn't going to happen either. She was still angry, but repented, and joined Kitty by the window. Although it was dark, she could vaguely make out some trees, scattered to the right of one of the fields. "What's that?" she asked, pointing to a rundown building opposite.

"Oh, the outhouse. It's in a terrible state apparently. I've never been in there."

"Oh. Who owns this house?"

"We do." Kitty proudly smiled. "It's one of our safe houses."

"To hide from the Unseelie?"

"*Yes*. Come, let me show you around."

Having toured the house, with many winding stairs and low ceilings, they came to the kitchen. A large room with an old-looking green stove and a white Butler sink. The cupboards were in relatively good condition, made from solid wood, though what kind she wasn't sure, possibly oak. Bea sat down on one of the carved chairs by the extra-large rectangular table, while Kitty pottered about preparing tea. The house had all the charm of a country cottage, but much bigger. Most of the rough-textured walls were painted cream but were peeling in large sections. Somehow, it added to a shabby-chic charm, which Bea loved. It dawned on her that she'd only been aware of their presence; no-one else was around.

Kitty handed her tea.

"Where is everyone?" Bea asked.

"They went to get some food, bet you're hungry?"

Bea dismissed the question. "What, all of them?"

Kitty shrugged then laughed. "Sidhe men and their stomachs, they're not that different to human men."

"The male species are a race unto their own," Bea mumbled, staring into the mug of tea. "I feel numb."

"It'll get better." She was about to say something else until they heard the car pull up.

"They're here, minus one." Kitty announced, peering out of the window.

"Who's missing?" Bea felt her stomach flip.

Kitty looked around at her and smiled. "Aulis."

She sighed with relief, though knew the feeling went against her stronger voice of letting go.

The back door swung open and Ulric entered first, carrying, almost effortlessly, several large bags of shopping in one hand. Bea's eyes widened at the sight. Saras followed, but his hands were empty. *Why does that not surprise me?*

Kitty got excited while putting away the food and kept showing Bea various treats, but she found it difficult to show any form of enthusiasm. Her eyes searched for Chance, but Saras smiled her way and shut the door. She instantly cut her eye his way.

"Where's Anathon?" Kitty asked.

Bea knew it was for her sake.

"Attending to some business." He looked over at Bea. "He shall return presently."

Bea gave him another dirty look, not caring if she offended. Something niggled her about him, she just wasn't sure what.

A slight smirk of amusement appeared on Saras's face.

Kitty continued to put the shopping away.

Bea got up from her chair. "I'm going to run a bath, then I'm off to bed, night Kitty." She couldn't remain in Saras's smug presence any longer.

Kitty bid her goodnight, as did Saras and Ulric.

Bea gathered some things from her room and made her way to the bathroom. On turning the bath taps, the pipes gargled and spat out cloudy water, but after a time, ran clear. The water gave an indication that the farmhouse had not been used in quite some time. She sat on the edge of the bath, waiting for it to fill, and tried to picture how it would've looked in its heyday.

Three knocks rapped on the door. Bea cautiously opened it and peeped out, finding Kitty with a supersized grin on her face. "I bear gifts." She placed various items in Bea's arms, bubble bath, shampoo and her favourite soap – Pears.

"How did you-"

Kitty winked and trotted off.

Bea quickly realised Chance had chosen her *gifts* while shopping. Part of her didn't want to use them. Another part of her remembered him in the bath, laughing when he had used too much shampoo, soapsuds everywhere. She threw the gifts into the sink and locked the door, forcing the memory away. Before climbing in the bath, she poured in the bubble bath.

As Bea laid back in the water, tears became lost in the delicate, forgiving bubbles. She'd told Kitty that she felt numb, but it couldn't be further from the truth. Any crazy hope of some kind of resolution in relation to their ending was nothing but a childish dream. Bea laid back further, permitting the water to completely cover her face, hoping it would remove every trace of her tears. She resigned herself to the fact that Chance had no intention of ever talking to her again. Wearily, she climbed from the bath and wrapped herself up in a towel. She unlocked and opened the door, ready to leave, but the door opposite also opened. Bea stopped in her tracks as Chance stood in the doorway across from her. The heavy thudding of her heart returned as his eyes met hers. She yearned for him, even after the devastating confession, and, ridiculously, the knowledge that she couldn't have him, made her want him even more. He started to cross the short distance to the bathroom, and as he got closer, Bea slowly moved aside to allow him through. She wanted to step further away, but her feet refused to move. They both paused when their bodies lightly brushed against each other, and now, within close proximity, their eyes refused to leave one another. Bea's breathing deepened as his lips instinctively reached out to touch hers, but in the last second of promise, he pulled away. Her pride, her heart, absolutely all of the feelings that she had for him, became more of a jumbled mess. She edged away from the door into the hall, too scared to look down at the floor for fear of seeing pieces of her scattered there. She closed her eyes, as her stomach turned at hearing the sound of the bathroom lock click. She then ran as fast as she could, back to her room. In her haste to escape, she didn't see Saras lurking at the other end of the hall.

The sound of a cockerel abruptly greeted the dawn, and Bea covered her head with her pillow, but it didn't drown out the screeching sound. She climbed out of bed and opened the window. The air was fresh, soothing on her skin. She had not seen the cockerel on their arrival and wondered why. *Maybe he was hiding in the outhouse?* The smell of the country and the memories it brought would usually give her a feeling of peace and calm, but once she caught sight of the car, she remembered Kitty words, that today *he* would be leaving. She hoped that by watching the annoying cockerel strut around, the despair that she felt of Chance's absence would disappear. Her distraction was short-lived, seeing him place luggage into the boot. Her heart sank to a new depth, she knew that he didn't love her, but she didn't know how to stop it hurting. She walked away from the window but rushed back, hearing a frantic beeping of a horn. Bea peered out, there were some figures in the car, but she couldn't tell if Chance was one of them. Tears formed in her eyes. *Have I missed him? Let me just see him, please... just once.* Her breathing momentarily stopped as she heard footsteps entering the room, which seemed to pause at her recognition, as did the fluttering of her heart. Then, the voice that she dreaded, yet longed to hear, spoke. "Bea." His weak call echoed in the tiny room, reminding her to breathe. She wanted to turn around, look at the face she had begged the void only moments ago to meet. The pain of his betrayal and recent dismissal, hurt. *Stay strong,* she mentally repeated over and over. She continued to gaze out of the window to the green fields. His footsteps got closer, finally stopping when they reached their destination, directly behind her. He felt so close, she swore she could feel his warm breath on her skin. *Please god, give me strength,* she silently begged.

The constant noise of the car's horn became almost non-existent when Chance placed his hand on hers, up against the frame of the window. *Noooo!* she screamed, *please, please, don't do this.*

"*I love you,*" he whispered, as his hand pressed a little harder against hers at the declaration.

Bea closed her eyes. "Are you married?" She kept her voice calm and hoped that he wouldn't see past the façade. She had to hear the words once more from his lips, a final confirmation.

After a brief silence, he replied, "Yes." His voice sounded full of pain, but unknown to Bea, it was the pain of the lie. She immediately untwined his fingers that had found their way around hers. She heard the gasp of anguish at her withdraw. *Could he feel hers too?*

His footsteps slowly retreated, but then paused. "I will always love you, Bea." Her stomach turned over at his words. The footsteps resumed their retreat, eventually fading away. Bea supported her trembling body by leaning against the window, desperately trying to muster all the strength she had to stop from calling out, and stop him from leaving. If he'd persisted and held her in his arms, refusing to let go, would she still have remained strong?

She bravely lifted her eyes and saw Chance got into the car. For a spilt second, her mouth opened to cry his name, until he stepped back, turned and looked up at her. She backed away from the window, and on hearing the car pull away, permitted her controlled façade to crumble.

CHAPTER 18

The Silence before the Storm

*B*ea's mind still refused her the sanity of sleep. Two weeks had passed, which felt like an eternity in the small world that she now found herself in. Kitty had found her sobbing on the floor by the window, and after that, Bea kept herself tucked away in her room. She felt awful for leaving Kitty to her own devices, but couldn't will the strange emptiness from her heart. She hated Chance for telling her that he loved her at a time when it really didn't matter. *An unnecessary cruelty.*

Kitty had given Bea a journal. "Just scribble down anything, it doesn't have to make sense. Just let it all out. It helps me when I need to let go." She was right. It'd helped, although it didn't detract from the fact that she still loved him. It was meant to be a form of moving on, but the only thing that moved was Bea's pen as it scrawled across the page.

The cockerel had gone at least. Apparently, it'd escaped from a nearby farm. That was the first time she had laughed since Chance left. How strange it sounded when surrounded by her sadness, but it felt good, and she decided that it was time to leave the past behind.

Bea mumbled as the mirror reflected one truth too many. She slapped on some foundation and some blusher, and felt a bit better. If only she could manage a quick make-over inside too. She dusted off the fallen make-up particles from her clothes, and went downstairs.

Kitty was in the kitchen, on the phone. She placed her hand over the mouthpiece. "I'm not encouraging you or anything, but I thought you might need one." She pointed to the pack of ten cigarettes on the table. "Better to be safe than sorry, the shop is miles away." She returned to her call.

Bea sparked up, and the first drag made her feel light-headed. Tea and cigarettes were a strange, homely type of comfort, a habit she had developed during school, not by peer pressure, but through curiosity. Curiosity was another habit she'd tried to kick, without success. She looked down at the cigarette. Wasn't it just another bad habit that she needed to kick? She stubbed it out, a metaphor of Chance, and threw the packet in the bin.

Kitty ended her call and looked down at the packet in the bin, but didn't comment.

"Jenny said Liza rung several times, checking you're okay," she said.

"That's good to hear. How's Jen coping?"

"She's enjoying every minute. *However*, she told me that she's encountered a certain couple."

"Mr. and Mrs. Brough." The thought of them immediately brought a smile to her face.

"Yes, she said they come in every day asking if there's been any luck with a certain book."

"The Andrew Lang series."

"So, Miss Wolstenholme, I thought that now you have left the crooked little room, that we could go on a little adventure…What do you think?"

"An adventure with a Sidhe? Sounds ominous."

"Ominous? Not at all. A little stroll, get some fresh air."

Kitty leant closer. "I found out some interesting folklore from the farmer and thought we could investigate."

"It sounds crazy, but I have no idea of *where* we actually are."

Kitty seemed to find that fact highly amusing. "We are in the Trossachs."

"Trossachs?"

"Scotland."

"I know where the Trossachs are, Kitty, and before any adventures…I need more tea."

Bea met Kitty outside. A car was on the drive.

"When did we get a car?" Bea asked.

"I asked a friend and *tada*…magically delivered. Never mind the particulars, jump in."

"I thought we were going for a stroll?"

"Once we're at our destination we will be. Are you aware that Sir Walter Scott's poem, The Lady of the Lake, was inspired by the Trossachs? Well, Loch Katrine."

"Yes. Have you heard of an English writer by the name of H.V. Morton?"

"No," Kitty replied, starting up the car.

"He wrote about the lake, too."

"*Really*, do you remember what he wrote?"

"Only a line or two."

"Do tell."

"He mentions the lake having a greyness that rose and fell in queer shadows." Bea tried to make her voice sound harrowing and Kitty laughed. "You might want to practice being scary. Is that all you remember?"

"Yep, my mind doesn't retain information too well, but that part stuck in my head." Her heart made room to pine a little for Liza. If she was still working up here, they could've visited. She felt a little too late for everything these days. Kitty must've noticed the slight change in Bea's demeanour and chatted more about the Trossachs history.

"So where are we heading?"

"I would really like you to see Loch Innis Mo Cholmaig, The Lake of Menteith," Kitty replied.

"Oh, I remember reading something about it being the only lake in Scotland."

"Yes, well, you're right. It's the only major body of water *referred* to as a lake in Scotland, but there are others, though lesser known. A mistake by a Dutch cartographer."

Bea looked impressed and Kitty preened.

"Well, we certainly won't need a tour guide."

"We Sidhe tend to know our history."

"Your history?"

"Yes, we've been here an awfully long time."

The drive wasn't long, and the conversation, added to idyllic scenery, lifted Bea's mood. They turned into a long road, and parked up in the Port of Menteith.

"Here we are. You're going to love it. Now, let's go and catch a ferry." Kitty led the way through a large cabin. Once they reached the jetty, Bea closed her eyes and savoured the beauty.

"Exhilarating, isn't it?"

"Yes, yes it is." There was something about the place that soothed, too. The lake was varying tones of blue, depending on where the light hit the water, and for a spilt second she felt a slight pang in her heart, remembering Chance's eyes. She blotted the vision from her mind and stepped into the small boat, where a young couple snuggled up. Bea turned away. "Is that where we're going?" She asked, pointing to an island.

"Yes. We're lucky, normally there're more people. We're on our way to the very heart of the Trossachs, Inchmahome Priory, built in the thirteenth century, mostly a ruin now, but it still has quite a presence."

"I didn't think the Sidhe had any interest in religious areas."

"Shhh," hushed Kitty.

Bea thought it odd that Kitty checked to see if any of the other people were listening. "It's a different story here. No matter our differences, the mythologies of a place are to be respected, even if the men of cloth do have a connection to it. There's over seven hundred years of recorded history here, but certain tales were not written down, but nonetheless, some stories are never forgotten." There was a bitterness in Kitty's tone she'd never heard before.

"What stories?" asked Bea.

"Look, the bell tower." Kitty pointed to the island. "We're almost there."

It had only taken around ten minutes for them to reach the Island, but before getting off the ferry, Kitty advised her not to mention the word Sidhe, explaining that the men of cloth and locals had long memories. Although puzzled, Bea agreed.

After visiting the shop, their tour started with the Priory ruins. Bea admired the beautiful archways on their way to the cloister, the heart of the priory. Next was the

Chapter house, where there lay a double effigy, which Kitty informed her were of Sir Walter Stewart and his countess Mary. A stone knight lay beside them. "Who's the effigy of the knight?" asked Bea. "And what are those slabs on the wall?"

"No one knows who the Stewart Knight is. That's Sir John Drummond's slab and the other, again, no one knows." Kitty shrugged.

"No one knows? Don't they have records?"

"Exactly." Kitty raised her brow.

Bea frowned and bent down to read the information given on plaques.

Kitty leant over her shoulder. "Not many are aware that there was a church here before the priory, called Insula Macholem. It's mentioned in the earlier histories, but not many talk of it. Rumour has it that Walter Comyn, the Earl of Menteith, found something of importance. He was the priory's patron in the thirteenth century. The Comyn family were one of the most powerful in Scotland at that time. The men of cloth prayed for the soul of the Earl and his family, even when the Earldom passed over to the Stewart family. They were obviously ensuring the salvation of his soul."

"Why?"

"That's the pivotal question isn't it? Why indeed? What did the Earl find that caused so much concern for his soul? Rumours have it that he found an ancient purple book buried under ruins of one of these islands, and that it contained secrets of other worlds. Food for thought." Kitty winked. "Would you mind if I disappeared for a while? Not for long, I promise."

"Of course not." Bea watched Kitty skip from the Chapel. Some of her comments seemed out of character, odd, probably due to being cooped up in the farmhouse too long.

Bea ran her hands over the Stewart knight's hand, his hilt was intact, but the rest of sword now gone. She wondered if the effigies had been moved from elsewhere on the island. Something felt out of place. She took one last look before exploring the grounds.

As she took a casual stroll, the one thing that hit her was the seclusion of the island. *If there was ever a place that had a Sidhe attachment, this would certainly be it,* she thought. She found herself on a well-trodden path. The guide called it Nun's Walk. A stone wall was covered by moss and lichen over the grey blocks. Kitty was right, there were secrets here, untold. Bea found herself passing ancient trees amongst carpets of Harebells, and then found a gnarled tree to rest under. She couldn't help but run her hands along its old bark. "You've seen a lot of things, haven't you?" Her eyes drifted out onto the lake. On seeing land opposite, she pictured Chance on the other side, in search of her. Strange she didn't feel sad. She shook her head, a silly daydream, but still, it made her eyes well. Even in the imagery, she was unable to reach him. It somehow felt like goodbye. Bea bent down, picked a Harebell, and gently placed it between the pages of the pamphlet guide. Odd, that in all the time here, she hadn't felt the starvation of Chance, until now. She was grateful when Kitty found her.

"A beautiful spot you've found here. Right by Nun's Hill. I've always had a soft spot for this part of the island." Kitty stood next to her. "And what a lovely sweet chestnut tree."

Bea glanced up, taking another look at its branches and

leaves. "Did you find anything interesting on your travels?" she asked, in the hope that her mind would become distracted once more.

"Nothing of significance. What about you?" Kitty stared out towards the lake.

"A little peace."

"Well, let me know when you're ready to leave that newly-found peace. No hurry, but I have more adventures planned."

"I'm ready."

Once they returned to the jetty, Bea took once last glance back at the Island. "Kitty look." She pointed out to the lake, where a swan swam close to where they stood.

"Thank you." Kitty spoke in a faint voice.

Bea thought that she saw Kitty's eyes glisten, and realised the gratitude was not for her.

"I need to show you something," blurted Kitty.

"What?"

"A deviation." Kitty pulled her, excitedly.

Bea was led to the southern shore of the lake. "Quite a trek," she gasped.

"Nearly there. It's a bit overgrown, more than I remember." She smiled at Bea. "But it's worth it, you'll see."

They continued to walk through trees and bramble, until they came to the edge of the shore.

"I was...we were standing right opposite. Look, the tree."

"Very observant, I'm impressed."

Bea didn't mention that the spot where they now stood was exactly where she imagined Chance standing. It disturbed her a little.

"Legend states that faeries built this piece of land called Arnmach. The hill over there is known as Bogle Knowe, a fairy abode. Folklore says it's where the fourth Earl of Menteith, Walter Comyn, read a book belonging to the fae, and in doing so released them into this world. Trust a human to take the credit," Kitty scoffed.

"The purple book? Hold on, are you trying to tell me that you're all *faeries*?" Bea found it hard to keep a straight face.

Kitty's eyes narrowed. "No, but humans like to label, so we became a twisted version of the truth. Oh, and let's not forget Shakespeare who made everything worse by delivering us as small, diminutive beings with wings – really insulting actually."

She looked directly into Kitty's eyes. "Okay, let me get this straight. Faeries are really Sidhe?"

Kitty cringed. "We hate that word. Well, our origins can be found in faery stories, but the really ancient myths, even older than the one I just told you, explain us more accurately." She checked to make sure no-one else was around. "Certain people here wouldn't want that remembered…I wanted to show you some of the places where our stories have been forgotten."

Bea giggled, grabbing Kitty's arm. "Your secrets are safe with me…*fairy*."

"Not funny, Bea, really."

When they got back to the car, Bea wanted to question Kitty about the swan, about the ancient tales of Menteith, but her instincts warned her to let it be. "So where are we off to now?"

"To explore Doon Hill and the Old Kirk in Aberfoyle.

The Reverend, Robert Kirk wrote a book called the Secret Commonwealth, back in the seventeen hundreds. The book is an essay of certain supernatural beings... *faeries*." She rolled her eyes.

"A reverend? The mind boggles. Wouldn't that be considered heresy?" Bea asked.

"Not really, this reverend documented faery folklore from traditional tales in the Scottish Highlands to promote Christianity. It's a biblical account of *non-human* spirits. He was also the first man who translated the Bible into Gaelic, but more interesting is that the Reverend was a seventh son, and because of that, supposedly, gifted with second sight. Legend states that he did not die, but instead entered into another realm via a faery hill. Others say his spirit is imprisoned in a pine on Doon hill. Humans can never stick to one story... No offence, adds to the intrigue I suppose."

"None taken."

As Kitty drove, she continued to recite some of the folklore. "Sir Walter Scott first published Kirk's work on fairies more than a century after his death. Andrew Lang later gave it the title, The Secret Commonwealth of Elves, Fauns and Fairies."

"I wasn't aware of that. I'll have to tell Mary."

It didn't take long for them to arrive at Aberfoyle car park.

"In a while, you'll see a sign for the Faery Trail. I must admit, when I first saw it I giggled."

"Why?" asked Bea.

"It has a toadstool painted on the sign, typical stereotyping." Kitty yawned.

The sun clouded over and Bea slipped her jacket on. "The weather here consists of several seasons in one day."

Kitty laughed. "Good Scottish weather."

Their first stop was at Aberfoyle churchyard, containing a church ruin. It was here that Bea saw the memorial of the late Reverend Kirk. A crook and dagger were etched on his tombstone that faced Doon Hill. Bea's eyes widened. "Are you serious? I thought it'd be a small mound."

"We're going to meet the Chaplain to the Fairy Queen." She giggled, and continued to lead the way from the church to the fabled hill.

"They say Rev Kirk walked this way every day. Doon Hill is also known as Faery Knowe, or Dun Sithea." Kitty continued her storytelling.

Bea felt uncomfortable, though wasn't sure why. The hill had a strange atmosphere. "It doesn't feel natural."

"It was an iron age fort."

Bea nodded, saving her breath for the climb up which became steeper. Twisted trees surrounded them on either side. Eventually, after a two short breaks, they entered a small clearing where a hand-made wooden sign greeted them by the foot of a tree. 'Look after our forest. Please stick to the path, more than just faeries live here.' Bea shrugged it off, but still felt uneasy.

They strolled into the centre of the hill where Kitty placed her hands on a large tree bearing dark green foliage. "This beauty is known as the Minister's Pine."

Bea felt apprehensive about approaching.

"It's alright. No spirit of the Reverend resides in this tree."

Bea still preferred to walk around the surrounding trees,

most festooned with small pieces of brightly coloured fabric, ornaments and floral gifts, though many had become faded by weathering. On closer inspection she noticed that the strips of fabric tied to the branches had messages written on them. "What are these?" Bea brushed her hand through them.

"Oh, it's an ancient custom. The rags are tied and left on the tree in the hope of a cure, a prayer of sorts, offerings to the local *supernatural* beings. They're known as Cloutie trees."

"What a lovely idea." Bea's fingers continued to play among the ribbons until Kitty pulled out a white rag and marker pen from her pocket. She handed them to Bea. "I knew you'd like it, so, I came prepared."

"What shall I write?"

Kitty shrugged. "Words of the heart the wind can carry." She smiled and left Bea to write her message. Bea sat down on the grass, and placed the pen to the rag, but found words difficult to find. She stared out into green and the tree on the island came to mind, bringing with it, the image of Chance standing by the lake. She remembered reading somewhere, 'never regret something that once made you smile.' Instantly, the memory of them both dancing in her flat all those months ago, filled her heart with a temporary joy that too quickly faded. Without thinking, her hand started to write.

It's been a while, but my heart still feels the same...yet I know, it's best to let you go.

The words were her own version of the song that they danced to, and in her mind, confirmed that their love was over before they had time to begin. *Why hadn't I seen clearer then?* She couldn't help but wonder if he chose the song as an early goodbye, knowing it wouldn't last. Another thought that hurt.

She turned the rag over and continued to write:

Keep your light bright, Anathon. Maybe, our souls will meet again. Goodbye x

The last word was the most difficult to write and she fought back the tears of closure. Bea kissed the rag, and then tied it to a branch with the many others, watching it blowing in the gentle wind. "Goodbye," she whispered, turning away.

Kitty asked if she was ready to return to the farmhouse.

She nodded. "Thanks for all this. You're quite a clever Seelie."

Kitty placed her arm around her. "You're welcome. Come, let's go get some tea."

"Or perhaps some mead?"

A big grin spread across Kitty's face.

CHAPTER 19

The Outhouse Encounter

$\mathcal{B}$ack at the farmhouse, Kitty poured them a drink. "Do you want to go home yet?"

"Not yet." Bea slumped back in a chair.

"No problem, Jenny, it seems, is quite happy filling in...I really enjoyed today. Possibly, we can fit more adventures in?"

"I'd like that. When did you tell Jen we'd be back?"

"I didn't. She was in her element, but I know that she'd love to tell you all about the Brough visits."

They both laughed.

Kitty went to pour more mead into their glasses.

"No more for me. I'm going up."

"Really?" Kitty pouted.

"I'm shattered." She gave her a re-assuring smile. "Thanks again...Night."

"Night, Bea."

It was the first time she felt Kitty had become a friend, not just an acquaintance. Her starvation of Chance was still present, but she'd overcome the major obstacle, mentally letting him go. Sitting under the tree not being able to reach him, the tying of the rags, were all symbolic and helped with her healing. Kitty wasn't so hare-brained after all.

Lying in her bed, she proceeded to jot down the day's

events. Her eyes became heavy, and she started to drift into sleep, until she heard shouting. She lifted her head slightly, eyes half-open, listening out, but heard nothing. She pumped up her pillow and got comfortable again, but as soon as she closed her eyes, she heard the arguing, again. Bea jumped from the bed and looked out of the window. Light filtered out from the outhouse door, and her mouth gaped open as two blond men, she assumed Seelie Sidhe, took turns in slapping a dark-haired man. Bea rushed down the stairs, and out the front door. She instantly recognised the two blond-haired men, Aulis and Ulric. "What are you doing?" she yelled.

The Sidhe heads turned, but dismissed her. The victim of their taunts began to edge his way towards her. His frame was broader than most of the other Sidhe she'd encountered. His hair long and dark, but it wasn't until she saw his eyes that she felt scared. They were full of rage, glinting her way, and she automatically stepped back from the fearsome glare.

Aulis stood in front of the man. "And where do you presume to go?"

"Human bitch. You have destroyed him!"

Aulis punched the man in the stomach. "Watch your tongue."

"Wh...Where's Kitty?" Bea asked, looking back towards the house. Suddenly, an excruciating pain travelled violently across her cheek, knocking her to the ground. She tried to see who had hit her, but everything blurred. The blond Sidhe were dragging something to the car. She gasped; it was the man with dark hair. She heard a familiar voice cry out her name, but before she could reply...her eyes closed.

Bea woke to find Kitty beside her on the sofa, pressing a cloth to her face. It stung and she winced. She tried to get up, but a tremendous pain shot through her face.

"Stay there… let me finish cleansing. Here, drink this." Kitty handed her a small glass containing a dark blue liquid, with what appeared to be gold specks suspended in its gooey thickness. Bea wanted to ask what it was, but knew it would hurt to talk. She took a sip of the otherworldly substance. It tasted vile, and she handed it back to Kitty.

"No, drink it all, the pain will go," she insisted.

Bea took the glass and quickly gulped the rest down. She wanted to heave, but couldn't, it would've hurt too much. She sat back and started to feel a strong tingling sensation travelling around her throat. It reminded her of pins and needles. The strange prickling then spread to every part of her face. She didn't like the feeling and started to rub her skin, avoiding the areas of her face that hurt. The tingling moved again, concentrating on where the pain was at its greatest. Within a few seconds, she felt the sensation completely stop, and she slowly opened her mouth, there was no pain.

"I had to place some of those sticky strips on the wound, but the wound will heal fast. You won't feel a thing." Kitty smiled, taking the empty glass and placing it on the table.

Bea's eyes followed her hand, where an assortment of pots, phials and crystals were strewn over the table. "What are those? And this?" She leant over and picked up a small, black velvet bag. Crystals were neatly woven into the fine fringes.

"Medicine." Kitty gently removed it from Bea's hand, placing it back upon the table.

Bea stared at her. "What's going on? Who hit me?"

Kitty poured some mead. "An Unseelie struck you, by the name of Delbaeth. Aulis and Ulric have taken him to the rings."

"Rings?"

"Portal. They're sending him back home," Kitty replied.

"Why did he hit me?"

"There's a war between the Seelie and Unseelie, you are human, but your soul is Alithia's, *Seelie*."

"He hates me because my soul is Seelie?" Bea couldn't believe what she was hearing.

"We have to be careful now." Kitty drowned the sentence in a glass of mead.

"Careful of what?"

Kitty kept her face in the glass. "They know who you are."

"The Unseelie?"

Kitty nodded.

"This war has nothing to do with me," Bea protested.

"It has *everything* to do with you."

"I'm not Alithia!" Bea snapped.

"You don't understand." Kitty softened her tone.

"Then, *please*, by all means, Kitty, enlighten me."

A stranger walked in the room. "I will explain, if I may?" The female was tall, gangly, and extremely pale. She stood at the other side of the coffee table, pouring herself a drink. Bea turned to Kitty as the Seelie placed her hand out to greet her.

"It's alright," assured Kitty, gesturing for her to reciprocate.

"I am Annalen, but please, call me Anna." Her gentle countenance eased Bea's apprehension and she loosely shook her hand. "I'm sorry that Delbaeth struck you, that should not have happened. He escaped from the vehicle on my arrival."

"Who, exactly are you?" Bea asked.

"I am a wanderer of worlds, like Kitty. It seems that you have caused quite a stir with my kind. It must all be rather overwhelming for you." Anna waved her hand and the chair from across the room placed itself in front of the coffee table. She sat down. "We really shouldn't use our powers here, but I think we are past that now. Wouldn't you agree?"

Bea looked at Kitty, wondering if she was also capable of such talents.

Kitty made a slight movement of her hand and the medicines on the table returned to the velvet bag.

Bea's eyes widened. "You hid this from me?"

"We are not permitted to use our powers here. It's not that Kitty wished to keep the truth from you." Anna said.

"I didn't see you outside, Anna." Bea remarked.

"Sadly, we were inside when the dreadful incident happened. We thought that you were sleeping."

"I was, until I heard shouting. Why were Aulis and Ulric taunting Delbaeth?"

"They were wrong in doing so, there's no excuse. All of this has obviously had an impact on the Sidhe psyche. The Sidhe experience heightened emotions in confrontational situations. Please allow me to apologise on their behalf." Anna smiled. "Your soul being connected to Alithia has inadvertently involved you. As you are aware, Alithia was brutally murdered, and with the essence of her soul finally returning, has caused old resentments to resurface. The Sidhe are on edge, and act in ways that are not usual for our kind.

Again, I apologise for the violent display and discomfort that you have suffered."

Kitty poured more mead, offering some to Bea, who declined.

Bea felt her eyes getting heavy; it'd been a long twenty-four hours.

"Will you be staying with us long, Anna?" asked Kitty.

"Only for as long as I am needed."

"Needed? *Why* are you here?" Bea was too tired to worry about appearing rude.

"I came to see Kitty before leaving this realm. This farmhouse is quite close to where the portals of our worlds meet. Most of the other rings are permanently sealed."

Bea distrusted the new arrival, but she was sure Kitty would be glad of the company. Anna would be a more suitable companion than herself tonight. She excused herself.

Bea stopped off at the bathroom to freshen up and examine her wound in the mirror, it had almost healed.

"Bea." A voice spoke behind her.

Bea jumped in the air. "God, my heart. What are you doing to me?"

"I can assure you *he* had nothing to do with it." Her shoulders shook as she giggled. "You're so funny. Did you know that your legs make bizarre movements when you jump?"

Bea frowned and waited for Kitty to finish her fit of giggles. "How has my face healed so quickly?"

Kitty grinned, her eyebrows bounced up and down. "Sidhe magic."

Bea rolled her eyes. "What's got into you?"

Kitty opened her hand, and Bea bent down, prodding the three, tiny, glistening purple mushrooms with her finger.

Kitty pulled her hand away. "Don't play with them."

Bea stared at her. "What are you doing with those?"

Kitty responded with another grin. "Try one."

"Oh, my god, they're a drug, aren't they?" Bea stood back shocked.

"No, no…A medicine." A cheeky grin followed.

"Sidhe!" Bea shook her head and barged past Kitty, out of the bathroom.

"I'll take that as a no…Don't say I didn't offer… Goodnight."

Bea changed into her nightclothes, sat on the bed, reached for her journal and started scribbling away. Her eyes still felt heavy, but she managed to fight the sleep off, until all the information of the last hours was written down. She placed the journal in the dresser and noticed the light still shining from the outhouse. She had forgotten about it during all the commotion. Anna had said they were inside, but Bea hadn't seen them downstairs before running outside. She decided to investigate and slowly crept downstairs, peeping into the living room as she tip-toed past. Kitty and Anna were both asleep, *too much medicine.* She shook her head and continued her journey outside.

The cold, early-morning breeze made her shiver, and she pulled her dressing gown closer to her body as she approached the outhouse door. Cautiously, she turned the handle. The door creaked as it opened, and she froze for a moment, wondering if anyone heard. She couldn't help but giggle at herself for being such a child, and dismissed her caution.

She entered a small hall. Kitty was right, the building was in a terrible state, plaster was missing from most of the walls, exposing the stonework, and some of the ceiling had fallen to the ground. The source of the light was coming from around the corner, beyond the end of the tiny hall. The light did not flicker, it was continuous, *electric*. The thought comforted her as she continued to investigate. She turned the corner and gasped, placing a trembling hand over her mouth to stop a scream. She stood terrified at the image in front of her. A figure lay slumped amongst the rubble, beaten and bloody on the ground. Her eyes followed the outline of the figure. The bundle was a man, and his blood stained clothes turned her stomach. She leant in further and saw shackles attached to his wrists. The chains that bound him were secured to the opposite wall, held fast by two heavy locks. Her eyes searched the room before attempting to move closer. Her whole body trembled with each step. The sound of her feet crunching on the rubble caused her to pause, nervously, several times. Eventually, she plucked up the courage to kneel down next to the battered body.

Now that she was closer, she could see his dark hair, matted with blood and dirt. She gulped, trying not to come into contact with any of the blood on the floor, while gently turning the body over. The heavy figure rolled and flopped over. Bea staggered back, tears of shock and horror formed in her eyes. *It can't be!* She glanced towards the small hall, checking no-one was there, before scrambling closer. She lifted his head and placed it gently upon her lap.

"Kari. Wake up, Kari." There was no response. She started to tremble more fiercely, at the realisation of the true purpose of the Seelie visit that night became clear.

Tears fell from her eyes as she looked down at his face. He was a mess, and what scared her most was that Kitty must've known. Her mind raced, *what can I do?*

She heard the door creak and gently returned Karian's head to the ground. Slowly, she got up from her knees, but paused as the debris of the outhouse cracked under the weight of someone else's feet. Bea's breathing deepened and as she turned to face the intruder, her fear turned to anger. "What have you done?" she shouted, storming over to Anna. "You people are sick!"

Anna's eyes glanced over at Karian. "I -."

"Don't bother. I don't want to hear any excuses. You apologised for the Seelie's behaviour, did you actually mean for this?" She gestured over to Karian's body.

That now familiar creak announced another arrival. Kitty turned the corner and her eyes lowered as they met with Bea's.

"I hope you're disgusted with yourselves?" Bea spat, pushing past them both.

"Where are you going?" Kitty cried, running after her.

Back at the house, Bea ran around gathering up bowls and cloths. She glanced over at Kitty hovering by the table. "The medicine, where is it?"

Kitty remained quiet.

"Where is it?" Bea demanded, eyes ablaze.

Kitty gave her the bag. "You'll need my help."

Bea looked over at the kettle. "You can bring that."

Anna was still standing in the same position when they re-entered the outhouse.

Bea walked over and dropped the things she'd gathered next to Karian. "Kitty, the water."

Kitty didn't move.

"Kitty, I need the water." Bea pressed, holding out her hand.

"She can't come any closer, Bea." Anna took the kettle from Kitty and held it out in front of her. "Neither can I."

"You refuse to help? *Even now?*" Bea couldn't believe what she was hearing. She got up and grabbed the kettle from Anna's hands.

"It is not that we do not wish to, we physically can't. It is the iron. The properties have been made with the skills of Seior by a Deisi of our world. The shackles are made of what human's refer to as cold iron," Anna explained.

Bea frowned looking at the iron then back at Kitty and Anna.

"Cold iron repels the Sidhe, we get ill from it. The medicine won't work while he is wearing the shackles." Kitty added.

"Where are the keys?"

Kitty glanced over at Anna. "I don't know."

"They left him here to die, didn't they?" The silence was confirmation enough. "*Why?*" Bea's voice became a whimper.

"We are at war," Anna reminded her.

"To hell with your war!" Bea shouted, starting to pace the room. "Right, I need to get him away from this iron...I need a hammer, a chisel, anything to get these damn things off. Or are they made of things that you cannot go near, too?"

"I'll go and look." Kitty left.

Bea ignored Anna and started to clean Karian's face. "Don't worry, I'll get them off."

When Kitty returned, she placed a toolbox on the floor. Bea opened it, tipping out the contents, grabbing a hammer and a chisel. She crouched down near the wall, which held the chains, and placed the chisel in one of the locks, bringing the hammer down onto the chisel as hard as she could, again and again. Bea yelled as she caught her thumb, causing her to drop the chisel. The sound echoed throughout the outhouse. "It's not working," she groaned, frustrated.

"Just hit it with the hammer. Forget the chisel. Hit it right in the centre, as hard as you can." suggested Kitty.

Bea stood over the lock, and took a deep breath before slamming it with as much force as she could muster. There was an enormous thud as the lock broke, parts of it scattered across the floor. She did the same to the other lock and unclipped the hasp. She felt ill as she removed the shackles from Karian's wrists, and retched. On his skin were severe burns; some had peeled away layers exposing weeping tissue, a reaction that must've been caused by the iron.

"Move the iron and we can help. We'll carry him into the house," Kitty said.

Bea threw the other shackle away from Karian's limp body, and pulled the chain into a heap on the far side wall. Kitty rushed to Karian's side, as did Anna.

"Can't you use that power you have to levitate him or something?" asked Bea.

Kitty shook her head. "It's the residue of the iron. I can taste it just touching him. We have to be quick. We'll weaken at the essence of it."

CHAPTER 20

A Different Perspective

A pungent smell filled the bedroom as Kitty mixed a number of ingredients from her bag. "Why did you not tell me?" Bea asked.

"You had too much to deal with already."

"*Really*... So what were you going to do? Just let him die?" She was still incredulous.

"It's not Kitty's fault, Bethany."

Bea glared at Anna. Kitty stopped mixing the concoction and faced Bea. "I don't approve of this either. Actually, I don't like a lot of things that have happened recently, but I have to follow orders."

"Orders? *Knowing* someone is confined in the outhouse, in iron chains, dying? Can you really justify that with the words, 'I was just following orders?'"

Kitty slammed the mixture down and stormed out of the room.

"We understand that you're upset. We were discussing Karian while you were upstairs last night," Anna explained.

"Before or after Kitty offered me the mushrooms? Guess you both needed some form of escapism, huh?"

"Bethany." Anna's voice was soft, submissive.

"Stop calling me that. Only certain people can call me by that name and *you're* not one of them."

"I apologise. Please, permit me to put the ointment on Karian."

Bea removed herself from the room, finding sanctuary out on the doorstep of kitchen. She was over the initial shock of seeing Karian at death's door, but her anger still brewed. She heard footsteps coming towards her.

"May I sit down?" Kitty asked, hovering beside her.

"Not too close." Bea hated being offish, but how else was she to handle their decision to allow him to die. She'd begun to look at her as a friend, someone that she could trust, but that'd changed now.

"I know you feel lowly of me, and I'm truly sorry for that…I want you to understand that the Sidhe have been at war for so long, that we've obviously lost something very important…You made me realise that tonight." She sat next to Bea, but left a gap between them.

"What have you lost?" Bea muttered.

"Our humanity."

She turned to Kitty. "You're not human. Maybe you're not meant to share our ethics of empathy."

"That's unkind, Bea."

"As unkind as allowing Kari to die?"

"We couldn't do anything, the iron. Okay, I admit, that's why I got off my head last night. I shut it out. Yes, it was wrong, and maybe I could've approached you."

"No doubt about it, you should have." Bea snapped, but felt guilty at doing so and sighed. "I *do* understand that wars change perceptions. It doesn't matter where we're from, war is ugly."

"I'm sorry that I didn't tell you. I honestly didn't know how."

"You start with the truth, the rest moves on from there." She was tired. Staying angry was draining what little resource of strength she had left.

"I want to help, Anna does too."

She looked at Kitty, her defences lowered. "Who did this to Kari?"

Kitty remained silent.

"Kitty?"

"Aulis and Ulric."

"So, who put the iron on him?" She knew the person had to be human, since Sidhe were repulsed by iron.

Kitty shook her head. "I don't know."

"The truth?"

"I honestly don't know."

Bea saw the sincerity in her eyes. "Delbaeth thought I knew what had happened to Kari, didn't he?"

"Not exactly." Kitty paused. "He blames you for Karian's capture, and resents the fact his *Lord* loves a Seelie."

"You mean Alithia. Why can't any Sidhe get that part?" Bea snapped.

"The Unseelie will not appreciate the return of Alithia's soul. They fear it will turn Karian away from the Court, he's to be their next king."

"So, all the Unseelie hate me... Great."

"Not all," Kitty mumbled.

"Comforting...Gimme a percentage?"

"Ninety-nine per cent not in favour."

"Just gets better."

"If Saras returns and sees that I have disobeyed his instructions, I won't see you again, and I want... need you to know… that you're the best human I've ever known." Kitty got up and walked back into the house.

Bea placed her head in her hands. She knew Kitty would be in danger, Anna too. They were putting themselves in that position for her and she found it hard to remain angry. "Truce it is," she mumbled into her hands.

They took it in shifts to tend Karian. The worst area was bedding, it reminded Bea of her uncle's passing and that scared her. Anna usually sorted that area, and Bea and Kitty were thankful.

Over the first few days, they saw no real improvement in Karian. It wasn't until six days later, he seemed to resume a normal Sidhe paleness, instead of black and blue. The majority of bruising was turning yellow, and the burns had scabbed over. Between them, they managed to bathe most of his body. His hair was the most difficult to get clean from embedded blood and dirt. Anna helped Bea for what seemed like hours. The majority of locks had to be gently soaked with a dampened sponge. Karian almost looked his old self.

Kitty took charge of the feeding. Luckily, she had an all-heal herb ground into powder that she mixed with a little honey and milk, which was syringed every few hours into his mouth. It wasn't much, but it provided him with all the nutriments he needed. Kitty also brought some clothes, now that she thought he was out of the critical stage. Bea was relieved once Kitty gave the all clear, and asked her when she thought he would come out of his comatose state.

"Depends on Karian."

From this point on, it was a waiting game. She knew Kitty

was worried about the possible return of the Seelie, although she never mentioned it. Anna seemed to handle the pressure more easily, and Bea made a conscious effort to get to know her better.

That evening they sat around the table to eat. Kitty retired early.

"What do you think Kari will say when he wakes up?" Bea asked Anna.

"He'll be disoriented. Confused, his head will need time to clear."

"Confused?"

"Two Seelie's and a human tending him. It will be interesting to see his reaction, to say the least."

"We'll need to get him out of here as soon as he's able to move."

"Yes," Anna agreed.

"Did they intend to come back for his body?"

"I don't know."

"They just left him here, not been in contact since?"

"Saras has been in contact with Kitty."

Bea was impressed with Anna's honesty. "Really? When?"

"Yesterday."

"Is he coming here?" She became anxious.

"No, no…He just wanted to know if Karian was dead."

Bea's eyes widened. "What did she say?" She started to feel guilty for being so harsh with them both.

"She told him that he hadn't moved. Obviously, we were unable to check, due to the iron. Kitty is quite protective of you. She didn't want you to worry."

"Why does Saras want him dead?"

"Old resentments."

"The war?"

"Partly… Karian has always been persistent and extremely bold, two things that Saras won't tolerate, especially in an Unseelie. But the main reason, he is the son of King Faryln."

"Why does he hate Farlyn so much?"

"After what happened with Alithia, he lost his way."

"Saras blames Farlyn and Karian for Alithia's death?" Bea knew neither had anything to do with her passing.

"Bea, the Seelie blames the Unseelie and vice versa. I can't see the cycle ending anytime soon. The main thing is to stop anyone from involving you in our politics."

"I won't get involved."

Anna gave her a gentle smile. "But you are."

"I know Alithia's soul is within me, or some essence of it, and I'm the present incarnation, but shouldn't my soul be referred to as mine not hers?"

"A good point, but it wasn't supposed to happen that way. It's complicated… I'm not educated in the higher teachings, but I'll try to explain it the best way I can." She pointed to Bea's hands. "Your fingerprint, it is unique to only you. Do you know why?"

Bea looked down at her hands. "No-one knows."

"Haven't you ever thought about it? Why each human's fingerprint is different?"

Bea shook her head and laughed. "No."

"It is very strange that so many important things are treated so nonchalantly in this realm. Yet, the material things, the unimportant things, are held in high regard… Those lines on your fingertips are your soul's imprint upon the body that it inhabits."

Bea frowned. "What are you saying?"

"The fingerprint represents *who* you really are. By the time of four months gestation, the human fetus has already established a connection with the soul, forming the fingerprint. This is the reason why no two humans have the same mark, even identical twins. The fingerprint, the soul's code, is recorded in the Akashic records, an otherworldly library, recording souls lives, deeds...Akashic in our tongue is Siarthia."

Bea looked down at her hands. "So, if I die in this form, and then get reincarnated, will my fingerprint be the same in the next form?"

"Yes. Well, it may alter slightly, as the records of your Vororbla, karma, are updated."

Something within her felt the truth in Anna's words. "The Akashic record is a library?"

"Yes... a non-physical library, containing the knowledge of a soul's life experience, over all time. It is the centre of a web that weaves all existence."

Bea sat in silence for a while. "Okay, that's kind of freaked me out."

"Why? Look around you. Nothing has changed."

Bea's eyes sheepishly scanned the scenery. "You're wrong, something has changed...I feel different."

"How?"

"More awake." Her eyes drifted to the stars.

"Is that a bad thing?"

Bea laughed. "Probably not."

"Well, then all is good."

"Anna? Do the Sidhe have fingerprints?"

"No."

"So, how does the soul know what Sidhe form to connect with?"

"I think that is something to talk about another day… It's gone twelve."

"I'm not sure I'll be able to sleep tonight."

"Everything is just as it was. You just have a better knowledge of how you came to be. Know that your choices are not mistakes, and take some comfort in that."

"Are you saying everything's predestined?"

"Not exactly, but again, a subject best saved for another day. I think we should both get some sleep, goodnight, Bea."

"Goodnight, Anna and thank you."

"You're welcome." Anna went inside.

She traced her fingertips with her thumb, and stared up at the stars. She felt a small sense of clarity amongst the turmoil of many questions racing through her mind that still required answers.

How old is my soul?

Do I even have a soul that is actually mine?

Is my soul more Alithia now, or has she changed to fit me?

CHAPTER 21

Time to Face the Past

Opening her eyes, Bea admired the faint pattern on the wall made by the sun's rays softly filtering through the lace curtains of the window. She felt good. The talk with Anna made her realise life was about having experiences, both happy and sad. It dawned on her, while scribbling the conversation down in her journal, that the soul enters a body to gain these experiences, to grow and develop, eventually evolving to some higher form, but why? That was as far as she had evaluated, but in some way it made her feel more alive. Maybe, in the profundity, she found a certain magic, a subtle allurement that stirred her senses.

"Bea?" Kitty poked her head around the door.

"Morning. What's up?"

"He's awake." She raised her brow. "Just thought I'd let you know."

"Oh…Thanks." The time had finally come for her to meet again with Karian, and she felt nervous. The last time she'd spoken with him, all those months ago, she was running away.

Bea slowly crept to the door across the hall, and quietly entered Karian's room. He was sitting up in bed, looking out towards the window, while Kitty was trying to convince him to eat something. Bea tried to make a silent exit, but Kitty got up and placed the bowl of porridge in Bea's hands. "He refuses to talk, eat or drink. Your turn, see you downstairs." She flew out the room so fast Bea didn't have time to object. She took a deep breath and made her way over to the chair by the side of the bed. "How are you feeling?"

Karian didn't reply, or even turn to look at her.

"Are you angry with me?" she asked.

Still, no reply.

Bea placed the bowl on the bedside table, and then spoke as softly as she could. "I know, this all must feel strange, but Kitty and Anna *really* do want to help. You're angry with me, and that's okay…We just want you to get better." She looked around the room, this was proving more difficult than she imagined. "Kari… that night of the play… I… I was scared and I didn't know what was happening to me. I'm so sorry for your loss of Alithia, but you need to get better, you're not safe here. *Please*, try to build your strength up, eat something."

He didn't respond.

She sighed. "I'll leave the bowl here, try and eat. I'll pop in again later." She got up and walked to the door, turning around before leaving. He remained in the same position, no expression.

Bea entered the kitchen. "He wouldn't eat or talk to me either. I think he's still angry with me."

"Angry with you?" puzzled Anna.

"Kitty never told you?"

Anna shook her head.

Bea glanced over at Kitty, quite impressed that her personal life hadn't been exposed in detail. "We met briefly in London and we…had a disagreement. It's the first time we've seen each other since." Bea thought it best kept simple.

"Oh." Anna replied.

"Time to indulge, I think." Kitty poured herself a glass of mead.

"How did you sleep last night, after our talk?" asked Anna.

"Very well. I felt quite refreshed when I woke up." She joined them at the table.

"So, what do we do with the Unseelie?" asked Kitty, already topping up her glass.

Anna and Bea looked at each other.

"I think we should just keep up the pleasantries, until he is ready to leave." replied Anna.

"Hopefully that won't be long," Kitty mumbled into her glass.

"Has Saras contacted you?" Bea asked, noticing that Kitty was applying her usual method of blotting things out using mead, and wondered what the drink problem was really hiding.

"As a matter of fact, he has. He will be gracing us with his presence at the weekend."

"So soon? We should tell Kari."

"Tell Karian." Kitty huffed. "It'll only encourage him to stay. The Sidhe love a touch of conflict. Do they not, Anna?"

"How many glasses have you had already, Kitty?" Bea examined the bottle.

"Not enough." Kitty took the bottle from Bea's hand.

Anna spoke, "I agree with Kitty. Karian would most likely prolong his stay if he knows Saras is due to return."

"So, what do we do?" *They had to get him out of the house, but how?* thought Bea.

"Keep him healthy and urge him to go as soon as possible. Kitty says he only needs his strength back, everything else is healed," Anna replied.

"It's the inside we should be concerned about," Kitty grumbled from her glass.

"Kitty, you are relieved of your duties today," Anna remarked, taking the bottle.

"Really? If I knew that, I would've drunk more days ago. I'm quite content to be removed from any responsibility of the Unseelie."

All through the day, Anna and Bea tried to communicate with Karian, but he would only close his eyes and block them out.

In the evening, Kitty was starting to get loud due to her excessive intake of mead, and Bea suggested that Anna stayed downstairs to keep an eye on her, while she attended Karian. Anna agreed.

Bea sat down on the chair next to Karian's bed, but did not speak. She hoped her silence would coax him into talking. After around ten minutes, it worked, and he opened his eyes. "Why are you still here?" His voice was gruff.

She was taken by surprise at hearing his voice, but didn't show it. "I could ask the same of you." She saw his lip twitch, *was he about to say something or was it a snarl?*

The room remained silent.

Karian turned over and laid his head on the pillow, facing the wall.

Bea rolled her eyes and made herself more comfortable in the chair.

After a while of sitting in silence, she was tempted to slip off her shoes and place her feet on the edge of the bed. *No. I will not give him the satisfaction of pushing them off.* Instead, she plumped up her cushion and curled up in the chair. It was uncomfortable at first, but she soon found herself drifting off to sleep in the monotony.

Entering a dream, she saw a vision of rolling hills, various shades of green. The leaves of surrounding trees danced as a warm breeze passed. She lay upon the grass, with her eyes closed, listening to the sound of nature. She heard footsteps and opened her eyes. The glare from the sun was bright, too bright, and she sheltered her face with her hand. She could feel someone very close. She sat up, and saw a faint outline of a face. It took a moment for her eyes to adjust from the sun, but once they did she saw *Karian.*

Bea suddenly woke from the dream, and became more unnerved seeing Karian staring back at her. The glint in his eyes gave her the impression that he seemed to be enjoying her discomfort. She distracted herself by straightening up the cushions. After regaining some composure, she turned around, and found him still staring at her. "Are you deliberately trying to make me feel uncomfortable?" she asked.

"Why would I do that?" he replied, laying his head flat against the pillow, now staring up at the ceiling.

"I don't know." Her eyes followed his. When she lowered them again, he'd returned his stare in her direction.

"Can't you sleep?" she snapped. Her frankness worked and he looked away.

Silence filled the room once more.

She closed her eyes. After a few minutes, she heard his voice.

"Am I that repulsive to you, *Bethany*?"

Karian speaking her full name strangely moved her. She opened her eyes and shook her head. "Repulsive, no." She saw his jaw tense, as if he wanted to say more but thought better of it. She got up from the chair, and hesitated before sitting on the edge of the bed. "I'm not Alithia. My choices have nothing to do with you. I'm human...I'm Bea." She gulped as his eyes briefly glared her way. "Thank you for explaining so eloquently."

"I don't understand why you're so angry with me?" she flapped.

Karian closed his eyes.

She was about to move from the bed when he grabbed her arm, but then quickly released his hold. Her skin felt tiny shivers linger where he'd touched. She sat back down confused by the sensation.

"I left everything to come here. To this wretched, dull realm. I even endeavoured to make it my home." His eyes looked into hers. "For you."

"For Alithia!" She got up and sat back in the chair.

"As you say, for Alithia." He bit his lower lip. "I can see it was all rather foolish of me."

After a few minutes of silence, she tried to break the ice. "I don't want to argue with you. We've *all* been hurt. It's just the way things are. The past should always stay in the past. Right now, all that matters is that you gather your strength and get out of here."

"Don't you feel anything for me?"

Bea's heart started racing, feeling the weight under the pressure of his words. "I don't know you."

He looked directly at her. "Forgive me, but you're mistaken. *You* know me very well."

Her stomach fluttered at his intensity. She cleared her throat. "Alithia knew you *well*. Not me."

"Why are you nervous?" His eyes seemed to take in her every physical response.

"I'm not nervous. I'm tired."

"That's not the reason." He leant his head to one side, as if trying to get a different perspective on her reaction.

"Really?" She looked away, her foot started tapping as her agitation grew.

"You know how close you are to finding what you seek, and it frightens you."

Her eyes flashed in his direction. "Don't presume to know me."

"I presume nothing," he grumbled. "But know that my heart has not known peace since I was last in your arms. At least I will not deny it." He turned his back to her, like a child, sulking.

Watching him, she realised she'd felt that way too, not so long ago. The ache of Chance slowly crept back. She wondered how Karian had managed to carry the burden of that pain for years, possibly lifetimes.

"I deny it because I'm not her...I'm sorry for your pain, but I can't help you." She couldn't sit in the room any longer. The conversation reminded her too much of the bitterness that love can bring, and she still felt fragile from her own estrangement.

Back in her room, she felt more at ease. She didn't realise how oppressive the atmosphere had been with Karian. She grabbed her journal, but placing the pen to paper, her mind went blank.

Just write what you feel, don't think... Kitty's words echoed through her mind. So, that's what she did...

It still hurts, and watching someone else deal with loss, brings my hurt back. I can't help Kari, and he can't help me. Where do I go from here?

She threw the pen onto the journal and sprawled over the bed, closing her eyes.

Bea woke up, half-asleep, shivering, pulling the quilt up more snuggly around her body. She remembered how warm she used to feel in Chance's arms and kept the picture of herself there. Feeling more relaxed, she nestled her head deeper into the pillow, and fell asleep. She dreamt of him lying next to her. His hand gently traced the outline of her face, then down her nose and over her mouth. Her lips parted as she felt the warmth of his naked body close to hers. His hand gently swept over her breasts, then down her side, and her body shivered in response to his touch. "Remember?" he whispered, before pressing his lips against hers, first soft, reserved, then more passionately.

"I remember," she whimpered. A wave of pleasure suddenly flowed through every inch of her body, as she felt *all* of him.

"Every part of me is yours. Remember?"

She groaned as his tongue gently caressed her.

"*Feel me.*"

Her mouth searched for his. "Where are you?"

"Here."

Bea suddenly woke, for the man making love to her in the dream was not Chance at all, but Karian. She pulled the quilt closer and looked around the room. It was dark, quiet, but she could sense someone in the room.

Slowly, Karian appeared from the shadows.

"Get out...and take your sick, Sidhe fantasy, with you."

"Bethany, I heard a noise from outside and I was concerned. I've only just walked in." he defended himself, stepping closer to the bed.

"*Really?* Well, now it's time to just walk straight back out again." She scrambled out of bed with the quilt wrapped tightly around her, and Karian retreated to the door.

"Good to see your health's so much better. Goodbye!" She slammed the door, just missing his face, and then pushed a chair in front of it.

Karian stood outside the room. "I haven't done anything wrong. You were obviously dreaming."

"You know exactly what I'm talking about, Karian. Goodnight!"

Karian gently placed his hand on the little wooden door. "You *will* remember me."

CHAPTER 22

Beyond Any Shade of Black

$\mathcal{I}$n the morning, Bea still seethed about Karian being in her room the previous night. "How dare he?" she muttered, while making her way downstairs. Her eyes narrowed as she passed his door. Lack of sleep was going to weigh heavily on her today.

Downstairs, she could hear laughter, mainly Karian's, and her blood started to boil. *Yes, laugh all you like Kari. You're going home today.*

Unknown to Bea, Karian had made an extra special effort to befriend his enemy, in light of them saving his life.

"Morning, Bea," beamed Anna.

"Morning, Anna." Bea deliberately barged past Karian. "Well, as you can see, Kari is feeling much better today. I guess he'll be saying his goodbyes. Hopefully, he's done so already."

Anna looked at Karian, who didn't appear fazed by Bea in the slightest.

"I'm sorry, would you like some tea, Anna?" asked Bea, about to cut her eyes at Karian, but a wave of hair slowly slid onto his face distracting her anger. Her fingers twitched at the thought of brushing it away, and she quickly turned, for fear of carrying out the act.

"No, thank you...Have you two already spoken this morning?" Anna asked, obviously confused by the hostility between them.

Karian enlightened her. "We had a little misunderstanding, Anna. I grew concerned when I heard a noise from Bea's room, so, I went to see if everything was alright. She had awoken from a dream and didn't appear to be happy about leaving it."

Bea paused from stirring her tea, he'd hit a nerve, but she was more angry with herself for having enjoyed his closeness in her dream. Her eyes dared to permit another glance in his direction. He was attractive, she admitted, and knew that the danger of the attraction lay mostly in his eyes. She reminded herself to stay well clear of them.

"A dream?" Anna asked.

Bea shook her head. "No. It started as a dream, and quickly changed into a nightmare. I think a better argument is required to excuse you from being in my room, don't you, Kari?"

Anna's attention moved back to Karian.

"As I explained." He ignored Bea. "A simple misunderstanding, Anna."

"Unbelievable." Bea grabbed her tea from the side, taking a sip.

"Please, feel free to explain the perversion that you accuse me of?"

She knew it was a dare. "Go home!" Bea snarled as she brushed past him. "This is a Seelie residence and *Unseelies*, are un-invited." While exiting the kitchen, she bumped into Kitty. "Sorry. God, I can't stand him, arrogant Sidhe." She continued her journey of escape up the stairs.

"Okay …what have I-" Kitty was shocked to see Karian standing in the kitchen. "You're up."

"Yes, and I want to thank you for showing me so much hospitality, considering I was a prisoner of your lord. I *promise* to return your kindness in any way I can, my Sidhe word." He slightly tilted his head in respect.

Kitty's eyes widened. "Wow. Great speech…Good morning to you too, Unseelie."

Bea tried to simmer down by writing in her journal, until there were three taps on her bedroom door, "Seelies only!" she shouted.

Karian poked his head around the door and grinned. "I'm extending a white flag and come in peace."

Bea huffed. "Please, just go away."

He ignored her, and walked straight in. "I didn't mean to intrude last night. If I knew how this was all going to be turned against me, I would've stayed in bed."

Bea sighed, not wanting to be harassed by his childish antics anymore. "Go away."

He continued to walk further into the room.

"Not another step!" she snapped, without looking up, continuing with her writing.

"I need you to know, I would never be so bold as to implant an image into your mind, especially while you sleep." His head tilted to one side, as if observing her more closely.

"Hmm, as I've said already… *leave.*" She was scribbling now rather than writing.

"You're being rather unfair," he protested.

She threw down her pen and stared straight at him. "What

do you want, exactly?" It was evident that he was trying to hide a smile, now that he had her full attention.

"For you to realise that I'm not some sort of otherworldly pervert. Once I realised what your dream was about, I turned to leave. Until, well, you saw me."

Bea held her tongue as he continued.

"I only came to see if everything was alright."

"You know, it's funny, because yesterday you were all woes and sorrow, yet, today, full of beans."

"Full of beans?"

"Happy, joyous." She was growing more frustrated at his presence.

He smirked.

"Go away." She was about to return to her journal, but he continued the annoying conversation. She huffed and looked up at him.

"Do you *really* want to know why I am so happy? Full of beans?" His eyes flickered.

"You get to go home today?" She gave him her most gracious smile.

"Oh, flippancy, I like that. No, that's not the reason." Karian edged his way towards the bed, "I realised that you were…"

"Yes?"

His face suddenly looked serious. "You said *my* name." His eyes fixed on hers.

"Yes, I said your name." She climbed off the bed and marched over to him. "Do you want to know why?"

"Yes." he replied, smug.

"It was a cry of disappointment. I wanted to see *his* face, not yours. So, don't get ahead of yourself." She marched towards the dresser to get some space between them.

"You think that's the reason, but it isn't," he coolly replied, turning in her direction.

"You're unbelievable. I remember my dream, I remember how I felt. I remember wanting someone else." Her heart was starting to race with fury at his intolerable arrogance.

"Then, why did you cry out my name, not his?"

"Disappointment, shock, horror, get it?"

"No. It's because you wanted, *needed* me."

"You're delusional." Her foot started tapping.

"What was happening in your dream, Bethany?" He started to walk towards her.

"None of your business."

"Was I touching you? Loving you?"

She gave a hollow laugh. "That's it, I'm bored. Time to go." She went to show him the door, but he moved closer, blocking her path. "You're fighting it." Karian's tall, lean figure was almost upon her.

"I'll show you a fight in a minute!" *What am I saying?*

"Alright you win, I'll go." Karian backed off a little, giving her some room. "But you need to start being honest with yourself, even if you need to hide that honesty from me."

"Is that right?" Her blood was boiling.

He began to advance more, until his mouth was inches from hers. "Yes."

"You're so-"

"Kiss me."

"What?"

"Kiss me."

"I'm not going to kiss you."

"What are you scared of?"

"I'm not playing this game, Kari, back off." She moved away.

But his feet kept edging forward, forcing Bea to step back further.

"Kiss me."

"I'm not going to kiss you. I don't even like you."

"One kiss." His blue eyes intensified beneath his chocolate locks.

She moved her head as his hand reached out to touch her face, and her legs hit the dresser, unable to back up any further.

"Did I touch you like this?" His slender hand gently traced the outline of her face.

She froze as his finger lightly ran down her nose, then slowly over her mouth. His touch was a replica of the dream, and all of her senses responded in ways her mind absolutely refused to act on.

"Kiss me." His sensual voice persisted.

Her heart pounded, her breathing deepened. Why she wasn't pushing him away? She had never kissed anyone that she didn't have feelings for, and she wasn't about to start now. "I don't love you." She managed to declare in a whisper.

"It doesn't matter." His mouth came closer to hers. "I want you, Bethany, *so* much." His searching eyes felt as if they were feeding her with his desires. "You deserve someone who is ready to love…who will give *now*…that person is me, not him…you do not have to wait for me."

She couldn't move, sensing within him anguish. She knew

that he was holding back, suddenly his jaw clenched, and he turned his face away.

She didn't understand. *What's he doing?* Her lips were his for the taking. She had become trapped in his web, but he didn't seize his prey, *why?* She remained still as Karian's arms remained either side of her on the wall. Suddenly, she felt a rush of anger, mixed with a taste of embarrassment and pushed past him. "Now that you've finished with your little game, be kind enough to leave." She stormed over to the door, holding it open.

"A game? Are you *still* not aware of the impact that your presence has on me? I have waited so long to be this close to you again. I can wait a little longer...until *you* admit that you want me, too."

"You'll have a long wait!" she snarled, folding her arms.

He hesitated in the doorway. "When I lost you...my world darkened beyond any known shade of black, and the only light that I have seen since...is you, and no matter the pain of hearing your rejection, I will continue to wait...for yours is the only light that I will ever see."

For a moment, it felt as if time had stopped, but on hearing his footsteps fading, the present finally caught up. *How could his words have penetrated her barrier? Why did she feel guilty for snapping at him?* She strolled over to the bed and flopped down, staring up at the ceiling trying to make sense of what had just happened. How strange she felt, the anger passed too quickly, and she began to question herself. *Did I want him to kiss me? Why didn't I move? I should've pushed him away sooner. What about Chance?*

There was a knock on her door and Bea sat up. "Who is it?"

"Me. Who else?" Kitty laughed on entering. "You look stressed. Guess that arrogant Unseelie really did piss you off?"

Bea was shocked. "You swore. I've never heard you swear before."

"I don't, as a rule. I'd rather not get into too many bad habits. Can you imagine using vulgarity in front of Saras? Living in this realm for so long, it's been a difficult rule to keep, I can tell you."

"What about you? You okay?"

"Well, having breakfast with the Unseelie King's son, a Sidhe that I presumed was my enemy...There's no denying it feels strange," Kitty shook her head. "I was wrong about Karian. I was ready to leave him to perish in the outhouse, and I want to thank you for making me realise that what I was doing was wrong. There's so much prejudice towards Karian back home. Most Seelies including myself, until now, believe he had something to do with Alithia's death. They think he murdered Alithia, and escaped punishment by running to this realm. Changing their opinion of him will be difficult. It would be so nice to have peace again, and to return home, but the animosity has been stewing for hundreds of years... What a mess."

"Would Saras listen to the truth?"

"His animosity runs the deepest. Saras and Farlyn have an even longer history. He would not aid any forgiveness of Karian. Saras will always hold the Unseelie accountable for the ills of our realm. I couldn't see that before."

"It's hard to believe such evolved people can suffer with the same problems as us."

"Wars?"

"Prejudice." Bea corrected. "How did they manage to capture Kari?"

"He was in the neighbourhood, so to speak."

"Near the farmhouse?"

"Yes. He deliberately got caught."

"What?"

"I want to be totally honest with you. I made the mistake of not being totally honest before, and I don't want to make the same mistake again."

"The Unseelie that hit me said it was my fault. He blamed me for Kari's capture, now I understand why."

"None of this is your fault. It was Karian's choice, not yours."

"What did he hope to achieve?"

Kitty looked surprised. "You...*his* Alithia."

Bea shook her head. "He has to move on."

"Karian is rash, single-minded. Apparently, takes after his father that way. Moving on is not an option for him."

Bea looked confused. "There is always choice."

"He grew up outside of the Seelie Court, without the proper spiritual training, it's normally given via the Court, through the Heaven Stone Order. Karian never received this guidance. His father broke off from the Seelie Court before he was born, and as far as I'm aware, there's been nothing to replace it. The training is no longer given to the Unseelie because of the war."

"You've spent most of your time here, how do you know so much?"

"It's my job." She shrugged. "I've been tracking Unseelies

for as long as I can remember. We gather every bit of information we can, and use it to capture them. I know more of Unseelie behaviour than that of my own Court. So, tell me, what happened with the arrogant Unseelie?"

"It was a misunderstanding, nothing important."

Kitty's eyes narrowed. "The truth?"

"Will you tell me why you've been drinking so much?"

"Another time maybe."

"You can trust me. I won't say anything."

"If I tell you, then it's like I'm admitting there's a problem. I'm not sure I'm ready for that."

"Maybe, being here together can be healing for us both."

There was a brief silence. Bea knew that Kitty wanted to say something, and whatever it was, it must still hurt quite a lot.

"I was quite hard on Chance when I found out he was developing feelings for you..." Kitty paused. "I felt awful being so self-righteous towards him, considering what I'd done."

Hearing Chance had feelings for her, stung. "What did you do?"

Kitty was quiet for a few seconds before speaking again. "I also fell in love with a human, and what's worse is that you know him"

Bea tried to hide the surprise on her face, but knew Kitty had seen it. "How could I know him?"

Kitty's eyes met hers. "He's the best friend of your ex."

Bea's mouth sprang open. "Tommy?"

"No-one knows."

She saw a flash of fear in Kitty's eyes. "I will never tell a soul...but how? When?"

"Quite some time before I was instructed to watch your shop. We bumped into each other at a bar. He was charming, cocky, but…I don't know…We just ended up seeing each other. If I'm honest it was more a type of defiance on my part. I wanted to experience a human male. Needless to say, I wish that I hadn't."

"Does he know you're a Sidhe?"

Kitty shook her head. "No…when I received the orders to observe you, I found out about your closeness with Brandon. I couldn't take the risk and broke up with him…it was horrible."

"Oh, Kitty, I'm so sorry."

"Don't fret…you did me favour, indirectly. We would've had to break up sooner or later. Best that it was sooner, especially with Saras back in this realm. He can sniff secrets out in an instant."

Bea's thoughts drifted back to when Tommy tried to stop her from going up the stairs of the pub, to prevent her from finding Brandon with the landlord's daughter. She knew that he was protecting her, not Brandon, and wanted Kitty to know it. "He's not lost like Brandon."

"No, he was quite the gentleman," Kitty replied. "So, enough of me and my pathetic love life. Tell me what happened with the arrogant Unseelie…I need a giggle."

"Oh, seriously, it was a misunderstanding, nothing important."

CHAPTER 23

As Seen Through Her Eyes

$\mathcal{K}$arian sat at the kitchen table, alone, until Kitty entered.

"So, Unseelie, how are your wounds?" She leant against the side, staring at him.

"Better, thank you for your concern." He sensed her animosity towards him, and decided to confront it. "You don't like me very much do you, Kitty?"

"Does it matter?"

Karian shook his head. *At least she was honest,* he thought.

"I didn't think so. Okay, let's get something straight, now that you are up and about. I know why you're here, but it's not going to happen...Do you understand?"

He wasn't accustomed to being spoken to in the tone that she used, but did his best to conceal the fact. "Anathon is your friend, a Seelie, and so has your loyalty."

"He has nothing to do with here and now."

"May I ask, why has he not been reprimanded?"

"I don't think that's any of your business."

"Of course, the rules only apply if one is Unseelie."

She shrugged. "Life can be unfair. Yes, I know that you were beaten and fled for your life, that you had nothing to do with Alithia's death, but at present that doesn't change anything... does it?"

He resented her attitude; it was cold, too forward. She

spoke about a love that he felt before she was even born. "Considering your Court claims to be the more…shall we say, righteous? Then, should they not practice what they preach? *Anathon* should not be here."

"If your father had showed his true worth, then maybe."

Karian briskly removed himself from the chair, her words stung. "You should learn to be more respectful."

"Why didn't you tell your father the same thing while his men were beating you, in front of him?"

Karian walked up to her and placed his face near hers. "Tell Anathon to go home."

"Unfortunately for you, I'd prefer him to stay. You do not intimidate me, Karian. Now kindly move from my space."

"Or?" his eyes dared.

"There will be one less Unseelie to worry about."

Karian burst into laughter. "Surely, you require a glass of mead first?"

Kitty flew across the room with Sidhe speed, and then back to Karian, holding a knife up at his throat. "Like I said, I don't intimidate easily."

Anna walked in, dropping the bunch of wildflowers she had picked. "Kitty, why are you holding a knife to Karian's throat?"

He tried to edge away from the blade to speak, but Kitty pressed it harder to his neck. He gulped. "She is expressing how my…technique of persuasion is inadequate."

Anna rolled her eyes. "Kitty, put the knife down."

She didn't move.

"Kitty! Now!" Anna raised her voice.

She slowly released the pressure. "Stay away from Bea." Kitty lowered the knife, throwing it in the sink.

"Protective, isn't she?" he remarked, wiping away the trickle of blood from his neck.

"Both of you really need to think about what's actually at stake. Personal feelings have no place in matters of the Court. If there is to be any future for the Sidhe, it starts with us. If we can't find a way to be civil to each other, how can we ever expect peace on a larger scale? End this, or kill each other now." She started gathering up the flowers from the floor.

He knew that Anna was right. Besides, if Bea came downstairs and found her friend splattered all over the kitchen, it would be rather hard for her to forgive him. He extended his hand. "To the start of peace?"

Kitty looked over at Anna, who glared her way, and she begrudgingly shook his hand. "I still meant what I said," she mumbled out of Anna's earshot.

That evening, they all had a drink, in merriment of a small truce between Seelie and Unseelie. The two different sects being together was unheard of, and it was a definitely a cause for celebration. Bea made a mental note to be civil to Karian. Ever since she had arrived at the farmhouse, it'd been stressful. Tonight, she wanted to let her hair down. Saras was due to return at the weekend, so it was time for everyone to enjoy what they knew would be a short-lived pact.

Kitty turned the radio on and started to dance. Laughter and taunts filled the room as she invited a reluctant Anna to join her on the imaginary dance floor.

Bea could feel Karian's eyes on her, she bellowed over the

music trying to distract his stare. "I wasn't aware that the Sidhe liked Madonna."

"Who knows? Madonna might actually be a Sidhe," Karian mused.

Kitty pulled him to his feet. "Let's make history with Madonna, Unseelie."

Bea giggled as Kitty danced rings around him. To be fair, Karian still had a fractured rib, so his movement was a little limited.

Anna quickly escaped Kitty's clutches and re-joined Bea on the sofa. "It's you that has managed to create this unity. I can't remember a time when the Sidhe have been together that didn't involve fighting."

She shook her head. "Circumstance, Anna, that's all."

"You should allow yourself more credit."

"Come on, you two, join us!" cried Kitty, showing off some rather flamboyant Sidhe moves.

Karian started to walk towards Bea and Anna. Bea averted her eyes, dreading him asking her to dance.

"Anna, would you care to join me?" Karian extended his hand.

Anna turned to Bea, but she had already disappeared, Kitty had pulled her up.

Anna accepted.

Laughter filled the air as they all started to jive.

Karian popped into the kitchen, grabbing another bottle, and returned, refilling everyone's glasses.

Bea sat back down and Karian later sat in a chair, furthest from her. She wasn't sure why, but his dismissal bugged her. *Is this a new game?* she wondered.

It was starting to get late and the music had changed tempo, and Anna retired for the night.

"Come on, you two, dance." Kitty glided across the floor with Sidhe speed, glass in hand, Karian joined her.

"I've had a wonderful night, thank you." He planted a kiss upon Kitty's hand, which put her off balance, but she managed, to their surprise, to quickly straighten back up again.

Karian turned and tilted his head. "Goodnight, Bethany."

"Very formal, Karian?" observed a merry Kitty.

"I wouldn't want to be accused of doing anything… improper."

Bea rolled her eyes…*go to bed.*

"Come on Bea, dance with me!" Kitty cried, dismissing Karian.

"One dance." Bea replied.

It wasn't actually dancing, Kitty was wobbling and Bea became her dance stabilizer.

"I've not felt *so* relaxed for a very, very long time," Kitty sung out.

"It's the mead." Bea giggled, pleased that Kitty seemed to be more relaxed than earlier.

"No. No, it's this." She waved her hand through the air. "We need you in our realm, to work your Seior."

"I have no Seior, Kitty. We're a team."

"Yep, a team. I like that." Kitty smiled and raised her glass. "Human, Seelie and Unseelie… What a team."

Bea could feel the effects of the mead starting to dull her concentration. "Kitty, I've got to go to bed. Will you be okay?"

"Of course, I'm going to dance the night away. I've aired a few things, and much feel better."

"Good…I'll see you in the morning." Bea gave her a quick hug.

"See you in the morning," Kitty sang.

Before leaving the room, she took one last look at Kitty, who was giggling and dancing away in her own little world. She smiled and made her way up the stairs, but paused on hearing Kitty singing the song that Chance and she had danced to at her flat. A flash of sadness swept over her. She wondered if he'd ever mentioned to Kitty that it was *their* song. Her mood changed quickly, from one of sentiment to resentment as she pondered on what his song to his wife would be. She blocked out the music and all thoughts of him, continuing her way up the stairs.

Karian's door lay open, and Bea curiously, walked over, and peered in. He was standing by the window, and must have sensed her, for he turned, blankly stared at her, and then returned his gaze back to the window. She wanted the floor to swallow her up, she had been caught, but instead of retreating, her feet carried her further into the room. "You're still awake?" *Obviously, stupid question*, she thought.

"I couldn't sleep." He turned back the window.

"Kitty told me that you allowed yourself to be captured, is that true?"

"A fleeting moment of stupidity." He stared into the glass of mead, before taking a large mouthful.

"Last night, did you use a type of glamour on me?" she asked, hovering by the foot of the bed, still feeling uneasy, wondering why she had bothered to enter the room in the first place.

He shook his head. "No."

Bea hoped, rather than believed, that he was being truthful.

"Can I ask you a question?" His voice, low.

"Yes." She replied, although dreading it.

He looked straight at her. "Do you remember us?" His cool persona was betrayed by the longing in his eyes. She could now see how vulnerable he really was, and found herself answering honestly. "Yes."

"Bad memories, huh?" He looked away. "Don't worry, I'm leaving tomorrow."

"They're not bad memories. They're just not mine."

"And Anathon?"

Chance's real name made her stomach turn. She didn't understand what Karian wanted to hear. "What about him?"

"Are they better memories?" He gulped down more of the mead.

"They're mine." was all that she replied.

He slammed down his empty glass and sat on the bed. "Goodnight, Bethany."

She was about to leave, but instead found herself sitting on the bed next to him. "I'm sorry."

"I know." He lowered his head, closing his eyes. "The most difficult part to say is the one that you don't want to hear… that I have always loved you."

"*Not me*…Alithia." she gently reminded.

His eyes met hers. "Why do you continue to resist *me*?" His stormy, blue eyes evoked Alithia's memories. She remembered seeing the same anguish in his eyes that fateful day at the well, and her own eyes started to glisten as the feelings of losing him returned. "It's the safest way, everyone needs to protect themselves." She tried hard to blot out the memory and the emotion it stirred.

He embraced her hands in his. "I'm finding it so hard to let you go." His face, his eyes, his posture, all mirrored his yearning.

"I'm not the person that you seek, Kari." But inside, she was finding it difficult to disassociate Alithia's feelings from her own. She watched a tear form in the corner of his eye.

"Is it so easy to walk away? To not to even try?" he asked.

"I know you're hurting, and I ... I'm sorry."

"You know, but you don't allow yourself to *feel*. You loved me once. You went against your family's wishes, giving up everything because you believed in me, *in us*. Why do you find it so difficult to love me, again?"

Bea lowered her eyes. She did feel something, but knew that everything she felt was down to Alithia.

His released his hold of her hands. "I'm too late...you love him."

"I'm sorry." She twiddled her fingers, nervously.

"Please leave."

"I...I don't want to leave." She felt torn, being this close to him, feeling his pain, caused emotions to surface, that she found hard to explain.

"Now, you torture me."

She was about to get up but he grabbed her hand. "I had it all planned. I would allow them to catch me, bring me here. I would declare my love, and you would remember everything and fall in love with me again." His eyes were holding back tears. "I still love you *so very much*."

Her eyes welled, knowing that he meant every word. *Here's a man offering his love and I'm turning him away. Yet, the man that I love, lied and left me.* "Have you loved anyone else, since Alithia?" She wasn't sure why she'd asked. What difference did it make?

"You need to understand. My heart belongs to my twin flame, *you*." His ran his hand softly down her face. "You are my Vororbla, my karma, and no matter the coldness of your heart towards me now as a stranger, I will *never* stop loving you."

"What is my Vororbla?"

He leant closer and whispered in her ear. "Me."

Her pulse raced at his being so close. Her mouth opened to speak but nothing came out. Their eyes met, as his mouth hovered by hers. His breath against her skin made her mouth move closer, but he tenderly kissed her cheek instead of her lips. She knew it was his way of saying goodbye. His eyes were transparent with the pain of pulling away. Instinctively, her hand stroked a strand of hair from his face, then her fingers ran through his thick, dark waves, and another memory of him replayed through her mind.

Karian started to pull away, but she wasn't ready to relinquish her touch. She'd became caught in the web their past memories. It felt good being close to someone again, and hearing him declare that he wanted her, with all his being, broke through her defences.

He shook his head, while moving her hand. "I'm not him." His eyes filled with agony.

"I know," she mumbled, as her lips suddenly met his.

Karian's mouth was hesitant at first, but she teased his shy, quivering lips with her tongue and he responded to her with such passion that she couldn't find the strength to fight the conflict within. His body pressed against hers and she had no choice, but to lie back on the bed. His arms were either side of her, eyes searching hers. Bea wondered if he was looking at her or Alithia, but as he gently nibbled at her neck, the question fled her mind.

One moment she was in the present, the next, in a previous sensual memory, unable to differentiate, as the two realms, souls, merged into one.

"I know you," she whispered by his ear while slipping her hand up his shirt. His skin was soft and his figure so leanly defined that she had to touch more of him. She ran her hand down his back, gently scratching his skin as his hand slid up her skirt, along the inside of her naked thigh. She gasped, and he paused just as his fingers were about to fully discover her. He looked into her eyes, she knew he was savouring the point of no return. His smouldering, needy eyes mirrored his memories, intensifying their connection. His tongue made a slow retreat from her mouth, travelling down her body where he continued to awaken her senses.

He was unlike Chance in every way. Open, uninhibited, silently daring her to break all the rules, and with every touch, every kiss, every lick, she felt his relentless need until she could take no more of his giving, and shuddered.

She invited all of him to her, and heard his groan as he readily accepted. Her body arched in surrender, luring him even closer. She allowed herself to want for the sake of wanting, to let go, allowing him to divulge every piece of his consuming love. His eyes never once left hers, even when he paused and jittered. Another groan of pleasure accentuated from him, as Bea took his bottom lip in her mouth, where her tongue passionately seduced his. She still wanted more and he obliged, leaving no part of her body un-devoured.

Caught now, she no longer wished to escape.

She watched Karian, as he lay sleeping. He looked so good, yet still felt dangerous. She couldn't quite place why her rational-self just couldn't let her feelings go, even now. Was she wrong to permit him to seduce her, did she seduce him? The whole experience became a blurred mix of fulfilling previously denied needs, and those of guilt – for betraying her feelings for Chance. As she lay next to him, her breathing deepened as she took in every curve of muscle exposed on his athletic body. Her eyes then followed the contour of his structured jawline, perfect nose, and the soft lips of his luscious mouth. *What about Chance?* Her heart sank remembering the different type of love that he had showed her, shy and tender. She felt confused, and reminded herself that he had lied, broken her heart. The conflict continued to grow as the memory of him refused to leave her. She shook her head, and climbed from the bed.

Karian immediately opened his eyes. "Where are you going?"

Her heart almost stopped at being caught trying to escape. "I thought you were sleeping."

"Don't go." He held out his hand, while his eyes pleaded.

Bea hesitated for a moment. One part of her wanted to dive into his arms, the other, to run away as fast as she could. "I *can't*. It's best that no-one knows."

He sunk his head into the pillow. "You feel you've done something wrong…in loving me?"

She wanted to be honest with him. "I…I don't know what I feel."

His slender jaw tensed as he withdrew his hand. "Am I not enough?"

She climbed onto the bed, and placed a kiss on his lips. "More than enough."

He looked into her eyes, holding her hand. "Don't run away…*please.*"

She gulped. "I just need to get my head round everything."

He resigned and nodded. "Of course, forgive me." He gently kissed her hand, slowly relinquishing his hold.

"Goodnight," she whispered, before walking out the door.

CHAPTER 24

The Night Brings the Dawn

When Bea woke, she found Karian sitting beside her, gently stroking the tattoo on her arm. "Morning." His voice soft.

"Morning." She felt a little uncomfortable about him being in her personal space and moved her arm. "Did you sleep well?"

"Extremely." His eyes glinted, searching hers.

Bea found him too intense. She hadn't even had time to gather her thoughts about last night, and quickly excused herself, grabbing some clothes, running off to the bathroom. She perched on the edge of the bath. *What have I done?* she thought, realising the enormity of her actions. The mead had definitely worn off, and her more rational self, began to surface. When she re-entered the room, he had gone.

Bea made her way down to the kitchen, where everyone was engrossed in conversation.

"Morning." Anna looked over and smiled.

"Morning, Anna." Bea joined them at the table. "So, what are you talking about?"

Kitty spoke first. "Karian has come up with a plan to evade Saras's wrath, concerning his escape."

Bea had forgotten that he was supposed to be leaving today. *That would account for him not wanting me to leave him last night,* she thought. Then the old fear of being alone haunted her, just a little.

He seemed to pick up on her vulnerability. "Morning." A smile pursed itself on his lips as her eyes shied away. "I was just suggesting that Kitty and Anna should inform Saras that they intercepted me when I managed to escape from the iron. Of course, they could not return me to the iron, being Sidhe. So, I was held captive in the house, and pretended to be hurt much worse than I was, and on the morning of Saras's return...I make my escape."

It didn't make sense to Bea. "How would you have escaped from the iron? You were too weak and-"

Kitty interrupted. "We could say you helped him."

"Oh."

"They can't do anything to you. They're bound, by oath, to protect you. You'll be forgiven, because you're a silly, weak human." Kitty beamed.

"So, the only difference to the truth is that you and Anna are kept in the dark?"

"Exactly. Saras won't be happy, but it would never cross his mind that we've aided Karian's escape." She proudly grinned.

Bea nodded, staring over at Karian. "So, you leave in the morning, not today?"

"One more night," he replied, with a cheeky smile.

Kitty and Anna were unaware of the undertone, and Bea lowered her head, to hide her blush. Her stomach fluttered at the unspoken promise given through his eyes, of again sharing his intimacies with her. It scared her, how much she wanted him.

Kitty and Anna went to stock up on a few groceries, and Bea rang Jenny, confirming that she'd return home within the next couple of days. She tried ringing Liza, but her phone was turned off. It had been too long since they last talked.

The house was quiet, she wondered where Karian had gone, and went in search of him. Bea found him outside. "How come you're out here? You okay?"

"Yes." He moved over on the bench so that she could join him. "Are you missing home, Bea?"

"In some ways. It's funny, I've never actually spent this much time away before."

"How do you feel now that you have?"

"Okay, there's been a lot of distraction." She laughed, at the understatement. "It *all* feels so weird."

Karian placed her hand in his. "I'll miss you."

"Not having you around... will be different too." She wanted to avoid any deep interaction of words between them.

He laughed, and she couldn't help but laugh too, knowing that he was amused by her avoidance of sentiment.

His eyes gleamed.

"What?" she cried, trying to fight the attractiveness she found in his smile.

"You're so...so precise with what you say."

"Precise? No, I'm not." Initially she felt indignant at his insight. "I just try to avoid saying the wrong thing. It's actually quite a skill." She couldn't help but laugh at his unbelieving stare.

"And what would've been the wrong thing to say?"

She shook her head. "No, I'm not playing."

Karian's lips suddenly met hers; he scooped her up in his

arms, and carried her inside to the sofa. She yelled for him to put her down, but actually felt aroused by his forthrightness, and allowed him to take control.

He laid her on the sofa, and leant over her. Their lips met again, as his hand slipped through her blouse and caressed her breasts. She found it hard to fight with the excitement racing through her body. It happened so fast. Her hands grasped at his brown locks, as he gently nibbled her lips, and slid his hand down to the button on her trousers, then slid further.

"We can't." She tried to resist him, but it was too difficult while his hand gave her pleasure.

Karian's tongue demanded hers, dismissing the weak plea. Her whole body now ached in anticipation of him. She slipped her hand into his trousers, but he pulled it away.

"I want to please you," he whispered, moving on to give her more pleasure.

Bea jerked, closing her eyes.

"Let me see you… look at me." His voice became a whimper.

She knew that he wasn't about to allow her to escape from him, not even in the most private of moments. She opened her eyes, and his were there to greet her, full of thirst. His mouth started to press hard against hers. She felt his entirety in that moment and her body welcomed him.

They lay on the sofa and he wrapped his arms around her. "Come home with me?"

This time, there was no way of avoiding the question.

"You'll want for nothing." He moved closer. "I need you. I don't know how to walk away."

His words tugged at her heart. Chance hadn't found it so difficult, or her mother. If only her heart would invite him in, but there was no use in pretending there was any room. It was completely full with Chance. Her heart had become a separate part of her, beyond any reasoning.

"I *will* miss you." She tried to bring Karian back to the present.

He gave her a weak smile, appearing resigned. Bea understood his pain – the fact that Alithia, the person he'd been seeking for several lifetimes, was now in a human that did not wish to spend more than a few nights with him, hurt. Little was she aware however, of how determined he was to find a way to work on that.

Bea could find no words of comfort, and instead hugged him, but he pushed her away. Then, she realised that he was staring at something. Her eyes followed his, and her mouth dropped open on seeing a small fiery ball of blue hovering inside the living room. It seemed to be emitting some sort of electrical charge. "What is that?" Bea's eyes squinted from its glare.

His voice became urgent. "We have to leave. It's Saras." He got up and beckoned her to follow. "Quick, there isn't much time."

She followed him into the kitchen, but paused. "I can't come with you." She glanced back at the orb, her heart thumping.

"Bea, the light in there is a probe, sent to check for any danger before Saras's arrival. Don't you understand? He's *seen us*. You can't stay here now."

"What are you talking about?"

"*Our* closeness. I don't want him to hurt you, *please*, you have to come with me."

She glanced down at her feet. "I have no shoes on."

"I can carry you." He managed a smile.

"I am perfectly able to -" Her sentence was cut short by the orb entering the kitchen.

"We have to go…now!" Karian took her hand in his and they started to run.

He led the way through a field. Her head was spinning, everything happened so fast. As they ran, she kept her hand in his, frantically looking behind for the orb and in doing so almost lost her footing.

"We must keep going… we're nearly there. Don't look back." They ran for what seemed like miles. They reached some trees, away from the open fields. She felt safer with their shelter. "Do you know where you're going?" she asked.

"To the stream."

"Stream?" She couldn't help but look over her shoulder for the orb.

"We need to get to running water."

Bea struggled to keep up as they continued to run, and by the time they reached the stream, she felt breathless and exhausted. Karian crossed first. He held out his hand from the other side, urging her to jump in. "Quick," he cried.

She hesitated, staring at the water, and then back at Karian. His hand still reached out in her direction. She dipped one foot in the water. "I can't," she yelled, feeling light-headed, as her thoughts drifting back to a memory, Alithia's fear of drowning.

"It's alright. It looks deeper than it is, hurry, Bea."

She took a deep breath and jumped in. There was a splash, and the cold, murky, green water washed over her. She started to panic, the memory of drowning in the well had violently returned in an instant. Karian cried out to her, but she didn't hear him. In her mind, the stone circumference of Alithia's deathly prison was closing in. "Karian!" she screamed, aware that she was about to go under.

"Alithia!" he yelled, jumping into the water, reaching her in seconds, but Bea was already under. Fear yanked at his heart, as he dived to find her. She was lying on the bed of the stream. He pulled her up, and swam to the other side of the bank with her. Frantically he started pumping her chest. "Don't you leave me, not again...Alithia!"

Bea began to choke, coughing up the remaining water from her lungs. He embraced her tightly within his trembling arms. "Don't let me go." She spoke Alithia's last words before the well sucked her under. He fought hard to keep the tears that had welled up in his eyes at bay. "Never." He'd managed to save her, his Alithia, in this realm, in this life form, but the torture of reliving his previous loss had weakened his facade. He closed his eyes, to hush the inner screaming cries of his past love, still haunting him.

Bea began to shiver, casting away the past. "What do we do now?"

"We'll be safe here for a while. Catch your breath, rest. Saras cannot cross a running stream."

"Why?"

"It's a paradox of our crossing over into this realm. A protective boundary made a long time ago by universal laws. No Sidhe can pursue a human over running water." He forced a smile. "Finally, you're coming home."

She looked up into his eyes. "You've won."

"I know." This time his smile was real.

Her eyes suddenly widened. Karian turned, and saw Saras preening on the opposite bank. "Time to leave."

She nodded, in agreement, taking his hand as she got to her feet.

"Karian. I must say, you have *miraculous* healing skills."

He threw a glare in Saras's direction.

"Bethany, you cannot trust Karian." Saras warned.

She looked straight at Karian, who shook his head and squeezed her hand. "We must go."

"The verbal poison will keep spilling from his mouth in the hope that you will listen."

Saras's voice grew louder. "I wonder, did Karian inform you that Anathon has not left this realm?"

Her pace slowed down, and the muscles in Karian's face tightened. "Bea, we have to go. This is his way of delaying us."

"Ask him, Bethany." Saras continued. "It is a simple question to answer before you take your leave. He is aware after all, that I cannot cross. Therefore, ask yourself, what is the hurry?"

Karian turned, not bothering to hide the agitation he felt. "Lord Saras, if you remember correctly. I was quite unconscious via the gift of friendship that you bestowed upon me, prior to my stay at the farmhouse."

A slight smirk pursed itself on Saras's lips. "I remember well, but you seem to have avoided the question."

Karian muttered under his breath, and placed his arm around Bea. "We're wasting time."

He was about to start walking, when Saras hastily added. "Who placed the iron on your person?"

Karian's eyes shot over at Saras. "Being unconscious, I would not know, Lord Saras. Are you saying that it was Anathon that beat and bound me?" he replied, quite smug.

The conversation had turned in Karian's favour. Saras's smirk quickly disappeared, as he saw the look of disbelief on Bea's face.

"She is not *Alithia*, Karian. Your hold will wane." Saras turned away.

"Now, who's avoiding the question, My Lord?" Karian shouted, but Saras had already disappeared.

"How could Ch...Anathon chain you? He's a Sidhe?" asked Bea.

"He did not tell you?" The question genuinely caught Karian by surprise. "I thought you knew *everything* about him? I'm sorry."

"Knew what?"

"He's only half Sidhe, his mother was human."

"Kaelen was human?"

"Yes...Are you alright?"

"I'm fine."

A few miles west of the lake, they found a small village, and entered a small, quiet inn. Karian asked a bartender if he could use their phone, and within the hour, a black Mercedes with tinted windows pulled up.

Karian introduced the Unseelie driver by the name of Soren. Bea thought he looked quite intimidating, not the usual slender build she'd grown accustomed to seeing in a

Sidhe. His face was not as demur either. It was cold and hard, his dark eyes looked bitter. He had greeted her with what appeared to be a rather menacing sneer, and she instantly distrusted him.

Karian climbed into the back seat to join her. Soren appeared rather put out by her presence.

"We'll talk later." Karian quickly appeased him.

Bea asked how Soren had got to Scotland so quickly.

"The Seelie are not the only ones with safe houses." He smiled, wrapping his arm around her.

"Where are we going?" She could feel Soren spying on her via the mirror, but ignored him.

"To the theatre," replied Karian, resting his head back.

"Why the theatre?"

"It's where I live."

"You live at the theatre?" Out of the corner of her eye, she saw Soren grin at her comment, and it made her feel both angry and uneasy.

"It's the safest place," he replied, kissing her on the temple. He rested his head back again, and closed his eyes.

Bea gazed out of the window. *What am I doing? I don't belong here. Everything's changed… but wasn't that what I wanted?*

CHAPTER 25

Decadent Living

*L*ittle conversation passed between her and Karian for the rest of the journey, by the time they reached the motorway he had fallen asleep, leaving Bea in the company of Solemn Soren. She tried making conversation with him, once. By his grunt, it was quite clear that he did not wish to chat.

On their arrival in London, it started to rain. The dampness reflected her mood, grey and dismal.

Soren called out to Karian. "My Lord, we're home."

He stirred, and opened his eyes. On seeing Bea, a big smile appeared on his lips. "You're still here, it wasn't a dream." The excitement in his eyes did not match hers and he must've noticed. "I apologise. I fell asleep, it was wrong of me. Did Soren not keep you entertained?"

"A little." Her eyes caught Soren's in the mirror.

"I know that you're tired. Everything's been prepared for you." He gave her a gentle smile.

"Prepared?"

"Soren notified everyone of our return."

"Everyone?"

"Of course, you don't know. Some of the other Unseelie of this realm live here, too."

Bea's mood sank further into darkness. All she wanted to do was go home, her home, her safe and happy place.

The car pulled up in front of the theatre. Soren was the first to jump out holding a huge umbrella over Karian, who waited with an extended hand for Bea. She took a deep breath, and got out of the car. Soren handed Karian the umbrella, and waited in the rain as they made their way up the steps to the theatre doors, where two burly Unseelie men stood guard. They too, looked menacing, thought Bea, but Karian paid them no heed, and with the sweep of his hand, they moved.

Inside, Karian handed his umbrella to a female Unseelie. Bea couldn't help but stare at her beautiful sapphire eyes, set in a clear, porcelain complexion. The Unseelie shied away.

Bea's heart thumped as they turned the corner, arriving in a crowded corridor, where two rows of Unseelie lined each wall. So many inquisitive, piercing, blue eyes scrutinised her. She couldn't help but snuggle closer to Karian as they walked down the long corridor. Not one of the Unseelie said a word. They only tilted their heads, to show respect, as they passed by. Through their eyes, she noted their greeting was a mixture of awe and suspicion. *Are they looking at me as Alithia?* she wondered.

Once they reached the end of the corridor, Karian opened a large, finely-carved, wooden door.

"Welcome to my *private* quarters." He smiled, gesturing for her to go in.

She felt nervous, but that feeling melted away on entering. "It's amazing," she gasped. Her mood lightened at the sight of the luxurious grandeur before her. The large room was decorated in the colours of teal and gold. The furnishing consisted of silk and co-ordinating tapestry, which adorned the elegant wood in room, all in Art Nouveau styling.

"Like it?" he asked, looking for her approval.

"I love it." She walked over to the huge antique four-poster bed that had first caught her eye, and ran her hand down the carving of one post. "It's enormous."

"Custom made. I like to be able to move around in bed." He gave her that famous Karian smile, as he joined her.

There was a knock at the door. Karian permitted entry, and a female Sidhe carried in a tray with a pot of tea. He pointed over to the sideboard, where she placed the tray down, tilted her head and left.

"Don't you talk to the other Sidhe?" She found the coldness he displayed towards the woman disturbing.

"Talk? Yes, why?" He looked confused.

"You just dismissed that woman."

"It seems a habit I'll have to get out of, around you." He embraced her. "I'm sorry. I have to be different here, in front of them." His eyes gestured towards the door.

"Why?"

"I am the King's son. I'm expected to act in a certain way."

"And I thought pomposity only existed among humans."

By the twinkle in his eyes she could tell Karian was amused. "It's not who I am, Bea. I have to oversee *all* of the Unseelie in this realm. I cannot appear weak. Let's not talk of this now. You're tired." His old self started to shine through as he ran around trying to appease. "This is the bathroom." He tapped on the door of the en-suite. "Some fresh clothes, here." He guided her eyes to the chair. "And let's not forget tea, here."

"Thank you," she replied, appreciative of the effort, although by someone else's hand.

"I have a few things to catch up on. Would you mind if I disappear for a while? If you need me, I'll be through there." He pointed to a door, opposite the bed. "It's my study."

"Sure, I think a bath and some sleep will do me good."

His hand swept over her cheek. "I know it feels strange, and I don't feel I've helped to make your initial impression a warm one. I *will* be more myself, I promise."

She smiled and nodded.

Karian gently placed a kiss by her ear. "Call me if you need anything, I'm just through there, remember."

"Got it." She watched his head slowly disappear behind the door of his office. Once she heard the door close, she poured herself some tea and leant against the sideboard. Her eyes scanned every part of the room. It was beautiful, reminding her of a grand, old, manor house, so why did she feel so deflated? She sighed, remembering – *the manor house, the Bluebell, him.* Bea slammed her cup down, *No...I will not think about him. He's a liar, a cheat and now, a bully.*

CHAPTER 26

Muswell Hill

*C*hance stared out of the window, down to the street below. He'd been held captive here, in Muswell Hill, ever since his return from the farmhouse. Two Seelie guarded the door outside. There was no way to escape, and even if he was able to find a way, he couldn't disobey an order, even from Saras. It wasn't a risk he was willing to take, placing more shame on his family, and The Order of The Heaven Stone. He'd paced his cell a thousand times, trying to figure out a way to gain his freedom, especially after failing at The Heaven Stone meditation, which normally enabled him to communicate directly with the Aos Si – the lesser of the Sindria. His mind had refused to remain clear enough for contact. Bea consumed every thought, he needed to see her again.

The worse recollection, that continued to play over in his mind, was that of being told Karian had been captured near the farmhouse. Saras had readily supplied him with the information that Karian had hidden in the trees, that a probe orb discovered him. Saras gave the order for his men to beat him.

"I'm surprised that you didn't dirty your own hands." The reply earned Chance a punch across the jaw. When he spoke again, it was to ask what they had done with Karian. He recalled the conversation led by Saras. "There is a rather slow, painful death in progress. Have you seen the effects of cold iron, Anathon? It burns. The effects are quite ghastly as it eats away at the skin. The iron then emits its Seior venom into the wound, and the bloodstream. Quite excruciating, I hear. Of course, the iron has to be at some point hexed by a Deisi." He remembered that Saras had shivered at the telling.

"Who placed the iron on Karian? Do you have human allies now?" Chance asked.

"Isn't it enough to know that he is dying? Is he not your enemy, too? An Unseelie fighting for Bethany's affections must add a certain insult to injury, does it not?"

"What does Queen Eliseis have to say of Karian's torture?"

"Don't *test* me, Anathon, I oversee here. He is a mere Unseelie, not worthy of the Queen's attention."

"He is still of royal blood, and The Heaven Stone is your keeper. There is a code of conduct." Chance had reminded.

Saras curled his lip. "The minions in your Order are dying out. The Order of The Court now carries the responsibility of our realm and this forsaken place. Eliseis is the queen of that Court and, of course, I will uphold whatever the majority rule. Though remember, Anathon, I represent the majority. Eliseis's personal opinion matters not." Saras recomposed. "The Heaven Stone maintain the universal balance, but what balance has there been in this world? The Aos Si and the Sindria left this realm. If they cared about the balance, would they not have stayed? Let these humans have their possessions, their self-absorbed lives, The Heaven Stone care not."

"You're wrong."

"We shall see."

Chance mulled over the conversation in his mind, *who could be Saras's human allies? Who could have placed Karian in irons?* The only explanation that made any sense was Brandon. He knew what they were, and he hated Karian, but how could such an alliance be made?

Chance was weary. He lay down on the bed and covered his brow with his hands. *Would it be worth trying to physically push the memory of Bea out from his mind?* He groaned, as he replayed her hands releasing his at the time of their goodbye at the farmhouse. *She hates me.*

He heard movement and voices coming from behind the bedroom door, and sat up. He tried to work out what they were saying, but the conversation remained too faint.

The door burst open. Kitty entered looking distraught. Her mouth opened, as if to say something, until Saras glided in.

"Bea?" Chance perched on the edge of the bed as fear coursed through his body. His attention focused solely on Saras who seemed to be in deep thought.

Kitty briefly glanced at Saras, and he nodded. "She's okay. We need to talk." Kitty sat on the bed. Her tone made him anxious. "Where's Bea?"

Kitty placed her hand on Chances arm, but he shrugged it off. "What's going on?"

Saras spoke. "Kitty, would you kindly explain. I feel the words will get stuck in my throat at any attempt of repeating your feeble excuse."

She shifted uncomfortably on the bed. "Saras told you of Karian being found near the farmhouse?"

He nodded, not liking where this was going.

"Well, Karian was…after he was beaten, Bea found him in the outhouse."

Chance jumped to his feet. "What?"

Kitty held her palms up, trying to calm him down. "Bea *is* alright."

His eyes narrowed. "But there's more."

She took a deep breath before continuing. "We brought him into the house."

"YOU DID WHAT?" he yelled.

"We had no choice. Bea removed him from the iron."

"I can't believe I'm hearing this." He started to pace the room. "So where is she now?"

Kitty gulped. "They ran away."

He tried to grasp what she was saying. "What? Who ran away?"

"Bea left *with* him," she replied.

"You mean he forced her…" He glared at Kitty.

She shook her head. "No."

"What do you mean, no?" He was finding it hard to remain calm and his hands began to tremble with anger.

Saras spoke. "Let me clarify the situation. Our dear Bethany left with the Unseelie quite voluntarily. A repulsive thought, I know."

"YOU LIE!" Chance spat. "What have you done with her?"

"I will forgive such a remark, once," stated Saras with an icy glare.

Kitty jumped up. "Stop, enough…Anathon, the orb caught them, we *all* saw them."

"May I add that, in a desperate attempt to win her back,

I informed Bethany that you were still in this realm. Needless to say, it did not have the effect that I hoped," said Saras.

Bravely, Kitty dared to send Saras a stinging glare.

Chance burned with a rage he had never felt before. "Where are they now?"

Kitty was about to say, when he mumbled, "The theatre… he has finally reclaimed *his* Alithia." Chance closed his eyes and permitted the long-awaited dread to fill him.

"There is a way… it might not be too late," Kitty urged.

He knew she actually meant, not too late for Bea to fall into Karian's bed. He felt sick, his stomach twisted with a gut wrenching mixture of hate and jealousy. "You're forgetting the Unseelie has Cynthia, their Deisi. We cannot get into the street, let alone the theatre," he snapped.

"We have *our* Deisi." She dangled the carrot.

His eyes met hers in an instant. "You know where she is?"

"Yes, and Saras said that he will let you go."

He looked over at Saras.

"There is no need to unnecessarily inform the Court of your… indiscretion, but there are two stipulations to your freedom."

Chance already knew what they were. "That I say nothing of your losing the one thing you came here to retrieve."

"Astute. The other?" Saras flexed his fingers.

Chance's jaw tensed. "No further indiscretion."

"Very good, so we understand one another?"

"Perfectly." Chance stated, though he hated complying to Saras's rules.

"Good. Kitty will make the introductions. You are free to

leave." Saras lowered his head to Kitty, but Chance received no such respect.

Chance rubbed his hands over his head, trying to focus. "Have you got the car?"

"Yes," replied Kitty.

"Where's my case?"

"It's in the living room, where it normally…" Kitty's words drifted off as he stormed out of the room. She quickly followed him.

Saras and the guards began to make their way out of the flat.

Chance found his case under the dining table. He could tell that it had been opened, but nothing was gone.

"You won't need anything from that…The Deisi is all the weapon you need."

He ignored her, placing various weapons in his trouser band and pockets. "Ready?"

CHAPTER 27

Safe House

Chance and Kitty made their way to another safe house in South-West London.

"So, where were you?" His eyes stared out the window.

She didn't need to ask what he meant. "I was in town with Anna."

"Who's Anna?"

"A Seelie that Saras dropped off, the night he brought Karian to the farmhouse."

"I can't believe you left Bea alone with him?"

"It was a part of the plan." She didn't like the hint of blame in his voice.

"Plan? What plan?"

"To save our arses…We hoped by going out, Saras wouldn't get suspicious."

"You *knew* Karian was going to escape?"

"What were we supposed to do? Bea gave me a lecture on torturing a *defenceless* Unseelie. Then, suddenly, he was in the house. I didn't know what to do."

"Did you know that Bea was planning to go with him?"

"No…I thought it was just Karian. Bea and I planned to go home. Believe me, I'm as shocked as you about the whole running-away thing."

"I doubt that," he spat.

"What's that supposed to mean?"

"Forget it." He pulled one of the weapons from his waistband, checking the load.

"No, I won't forget it, what are you implying?"

"Must've been quite cosy with you all being nice to the Unseelie."

Kitty raised her brow. "I swear… I had no idea that Bea was going to run away with him. I think Saras may have scared her, the orb went into the house."

"Did you see all the footage from the orb?"

"I saw what Saras showed me." Kitty dreaded answering anymore questions.

"Which was?" His eyes burned into her.

"Do we *really* have to do this now?"

"When do you suggest we talk about it? In front of the Deisi, over tea?"

"No need for sarcasm," Kitty snapped.

"You don't want to tell me… do you?"

"Look, I didn't see anything, apart from them running out of the house," she lied.

Kitty pulled up outside the safe house, and Chance jumped out of the car. His mind was working overtime, *was Kitty lying to him? Was Bea really just scared and confused, so ran?* But it was his last thought that hurt, that cut like a knife. *Has Bea, Alithia, fallen in love with Karian all over again?* The normally deeply-hidden human side of him started to rise to the surface, as he became consumed by even more jealousy.

CHAPTER 28

Theatre

$\mathcal{B}$ea strolled into the bathroom. She had imagined the room being quite small from the outside, but on entering, it opened up, like the Tardis. The beautiful high ceiling boasted its original plaster coving. Two tall, sash windows were simply dressed with delicate white voiles. Plain fairy lights hung lazily around a massive gilded mirror that leant against a wall, directly behind two free-standing, roll top baths. A strong, floral aroma filled the air.

As Bea stepped closer to the baths, she saw that one had already been run, and also identified the aroma's source — rose petals floated on top of the water. It looked incredibly inviting, and she tested the water with her hand. Her mood had certainly improved with the prospect of a warm, scented soak. She ran the cold tap as she got undressed, and then eased herself in. It felt heavenly, and her eyes closed in the petal lagoon. There were no more thoughts of the day, her troubles temporarily melted away.

The water eventually got cold, and her skin had become wrinkly, indicating it was time to climb out. Begrudgingly, she got out of the bath, and covered her wet body in a new robe, which was kindly left for her. She felt content, with the discreet pampering that Karian had so considerately arranged.

When she returned to the bedroom, her nightclothes were

laid out on the bed, accompanied by a light purple rose. Bea picked up the long, sheer gown and slid it on. She laughed noticing how transparent it was, *only you, Karian*. Then, something caught her eye on the bed, an envelope, it must've been left under the gown. She sat down and opened it.

It read:

My dearest Bea,

I love you.

Always yours,

Karian.

She remembered that, in the past, Karian had sent Alithia letters with words of love. Usually of secret meetings, arranged via her handmaiden and his squire. Which were always destroyed to avoid anyone finding them.

There was a knock at the door, and she scurried around trying to find something to put on over her see-through nightdress. The damp dressing gown had to do.

Casually, she called out. "Come in."

A female Unseelie walked in, her hair jet black, with eyes almost as dark as her hair, a midnight blue. "I'm Masas. I hope you don't mind the interruption, but Lord Karian said that you might be hungry." She carried in a tray piled with food.

Bea's eyes widened at the amount, all perfectly displayed.

"Lord Karian would say it's better to have more than less." Masa placed the tray on the bed next to Bea. "He sends his apologies for the delay in joining you."

"Lord?" Bea mused, but noticed that Masas looked quite indignant at her remark.

"Our King's son." Masas tilted her head and left, closing the door behind her.

"What century am I in? So odd," she muttered, nibbling on the grapes.

After she tucked into her feast, she rested on the bed amongst the dozens of feather-filled pillows, and once more, took in the surrounding grandeur. She could hear the faint sound of talking and, following the distraction, found herself outside Karian's study door. *Should I go in?* she pondered, but the voices got louder and on recognising one being Soren, she quickly moved away, deciding against the idea.

"You do know that eaves-dropping is wrong, don't you?"

Bea spun around and saw Asta standing by the other door, her surprise was greeted with a cheeky smile. "Bet you didn't think you'd see me again, huh? Nice gown, by the way." Asta helped herself to some of the grapes.

Bea had forgotten the see-through nightie, and grabbed her dressing gown, slipping it on. "What are you doing here?"

Asta laughed, running her hand down the wooden post of the bed. "It's my home. I sensed you were up and thought you might like to see how the *Earth* Sidhe party?"

"Party?" Bea didn't like the idea, remembering the wall of eyes on her arrival. "I can't, I don't have anything else to wear." She sighed, pointing to her old clothes.

"Just keep the gown on and you'll be fine." Asta's eyes drifted over to the study door. "The male Sidhe's testosterone is *so* much fiercer than any humans, but of course, you must be aware of that already." She grinned. "Come on, at least with me, you'll be safe. There are so many strange Sidhe that frequent this place, any one of them could accidently wander in. Karian won't mind. Just one drink."

"I wouldn't feel comfortable in just my gown, Asta."

"Then let's swap clothes." Asta started to undress, throwing her attire in Bea's direction. "Karian won't be back for hours. Hurry, we're wasting valuable drinking time. Get changed."

Bea sighed and held up the PVC dress trying not to cringe. Gingerly, she slipped out of her night clothes into the Sidhe garb.

Asta spun around. "Ta-da!"

Bea gave her a weak smile, not feeling quite as pleased with the swap, especially when accessorised with slippers.

After climbing up what seemed like endless flights of stairs, they arrived in a crowed hall, which immediately became silent once Bea entered.

"What are you all staring at? Is that how we treat our guest?" Asta bellowed. "Seriously, have none of you seen a human before?" She rolled her eyes and the noise resumed. "Come and meet some friends of mine." Asta led the way.

From the outside, the theatre appeared quite small, so when Bea saw the sheer size of the hall it took her by surprise. It wasn't as grand as any other part of theatre she had seen. The walls were all bare plaster, and in many places, the brickwork lay exposed. Nonetheless, it had a sense of its former glory and she imagined how it would've looked before it fell into disrepair. This must've been the area that Karian mentioned, when they first met, that required work.

They weaved their way through the hall, which was filled with tatty sofas, several chaises longues, and an assortment of tables. Asta headed towards a large bar, where a woman was staring intensely at Bea.

"What are you doing here?" Masas suddenly appeared in front of them.

"It's alright, M. She's with me. Come on, Bea," she urged, giving Masas a scolding glare.

Bea looked back over her shoulder at Masas who stood staring at them, shaking her head.

Once at the bar, Bea looked for the woman that had been eying her, but she was gone.

"Here try this." Asta passed her a glass filled with a black liquid.

"It really doesn't look appealing."

Asta shook her head, taking the glass back from Bea. "You don't trust me? I can't say I blame you." She laughed, tossed back the drink, and then shivered. "Wow…I've never got used to it's kick. Try one." Asta eagerly ordered another two glasses.

The Sidhe behind the bar served two more. Bea had a feeling that the woman wanted to see her reaction too, a human one. "What's in it?" She stared down into the glass.

"Does it really matter? After three. Ready?"

Bea nodded, wondering what she'd got herself into.

"Three!" yelled Asta, and both downed the drink.

Bea cringed at its taste. "Eww." Then shivered.

Asta couldn't stop laughing. A few heads turned in their direction, but then returned to their business. Bea expected her presence to cause more of a stir, as it had on her arrival, but instead, the majority of Sidhe seemed to tolerate her presence, by a way of dismissal.

"Where's the ladies?" she asked, wanting to go in search of Masas.

"Over there." Asta pointed. "Stay left, you can't miss it."

As Bea sifted her way through the hall, she caught sight of Masas in a corner, and started to approach her. She appeared anxious. "Masas, are you alright?"

"Oh, she'll be just fine Bethany." The woman that previously stared at her from the bar joined them. Her long, wavy, blazing red hair, complimented her stunning Malachite green eyes.

"Do I know you?" asked Bea, as Masas's head lowered.

The woman laughed. "Doesn't everyone here?"

"Who are you?" Bea sensed something was out of place.

"Why, I'm Cynthia. You know, the witch lover duped by Alithia's reincarnation…you."

Bea's mouth dropped open, and her heart started to thud.

"Leave her alone, Cynthia." Asta appeared and Masas scurried off.

"Asta… Bea and I were about to have a little chat. Really, there's no need for concern."

"And what would you have to say to a reincarnation of Alithia?"

Cynthia smiled, but her flickering green eyes never left Bea. "I thought you detested humans, Asta?"

"Oh, she does." Pia was now by her sister's side. "However, Bea is under our roof, and a guest. She cannot be harmed."

"Harmed? Oh, Sidhe-lings, I have something much more exciting planned."

The music came to a halt, followed by a silence of all the voices in the hall, as Karian and Soren entered. The small, dark corner quickly became the stage.

Cynthia's grin disappeared when Karian stood next to Bea. "My Lord. My bed has been cold of late."

He turned to Bea. "*Please,* meet me back in the room."

Bea didn't want to get into a female bitching contest, and readily agreed.

Cynthia laughed as she started to walk away. "What a good little girl you are. Oh, and do remember, that when he next beds you, he sees *only* her, his Alithia."

Karian's eyes flickered blue. "Enough!"

Cynthia's eyes met his. "Oh, touchy." She moved closer. "Be mindful of how to speak to me Karian. Remember, I am not one of your Sidhe."

Asta and Pia looked nervously in Soren's direction, as he twitched beside Karian, a sure sign that he wanted to attack.

Cynthia swiftly moved away from them, suddenly appearing in front of Bea, causing her to stop in her tracks. "Bethany, tell me, does Anathon approve of you being here?"

Karian sped across the hall and stood in front of Bea. "We can discuss any problems without Bea present, can we not?'

Cynthia ignored him, and once again regained her position in front of Bea. "You need to be an honest human, Bethany. Tell our Lord, it is Anathon that you love, and *his* touch that you imagine when our Lord expresses his…admiration."

Bea saw the sting in his eyes, and heard the mumbles of low chatter echo throughout the hall.

Asta charged in Cynthia's direction, but yelled as her hand started to turn black, burning from the inside out. Pia rushed to defend her sister, but thick black smoke started flowing from her mouth, and she fell to her knees choking.

"Tell them to back off," Cynthia warned on seeing Soren's approach.

Karian did so, with one look.

The burning stopped and Asta, who was still choking, went to help Pia to her feet,

"How easily you all forget," Cynthia spat, addressing the crowd of Unseelie. "I can remove every single piece of protection I have ever granted." She turned to Karian. "For you…no longer hold my favour."

Unknown to Bea, she was threatening to remove the shield of Seior around the theatre that prevented Seelie entry, and Karian had no option but to play along. "What do you want?"

"You see, Bea. He can be quite tame." She was obviously appeased, for now.

Bea stood frozen, staring at Asta's hand, as it returned to its normal pale colour.

"Oh, those eyes, how quickly they betray you, Karian. What do I want? I want you to tell her the truth." She smiled, as the blue electric glare from his eyes reflected into hers.

"I'm waiting." Cynthia's voice got louder for the crowd.

He remained silent.

"Well, it would appear that your Lord has a preference for his own interests, rather than that of the Sidhe that he takes charge over. I hope that you *all* enjoy the future siege of your home by the Seelie. Are you all ready to return home?" She started to utter the spell for the shield's removal.

The Sidhe in the hall shuffled closer to Bea.

Asta, Pia and Soren stood ready.

"Wait!" Karian shouted. Everyone, apart from Bea, knew that the majority of the Sidhe wouldn't hesitate to turn on the human if their only sanctuary from the Seelie was to be taken away.

"Karian, you surprise me. Are you really about to choose

your people over Bea, your Alithia? Well, I suppose now that the walls are closing in. What a *great* Lord you are...ready to tell Bea, to tell us all who you truly love?"

Karian glared at Cynthia, his hate for the Deisi visible to all. "It *is* Alithia that I love, not this human."

"That's not enough!" Cynthia snapped. "Don't bore us with what we already know of your *feelings*. You can do better than that... you *lied* to me enough times."

He remained silent.

Cynthia looked around at the Unseelie, and then at Pia and Asta. "Do your people mean nothing to you, Karian?"

His whole body tensed, and he drew a deep breath. "This human means nothing to me. She is only the vessel that I seek Alithia through, and I will do whatever is necessary to get Alithia back." His eyes met Cynthia's, and she gave him a massive grin, and then roared with laughter, which eerily echoed throughout the hall. "Will you not also tell Bea of your deceit?" Her eyes quickly glanced towards Bea, then back at him. "Oh, Karian, if only you could see the expression on your face. You are obviously trying to decide which to reveal?"

Bea had heard enough and started to walk away.

"Little human, you haven't heard the best part of our Lord's confession."

Bea ignored her, and continued to walk towards the door.

"I doubt if Karian has told you that Anathon is not married?"

Bea paused, and the Sidhe in the hall began mumbling amongst themselves.

Karian rushed to Cynthia's side. "It is a dangerous game that you play, Deisi."

Her eyes met his. "My Lord, those are the only ones that this Deisi enjoys…remember?"

He whispered close to her ear. "Get out, while I still care enough about my people to keep my hands from wrapping around your throat."

Soren loudly announced to the crowd, "Our Lord has secured the theatre. You can go back to your merriment." He turned, facing Cynthia, ready for his Lord's command.

"Oh, Soren. No need for such aggression. I have accomplished one part of my *evil* plan. The other I'm saving for a select few." She sneered at Pia and Asta as she brushed past them.

"I'm going to get her back for what she did," groaned Asta, looking down at her hand.

"Sister, we'll do it together." Pia's eyes flashed blue.

When Karian entered the bedroom, he saw Bea sitting on the edge of the bed with her head lowered. He knew that she'd been crying. The tears hung in the close air like shivers of glass ready to pierce his heart. His feet numbly strode towards her at a pace where time stood still, and every lie became entwined with his dark fate. Karian held out his arms, the palms of his hands facing upwards in total surrender. Slowly, he dropped to his knees. "Forgive me."

She lifted her head, and he saw her eyes full of deep wounding which needed no words to understand. His heart sank at receiving the silent message, and a rushed mix of fear and self-loathing raced through his veins. He looked down at the floor to hide what he considered his greatest weakness… failure to be honest.

Bea tenderly placed her hand under his chin and lifted his gaze to meet hers. "You didn't tell me about Anathon, and I understand why, but, please, no more." Her voice was strained. "No more pretending. No more regret…you forget, Karian, I *know* what it feels like to love someone that will never love you in the way that you need. So, *please*, promise, no more lies, no more deceit… *you* love Alithia, and need to find her through me. I love Anathon, and need to forget him through you." Tears fell from her eyes as she continued to speak. "Can we not just see each other for who *we* really are?" She placed her hand upon his cheek, and he pressed his face hard against it. "I promise." His hand reached for Bea's, and his fingertips swept over hers and, on touching, he grimaced and shook his head, refusing to believe what he saw there. "If only I could shed this skin, and be rid of the shadow that *relentlessly* torments my soul."

Bea sat on the floor beside him, entwining her fingers with his. "What shadow?"

He stared down at her hand, fighting against the avalanche of emotion building up inside of him. "*Vororbla.*" His trembling hands clenched hers tighter, and he gently kissed her knuckles. "I've been so empty…lost without you." He lifted his head, eyes staring into hers. "There is one thing that I've *never* forgotten…the goodness that fills me, when I'm with you."

She brushed her cheek against his, wiping away a tear that escaped. Her touch of tenderness after all the lies, caused him to crumble, and with his release, came hers.

They permitted the tears of raw truth to flow onto each other's skin. Karian's sobs of honesty enabled a new truce between them, and he saw, in her eyes, an acceptance of his love.

As they lay in each other's arms, each look, brought a reward of deeper understanding of what they truly wanted, and both were prepared to surrender to the fact that they needed each other to overcome their Vororbla, karma, in love.

It was the first time that he felt complete since Alithia died. He didn't have to pretend anymore. Bea had seen him at his weakest, in a way that Alithia had not. His sobs released the pain that he had held onto for so long. Hurt, regret, anger, had been the only emotions that had kept him going, until this night. He was able, finally, to just *be*. The fear and the persistent foreboding shadow were cast away by her light and forgiveness. With the torment gone, all he needed, wanted, was her love in the form of a long, warm embrace. He wished the night would never end, that they could lie in each other's arms until all healing was complete. The touch he sought was not sexual, nor did he feel his usual need to impress, it was about honesty, revealing his inner most core. He had overcome something precious this night – impatience. Time was finally was on his side.

CHAPTER 29

The Preparation

*B*ack at the safe house, Chance was wearing away the carpet with his frantic pacing. "Where is this Deisi?"

"She'll be here." Kitty was exasperated, rubbing her neck, which ached from sleeping for a few hours in the chair.

"So you said, two hours ago."

"I told you to get some sleep, she's been delayed."

"How can I sleep?"

"Okay, maybe, it was a stupid suggestion." It was going to be a long night.

Chance sat down, placing his head in his hands. "I'm losing her. I can feel it." He didn't care if Kitty knew his feelings, the waiting was driving him crazy, and he couldn't help but think the worst, as images of Karian touching her kept flashing through his mind.

Kitty sat next to him. "I wish I could do something, give you some words of comfort. I'm just no good at all this stuff...I'm sorry."

"I don't need the comfort of words, just the Deisi," he snapped.

Kitty's phone rang. "Hello...*Oh, thank goodness.* Yep, I'm coming down." Her eyes met Chance's. "She's here." Kitty shot out the door to let her in.

Chance's pacing resumed, until Kitty re-entered the room, followed by the Deisi.

His face dropped. "*Jenny?*"

"Hello, Anathon." A brief shrug, followed by a smile, caused him to glance over at Kitty for confirmation. She nodded.

"Sorry, I'm late. It's a ridiculous hour, I know, but better late than never, huh?" She winked in his direction. He was speechless. *How did he not pick up on her being the Deisi?* Saras's words of the Heaven Stone being a dying breed repeated in his mind. *Are we?* he wondered.

"Stop fretting, Anathon," Jenny interrupted his thoughts. "You'll need to remain balanced to enter the theatre undetected. Come, sit down, let's talk." The gentle Jenny from the bookshop disappeared, and an assertive Deisi had taken her place. He wasn't sure how he felt about that, but he didn't argue, too much time had been wasted already.

Jenny started explaining what was expected of him. "So you understand? It's Bea's choice either way. She can choose to stay or go of her own free will."

Reluctantly, he agreed.

"Good. Now, we need to prepare you."

"Prepare me?"

"You have to bathe, with this solution." Jenny handed him a glass bottle containing an abundance of herbs and crystals. "Stop examining it and go."

"Do I put it all in?" His eyes were still trying to make out what was in the bottle.

"In?" She laughed. "No, not *in* the water. You apply it to your body, and then lay in the bath for seven minutes. Have you got a watch?"

"I have the training, I don't need a watch," he grunted.

"Great, off you go then." She stood, hands on hips, eyebrows arched, indicating the direction of the door. He sceptically looked down at the bottle in his hand. "*This* will keep the Unseelie from seeing me?"

"I'll run through everything once you're done." Jenny's eyes gestured to the hall.

He sighed and disappeared into the bathroom.

Once he was out of earshot, Kitty asked what the solution did.

"Absolutely nothing."

Kitty sat back in her chair. "You're joking, right?"

"No, it's what I call a mental preparation. He's surely in need of it. I felt his vibe from the car. Not good."

"So, what are you going to do?"

"What a Deisi does, use the power of Seior."

Kitty gave a nod, she knew magic would be involved, and sometimes it was best to stay ignorant.

Chance marched back in. "Seven minutes completed."

"Do you feel better?" Jenny asked.

"Am I supposed to?"

"It helps." Jenny replied, while digging around in her bag.

Chance leant closer to Kitty. "Are you sure she's the Deisi?"

She kept her voice low. "Yes. Though I agree. She isn't what I expected either."

"I feel no different," he stated, looking down at himself. "I don't think this is going to work."

Jenny pulled out another bottle. "Here, drink this."

He snatched the bottle and gulped down the liquid. "Now what?"

"We wait."

"More waiting," he muttered under his breath.

Kitty offered everyone some mead.

"No, thank you, and by the way, Anathon can't have any either. It might cause a reaction."

Chance glared at Jenny.

"Do you feel any different, yet?"

"No," he grumbled.

"Hmm...maybe, I got the bottles mixed up." Jenny appeared deep in thought.

Chance looked as if he wanted to retch.

"It's okay, relax, I'm only joking." This time her smile broadened, exposing all her white teeth.

Kitty laughed, until he glared at her.

"Okay, next is the list of triple seven. This is a difficult task, do you feel ready?"

"I was ready hours ago."

Jenny pulled out a notepad and a pen. "Here you go."

He waved them around in the air. "This isn't *Seior*. Why are we wasting time?"

"I'm here to help you. If you do not wish to have my help, simply say so now, and I'll go."

He was tempted, but knew that he couldn't gain entry to the theatre without her help. So he agreed to play the silly game, and waited for her to continue.

"Write down seven things that warm your heart, seven that anger, and lastly, seven things that you would change."

He didn't see the point. "Why?"

"Now, who's wasting time?" reminded Kitty, brows raised.

"I'm not in the right frame of mind." He threw the paper and pen on the table.

"What is your present frame of mind?" Jenny asked, the fun had left her eyes.

He remained silent.

"Do you wish to continue or not?" Jenny leant down, about to grab her bag.

Kitty's head gestured over to the writing bureau in the corner. Chance gritted his teeth, grabbed the pen and paper, and sat down at the bureau. "Do I have to show you the list?"

"Not if you don't wish to," replied a nonchalant Jenny.

"Good," he mumbled, wriggling around in the chair, staring at the blank sheet before him. He tried to concentrate, but his mind kept picturing Bea with Karian. Eventually, he'd stared long and hard enough at the paper, that answering the first seven were easy, which he wrote in Lifprasira characters, a language he felt more comfortable with than human lettering. He found himself pausing many times to reflect. The list read:

Seven things that warm my heart –

1. *Bethany*
2. *My mother's name*
3. *My parents*
4. *The flower of souls*
5. *My realm*
6. *My duty*
7. *My honour*

Seven things that anger me -

1. *Him!*

2. *Saras*
3. *Theatre*
4. *This test!*
5. *Lying*
6. *The night*
7. *Myself*

Seven things I would change –

1. *His hold on her*
2. *Myself*
3. *The nights*
4. *Time*
5. *Our realm*
6. *The Court*
7. *The Order*

On completing the list, he stared at it for a while, and as he read it over, he felt strangely calm in spite of everything.

"*Now*, do you feel different, Anathon?" Jenny asked.

He smiled, realising the test was to get him to re-focus, to let the anger pass. "Very clever."

"You can keep that list," Jenny replied.

Kitty looked lost. "I don't get it, what did I miss?"

"Only a little insight to the self." Jenny replied, smiling over at Anathon.

Kitty still looked puzzled as she poured more mead. "When will he be ready to leave?"

"Oh…I think now is suitable."

A big grin appeared on his face.

CHAPTER 30

The Material Release

"*W*ouldn't it have been better to attempt this earlier?" Chance's eyes kept a steady watch across the road, towards the theatre.

"Sidhe senses are more in tune at dusk. The early hour is better for us."

"You still haven't explained how you are getting me in."

Jenny eyes fixed on Chance. "If I told you that Bea loves you, would it make a difference?"

He lowered his head feeling uncomfortable. Just hearing her name made his heart ache. "If I dared believe it." He didn't feel as if he had to hide his feelings from the Deisi. She used Seior, and would know the truth, no matter what he replied.

Jenny started to chant in Seior, the words from her lips chimed, conducting a sweet serenade. *Can you see a floor plan showing you the way?*

Chance could see Jenny's mouth still chanting and hear the sound, but she appeared to speak with two voices. It was then, he realised that she was using a form of telepathy. A detailed map appeared in his mind, and he nodded. "Yes."

Then go now, follow your heart, Anathon…remember, what you seek is seeking you.

He looked over at Jenny, still engrossed in her chant.

Go! she repeated.

He ran across the road to the front of the theatre, but halted on seeing the two burly Unseelie guards at the entrance, and slid behind a van.

All you have to do is follow the instructions given to you, no more, no less. I'll do the rest, she reminded.

He took each step towards the Unseelie with care, until one of them suddenly moved away from the door. Chance sped past, finding himself in a long, dim corridor. The Unseelie were all around him, but there was not one glance in his direction. His feet followed the directions on the mental map. His heart was beginning to pound as he got deeper into the theatre. He continued to weave through the Unseelie.

Chance stopped at an ornately-carved wooden door. He could feel her close now, his senses were going wild, stronger than any training had previously provided. He slowly placed his hand on the handle. *What will I say to her? Will she listen?* He took a deep breath in preparation of seeing her again, and opened the door. He cautiously entered the room, closing the door quietly behind him, just as Jenny instructed. His heart jumped a beat as his eyes rested on Bea sleeping in a huge bed. He took another deep breath as he felt the familiar pang of jealousy. He reminded himself that it was her choice, and no matter the outcome, he'd have to accept it. Chance made his way closer, down the side of the bed, finally taking a seat in a chair opposite Bea. She looked so peaceful, which stung a little, for he hadn't had a full night's sleep since leaving her. It seemed so long ago, now. He sat willing her to wake, hoping that she'd sense his presence, but she didn't even stir – another sting. A part of him wanted to watch her sleep, simply remembering their togetherness, but he knew time was against him.

"Bea?" His voice was a low whisper. "Bea?" He called out again, nothing. Chance ran his hands over his head, but then heard Jenny's voice – *You must hurry, their Deisi can feel my presence. Follow your heart, Anathon. What do you need to say to her, wake Bea... now!*

He went to whisper in Bea's ear, but her scent distracted him. Chance closed his eyes savouring the aroma, but being that close and not able to touch her was pure agony. He opened his eyes, lips still tight from needing to scream her name. He sighed, and then let his agonising pain travel on his words. "What you seek... *is* seeking you."

Bea murmured and he stepped back.

"*I seek you.*" His voice became louder, as did his thoughts. *Am I in your dream?*

Suddenly, she opened her eyes and they both froze as their gaze met.

There was a commotion outside the door, causing them to break their silent bond. Bea sat up, pulling the bed sheet close to her chest. Chance noticed her effort to hide the fact that she was naked underneath the covers, followed with a look of guilt. His heart sank, knowing that he was too late. He wondered if he managed to conceal his disappointment, or maybe it was disgust, he wasn't sure. He turned towards the door on hearing Karian's voice, still trying desperately to control the hurt and anger rising within.

"I always seem to be asking you the same question...Why are you here?" Bea asked, still avoiding his eyes. He knew that she was trying to disguise her embarrassment with coldness, for he would act the same way.

Karian called out her name, still trying to get in.

Chance cupped her face in his hands. Bea tried to wriggle away, but he kept his hold firm. It took a lot for him to resist the impulse of placing his lips on hers, denying Karian any further claim. "THIS..." His eyes moved briefly around the room. "Is all a lie, an illusion, keeping you spellbound. Pretty little trinkets, material objects to keep a human's interest."

"What are you talking about?" Bea struggled to release his hold.

Chance realised that he was beginning to scare her and made an effort to speak more softly. "You're a *human*, Bea. Karian is using Sidhe glamour, an easy entrapment for ...for the weak minded. *Open* your eyes."

Karian's men began kicking the door. Unaware that it was protected, sealed by Jenny's magic.

Chance pleaded. "*Please...* just open your eyes."

Bea pulled away, and ran into the bathroom, tripping on the sheet draped around her body in the process. Chance knocked on the bathroom door. "You'll need these." He held out some clothes, the ones that he recognised as hers. Bea's hand extended through a slight gap in the door, grabbed the clothing, and slammed the door, just missing his fingers. He gritted his teeth.

Suddenly, there was a loud crash as the main door fell to the floor. Jenny's protection had gone. Chance braced himself and stood in a stance as Soren bowled towards him, but Karian overtook him and ordered a retreat. He appeared strangely calm, but his eyes revealed the truth, filled with hatred. Karian looked around the empty room. "Where's Bethany?"

Chance didn't answer. His rage growing at the image stuck in his mind, of Karian's hands all over Bea.

"I'm here." She announced, exiting from the bathroom, breaking the stony silence.

Karian rushed to her side. "Did he hurt you?"

Chance's hands tensed, and began to shake on seeing his enemy so close to the woman he loved.

"No," she replied, slowly edging away from Karian.

"Bethany?" Karian reached out to her, but she pushed him away. His eyes flashed an electric blue towards Chance. "What have you done? What have you told her?"

"Only the truth," Chance replied.

Bea backed further away from Karian, towards the fallen door. Her eyes wide. "What's happening?"

Everything started to fade. The wallpaper darkened, becoming stained, and parts were torn, some pieces falling from the walls. Most of the furniture had disappeared. The sideboard, the chair, turned to dust and vanished. The grand four-poster became dull, dusty and broken. Bea reached out to touch the decorative carving, but it crumbled in her hand. She looked down at the floor. The carpet was worn too, and emitted a strong, musky smell.

Tears filled her eyes as she glanced over at Karian. "More deceit?"

He shook his head. "I wanted you to have the best that I could give. I didn't think..." He reached out.

"Don't you *dare* touch me!" Bea snapped. "Seelie, Unseelie, you're all the same, I can see that clearly now, nothing but lies." She slapped Karian, and marched over to Chance.

He turned his cheek ready to receive the same punishment.

"It's *you* who's disappointed me the most." Her damp eyes condemned him, before turning away.

Chance lowered his head. A slap would've hurt less.

Soren tried to control the crowd of Unseelies beginning to mass at the door, but Bea, fearlessly, pushed the crowd aside and disappeared down the corridor. Karian was about to follow her, but Chance stood in front of him, blocking the way. Karian nodded over to Soren, and then stared directly at Chance. "I guarantee, you shall not leave as easily as you entered." His eyes were aglow, seething with Sidhe anger.

Chance stepped up to him. "What other mind tricks did you *need* to play, to entice her into your bed?"

Karian smiled at his obvious jealously. "Do you *really* want to talk about our bedroom activities, Anathon?"

"You're missing the most important point," said Chance, his lips tightened to avoid a bombardment of abuse.

"What point is that?"

"That it wasn't real." He taunted Karian's insecurities.

Karian moved closer. "When my tongue caressed...*tasted* every part of her, it felt very real." He suddenly stumbled back as the full force of Chance's anger, a punch to the jaw, came from nowhere.

"Like the taste of that?" Chance asked as Karian landed on the floor. "Your reality check."

Karian wiped his mouth dry of blood. "I preferred the taste of Bethany," he sneered.

"Keep the memory. It isn't going to happen again," Chance spat, turning away in disgust.

Karian slowly eased himself to his feet, but it was only a distraction, while he drew a knife from his shoe, throwing it at his enemy. It swiftly glided through the air and caught the side of Chance's temple.

He glared at Karian.

"You will never have her." Karian's eyes became an opaque blue that surged with sparks.

Chance nodded, and within seconds, both men ran for the knife.

All the watching Unseelie jumped back, as they came kicking, blocking and punching their way across the room.

Chance received a sudden jolt from a punch in the throat, collapsed and gagged.

Karian used the moment to retrieve the knife from the door frame, and stood over Chance, thrusting the blade, but Chance flipped back, landing nimbly on his feet. His hands attempted blows to Karian's chest, but Karian swiped at Chance's hands with the weapon. They reached a stalemate, both out of breath. They paused, their eyes anticipating the opponent's next move.

The crowd encouraged their Lord on, especially now that he seemed to have the upper hand. Chance realised that Karian would not be satisfied without more bloodshed, that he wanted him gone, and the idea seemed to please the overzealous crowd.

Chance was planning his full attack. He didn't want to kill Karian. It was not The Heaven Stone's way. Hurting him would be enough...for now.

Karian advanced to Chance's left, then suddenly, changed direction, and hit him with the hilt of the knife in his stomach, as a warning. Chance quickly recovered, and counter-attacked, his leg lock managed to drop Karian to the ground. In a fit of embarrassment and rage, Karian threw the knife at his enemy with such force that Chance's arm swallowed the whole blade, up to the hilt. He staggered as Karian got to his feet.

Chance pulled the knife from his arm, and blood dripped onto the floor. "The time for play is over."

"Not until I say it is," smirked Karian.

Chance grimaced, before running at Karian. He slid to his knees just before impact, and delivered a powerful blow to Karian's scrotum.

The crowd went quiet.

The only sound heard was Karian groaning and gasping for breath in a heap on the floor.

Chance knelt down on one knee, next to him. "Like I said, playtime is over. You deserve no Heaven Stone conduct of fair play."

A voice shouted out from the crowd. "It was a fair fight, no Sidhe can harm him. Allow him to leave."

Chance turned around and saw Cynthia, the Unseelie Deisi, gesturing safe passage.

He glanced down at Karian. "We'll settle this in Coldfall, Seelie against Unseelie. I'll be in touch." He threw the knife at Karian's face, deliberately catching his temple. "Sons of Kings shouldn't play with sharp toys," he muttered, before walking towards the door.

The crowd backed out of his way.

Chance tilted his head with respect in Cynthia's direction, and continued his walk down the corridor. His arm was throbbing, but he would not permit them to see his pain.

The Unseelie muttered and snarled abuse as he passed. Their eyes an opaque, electric blue. The corridor alight, lined with angry Sidhe. He ignored them, and before exiting the theatre, he shouted, "Until our meet in Coldfall."

Soren suddenly appeared in front of him. Chance wasn't in the mood for more delay, and with one jab of his hand to Soren's throat, and another to his temple. Karian's aide fell, hard, to the floor.

When Chance descended the steps of the theatre, he saw a flash of headlights down the road.

Once he got closer, he saw that it was Kitty. "Where's Jenny?"

"She took Bea home. Oh, my goodness, look at you." She noticed the fresh blood streaming through his shirt.

He climbed in the car. "It stings less than Bea's tongue."

Kitty threw her scarf at him. "Please. Don't bleed over the car, there's nothing worse than trying to get blood out of fabric." She reached for her bag. "I have some healing compound in here. I was hoping it wouldn't be needed, that everything would be handled peacefully…silly I know." She handed him the bottle. "What happened?"

"Karian. I need to see Bea."

"I can't take you."

"Then, I'll get out and walk." He reached for the door handle.

"Wait." She stopped him. "You can't walk anywhere in that condition. Let's go home first, give you some time to heal."

"Will you take me to see Bea or not?"

Back at the theatre, Karian shouted at everyone to get out. His eyes raw with rage, and filled with tears of humiliation and frustration. The last Sidhe that he bellowed at was the one informing him of Soren lying flat out on the floor, by the entrance. Karian slammed the door to his study.

He sat on the bed, enervated. He'd lost his Alithia, *again*. He did not hear the light footsteps of his old consort, the Deisi, Cynthia, entering the room. Her eyes burned into his back.

Karian felt the spite in the room and lifted his head a little. "I told everyone to get out. That includes you." His was voice bitter, full of contempt.

"You forget, Karian, *I'm* not everyone."

She rested her hand upon his shoulder, but he brushed it off with distaste. "Leave me, I don't need your gloating."

"You want to be left alone to lick your wounds, in private? Only now do you realise that your Seelie human does not love you. All your dreams, your hopes of being together, dissipate into shadow." She faded out her voice to emphasize the distance of shattered dreams.

He turned to face her, his eyes surged. "Just as I have never wanted to say that I loved you." His tone icy cold, but she did not recoil from its stormy blast.

"Your *agony* is only just beginning, Karian, son of the King. You will never again hold your *dear* Alithia."

"Leave me... now!" His eyes flashed, causing her to retreat a few steps, but her tongue remained tart. "You sad, stupid, Unseelie prince. Yes, I loved you and you threw that love away, for what? The inner deprivation that now awaits you. Alithia is not your twin flame...she never was. You're blinded by a self-obsessed need, just like your father, and, like him, you will wear a fool's crown."

Karian flew from the bed and pinned her up against the wall, his hand pressed hard against her throat. "I warned you that your sharp tongue would get you into trouble, Deisi." His eyes continued to glow with Sidhe wrath. "I will not warn you again, leave." He released her.

Cynthia backed away, choking between words. "It doesn't matter whether or not you believe my words. She has found her twin in Anathon." She paused, sensing something. "But you know that already don't you?" She gasped at the image in her mind. "Of course, when you touched her fingertips, the Siarthia, the library, permitted you a glimpse didn't it?"

"Get out!" he yelled, trying to stop himself from ripping her to shreds.

"Oh, Karian, you are full of surprises. If I wasn't so vengeful I might've even felt a slight pity for you." She laughed, and it echoed throughout the room. "But I think there is something that you didn't see, My Lord. Your enemy's seed will soon be in her womb, I've seen it...What a stupid Unseelie you are."

Karian charged at her, but Cynthia used her Seior for invisibility.

"You lie!" He raged around the room, her laughter drove him crazy.

Soren came running in. He watched as Karian seethed at the emptiness around him. "My Lord?"

Karian ignored him. Cynthia's laughter had stopped, and he realised that she had gone.

"My Lord?"

"It would seem Vororbla and I are old friends once more...Now let me be." Karian sat down at the desk, his arms stretched out in front of him, fists clenched. His eyes refusing the release of tears in front of Soren, and not one sound escaped him during the internal fight.

Soren retreated to the door, looked back at his Lord, whose face wholly revealed his growing turmoil. The stench of regret began to seep into every crevice of the room.

Soren tilted his head while closing the door, but as walked away, the loud cry of his Lord's despair echoed through the theatre.

CHAPTER 31

Weakness in Me

Jenny took Bea home, initially acting surprised at seeing her wandering the streets, with no shoes on, as had many passers-by. Bea simply stated that they gave her blisters and, in a mad fit of frustration, had thrown them in the bin. Jenny told her that she had been visiting relatives in the area, a few streets away from the theatre, and accepted Bea's apology for not wanting company.

Bea sat in the kitchen, drinking tea. She longed for everything to be as it once was before Chance and Karian had entered her life. She'd wanted change, and now that her life had taken a different path, she had no choice but to accept it. Her inner wall, her heart's invisible shield, stubbornly reinforced itself at the thought. The wall had its drawbacks, for even though it refused to let anything penetrate, in the same way, it refused to let any of the pain out. The only way for the hurt to be released would be to let the wall fall.

She shook her head. *I won't let my guard down. I will not be hurt again.*

The expression on Chance's face refused to leave her. Her gut turned over repeatedly, remembering the look in his eyes as he noticed that she was naked under the sheets, the disgust so evident. He'd already judged her, *he*…the one that told the biggest lie of all. She slammed her cup down as the guilt of sleeping with Karian coursed through her veins. *For god's sake, get a grip. He lied, they both lied.*

Her thoughts drifted to the relief she felt on leaving the theatre, leaving Karian and his mind tricks, after everything they'd said. There were still more questions. *Did he make me want him?* She ran her hands down her face at the thought of him touching her. *What have I done?* A sense of betrayal brought the guilt flooding back.

"It's not your fault." A voice broke the silence.

Bea nearly fell off her chair, Chance stood in the doorway of the kitchen, his face bloody and bruised. Then, her eyes caught sight of the fresh, blood seeping down his arm. She gasped, eyes wide. "Kari?"

"He was alive when I left him," he mumbled.

"I didn't mean..." She sighed. *What was the point in trying to explain?* "How did you get in?"

He put his key on the table, and Bea remembered, she hadn't asked for its return.

"I had to see you... one last time," he said.

Bea felt her heart beating at her inner wall, but refused to acknowledge it. "In that condition?"

"It looks worse than it is." He winced, as his wound released more blood.

"Sit down." She pulled out a chair. "Where's Kitty?"

"She dropped me off, and gave me this." He pulled out the medicine bottle.

She remembered it from the farmhouse, and prepared the mixture in silence. She wondered why he made a point of saying goodbye, had they all not gone through enough to last them a lifetime? But still, even with all the craziness, she couldn't turn him away, not like this. She asked the void inside if her Vororbla had become a haunting shadow chasing her too. Two men, three hearts, caught within the invisible web of lies.

She watched as Chance struggled to remove his shirt, and helped him. She gasped when she saw the gaping wound the blade had left.

He removed the mixture from her hand. "It's alright. I'll do it."

His vulnerability had made her defences weaken, but she fought every ounce of feeling. He began to spread the mixture over his arm, and gritted his teeth when placing the mix in the open wound, dropping the bottle from his hand. He groaned, and gripped the table.

Bea reacted without thinking, and ran over to him. He whimpered.

She lifted his face to hers, but quickly released her hold when she saw his eyes. They'd become an opaque mass of glowing blue, and as she stood in shock staring at them, they began to change. The opaqueness disappeared first, and then the electric blue simmered and faded away. "What just happened to your eyes?"

"When we are in pain, or get angry... they change."

She stepped further back. "Yet another thing I didn't know."

"You don't remember, as Alithia, Sidhe's eyes changing?"

"No."

"Yet, you remember *him?*" His voice was low, but she heard the words.

"Like you remember your pretend wife!" she snapped, turning away.

She didn't see him cringe. "I didn't want to lie to you."

"Oh, and what about the message, the one you gave Saras in front of me, in this very kitchen? So brilliantly executed... for a novice."

"I had no choice."

"Why are you really here?" She leant against the side, arms crossed in front of her.

"I had to see you again."

"To say goodbye..." She nodded, realising.

He said nothing, he didn't have to. She felt his leaving the moment he came in. "I don't want to argue anymore. I just...I can't do this anymore, none of it." She tried to stay strong, to make sense of why she still had feelings for him after everything that had happened.

"Do you love him?"

Hearing him ask both angered and hurt, more than she wanted to admit, but she knew that he feared the answer. He looked scared, but she had to be honest for both their sakes. "Yes."

He winced and his whole body tensed.

"You lied to me, and I can't tell which emotion is real anymore." She placed her hand over her mouth to muffle a sob. "All I wanted was to love you." She still did, but something inside wouldn't allow her to say it.

"I know it's my fault...I...you thought that I betrayed you." He looked straight at her, struggling to speak. "I have never felt such a loss, *Bethany*... as when I saw you in his bed."

Her tears started to fall at seeing his. "I thought..." she broke off. "All this might not have happened if you'd just... been honest with me...Why is it the simplest things, like love, are the hardest to sustain?"

He cleared his throat. "Then, I'll be honest now. Everything I thought was important means nothing...The Order, The Court...*nothing* without you." He bravely reached out to her. "I know that it's too late, and I'm sorry."

Bea slowly walked over and held his hand. He wrapped his unwounded arm around her waist and squeezed tightly, burying his face in her chest. "I lied to you, and that will *always* be my biggest regret."

She cradled into him, staring into the air. "And so this is to be our goodbye."

It was still early when Bea climbed from the bed, leaving Chance peacefully sleeping. She preserved his image in her mind, as she quietly got dressed. She knew that she shouldn't have slept with him, but it felt right. *How do you keep fighting yourself? Deny your soul the need to say goodbye?* His touch, his kiss, had been as tender as the first time he stayed. Every caress was a gift of parting. They shared in each other's sadness, both regretting that it had come to this, but had to be strong and go their separate ways.

It was time to listen to the quiet voice within, the one that whispers to her, when she's alone. No matter how much it hurt. It was time to move on, to stop being scared – to trust that she was strong enough to continue, alone.

She sat down in the kitchen, staring down at a pen and paper.

Writing a letter of goodbye wasn't easy. She loved Chance, Karian too, and the only way forward was to let them both go. She hated herself for not being able to choose between them. It was the sort of situation that you only read of in agony-aunt columns, not something that happens in reality, but then, nothing of these last months was a normal reality.

She felt a different connection with each Sidhe, and wondered how and when she had become so lost in her own emotions. *Was it a fault in her? Was it down to Vororbla? Why did she find it so hard to turn either away?* Both had lied to her, both had wormed their way into her heart, and she was breaking under the strain of their love…but not anymore.

She wiped her tears away with the back of her hand, picked up the pen and wrote the first line.

As I write, you sleep.

My hand fluidly moves across the page, for it appears to know before I of what to write. I was afraid to keep my eyes closed lying next to you, for fear of never wanting to leave.

This heart does not readily meet the loss of you within the darkness, again. No part of me regrets loving you, nor you loving me, but I feel we both have untold stories yet to tell. Why else would Vororbla place so much difficulty between our love?

The veil that drifts between our two worlds, speaks to us in half-truths, but know that I shall wait for the elusive veil to part once more, and one day, I will join you again upon the hill of Calageata, amongst a carpet of purple flowers. I only hope that I am able to find you, and that the mist does not blur my vision. Keep the light in your heart bright, so that I might see it clearly through the veils that mist our two worlds.

For what I seek, seeks me… and what you seek, seeks you.

I love you eternally, goodbye.
Bethany xxx

Creeping back into the bedroom, she laid the folded letter next to Chance, and crept back out.

Chance opened his eyes. He'd been awake the whole time. His hand reached for her letter, but he did not open it, instead he lay staring, twirling it between his fingers. He heard the door of the shop close, and the little bell prolonged the declaration of her departure. Chance stared over at the window, wondering when she would find the note that he'd slipped in the front of her bag. He closed his eyes, basking in her scent that still lingered on the pillow beside him. An overwhelming forlornness started to smother him, and he turned and snuggled into the pillow, his hands clenched knowing that he would never hold her again.

CHAPTER 32

Talk of Change

𝓑ea waited near the alley by the shop for Jenny to pick her up. Her heart pounded at the thought of Chance discovering her absence too early, and she texted Jenny to hurry. After a few minutes she received a text. Jenny was waiting around the corner. Bea glanced up at the window where she knew he lay, and whispered goodbye.

"You okay?" Jenny asked as Bea climbed in the car.

She nodded, avoiding Jenny's inquisitive stare. "Yep."

"Sure?"

"I just needed to get away for a bit. Sorry it's so early." Bea put on a brave face.

"Like I said, anytime." Jenny started up the car.

After a silent journey, the car pulled up in a beautiful, tree-lined street, outside a large Victorian house.

"My humble abode." She was welcomed with a huge smile.

Far from humble, thought Bea, as she stared up at the impressive façade. "Is it converted?"

"No." Jenny laughed, beckoning her up the steps.

Two enormous black doors greeted them, which were made even grander, if possible, by their polished gold fittings.

"Is that what I think it is?" Bea pointed to the door

knocker, taking a closer look at what seemed to be a gold fox, its tail curling round to form a circle as the knocker.

"It is. Do you like it?"

"It's great."

Jenny gestured her in.

On entering the wide entrance hall, Bea's eyes widened at the lavishness. Skilfully draped curtains hung above the doors and windows. Beautiful, large, ornately framed pictures adorned every wall. "Your home is…incredible."

"Thank you." Jenny guided her into the living room.

The high ceilings and original sash windows were the first thing Bea noticed. Then, her eyes became drawn to a deep-purple, velvet chaise longue, which proudly sat in a nook filled with books. Bea smiled.

"I thought you'd like that space."

"Do you mind?" Bea pointed over to the books.

"Not at all, make yourself comfortable. I'll get the kettle on."

Bea looked around the room again in awe, before going to investigate Jenny's reading material. "I didn't realise that you loved the classics." She shouted out, while her fingers ran over the vast array of books. The familiarity made her feel comfortable. A book suddenly caught her eye and she pulled it from the shelf and smiled. "The Coming of the Fairies, by Sir Arthur Conan Doyle."

Jenny came in with two mugs of tea. "Have you read it?"

"My mother used to read it to me. You're aware this is a first edition."

"Yes…A lot of the books were already here when I moved in. I haven't touched the place really, just a few bits here and there. Come, there's a something I want to share with you."

"What's that smell?" Bea asked, as a strong aroma filled the room. "Is it joss sticks?"

"Yes, Frankincense and Myrrh, is it too much? I know some people don't like them."

"No...no I like it." She didn't bother mentioning that her mum used to burn the same incense. It felt homely, but odd that the habits of someone so young would evoke fond memories of the past.

"Are you ready?"

Bea nodded. Jenny made a strange noise and a rather odd-looking fox appeared from behind a chair. The way it had responded to Jenny's call was astounding. The cute, tiny fox now sat in front of her, rubbing its head against her leg.

"It's alright, you can stroke him. He's quite friendly. I know it's a little strange. I usually keep quiet about our little friendship."

"Does she have a name?"

"He does, it's Fez."

"Oh, *she's* a boy. He doesn't look like a normal fox. Will he grow into his ears?"

"He's a Fennec, means fox in Arabic. A species called Zerda. Cute, isn't he?"

"He is." Bea stroked behind his ears. "Hello Fez. How were you introduced?"

"I found him as a cub, starving to death, bless him. So, I brought him home, he ended up staying. I managed to give him a bath, and he slept above my head to keep warm. His tail kept falling down by the side of my face. It reminded me of wearing a Fez, the name stuck."

"That's a lovely story. I must admit, I've never seen a pet fox."

"Oh, he's not my pet. Fez is a dear friend, who chooses to keep company with me.

So, what did you feel the need to escape from?"

Bea was taken aback by Jenny's forthrightness. "Emotional turmoil, you know, crazy life stuff."

"Anathon?"

Bea's smile vanished, stunned at hearing Chances real name. "Wh...What did you say?"

"Anathon, you were with him last night, after leaving the theatre." Jenny continued as if nothing was unusual about her statement.

Bea slowly edged away from the sofa. "How do you know that?"

"*Please,* don't be alarmed. I've wanted to tell you for a while, but the time was never right. Yes, I'm Jenny, but... I'm also the Seelie Deisi."

Bea could hardly speak. "What?"

"A type of witch, like Cynthia, I really hate that word by the way."

Bea stared at her in amazement. "You were lying to me, all this time?" The warm, homely feeling quickly disappeared. "Is no-one trustworthy?" She'd heard enough and stormed out the room, heading towards the front door.

Jenny ran after her. "Bea, I'm sorry... I had to tell you. I never lied. I just...just didn't tell you everything."

"Everything. Oh, the insignificant part, that you are one of them. I don't believe this." Her hands reached to open the front door.

"You're pregnant."

Jenny's words kept her feet from going any further.

"I'm a Deisi, Bea. I was sent here to guide you, to keep you safe. That's why I came to the shop, so that I could be close when you needed my help." She spoke more softly.

"Is that what Deisi's do? Snoop and betray?" Bea shook her head. "And I'm not pregnant."

"I didn't want to tell you like this. Being a Deisi, I immediately picked up on the baby's presence. I want to help you."

Bea stood motionless. Her heart somehow knew that Jenny's words were true. "I can't trust anyone."

"You can trust *me*. I gave safe passage to Chance, so that he could get you out of the theatre. I was also there the night you ran out of the theatre and collapsed in the rain. You were dazed. I took you home and put you into bed. I was here when you went to the farmhouse, keeping the shop open so that you would have some peace from all of this. I was there the day those teenage girls, those horrid bullies, followed you home from school. One of them suddenly fell over? It was because of my well positioned foot. Bea, I have always been there. You *can* trust me."

She gulped, listening to Jenny speak of more things that no-one else knew. Bea slumped on a chair beside the main door. Unconsciously, her hand remained on the door handle. "Who are you?"

"I was a friend to your mother, Ellen. I look younger than my true age. My name then was Marlene."

Bea vaguely remembered a red-haired woman named Marlene that used to babysit her. She could see the resemblance now and released her grip of the door handle. "I don't want to hear anymore, *please stop.*"

Jenny moved closer, kneeling down in front of her. "I'm a friend. I made a promise a long time ago to Ellen that I would watch over you. *Please*, don't be afraid of me. I'm here to help you in any way I can."

"I'm carrying Kari's child." Bea let her anguish fall in the form of tears. Just as she thought she'd escaped…The Sidhe, Vororbla – had pulled her back in. Bea felt Jenny's hand on hers, with the words 'It'll be alright.' and she pulled away. "How? How will any of this be alright? You should've told me who you were sooner." Bea stood up about to open the door.

"*Please.* This is the safest place for you and the baby. No-one knows where you are. Stay and rest. Give yourself some time to think…I'll put the kettle on."

Bea's hand paused on the door handle. Jenny was right. Chance might still be at the shop, and with Liza away, where else was there to go. Her hand slumped to her side, and she made her way back to the living room.

"How are you feeling?" Jenny sheepishly asked, entering the living room with hot refreshments.

"Numb."

"This might help." Jenny passed her a cup of herbal tea.

Fez sat beside Bea.

"He likes you," chirped Jenny. "It's not often he meets someone new."

"You mean a guest that breaks down?" Bea forced a smile. "I don't know what to do. I thought I had time to sort my head out, but now…When did you last see my Mum, *Ellen*?"

"Shortly after she dropped you at the bookshop as a child."

"Were you with her…when she died?"

"No, but I know that it was the hardest thing she ever had to do, leaving you with your uncle. Ellen needed to know that you were safe. You were *everything* to her, Bea."

"What would she need to keep me safe from?"

"Pain…the pain of you seeing her ill. She thought that she was protecting you."

"And you were there to protect the soul of Alithia in Ellen's child."

"Initially…yes." She admitted.

"Who sent you?"

"Queen Eliseis, the members of The Heaven Stone notify her of everything."

"What does she want from me?"

"To know that you're protected."

"That Alithia is protected." Bea corrected.

"*No*, you're the next stage of Alithia, and Eliseis is fully aware of that fact. She is a good Sidhe, and is consoled that her daughter has passed over."

"So why protect me? A human? Does Eliseis want me to return to your realm and take Alithia's place?"

"Not if it's not what you wish. Alithia was not meant to leave her realm so soon, her soul waits for rebirth in our realm, not here. But it's your choice whether or not you return, not ours…but you would be most welcome."

"Did…did you tell her of my condition?"

"No…I'm here to help you, not inform Eliseis of your private being. I receive certain knowledge…" Jenny shrugged.

"As to whether I want it or not is another matter, but I promise not to tell anyone unless it is what you wish. Try not worry, Kitty is doing all she can, too."

"Kitty? Does she know?"

"No. She's dealing with Saras."

"I don't like that Seelie."

"Not many do, you have good taste. Do you want Kitty to know? About the baby?"

"I've always preferred truth over deceit. Though I'm not sure I'll be able to tell her."

"Would it be easier if I did?"

"I doubt if it matters who she hears it from, the shock will be the same." Bea couldn't imagine telling her that she was pregnant by Karian, and changed the subject. "How did Chance take the news of you being a Deisi?"

"It took him quite by surprise. You should've seen the expression on his face. He said that I was bossy."

"I wonder where he could've got that idea from."

"Exactly what I thought... Bea, there is someone that I would love you to meet."

"Who?"

"A human, named Jonathan, he's visiting this realm."

"From your realm? I thought that humans didn't know of the Sidhe?"

"You're mostly right, but in Jonathan's case it was permitted. It's a long story, and not mine to tell. Maybe he'll entertain you with the tale tomorrow. A few humans do visit our realm, sometimes to stay, but that hasn't happened for a very long time. Jonathan has lived in our realm for ...well, quite a while, but I think he gets a little homesick from time to time. I wanted to invite him over before he returns."

"I'd like that. I hope he doesn't mind a lot of questions, talking with another human about the Sidhe will be enlightening. No offence."

"None taken. So, you're staying a while?"

"I don't know. My head's all over the place."

"Take as long as you need. Meanwhile, have your pick of rooms. If you want, I'll get Kitty to come and keep you company while I open the shop. She can bring some bits over if you scribble down a list of what you need."

"No. Leave the shop closed."

"Closed?"

"I'm going to sell it."

"Sell the shop? When did you decide?"

"When you told me that I was pregnant."

"We could help, financially."

Bea shook her head. "No, thank you. I'd rather sell, start again somewhere else."

"Perhaps you need some time to think about it? It's your home, and I know you've stayed there because of love, not money. Do you want to talk, about Chance or Karian?"

Bea looked down at her hands, twiddling her fingers. *What was there left to say?*

"I know that you love him, Karian too." She placed her hand on Bea's.

"It's alright, Jen." She moved her hand, tired of pity. "I made up my mind before coming here, to let them go. It's the best thing for us all…breaking away."

"No Sidhe?"

"No Sidhe, I plan to sell up and move away. Start afresh...I wanted change, now I have it."

"Then, Kitty and I will help you."

"Thank you, Jen...I can't risk anyone else finding out."

Jenny nodded, in agreement.

CHAPTER 33

A Stranger, a Conversation, and Tea

It had been a long night. Bea tossed and turned as her choices repeatedly collided, like two whirling tornados, each representing a person she loved. Maybe, if it hadn't have been for Karian's deception she might have tried to love him, even though her heart was filled with Chance. She desperately tried to force away any thoughts of him, feeling physically sick at imagining his repugnance at finding out she carried his enemy's, Karian's, child. She was aware that her heart would never be the same, and Karian's words haunted with a bitterness — *Vororbla becomes the shadow that forever haunts.* As she lay awake, her feelings drifted to those of regret. Regret at not picking up her bag before leaving the farmhouse with her contraceptives in, regret at not refusing Karian at the theatre.

She'd never forgotten to take her pill, not once. Every day, at 6.30 pm, that little pill was sipped down with a small glass of water, done, gone. She sighed. *What is the point of beating myself up now?*

She refocused on a more positive mental imagery — moving away. Where would she go?

She closed her eyes and pictured a place that brought her peace. She was back in Devon, her original home. The narrow streets and quaint, different-coloured cottages filled her mind. Hanging baskets outside nearly every home. The Gulls screeched and harassed tourists for food. Suddenly, she was on the beach, sand beneath her feet. She wiggled her toes, and looked out towards the sea. The sun was setting. The water was calm and shimmered with colours reflected from the orange sunset. She breathed in, and slowly exhaled. How beautifully silent and still this world was. She'd forgotten how the simple things brought peace. The blandness that she used to complain about, and always wanted to change, was now what she most longed for, removed from the emotional chaos that currently surrounded her. At least there were no more lies. Every truth was out and aired, and she was grateful for that.

Climbing out of bed, she noticed the smudged mascara on her pillow, and quickly flipped it over not wanting to be reminded of last night's sadness. She diverted her thoughts to meeting Jonathan and Kitty. It'd been a while since she'd last seen Kitty. She missed her and the only human left in her life, Liza. Their calls were less frequent these days, due to Liza's work commitments, and she was glad in part. Liza would've noticed that something was terribly wrong. She needed to talk more than ever with her oldest and dearest friend, but knew that she couldn't open up, even to her. She could barely believe everything herself. Her life had become a bizarre mix of incredible events. How would she even begin to explain to someone...human? But the most important reason of all, she didn't want her put in danger.

Bea followed the smell of something cooking downstairs.

"Hi Bea, tea on the table, fry-up on its way." Jenny beamed from the stove.

Bea's mouth watered. "What time is Jonathan coming?"

"In about an hour." Jenny served the food onto two plates.

Bea was alarmed. "An hour...So early?"

"Early? It's four o'clock."

"What?" Bea looked up at the clock on the wall.

"I thought you needed the sleep, it's been a long twenty-four hours."

Tactful, thought Bea.

"Here you go." Jenny put the plate of breakfast in front of her.

"Thank you."

"My pleasure, Kitty said she'll be here this evening."

"Good." Bea tucked in. "Yum...this is great." She was hungrier than she thought.

"The Seior is in the cooking." Jenny joined her at the table.

The saying reminded Bea of Elly, and the picture of her smiling eyes warmed her a little. "Magic?"

Jenny nodded. "A good chant or two has to be muttered while you cook."

"Sometimes, I say a word or two when I cook, too." Bea laughed, remembering the time that she'd managed to make boiled eggs explode over the ceiling.

"I must admit your cooking skills do precede you, by word of Kitty."

"Chance told her how bad I was, huh?"

Jenny nodded, devouring another forkful of food.

Bea sat in the reading nook with the fairy tale of the Cottingley girls propped on her lap, waiting for Jonathan. She was enjoying the memory of reading with her mother when the bell chimed. She felt strangely nervous when Jenny scurried off the answer the door, and heard the muffled sound of them talking before they eventually entered the lounge.

"Permit me to introduce Jonathan, Jonathan *this* is Bea."

Bea observed his shy, earthy brown eyes, half-hidden by his long, mousey fringe which had dropped over his face as he moved forward to greet her. He appeared to be in his early forties, looked tired, perhaps from his travels. His clothing appeared dated, a white, stiff-collared shirt, with a black cravat.

Jonathan extended his hand. "It is such a pleasure to finally meet you, Bea. My apologies, would you prefer Bethany?" He appeared nervous.

"No, Bea's fine. It's nice to meet you, too. Jenny told me that you are visiting?"

He smiled, still jittery. "It is my first return for many years, and it feels rather strange, but still, quite delightful."

Jenny disappeared, declaring that she was making tea.

"When did you return?" Bea didn't know what to do with her hands and automatically crossed her arms in front of her, but realised that the action could be misconstrued as defensive, and quickly let them fall to her side.

"Yesterday." His eyes scanned the room.

"Oh. I thought you'd been here longer."

"You did?" He looked puzzled.

"Yes, I thought Jenny meant that you were in a hurry to get home, having being here a while."

"One day is while enough."

"One day?" She was surprised.

"Yes, I return home tomorrow."

Why would a human call the Sidhe realm home? she did not voice her curiosity. "Oh, well, I can see why Jenny wanted to see you with some urgency, I mean, before your return." His jitters began to make her feel a little awkward too.

There was an uncomfortable silence until Jenny returned, holding a tray of tea. She looked at Jonathan. "In here or the study?"

"The study please, is that alright with you, Bea?"

"Erm, yes." She felt like a child in his presence, probably due to his old-fashioned manner, just like her uncle's.

"Please, join me." He extended his arm, and Bea courteously placed her arm in his.

Once they entered, Jenny dismissed herself. Bea's eyes were begging her to stay, but her plea was ignored.

"If you would be so kind and sit with me?" Jonathan gestured towards a chair.

"Of course, shall I pour the tea?"

"Thank you." Jonathan still seemed on edge, tapping his hands lightly against the desk.

He eventually settled in a large, orange leather chair next to the desk. "Is there anything you wish to ask, about the Sidhe? You must have many questions?"

She handed Jonathan his tea and sat opposite him. "There're so many, I've probably forgotten the most important ones." She laughed, hesitantly.

"Then, start with the one that enters your head first." He appeared more relaxed.

She unconsciously scratched her head, making him smile. "Are there any humans, well, apart from you, in the Sidhe realm? I mean, are there many?" *What's wrong with me?* thought Bea.

"Many, no, but some, yes." He took a sip of tea.

"Whose side are they on?"

"Whose side? We humans are tolerated and we are not expected to get involved, or *choose* sides. To us, one Sidhe is no better than the other."

"I think I've discovered that, too."

"Really?" He looked curious.

She didn't wish to explain how and asked, "Why did you go to their realm?"

"To escape this one." His reply was quick, too quick.

Bea was not put off by his evasiveness. "But *why* did you wish to escape?"

"A better question. I went in search of new knowledge."

"Didn't you miss being here? Home?"

Jonathan's jaw twitched and his eyes drifted from her stare. "I had to relinquish *all* connections. The Sidhe invitation... did not extend further than myself."

"Didn't you have a wife? A family? Someone that'd miss you? Ask questions?"

Jonathan wiggled in his chair, taking another sip of tea before answering. "I did, but as I say, I had to relinquish all ties. I was..." He loosened his collar a little. "I loved someone...but it was important that I learnt more of this new realm and its people. So, I chose knowledge over love."

She found it hard to comprehend, leaving someone you love for knowledge. "That's sad. Maybe you did not love her as much as you thought." Bea bit her lip, shocked that the words escaped.

Jonathan looked straight into her eyes. "Don't misunderstand me, I loved her, I have never stopped." He lowered his gaze.

"So, you do regret leaving her?"

"Regret, no, but I would have done things differently."

"Did you ever return, to see the woman you loved?" She couldn't understand why she was hounding the stranger.

"I did, but…it was not as I…as I hoped."

Bea heard a strain in his voice, and released him from the subject. On asking her next question, she realised why she had quizzed Jonathan on leaving his love so freely. She did not have that choice. It was made for her. "Do the Sidhe and humans ever fall in love?"

Jonathan look shocked at the question. "It is frowned upon. *However*, if they are not of the Court, it could possibly be, shall we say, overlooked."

"What if someone of the Court falls in love with a human?"

"It has never happened to my knowledge." He took another sip of tea.

"Never?"

"Humans are the minority in the Sidhe realm. We are only permitted at Court by invitation. So, the likelihood of that ever happening is more or less non-existent."

"Sounds more like a prison," she mumbled, looking down at her hands.

"My dear…it is the most wondrous place that you could ever imagine. No human form of art or poetic words could ever capture its most absolute, marvellously serene environment. No, Bea, it is not a prison, more a type of Arcadia."

"But the war?"

"Ah, yes...the war. It is kept far from the Courtly houses. There has not been a significant battle in quite some time, although a few minor conflicts do still take place. The war is more a bitterness that fills their hearts now. They need to realise that a division of a race weakens it, a worrying time indeed. The abductions of the past could take place again."

"Abductions?" Bea was alarmed.

"You have not researched Sidhe lore?" He looked surprised.

Bea felt ignorant as she shook her head.

"In ancient times, babies were taken from their cribs, young women from their homes, men too. Humans blamed the Sidhe, sometimes rightly so, often not. It was usually done out of desperation, you understand...to further their existence. Though the Court never became involved in human...relationships." He cleared his throat.

"That's awful, I'm not sure I want to hear more."

"But you must...to understand. The war is a relatively recent divide, and can cause *such* desperation as their numbers decrease. A member of one Court not permitted to be with someone of the other Court. Occasional allowances at such times could be made, such as pairing with someone not of the royal line, but *never* a human. Their race has been endangered more than once, which in turn affects the lineage. Maybe it is again, I don't know."

Bea sat in silence. That might explain the reason for Chance's reluctance to get involved, he said that she would be classed as Alithia, not Bea. She still wasn't happy about hearing of kidnapping, whatever the reason.

Jonathan must've noticed the dismay on her face. "What would humans do if faced with extinction? They would do absolutely anything to ensure their survival. That's why we have lasted this long."

She couldn't argue with that. "From what you say, the Courtly ruling system appears as outdated as it would here. Everyone should be equal, none higher or lower."

"You're quite right, of course, but how would this change develop? Especially now, with the division of the Sidhe Court."

"The elementals?" She was grasping at straws.

"They are the guardians of souls, and serve a higher purpose."

She disagreed. "A higher purpose? Higher than a race on the brink of self-destruction?"

"How long have humans been self-destructive? Do you see any Aos Si or Sindria here? Their connection with Earth began long before our presence. Legends around the world have recorded our meetings with them, all referred to as myths. You must read more, Bethany. Piece together what has been misplaced."

She briefly looked down at the tattoo on her arm. "Why did the Sindria leave our world?"

"The world was changing. The remnants of their teachings are still all around, if you care to look. They showed us the way forward, but later, the people they taught were penalised. The Sindria are not aggressive beings, so they simply left. They hoped we would be compensated by leaving the people of the mounds, the Sidhe."

"Why did they come here at all?"

Jonathan was matter of fact. "To teach us that eventually we become an energy requiring no form."

Bea's eyes widened. "Do other worlds exist that require no form?"

"They do indeed, they are made of the purest light... all energy. The Heaven Stone ensures the journey for these energies is as it should be, in keeping with the universal balance. The cycle of life contains equal amounts of both matter and non-matter. One cannot exist without the other...a marrying at the time of creation. In death the two separate until a natural, new, union is made."

"Reincarnation...*like Alithia?*"

"Yes, a unique blending of biological and spiritual. The unseen, universal language is written everywhere around us, within us. Though, Alithia's path changed, she became lost in her passing, and returned to a light within you."

"It's quite a lot to take in."

"I don't mean to over-complicate, but it is quite difficult to combine the complexities of the Heaven Stone and the Sindria into one simple explanation."

She sat on the edge of her seat. "So, our fingerprints are a part of this universal language?"

Jonathan looked surprised. "You know of the fingerprint connection?"

"Anna told me."

"I see, good, very good."

"Is there a universal place that *all* souls return to? I mean do we all return to the same place when we die?"

"Of course, there is only one source, the Sidhe call it

Calageata, the home of the Sindria. There is a sacred area in their world where a well is said to reside. Its cosmic water is…shall we simply say, *magical*. The Elders say that the well leads to the heavens, where *all* souls complete their journey."

"Why did Alithia not return to Calageata, the source?"

"Due to the way she met her demise, caught between two worlds."

"What happens once a soul does return?"

"They make the decisions about their future and eventually, if they wish, return to a material form. The journey, their previous life is recorded, as are the lessons they learned, as too are the lessons they still need to learn. A lot depends upon our karma."

"Our Vororbla?"

"Yes. I take it Anathon informed you?"

Bea nodded. "Why was Anathon chosen to be one of the Heaven Stone, especially if he is half human?"

"Again, most is beyond my knowledge. I can tell you that he is an observer of souls. A kind of spiritual warrior, and will do whatever is asked of him to keep the balance of a soul safe, including its karma. It is of the highest priority."

Bea felt a lump form in her throat at the revelation. She was beginning to understand his conflict in loving her. "Ch…Anathon, did tell me of Calageata." The memory of his tenderness, his every touch, as they lay on a carpet of purple flowers, still ached.

"Do you know what Calageata means?"

"No."

"The swan gate," he replied.

"Why is it called that?"

"It is too long a story to tell now, but I can say that our earthly swan originates from their realm. Hence, the reason it is held in such high esteem here. As with the majority of our histories, the tale has become faded over time."

"Anathon told me that some Sidhe visit Calageata, but how can they visit if it is not made of matter, not solid and souls live there?"

"The Sidhe form is different to us humans. Yes, we look the same, but they are able to manipulate non-matter and matter in a way that we cannot. The souls in Calageata are present only when the soul flower emits it mists. All know to leave, or they fall into a deep sleep until the mists clear. Have you seen Seior used?"

"Yes…glamour."

"Ah…The Sidhe mastery of tricking the human eye, quite unfair of them. They bend space, manipulate time."

Jenny knocked on the door. "Sorry to disturb you, Kitty's arrived. Shall I leave the tea in the living room, or give you both a bit longer and bring it in?"

"A moment longer please, if you don't mind?"

"No problem." Jenny smiled and left the room.

"What…what about Sidhe children?" Bea asked.

"Children?" He looked a little bewildered.

"Do they use glamour? I mean, do they have these powers when they're born?" It dawned on her that she might have to later conceal her child.

"Well, of course, but guided by their parents, the teachings are easy to master."

Bea remained quiet. Why hadn't she thought of this before? "What if the child is half-Sidhe and half…*human?*"

She was too scared to look at him, for fear that he might see the reason behind her question.

"I only know of one," he replied.

"Anathon?"

"Yes, and I don't know him well."

"I'm sorry, it must seem like I'm asking the oddest of questions…Is there anything else you can advise me on, that you feel I should know?"

He got up from the chair and walked closer. "Listen to the voice within…it knows the way to your happiness and to the truth."

As Bea looked into his eyes, she saw tenderness, a genuine concern for her welfare that she didn't understand.

Jonathan cleared his throat and looked away.

"Can I tell you something?" She couldn't believe what she was about to say. "It's …embarrassing…difficult."

"Of course." He sat back down.

God what am I doing? she thought, and took a deep breath. "I…I'm pregnant."

A look of shock tightened the fine lines on his face. "Oh, erm…congratulations." The way he overly pronounced congratulations appeared to be more a question.

Bea gulped. "…by Karian." She couldn't look at Jonathan, but heard the leather creak as he shuffled in his chair. She slowly lifted her eyes. "I'm sorry, I don't know what Pos-"

He held up his hand to ease her. "No, please, don't apologise. I…I am…honoured that you feel that you are able to trust me enough to… bear such…such confidences. I… um, does Jenny know?"

"It was Jenny that told me, Deisi thing." She didn't understand why she told him, a stranger, of the one thing she knew that should be kept secret, but something inside told her he was safe.

Jonathan's small frame fidgeted about in the chair. He stood up and cautiously walked over, sitting down beside her. "What are you going to do?"

With him being close, she could smell his aftershave, a woody aroma, similar to what her uncle used to wear. "Hide...run away." She forced a smile but then looked away. His hand trembled as it reached for hers. "If there is anything that I can do? *Anything.*"

"You can tell me that I'm doing the right thing by staying here. That going to the Sidhe realm with a child that is half -Unseelie would be a bad idea."

She saw him gulp. "I cannot advise you, I...I'm not knowledgeable about such things."

"*Please,* tell me honestly, would my child be in danger? You're human and I feel I can trust you."

He blinked his eyes. "The Courts should protect you. The...they would not harm a child."

"Would the baby be accepted, or treated as an outcast?"

He looked surprised. "Do you intend to return to the Sidhe realm?"

Bea knew, even if she wanted to, like she did once, it wasn't an option, not now. "No, but one day my child might."

"The Sidhe do not harm innocents. The child should be safe."

"Thank you, Jonathan. It has been difficult for me to trust anyone lately."

"Who else knows of this, Bethany?"

"Only Jenny, but I want Kitty to know. Jen said they would help me to escape any further Sidhe *attachment.*"

"I see…and…you don't wish Lord Karian to know."

"Or Anathon," she quickly added. "No-one else must know."

"You can be assured that your secret is safe with me."

She squeezed his hand and kissed his cheek. "Thank you for being honest."

"You're welcome…I'm afraid I really must be going. I have a long journey ahead of me, and I fear I have filled your head with enough nonsense. There is quite a bit for you to consider for now, I think."

Bea wished he could stay longer. She wanted to know more about Jonathan, the man who went to live with the Sidhe, and hoped that her secret wasn't the reason that he decided to leave.

Jonathan held out his hand to escort her to the lounge. "You have one more question? I can tell."

She lowered her eyes before asking. "What if your heart feels something, but it's not possible to act on it, or there are things in the way?"

He lifted her face to meet his. "Separate the feelings your *mind* tells you that you're experiencing, and only *feel*. *Nothing* can ever diminish the voice of the heart. It is where your soul resides. All you need do is remain quiet and listen."

"Is that what you did?" Her eyes searched his.

"No… I made the mistake of listening to my mind." He placed her hand in his. "It will be alright, you'll see…I…I wish that I could stay longer, help you more."

"It's me that should thank you for putting up with all of my questions, and er…revelation."

"May I ask one thing of you, Bea?"

"Of course."

"Educate yourself in our histories. It may help guide you on your… journey."

"I will, I promise."

"Look after yourself, Bethany."

"I will, have a safe journey, Jonathan." Bea thought that she saw a deep sadness in his eyes, but before she could say another word, he left the room.

"So where is the human?" Kitty called out before poking her head around the study door.

Bea smiled, strolled over and gave her a big hug. "Oh, I've missed you. Where's Anna?"

"She returned home. This isn't a place a Sidhe would choose to stay if they didn't have to…I should know." Kitty looped her arm in Bea's, leading her through to the lounge. "So, let me fill you in on what happened after you left the farmhouse."

Jenny escorted Jonathan to the front door.

He looked directly at her, keeping his voice low. "Why did you not warn me?"

She had never seen him so perplexed. "What did she tell you?"

"That she is carrying an heir to the Unseelie throne."

"Oh that…It was not my place, I'm sorry, Jonathan…Did you tell her who you were?"

"No, she has too much to contend with." His voice became distant.

"It may have helped." She rested her hand gently upon his shoulder.

"No…It is not the time, she is not ready."

CHAPTER 34

The Plan

*T*hrough the night Bea really laughed for the first time since the farmhouse. Kitty was her usual self, free with speech, and cheeky. Jenny started to open up, too. So much had changed. Jenny the sweet volunteer turned into witch supreme. Kitty, Chance's 'sister' became a good friend, again. She sat admiring the unusual alliances and felt a strange sense of belonging.

Jenny served champagne and another herbal drink for Bea.

"Really?" Bea whinged when handed the drink, then, quickly looked over at Kitty wondering if she'd noticed the difference in beverages, but she was too busy complaining about the champagne being a human type of squash compared to the finesse of Sidhe mead.

"To togetherness." Jenny raised her glass.

"Togetherness," Bea and Kitty echoed.

"Eww…that's disgusting, Jen." Kitty pulled a face of repulsion. "I honestly don't know how you drink the stuff."

"It's a rather expensive vintage, I'll have you know." Jenny defended.

Bea remembered Karian saying something similar on her first visit to the cinema, and resisted a smile.

"No accounting for…no taste." Kitty muttered, sipping more. "Are you alright, Bea? You've gone rather pale."

"I'm fine. The champagne has affected your-" Bea felt a

sudden urge to be sick. "Excuse me." She retched and ran off to the bathroom.

"Too much champers, I told you it's revolting. See, it's not even fit for human consumption."

"She wasn't drinking champagne." Jenny appeared sombre.

Kitty gave her a puzzled look. "What was she drinking?"

They both heard Bea retch again.

Kitty jumped up, Sidhe speed, and ran to the bathroom door. "Hey, you okay? Jenny gave you one of her herbal concoctions didn't she? Nasty things."

"Seriously, I'm alright. I'll be out in a minute," Bea assured between retches.

"What did-" Kitty felt a tugging at her arm.

Jenny placed her finger to her lips. "Shhh."

Kitty frowned. "What are you doing?"

Jenny guided her away from the bathroom door.

Kitty's eyes narrowed. "What's going on?"

"I'm not sure I should say, yet."

"*What?* Tell me."

"Shhh." Jenny gritted her teeth, looking over towards the bathroom.

"What do you mean, shhh? Stop telling me shhh. What's going on?"

"Bea has a sickness…due to…a condition that soon passes." Jenny glared at her stomach.

It took a minute for the message to sink in. Kitty's jaw dropped.

"She's still coming to terms with it. Now, shhh!" Jenny demanded.

Kitty refused to stay quiet. "…It's *Karian's*."

Jenny nodded. "There's more."

"More!" Kitty exclaimed too loudly and immediately covered her mouth with her hand.

"I was unsure at first and haven't mentioned anything to Bea. She gave me permission to tell you that she was pregnant, so, I can also tell you..."

"What?"

Jenny took a deep breath. "She carries a second seed."

Kitty's jaw hit the floor a second time. "Seed? You mean two seeds...twins?"

Jenny nodded. "Although...the other is not Karian's."

Kitty looked confused and started waving her hands around. "What are you talking about? How can it not be Karian's? Is she pregnant by him or not?"

Jenny moved closer. "One is Karian's seed, the other... Anathon's."

Kitty shook her head. "That's not possible."

"It's known as superfecundation."

"Super what?" Kitty couldn't even begin to pronounce the word.

"Superfecundation... seeds that have the same mother but two different fathers."

"No, you're wrong. *How* could that even be possible?" asked Kitty, staring over towards the bathroom incredulously.

"If a woman sleeps with two men within five days of each other it's quite possible. Rare, but possible."

"How do you know that? Well, apart from being a Deisi."

Jenny raised one eyebrow and stared at her.

"I need some mead." Kitty made her way to the kitchen and started searching the cupboards. "Where is it? I know you have some tucked away for mind-blowing occasions such as this."

"Second cupboard, next to the sink." Jenny perched herself on a stool.

Kitty gulped her first glass down with incredible ease and speed. She leant over the table, glass in hand. "Okay, I'm ready...Tell me more, like when you think Bea *should* know."

"Know what?" Bea asked, joining them in the kitchen.

Kitty's eyes widened as she quickly poured more mead, and then sunk her eyes down into the glass, hoping it would provide a place to hide.

"That *Kitty* refused to drink the expensive champers and then hounded me until she found my secret stash of mead. There should be an AA for Sidhe in this realm." Jenny pulled the bottle away, throwing Kitty daggers for being so loud.

Bea laughed. "Jen, let her have the mead, she looks paler than me."

Kitty smirked, swiped the mead from Jenny's hand and wandered off to the living room.

Jenny and Bea rolled their eyes and followed her.

Kitty's face filled with disgust. "Oh, yuck. It's that dreadful fur ball."

"You *mean* Fez," Jenny reminded her, within earshot of the door.

"You should send it back to wherever it crawled out from."

Fez hissed at her and ran off.

Jenny huffed and went in search of him.

"You seem to be drinking an awful lot. Is everything

alright?" Bea asked, remembering their conversation back at the farmhouse, but something was still wrong.

"Never mind me, how are you? The sickness?"

Bea remained silent and Kitty plonked herself on the floor. "Jen told me."

Bea gulped. Her eyes looked around the room, anywhere but at Kitty.

"Talk to me." Kitty patted the space next to her and Bea begrudgingly sat down.

"Do you really want to talk about my pregnancy by an Unseelie?"

She gave Bea an enormous hug. "Hey, you have us."

"I know." Bea forced a smile. "But I can't risk anyone else finding out."

"No-one else has to know." Kitty shrugged.

Jenny stood listening by the doorway. "Bea there's more at work here than you know. It concerns the Unseelie Deisi."

"Cynthia?"

"Yes. She used to be Karian's consort. She helped him escape to this realm, after Alithia passed away...and now that you've taken her place, she's bitter."

"You're saying she might know? Has told Kari?" A panic started to flow through her body.

"No...no, it's actually worse than that."

"Worse? What? How can it be worse?"

"She doesn't want you to have Karian's child. She will do whatever she can to cause the unborn baby harm."

"Cynthia's put a spell on my baby?" Bea stared at her incredulously.

Kitty's face filled with horror. "But she is a Deisi? Sworn to harm none?"

"I know. I wasn't sure at first. There's been so many mixed messages coming through lately, I was unable to understand what they all meant."

"Can you stop the spell? There must be something that *you* can do?" Kitty insisted.

Jenny sighed. "Karian knows something already, but it's not coming through clearly whether its knowledge of the baby."

Bea gasped and placed her hands over her mouth.

"Try harder, Jen," said Kitty.

"I think Cynthia's blocking me." Jenny placed her hands on her temple and closed her eyes.

"You have to do something, and quick." Kitty began to panic.

"It's no easy task, Kitty. It'll take a lot of energy...let me have a minute." Jenny took the bottle of mead and gulped down a mouthful.

Kitty's face dropped. "That was the last of the mead."

Jenny ignored her and started searching through several drawers.

"What are you looking for?" asked Kitty.

"Papers that contain spells...the words of Seior." She grabbed an old book and frantically turned its pages. "Okay, I'm nearly ready. Kitty, get me the tub of salt from the kitchen."

Kitty scurried off and hurried back.

Jenny made two large, unbroken rings of salt on the floor.

Bea and Kitty looked at each other in bewilderment.

"Bea, Kitty, sit in that circle," she ordered.

They did as she instructed.

Jenny sat alone in the other. "You must both stay in the circle. It *must* not be broken. No matter what you see or hear, *stay* in the circle. Got it?"

They both nodded.

"I'm going to need another drink after this." Jenny mumbled, before closing her eyes and took a deep breath.

After a few moments of silence, Kitty's eyes scrutinised Jenny. "She's not doing anything," she whispered.

Bea nudged her in the ribs.

Jenny started to utter words of Se𝑖or, a fragmented, magical speech with a harrowing tone.

After a few minutes, they began to feel a slight breeze in the room. There were no windows open and Jenny had closed the door before they started. Kitty and Bea noticed that the breeze started to move around the room in an odd manner, though it never once entered the rings. Bea snuggled up to Kitty, who'd started to look as nervous as she felt.

Jenny's words became louder and the breeze got stronger. Ornaments started shaking, some falling off pieces of furniture. The curtains bellowed in what now seemed like a mini tornado sweeping across the room. Kitty and Bea froze, eyes wide, as the windows rattled and the chanting got louder, books started to fly across the room.

"I don't like this," Kitty gulped.

They watched, as Jenny started to speak in a different form of Seior. Faster, more aggressive, and in the distance they could still hear Jenny chanting as before. The two chants filled the room.

Slowly, an image started to form outside the circles.

Bea gasped as she saw a re-enactment play out before her eyes of Karian and Cynthia arguing in the bedroom at the theatre. The figures faded in and out as Jenny continued her chant. Suddenly, Cynthia's image floated in the air. A deep crimson, silky fabric covered her body, yet held no true shape. Her fiery, red hair moved eerily around her pale face. She seemed to be looking for something.

Kitty and Bea's mouths gaped open, as Cynthia's green eyes flashed with anger in their direction. Her long talons tried to claw their way past the circumference of the circle. Frustrated at not succeeding, her attentions fled back to Jenny, whose mouth wasn't moving but the chants could still be heard. Cynthia was about to speak, but her eyes flashed bright green, tinting everything in the room and her face twisted in anger, her mouth couldn't open. Her face distorted as she kept trying. Jenny chanted faster and the green light slowly began to fade along with Cynthia's image. The breeze became non-existent, and only one chant of Jenny's could be heard, her lips were moving again.

Bea and Kitty sighed with relief, as the chanting ended. Everything remained still and silent, an un-nervy feeling filled the room. Bea wasn't sure why, but she felt more afraid than before.

After a few minutes of Kitty scanning the room, she spoke, "Jenny... Psst! Jenny, wake up... Cynthia's gone."

Bea nudged Kitty. "What are you doing? Wait until she's ready."

"I'm getting bored." Kitty moaned again after ten minutes. "My bottom's gone numb."

Bea rolled her eyes. "Just wait."

Half an hour had passed. "Something's not right," Kitty muttered.

Bea agreed looking over at Jenny, who was still silent, eyes closed.

Kitty got up.

"What are you doing?"

"Stretching my legs," she replied, while placing one foot out of the circle. Suddenly, she let out an almighty scream and continued to cry out in pain, as her leg was attacked by something unseen. Kitty was being pulled out of the circle. Bea jumped up and pulled her back in. She collapsed on the floor.

"Your foot!" yelled Bea. Blood seeped from deep, raw scratches on Kitty's skin. Bea glanced over at Jenny, whose eyes were now open, but glazed over in white.

Within seconds, Jenny started to chant and Cynthia re-appeared, hovering in front of her, speaking words of Seior. Cynthia turned, smirking at Kitty, lying in agony on the floor.

Jenny stood up, her eyes now a glowing, seething green, which emitted a piercing light upon Cynthia, who cringed at its brightness. Jenny and Cynthia started to speak in the same tongue, evidently a war of Seior power. Cynthia snarled and spat in Jenny's direction, but she could not penetrate the circle. Jenny smiled and then lowered her voice to such a deep tone that Bea felt its vibration penetrate her whole body. Cynthia jerked, and Jenny made several quick movements of her hands. The movements were poised and with every shift of the hand, Bea noticed that her fingers were positioned differently. The systematic hand gestures reminded Bea of

Indian Mudras. Jenny repeated the Mudras while chanting, and Cynthia recoiled upon every one formed. Jenny placed her palms out facing Cynthia and a small green ball of light flared out, racing into Cynthia's chest. In a flash, she vanished. Jenny slumped to the floor.

"Jenny!" Bea cried, running out from the circle.

Kitty looked stunned that Bea wasn't hurt.

"Jenny. Jenny." Bea held her, gently tapping her cheek.

She groaned opening her eyes. "I...I thought I told you both to stay in the circle. You're like children, honestly."

Bea shouted out to Kitty. "She's okay."

"I'm in agreement with you, for once, Jen. Bea, you could've been ripped to pieces." Kitty scolded, still wincing in pain.

Bea helped Jenny to her feet. "Would she really have hurt the baby?"

"Yes. Most of us are bound by certain laws of the Seior, the magic that binds all. If Cynthia was still present, she would've hurt you. You saw a different form of her usual self." Jenny hobbled over to Kitty, with the help of Bea.

"It's nothing but a scratch." Kitty's laugh cut short as soon as Jenny touched the wound.

"I have some healing-"

"I'm not having any of your concoctions, Deisi...Bea, pass my bag." Kitty rummaged around for the blue bottle, but couldn't find it. Her expression looked dismal. "It might have to be the Deisi's concoction after all. I gave my last bottle to Anathon," she grumbled.

"Where is it, Jen?" asked Bea.

Jenny's eyes gestured to a corner of the room. "It's in the top cupboard, middle shelf, orange bottle."

Bea found the bottle and gave it to Jenny.

"She took a good swipe at you, didn't she?" Jenny remarked, while applying some of the cream.

"Ouch! That hurt." complained Kitty. "Be gentle."

"It's your own fault. Whatever possessed you to walk out of the circle during a summoning?"

"Boredom," replied Bea, shaking her head.

Kitty pulled a face and they all burst out laughing, relieved at some normality.

"So, it's all sorted, Cynthia can't harm the baby or speak of the pregnancy?" Kitty awaited confirmation.

"All is corrected," replied Jenny.

The spell casting, and the confrontation with Cynthia had exhausted Jenny, and she went to bed. Kitty hopped into the room to ask her a question, before taking to one of the spare rooms to heal her wounds. "Jen...Jen." She whispered into the darkness, now hobbling by the side of the bed.

"What?" Jenny groaned.

"Jen...*please,* tell Bea that one of the babies is Anathon's. It feels wrong to keep it from her."

Jenny tapped her lamp on. She looked weary. "Oh, Kitty, if only if were that simple, but there's more. When I performed the spell...I...I saw a glimpse of Bea's future."

"Then speak, what is it?"

"I can't, I'm bound by my oath."

"Your oath is to Bea, protecting her. Believe me, lies have been too plentiful, causing nothing but trouble."

"But that's just it, Kitty. I am protecting her."

"How much more could there possibly be that you can't tell?"

"Something that has the power to heal or destroy our race."

Kitty sat on the bed. "Like what? I don't scare easy, Jen."

"We're entering the final phase of an age, Kitty. We all need to build our strength."

By the look in Jenny's eyes, Kitty knew it frightened her. "What have you seen?"

Jenny sighed, placing her hand on Kitty's. "No matter what happens in the future, we have to protect Bea. Agreed?"

Kitty nodded, gulping, too scared to ask anything further.

Bea sat in her room, scribbling away in her journal. Her pen finally ran out of ink. "For heaven's sake," she muttered, grabbing her bag in the hope of finding a replacement. Her searching fingers felt a piece of paper. Inquisitive, she pulled it out of the front flap, and her heart skipped a beat when she saw Chance's handwriting on the outside of a folded note, which simply read, *Bethany*. She quickly shoved the note back in the flap, and sat staring at the bag. *When did he put the note in?* Her stomach turned over, wondering whether to open it. *I could just rip it up, yes, that's what I should do.* But she knew that she didn't have the heart or strength to throw away his words so easily. Didn't she owe it to him to read it? She wondered if this was how he felt, finding her note by the pillow, the morning she left him. Feelings of guilt persuaded her hand to retrieve the note. She slowly ran her fingertips over her name, and hesitantly, unfolded the paper, bracing herself. Inside a poem lay written in the symbols of Lifprasira.

Bethany, the light that you shine
-guided my light to you.
My flame became one with yours . . .eternal.
But now, your light is drifting from view,
-I find myself slowly fading into nothingness.
I watched you falling, your hands reached out
-beyond my grasp.
But know, I am with you in that void
-seeking you, as you are seeking me.
The nadir of nothingness is where the heart goes to die
-and the light that once shone so brightly, fades.
I am lost in the falling
-from which I see no recovery.
Yet, I seek your brightness still. . .
Never let your light fade.
Your dying flame,
Anathon x

Bea held the letter to her chest and wept.

CHAPTER 35

The Agreement

*K*itty had left the house before anyone woke. She needed to see Chance, now everything had changed, and hoped that Saras wouldn't question her too much about events at the house. She hobbled out of her car, grumbling, because she couldn't slip her shoe on her foot, still too painful. She already knew who she would blame for the wounds – *Fez*. She grinned.

When she entered her flat, Saras, Valu and Rigmar were awaiting her arrival. Saras's eyes stared down at her feet as she hobbled in.

"Yes, that beastly creature that I abhor, *Fez*, attacked me, without provocation I may add. Horrid little fur ball."

Valu laughed, but shut up with a glare from Saras.

"A cat?" Saras sounded sceptical.

"A fox, actually. Why on earth the Deisi keeps the vicious thing is beyond me."

"It is obviously her familiar." Saras gave a hint of a smile. "The Deisi use these *vicious* creatures, to assist their Seior. It is the creature that finds the Deisi. You must be careful, dear Kitty, a Deisi's familiar should not be mocked."

She became quietly un-nerved by this new revelation. "I can assure you…this attack was not provoked, in any way."

Saras told Valu to fetch Anathon from his room.

"Why is he in his room?" she asked.

"*His* choice. Sadly, I feel he detests our company, is that correct, Anathon?" His eyes spied Chance entering the room. "How is our Bethany, Kitty?"

"She's well," Kitty muttered.

"Good. Keep her safe. We have new plans since Anathon declared a meeting of Sidhe at Coldfall woods. Very clever of you, Anathon, no doubt you want this to be over as quickly as I. We shall finally meet and the son of King Faryln will be within our grasp. Kitty, send word to Jenny that we will need protection from Karian's Deisi. This Cynthia has given him an escape route before, it will not happen again."

"I'll *ask* her." She pictured Jenny's face at hearing the command. A faint smile appeared upon her lips as she imagined Saras getting green bolts shot at him.

Chance grabbed his jacket.

"Where are you going? Saras's eyes followed him.

"Out," Chance blurted, searching for his car keys.

"You're very droll today, Anathon."

Kitty's eyes narrowed, surprised by Saras's cool response. "Do you want me to come with you?" she asked Chance, hoping for an early escape.

"No." His reply was sharp, and Kitty's hope quickly faded into oblivion.

He headed towards the door where Valu stood. They eyed each other and Chance pushed his way past. Valu's eyes scoured after him.

Chance stopped the car in a side road, near The Mitcham

Castle, where Roel, Kitty's spy, was waiting. He jumped in the car and Chance asked for an update.

"There were a couple of men in suits that I haven't seen before. They came a few days ago. I informed Kitty, she said not to worry, but they carried themselves differently. She told me to just concentrate on Brandon. So, I did."

Chance shook his head. "She didn't send someone to follow them?"

"Not that I'm aware of."

"I'm going to talk to Brandon, stay in the car."

"Want back up?"

"No. Brandon and I have an understanding."

"From what I hear, he hates your guts." Roel replied.

"Then I'm lucky he doesn't mix business with pleasure." Chance grinned, before getting out of the car.

As he entered the pub the chatter lowered, but continued. He almost felt like a local.

"Chance, where yah been?" Brandon bellowed, beckoning him to the bar with the wave of his hand.

As he got closer, Brandon lowered his voice. "We'll talk in the back." He led the way to a small room and sat in an old, decrepit chair, gesturing Chance to take a seat as he lit up a cigar.

"So, apart from Bea keeping company with the Unseelie, what else has been 'appening?" he asked.

"You know about that?"

"Told yah, I'd be keeping an eye out." He took a long pull on his cigar.

"She's not at the theatre anymore."

Brandon nodded. "I know that too. Well done, mate. He looked a bit worse for wear when my blokes saw him."

"When did they see him?" He'd previously warned Brandon to stay clear of the theatre.

"A few nights ago...alone in Coldfall woods, any idea why he'd be there?"

"We're to meet there soon."

Brandon leant forward. "Who?"

"The Sidhe. That's why I'm here."

"Go on."

"After my...encounter with Karian, I suggested that we all meet, to settle matters once and for all."

"Do yah think they'll show up?"

"Karian can't ignore a direct challenge."

Brandon scoffed. "If I'd known...I would've 'ad him sooner." Brandon grinned, piles of smoke escaped his mouth.

"You wouldn't be worthy, in *their* eyes."

Brandon's cocky grin left his lips. "I know we're human, mate, but we've got balls."

"Balls you may have, but they wouldn't last very long." Chance smiled, he was starting to get used to the banter.

Brandon roared with laughter. "So, what do yah want from me?"

"I want your word that you'll protect Bea."

"I told yah, I'll *never* let anything 'appen to 'er. Even that bit of 'er from your world."

"From my world?" Chance wondered what he knew.

"You lot think she's some bird called Alithia?"

"Who told you?"

"Nah, mate, I ain't a snitch."

Chance gathered he meant that he would not reveal his source.

"What else d' yah want?"

"If the Seelie should fall, I want your assurance that you'll take care of things."

Brandon took a pull of his cigar, slowly exhaling the smoke. "Let me get this right. You say that we're no match for your kind, but if you get fucked up, yah want us as back-up?"

Chance nodded, not liking the sound of it much either. "Initially things have to be kept between our kind, but no-one says you can't observe the woods. If the Unseelie win, they get to run the show here."

Brandon's face changed. "I can promise you this…no Sidhe will *ever*…run the show 'ere. Got it?"

"We still have an understanding then?"

Brandon concurred with a nod. "If the Seelie win this meeting what 'appens then?"

"We go home as promised."

"And Bea?"

"She stays." He found the words acrid.

Brandon smiled and held out his hand. "To the understanding."

Chance reciprocated, and gripped Brandon's hand, forcefully. "Look after her."

Brandon winked and squeezed Chance's hand with equivalent force. "Oh, I will."

Back at the car, Roel questioned Chance, but he refused to give anything away, becoming pensive. "Are you ready to go home, Roel?"

"I count the days."

"As do I." Although Chance meant in a different context.

He asked Roel to ring Kitty and arrange a meet. It would be better for Roel to call, the less Saras knew of his plans the better, especially now that Brandon had been updated.

"She said to meet at a place called The Jazz." He typed the postcode into the sat navigator. "I hate these primitive things," he griped. "There, and we'll catch up at Coldfall."

Chance answered with a nod.

On entering The Jazz, a pokey little club with a long bar, he saw Kitty sitting at a small table by the front window. He wandered over and slid in the seat opposite her.

She looked surprised to see him. "Anathon. Where's Roel?"

"I asked him to call you. I didn't want Saras to get suspicious. What's Saras planning?"

"I think you know the answer to that." She slumped back in her chair, as her fingers played with the menu.

"Revenge on Farlyn?" he asked, glancing out the window.

"Yes, and before you say it, I'm fully aware we can't let that happen. *You* need to talk to the Heaven Stone."

"I already have." Chance observed her face.

She looked taken aback. "What did they say?"

"They'll be ready."

"Where did you go to when you left the flat this morning?"

Chance avoided the question. "How's Bea?"

"She's good."

He noticed her looking restless. "The truth?"

She shook her head and rolled her eyes. "I don't know what you expect me to say. Her world's been torn apart, you're disappearing for good. Yeah, she's just dandy."

He knew got up from his seat and stood by the table. "The night at the woods will give her the opportunity to escape us all...for good. Ask Jenny for help."

"What exactly are you saying?" Kitty looked confused.

"The Sidhe's time here is done."

Her mouth dropped open. "The Sindria?"

He nodded, lowering his eyes.

Bea lifted her nose from a book at hearing someone frantically banging on the front door.

"I'm coming!" Jenny cried.

The front door slammed and Bea sat up wondering what was going on. Within seconds Kitty marched in, quickly followed by Jenny. "We all need to talk," she announced, removing her jacket, throwing it on the sofa.

The women gathered around the coffee table.

"Do you really want to start a new life with no Sidhe involvement at all?" Kitty asked Bea.

"No Sidhe?" Bea looked confused. "Why? What's happened?"

"I found out that we will *all* be returning home very soon. Jenny can help make sure it stays that way." Her eyes wandered over to Jenny, who appeared hesitant to agree.

The thought of the Sidhe leaving made Bea a little dismal. Yes, they'd made her life a misery, but she'd also gained two friends.

Kitty continued. "You can sell the bookshop and start somewhere new, just as you wanted. The Sidhe, *no-one* would find you or the baby."

"If the Sidhe return home, who else would I need to avoid?" Bea asked.

"There's been some talk. Men asking questions." Kitty's eyes met Jenny's.

"By men, you mean Humans?" Bea said.

"Yes, and none of us know who they are. You're carrying a *Sidhe* child and have to be extremely careful now."

Bea became edgy. "You're saying we're in danger?"

"It's just best to be careful, at least until we find out who they are. If the Unseelie find out that you are carrying Karian's child...A child in line to the throne, some may want to hunt you down."

"Kitty, you're scaring her." Jenny scorned. "What do you mean, you don't know who these men are? Someone must know. You've never mentioned them before."

"I was informed firstly by Roel, then through another contact of mine, today. These men keep showing up in Sidhe places, asking questions, observing. I found out they'd been seen around the bookshop."

"What were they asking about?" Jenny asked.

Bea wondered why Jenny had not picked up on their presence, but said nothing.

"Mainly about Bea," Kitty replied.

"And they were human?"

"Well, they're not us." Kitty exasperated.

"Your contacts must be mistaken."

"They're not mistaken, Jenny." Kitty insisted.

"It's okay." Bea put her hands up, ending the squabble. "I'll make the necessary arrangements and stay at the shop until I find a buyer."

Jenny placed her hand on Bea's. "You have to do what you *feel* is right, but I would prefer you to stay here."

Kitty nodded in agreement.

Bea shook her head. "I'm going to stay at the shop, for now, anyway." Her whole world was turning upside down, but she was determined to change it her way.

Jenny sighed and sat back in her chair. "So be it."

"Can you seal the portals, Jen?" asked Kitty.

"With Bea's help, but how do we know that Saras hasn't conjured all this up? *The men*? Just to try and get Bea back to our realm?" Jenny replied.

"I met with Anathon." Kitty briefly glanced over at Bea. "He told me that the Heaven Stone would be present, with the *full* backing of the Sindria. Saras will not be able to manipulate this meeting."

"Indeed," Jenny agreed.

Bea broke from her thoughts. "What does that mean?"

"It means you'll be *very* safe," smiled Jenny, obviously brightened by the news.

"How?"

"Just as your mark, your fingerprints, link you to an energy source, so does the Sidhe's. Not only do the Sindria have access their energy's records, they can also call on them. Command them, but only if their behaviour threatens the karmic balance. If Saras has anything untoward planned, the elementals will have full control," Jenny explained.

"I thought they practiced free will?"

"It's a complicated arrangement...It's our will that permits the Sindria that power."

"I have never seen a mark on any of you," Bea said.

"You won't. It's not visible until it's called upon. The mark is similar to the one that you wear around your neck, the seven pointed star, and shows itself in the middle of the breastbone." Jenny's eyes drifted to the little silver star that Bea wore.

Her hand instinctively touched the pendant. "My mother gave this to me."

"Yes. Ellen told me that she would place it around your neck when you turned seven, adding to its power." Jenny replied with a smile.

"That's when I went to live with my uncle. She gave it to me just before we left home."

"It's a form of protection, like a talisman. Any Sidhe seeing the mark of the Sindria on a human would think twice about harming them."

"Chance never told me."

"He probably didn't feel it was important."

"What does the star mean to the Sidhe?" Bea asked.

"It's the star system that they pass through to journey here. You know it as the Pleiades. Whenever the Sidhe miss their home or feel they've lost their way, they look up through the darkness to the light. The stars represent the seven Sindria that gave birth to the first material beings, the Aos Si. They are known as the star of stars, the Amanara. It's what your pendant represents – home."

"You said *their* home, is it not yours too?"

"We've lived with both races so long that both Emerias and Earth feel like home. The Deisi originate from beyond the stars of Orion. So you see, us Deisi can look up and see the light of our true home, too."

"Can you see the stars of Earth from Emerias?" Bea asked.

Jenny placed her arm around Bea. "Light can travel to the furthest of places. We *all* believe that our light can communicate with all other light in the universe, if we're open to receive. In the days of our elders we would light candles to help guide souls home. All light can be used as a form of communication in some way."

Kitty piped up. "Okay, enough talk, where did you hide the other bottles of mead, Jen?"

Bea laughed as they both raced off to the kitchen, but soon broke off, realising how much she would miss them. The time to say goodbye was getting closer and she held her pendant tightly hoping it would help give her the strength to see everything through.

CHAPTER 36

The Parting Gift

Soren was helping Karian slip on his jacket. "My Lord, forgive me for asking, but why risk going *there*, before the meet?"

"I have to leave something for her, Soren." Karian pulled at his cuffs, straightening them.

"I feel it is my duty to inform you that the humans keep a watchful eye. Many Sidhe say that they use Glamour, but these *humans* appear to see through it."

"Yes. However, after our meet, that will not matter."

"My Lord?"

"I intend to meet my Vororbla head on. I no longer wish to be at its mercy." Karian patted him on the back. "Do not fret, Soren. It's time to go…" He headed towards the door but paused. "Soren."

"My Lord."

Karian took a deep breath. "You have served me well. Thank you."

Soren tilted his head. "It is an honour, my duty. May I ask a question?"

"Of course."

"What did the Deisi say?"

Karian stared down the hall. "She predicted my future."

Soren stopped the car outside the bookshop, and opened Karian's door.

"Wait here. I want some time alone."

Soren nodded.

Karian uttered some words and the door of the bookshop flew open, he walked inside. The smell of books and *her essence* was present. He deeply inhaled to savour every memory that the aroma evoked, but quickly exhaled when he picked up Chance's scent. His eyes narrowed and wandered over to the stairs. His jaw tightened as Cynthia's words once again tore through his heart. He composed himself before continuing his stroll to the counter.

He slowly ran his hand over the wood, remembering the time when he gave Bea the invitation to the play. Cynthia was right, he had been a fool. If only he had not been so impatient back then, Bea may not have fallen prey to Anathon, the Seelie, half-human, pretender. In his eyes, Anathon was not a true Heaven Stone warrior. Yes, his fighting skill showed prowess, but taking Bea to bed wasn't how a true Heaven Stone would behave. He should know, his father used to be one. Anathon was an abomination to their race and to the Orders. He flexed his fingers, then curled them into a ball, bringing his fist down onto the counter. The sound of a thud brought Soren running into the shop. Karian held up his other hand to stop his approach, and Soren halted on the spot.

"She is mine…she simply forgot," Karian mumbled. He placed his hand into the inside pocket on his jacket, and pulled out a small, deep-red, fabric-bound book. His fingers pulled at the ribbon bookmark, and the book spread open before him. "Have you heard the poem, 'When we two are parted' by Lord Byron, Soren?"

"No, My Lord."

"You must read it sometime." Karian kissed his fingertips and tenderly placed them over the fragile, pressed, Voror flower, which rested upon the poem's page. He started to read aloud, more for himself than Soren. "The vows are all broken, and light is thy fame…Long, long shall I rue thee too deeply to tell…In silence I grieve, that thy heart could forget…Thy spirit deceive…How should I greet thee? With silence and tears."

"Oh, that was beau'iful mate…just beau'iful!" declared a bellowing voice from the doorway.

Soren charged, Sidhe speed, grabbing hold of Brandon by his neck, dragging him outside. Where Tommy was waiting, gun in hand, and within seconds, he placed it on the back of Soren's head. "Best put 'im down now, mate." He twisted the barrel of the gun down even harder.

Karian casually strolled outside, unamused. "Release him, Soren."

Soren hesitated, his face filled with anger and resentment, but with one deathly glance from his Lord, let go. Brandon cleared his throat, and grinned at Karian. "Never mind, mate. Yah, just weren't 'er type."

Karian wanted to wipe the smirk from his face, but time was limited. It took all his strength to stop from snapping Brandon's neck in just one movement. "Soren." His eyes gestured towards the car and Soren opened the door.

Karian's calm, blue eyes, met Brandon's. "We *will* meet again."

"Oh, you can count on that mate, maybe sooner than you think." Brandon winked, and then looked at Tommy. "Ere, Tom, *if you go down to the woods today, you're sure of a big surprise.*"

Tommy started to hum to the song, moving his gun to the rhythm, impersonating an invisible trombone. Brandon rested against the shop wall, hands in pocket and continued to sing.

Soren started up the car.

Brandon and Tommy burst out laughing as the car drove off.

CHAPTER 37

Coldfall Woods

"*W*ake up…its time."

"Time?" Bea groaned, struggling to open her eyes, but rolled back over to return to sleep.

"The meeting at Coldfall Woods," Jenny announced.

Bea's eyes sprang open. "Today? What, now?" She lifted her head and looked over at the window, it was still dark outside. "What time is it?"

"You don't want to know. It's morning, but not long into it."

Bea grabbed Jenny's hand as she was about to leave. "I'm nervous."

"I promise…there's nothing to be scared of. You'll be safe." Jenny smiled. "Meet you downstairs."

"It's not *me* I'm worried about," she mumbled, as Jenny left the room.

Downstairs in the kitchen, Kitty grumbled. "Why so early?"

"We need the cover of dark. It's when most humans sleep. You're a Sidhe, you should know these things." She shook her head.

"How are you so calm?" Kitty asked.

"Calm? Oh, only the exterior. When was the last time *all* the Sidhe came together in this realm? During your time here?"

Kitty shrugged. "Never."

"Exactly. Has Saras asked you to join him at the woods?"

"No, I'm to stay by Bea's side. Wherever that may be."

"That's a relief."

Bea entered, joining Kitty at the table. "Morning."

"Morning. You ready for this?" Kitty asked.

"Let it be done," Bea grunted, still half asleep.

Jenny handed her a cup of tea. "We have to get there before the others."

"I'm going to start the car, see you both in a minute," Kitty said.

Jenny sat down next to Bea. "Shall I bring you back here, before they all arrive?"

Bea shook her head. "I have to do this. It's a part of moving on, right?"

"Yep, I guess so. I'll meet you in the car."

Bea nodded and waited until Jenny had gone, and let herself quietly grieve.

She lowered her head, resting it on the table. "I don't want *you* to go," she whispered into the wood.

On the journey to Coldfall Woods Bea requested that the radio stayed off. Her normal love of music still hadn't returned. Kitty's eyes kept peering over at the radio. The silence in the car was starting to drive her crazy. Jenny tapped Kitty's creeping hand as it reached for the button.

She retreated her hand and sulked. "I was only going to listen to it quietly."

Once they arrived at the woods, Kitty went to check out the

glade where the meeting was to take place. Bea and Jenny went to uncover the iron pieces that Jenny had buried a few days ago. She explained to Bea, that being a Deisi, she was unaffected by the iron enchanted by Seior.

Jenny and Bea arrived near the clearing and saw Kitty frantically waving her hands, a signal that they were too close, that she could feel the effects of the iron. They dragged the bundle further away, to some brambles, far from the walkways that the Sidhe might use, and Kitty gave the thumbs up.

They re-joined Kitty and stood in the middle of the glade.

"Where are we going to hide?" Bea asked.

"A tree will do," Jenny replied.

"What time is it?" Kitty asked.

"Two o'clock, they'll be here soon," Jenny replied, suddenly tilting her head.

"What's wrong?"

"I thought I felt something…No, it's alright."

Kitty raised her brow. "A Deisi paranoia thing?"

Jenny ignored her.

"What about over there?" Bea pointed to a huge tree. "We can all hide behind that."

"Perfect. Kitty, what way do the Sidhe normally enter?" asked Jenny.

"Over there…I agree that tree is the best situated, let's go." Kitty marched off.

Jenny and Bea followed.

"She seems to have cheered up," remarked Bea.

"She thinks that she's going home," Jenny whispered.

"Isn't she?" Bea's heart sunk.

"No."

"How do you know?"

"Another Deisi thing."

"It's because I'm staying isn't it?" Bea stopped walking.

"We've been elected as your guardians. It's quite an honour."

"I'm so sorry."

"Don't be. Kitty doesn't know her homeland. She thinks she misses it, but this is her home now."

The women made themselves comfortable by the base of the tree and waited.

"They're here," Jenny announced.

Bea felt her stomach turn over.

One by one, the women poked their heads from behind the tree, using the long grass as camouflage. Bea had to remember to breathe, she was so nervous. She saw several figures moving at the entrance to the glade, but it was still too dark to make anyone out. The moon was still present in the sky, but its light was dimmed by dark, drifting clouds.

"You will be safer coming out from the darkness Kitty, Jenny and Bethany. Allow us greet you in the proper manner, as is our custom."

The women all looked at each other in bewilderment on hearing the stranger's voice, too scared to speak.

"We are the Heaven Stone, we will not harm you." The voice did not sound menacing and Jenny was the first to build up the courage to stand.

"I am the Seelie Deisi of Emerias, with whom do I speak?"

Bea stopped Kitty from pulling at Jenny's leg, almost

causing her to trip as she walked out from behind the grass towards the glade. Suddenly, the whole area lit up as several small balls of bluish-white flame floated in the air, and remained suspended. Bea's mouth dropped open in awe.

A black-clothed figure approached Jenny. Bea couldn't see his face, the black hood covered his entire head, and hung in way that formed a type of stiff fabric veil.

"I am Beithir." He bowed, and then spoke a word Bea could not make out. Jenny also bowed, gesturing for them to join her.

Kitty stood up and Bea, gingerly, followed.

The glade was almost as bright as day now, and Bea could see a black figure in every section of the clearing, and hovering above each figure was one of the bluish-white flames. Bea was so distracted by them that she bumped into Kitty, and came to a sudden halt. "Sorry," she whispered, still staring at the flames. The lights reminded her of the old will-o"-the-wisp fable, drawing travellers from safe paths into danger. A shiver ran down Bea's spine. Her nervousness was finally put at ease, when Jenny re-joined her side.

Kitty advanced towards the figure. "I am Kitty, Kitholena of Emerias."

It was the first time Bea had heard Kitty's true name.

"I am Beithir, of the Heaven Stone." His voice then muttered the same word as before. Bea still couldn't make it out.

It was now her turn to stand before the ominous figure. As she moved closer, she could only vaguely see his lips, which remained quite still. Jenny gently prompted her with a nudge, and then Bea realised, he was waiting for her to introduce herself. "Hi...I'm Bethany, Bea of London...of Earth" She pulled a face, feeling embarrassed at the whole palaver. The figure before her dropped to one knee. Startled, she stepped back.

"I am Beithir, of the Heaven Stone. We are all here to serve you Bethany, Bea of London, of Earth." He muttered the strange word, but this time all of the other figures joined in.

Bea looked back at Jenny, who seemed in awe of the whole affair.

Beithir rose to his feet. "Return to your tree, but do not hide in the grasses, it is better to be seen on this morning." He turned away, as more figures started to approach from the darkness.

Jenny nodded in agreement and quickly guided Bea and Kitty back to their spot by the tree.

"What was all that about?" Bea asked, baffled.

"They are bound to protect Eliseis's lineage. *You*, Bea," Jenny replied.

"And who are *they*?" Bea stared past Beithir to the new figures entering the clearing.

It was Kitty who answered. "The Unseelie."

In that moment, she'd forgotten to ask of the word Beithir muttered. Her heart raced as she saw Karian lead the other Unseelie into the glade. He looked calm, maybe a little too calm, thought Bea.

"What do you think Beithir is saying?" Kitty asked.

"He's greeting them," Jenny replied.

"What!" Kitty exclaimed, so loudly that all eyes in the glade briefly, turned towards them.

"Well, so much for our cover!" Jenny glared at Kitty, who shrugged and mouthed 'sorry'.

Bea maneuvered herself behind Jenny, hoping that Karian wouldn't see her. She wished that the flames would diminish and place them in darkness again.

"Look, they're taking their formations. If you want to leave Bea, now's the time to say."

Even though the proposal sounded tempting, she had to know what was going to happen. "No, I prefer to stay." Her eyes drifted back to the Unseelie as they positioned themselves around one half of the glade between The Heaven Stone. The Unseelie did not look as menacing as the hooded figures, but their eyes were intense, edgy.

"Why are they going into formation?" Bea whispered, her hands abreast the tree.

"In preparation," Kitty said.

"Of what?"

"The inevitable…Look, Saras has arrived."

The Seelie were entering the glade, and Saras was proudly leading them.

Bea recognised a few of them from the Bluebell and the farmhouse.

Saras was greeted by Beithir.

Bea turned to Kitty. "Are the Heaven Stone the mediators of the Sidhe?"

"Something like that," replied Kitty, looking distant, now that her Lord was present.

"That depends, Bea," Jenny added.

"On what?"

"The events which take place. Remember, it is all about *balance*. The Heaven Stone will remain neutral, but if any Sidhe break from the traditional rules of conduct, The Heaven Stone become the higher power because they are Sindria warriors...the balance keepers."

"What's with the black clothing?" Bea asked, avoiding any further conversation of what *could* take place.

"It's worn mainly due to its protective qualities. Black repels Seior."

"Why do they keep their faces hidden, don't all the Sidhe know who The Heaven Stone are?"

"They prefer to remain anonymous in battle. The face is not important, to be seen as united, as one, is." Jenny returned her focus to the glade.

The Seelie took their formation opposite the Unseelie. Each half of the ring represented a Sidhe Court, and Beithir remained in the middle. Saras took his place in front of his men, and Karian his. Beithir spoke in the strange tongue and a deathly silence followed, which chilled Bea. "What's going to happen now?" she asked, wondering in what part of the glade Chance was in.

"The Eilada." Kitty's eyes widened.

The atmosphere grew more intense with every second of silence. Bea was sure that her heart made up for the missing drum roll as it pounded in her chest. She couldn't form any words, let alone ask about Eilada. Beithir bent to one knee and the glade roared with the same word that he had previously spoken in their greeting, but now it filled her with dread.

"What does Ameusouya mean?"

"It means, 'the light within me honours the light within you,'" Jenny whispered.

"Oh." Bea's eyes returned to the glade as Saras moved to take Beithir's place in the centre. "What's he doing?" Bea asked, as she saw Saras walk towards Karian.

"Showing his respect." Kitty replied.

Saras and Karian bowed their heads in each other's direction. Saras began to remove his shirt. His skin was as pale as the moon. His long hair shone, like fine threads of yellow silk. He knelt down, as Beithir had done, silence filled the glade.

Jenny whispered, "The Eilada is a dance of the seven Sidhe virtues. The highest rank of the Courts shows his prowess. It's a kind of warning, giving the enemy a chance to surrender. It is where the humans' old chivalric code originates."

"That's not going to happen, is it?" Bea knew the Sidhe were too proud, vain. "And so it begins..." Bea tried to gulp, but her mouth was too dry.

A bright light suddenly erupted from where Saras was kneeling, and as it faded he drew a long, thin sword from the ground. He flipped into the air, sword in hand, spun and landed steady on his feet. His hands then played with the sword, swaying it from one hand to the other. The twists and turns of his blade were so artful, swift, that Bea found it difficult to keep her eyes focused on it.

Saras ran towards the Unseelie, somersaulted through the air, and landed about a foot away from them. Not one of the Unseelie moved as he continued his dance.

It's Saras's moment to shine, thought Bea, hating every minute.

He ran up the trunk of a tree, hovered there for a moment, before springing into a triple somersault and landing by Karian's feet. Saras lowered his head as he bent his knee to the ground. Only then did Bea notice the symbols of Lifprasira, glinting on the sword in the moonlight. It was beautiful.

"He's challenging Karian," Jenny warned.

"What?" Bea gasped.

An Unseelie suddenly leapt over Saras, appearing just as skilled in his manoeuvres. Bea instantly recognised him, it was Soren. She had thought him terrifying enough as Karian's driver.

"Karian is permitted to have someone to fight in his stead. The challenger, Saras, has to prove he's worthy of challenging a Sidhe of royal blood." Jenny explained.

Bea felt a tinge of relief that Karian did not have to fight the well trained Saras. Her eyes quickly refocused.

The two Sidhe now stood opposite each other, in a stance, ready to strike. A smirk appeared on Soren's face as he drew his sword, it was wider, darker, Bea knew, just as deadly. Each Sidhe ran towards the other, leaping into the air. Their swords clashed and Saras made one more swipe, before landing back on the ground. Soren looked down at his slashed shirt, growled and charged again. This time they kept their dance to the ground. They moved with grace and finesse, reminding Bea of shaolin monks, but the Sidhe being much faster, more agile. She felt dizzy trying to keep up with their speed. Saras and Soren dived and bounded all over the glade, their swords clashed and swayed until all of sudden, the movement stopped. Soren slumped to the ground, and unrest came from the Unseelie Court. Saras strolled over to the jittering bundle on the ground, and without mercy, drove his sword straight through Soren's chest while staring at Karian.

Bea tried to fight the sickness rising from the pit of her stomach, but the imagery would not permit and she gagged, turning away to vomit. Everyone shouted Ameusouya, and yelled it once more, but this time she was sure it was only the Seelie that could be heard.

"Is the slaughter done?" Bea retched.

"For now, Saras is busy preening," Jenny replied.

Bea turned around and saw Saras with his blood-stained sword, strutting in front of a seething Karian. "Why doesn't anyone tell him to stop now?" asked Bea. Fear spread through her body as a wild, biting storm.

"He is the victor. They have to wait, until he is ready."

Bea was sure she heard a sense of pride in Kitty's voice. "Ready for what?"

"To challenge Karian, of course." Kitty stated, as if it were obvious.

"I thought the fighting was done?" Bea glanced over at Karian, whose eyes burned with blue flickers of light in Saras's direction. "You have to stop it…Kitty, Jenny?" She couldn't believe everyone was just waiting for the fight to happen. She felt sick.

"We can't," replied Kitty with seemingly no remorse.

"Jenny?" Bea could hear the desperation in her own voice, and hoped Jenny might use her Deisi influence to diffuse the situation.

"It is a Sidhe matter. There is no imbalance. I cannot interfere." Jenny replied.

Bea's heart sank, as Saras knelt before Karian. *Please god, no*, she pleaded in silence. Her mouth trembled as she fought back the overwhelming emotion of losing him. She'd already seen Saras's display of fighting skills, and remembered her conversation with Jonathan concerning Karian not having any Heaven Stone training, unlike Chance. Her heart pounded in her chest. She didn't know what emotion to conquer first, the barbarity of it all, the compulsion of wanting to run to him, or facing the fear of possibly never seeing him again. *Is it me or Alithia feeling this?* Her mind raced as Saras remained kneeling, but Karian spun through the air over him, and landed steady, maintaining his stance. Saras got to his feet. A smug look of contentment filled his face as he casually began to taunt Karian with the blood on his sword.

"He's trying to get Karian to lose control." Kitty mumbled.

Bea wasn't sure if she could continue to be a spectator for much longer.

"Yes, hoping he'll become more vulnerable." Jenny replied, but then looked at Bea. "But Karian is a skilled swordsman, apparently his father taught him. Don't lose hope."

Bea's head swarmed with questions as Saras continued with his jibes. *Do I want Karian more? After all, he's the father of my unborn child.* She forced the daunting prospect from her mind, as she watched another war dance begin.

Karian stepped back, throwing his sword into the base of a tree trunk and leapt into a series of backflips, avoiding the lunge of Saras's sweeping sword. Karian leapt into the air, grabbed his sword and propelled himself from the tree, flying by Saras, catching his arm with the blade. Saras's eyes became an electrified blue at its sting.

There were some mutters from the Seelie formation.

Karian rolled over the grass and crouched on one knee, a slight grin appeared on his lips as he waited. His eyes electrified in waves of flashing blue.

Saras flexed his limbs, his head bobbed from side to side, and slowly he twisted his sword repeatedly in his hands. The spinning movement hastened. His wrists began to move in such a way that all Bea could see was a whirling wheel of silver metal, spinning incredibly fast from one hand to the other. Her heart skipped as Saras charged, sword in hand, yet Karian remained still.

Move! Bea silently cried out …*Move!* Her heart stopped as Saras suddenly leapt in the air, his sword held below him, thrashing out in Karian's direction.

Move! Bea silently screamed, and in the very last seconds of Saras's descent, Karian flipped and rolled to the side, leaving Saras surrounded by emptiness.

"I can't take this." Bea blurted, "He's hurt."

Jenny looked confused. "Saras?"

"No, Karian, look."

Jenny glanced over at Karian.

Bea's eyes filled with fear. He had landed unsuccessfully after the deflection. Something was wrong with his foot and his leg buckled beneath him. As he lay trying to reach his sword, Saras leaped in for the kill.

"Nooooo!" Bea yelled.

Saras turned and paused, looking incredulous as Bea started running towards them. Jenny chased her and held her back. Kitty, Sidhe speed, stood in front of them, and from that moment, everything became chaos.

The Unseelie lunged towards Saras, but The Heaven

Stone intercepted the attacks. Then the Seelie leapt towards the Unseelie, swords and punches flew from every angle.

Jenny started to chant as she watched the onslaught.

Saras had broken free of his Unseelie attackers and headed towards Karian, who was now on his feet, limping.

Bea's eyes widened as a Heaven Stone intercepted Saras's sword as it was about to come down on Karian. Saras and The Heaven Stone figure circled each other.

"Chance."

"What?" Kitty said.

"The Heaven Stone fighting Saras…is Chance."

Kitty looked back towards the Sidhe. "Bea, stay here." She ran out into the glade.

Jenny had stopped chanting. "Bea, we should leave now."

"I'm not going anywhere."

"You have to think about the baby." Jenny grabbed her arm.

"I am thinking about the baby." She tried to pull away, but Jenny wouldn't loosen her grip. "Jenny, let go."

"Bea, look out there…What are you going to do?"

Her eyes turned to the glade. "I'm sorry Jen." Bea suddenly yanked free from Jenny's grip and started to run. As she entered the glade, she managed to slip between two warring Sidhes and almost reach Kitty, until a sword came flying through the air, aimed directly at her. Karian leapt into the air, to obviously try and stop the sword's momentum, but a Seelie attacked him. Bea closed her eyes ready for the impending blow. There was a loud clash, and straight after, a voice whispered near her ear. "Your light still shines bright."

Chance…Bea remembered to breathe as her eyes met his.

"*His* light still shines too," he muttered, eyes glaring briefly in the direction of Karian.

Kitty now stood beside them, unscathed.

"Get her out of here!" Chance yelled, his eyes now the same colour as the Sidhe surrounding them, a glowing, howling blue. Bea's heart ached as he sped away, re-joining the other Heaven Stone. His comment seemed to be an admittance of his withdraw, as if his affections had waned, reminding her of when he had disappeared before. *He always walks away,* she thought.

"We have to go," Kitty said.

Bea's eyes suddenly widened, as she saw Saras and his men being held at bay by a crowd of Unseelie trying to protect Karian, who now lay crippled on the floor in pain. Blood was streaming from his ankle.

"He's hurt!" cried Bea.

Kitty's eyes followed hers. She gasped. "That wasn't caused by a Sidhe, it's a bullet wound!" She stared out into the woods, swaying the sword out in front of her. "Bea, we have to leave. NOW!"

Bea refused to move. "Look!"

The Heaven Stone were divided. Chance stood ready to defend Karian against Saras, but some of The Heaven Stone had joined Saras's side as more and more Unseelie tried get their Lord free of the glade.

"We have to do some-" Out of the corner of her eye, Bea saw an Unseelie dive towards them, sword gleaming. Kitty pushed Bea out of the way as he lunged. He knocked the blade from her hand, and it spun through the air. Kitty frantically looked for something to defend herself with, but no weapons were near on the ground. Flustered, she picked up a small branch and gulped as the attacker continued his advance. Within seconds of the Unseelie swinging for her, she flipped over him, grabbed his head from behind, and stabbed him in the eye with the branch. He dropped to his knees screaming, and she stood staring in disbelief at what she had done. Suddenly, a Seelie glided past on his knees, and swept the injured Sidhe's head straight off, and it tumbled to the ground. Kitty stood frozen as the Unseelie's blood sprayed over everything in it's immediate vicinity, including her. Her Seelie saviour winked, and then started his attack on another Unseelie.

Kitty turned to grab Bea, but she had gone. Her eyes scoured the glade where she saw Jenny ducking and diving, shooting bolts of green-sphered lights protecting herself and Bea, who was running towards a crowd of Seelie, approaching Karian.

After retrieving a sword, Kitty joined Chance, Sidhe speed. Even with The Heaven Stone, the fight was in Seelie favour, and she was quickly faced with fighting a member of her own Court. Chance protectively stood in front of her. "THIS STOPS NOW!" he shouted, and a few Seelie backed off, but Saras and his men continued their advance behind them.

Kitty tugged Chance's top to ask him what to do, but his stance gave her the reply she needed.

Meanwhile, Bea weaved her way past the onslaught of Seelie, when she suddenly stopped. Jenny caught up with her, and was about to pull her to safety, when they both saw Karian surrounded. They watched stunned, as he slowly extended his arms outwards, balancing the hilt of his sword between the tips of his two fingers, in what seemed to be a gesture of surrender. His surging blue eyes met Bea's from a distance, and he widened the space between his fingers, letting the sword fall, waiting for the Seelie onslaught. Suddenly, a sword pierced Karian's side, and blood spurted out in a gush.

"Noooo!" screamed Bea, running towards him.

He fell to his knees and Saras's men dived in for the kill, a mad pack of frenzied dogs.

Bea kept yelling out, but her cry could not be heard through the warring Sidhe.

Jenny ran after her, glancing over at Chance and Kitty, but they were still engaged in their own fight.

Bea fought through the crowd that kicked and punched Karian's body, which lay lifeless on the ground. She had managed to dodge the blows, and was prepared to use her body to shield Karian from any further harm. The Seelie in the perimeter, instantly backed off, and the Heaven Stone warriors were by her side in a flash, including Chance, who stood, eyes wide at Bea.

Valu also retreated, lowering his sword, and stood by Chance. "No-one will care of your...*indiscretion*, not now Alithia has publically shown that she's a traitor." In an instant, Valu dropped to the ground. Everyone turned around. Valu glared at Chance while rubbing his jaw, but didn't say another word. Beithir eyed Chance and grinned before offering Valu a helping hand up. Chance knew he had seen the swift blow of his elbow connect with Valu's chin, and the look given, was one of silent approval.

"Nooo...*don't die.*" Bea cried, as she knelt down, gently

placing Karian's head on her lap. Her fingers brushed over his cut mouth. "Don't leave…Please, wake up. I'm here." Her hand felt sticky, and she tried to wipe it clean on her jeans, but everything, including the grass was smothered red where he lay. The warm dampness of fresh blood seeped from his body, through her clothes, onto her skin. "Noooo…" She sobbed, lowering her head onto his.

Jenny crept by her side and whispered. "Bea, close your eyes, now."

On closing her eyes…all of the surrounding noise suddenly stopped. The snarling, the painful cries, the yelling, the clashing of sword upon sword, every sound ceased. Bea waited a few seconds before lifting her head and opening her eyes. All of the Sidhe, apart from The Heaven Stone were totally still. "Karian?" Bea gasped, as a bright light appeared on his chest. She looked around the glade, the Sidhe were all facing the same direction, and each had a symbol just like Karian's, a star, shining brightly from their chests, too. The light from the illuminated symbols appeared to all join at a certain point in the clearing. Bea placed her hand above her eyes to protect them from the glare. "What's happening Jenny?"

"It's the elemental form of the Aos Si, the Sindria… they've come to take the Sidhe home. What you see is the light of the stars Amanara, which readily meets the flame of the portals." Jenny pointed to the far end of the glade.

Bea saw a ring, formed by blue flames, and as the flames started to fade, an outline of several female figures descended. She squinted at their brightness.

The women were semi-transparent, extremely pale-skinned. The only comparison she could think of was that of an ethereal Albino, breathtakingly beautiful. They were slender with long hair of pure white, and their eyes a translucent mix of purple and blue hues. Their unearthly figures were draped in flowing, thin, white, Grecian-type gowns, and as they moved, silver threads glistened within the fabric. They seemed to glide, not walk, across the glade, and grew more opaque the closer they got.

"They look like angels." Bea said.

Jenny kept her voice low. "Yes...with no need for wings."

The Sindria crossed the grass and approached the Sidhe bearing the star-shaped marks on their chests. They gently placed a long, slender finger upon each Sidhe in turn, and when touched, they started to walk into the several, newly-formed, flaming circles that had now appeared within the glade. The lights of each mark faded as the Sidhe entered the rings.

"Doesn't it burn?" Bea asked, holding Karian's hand in case they tried to make him leave too.

"No, it's a flame of energy, not heat." Jenny replied.

"So, they're returning home?"

"Yes, where they belong." Jenny's eyes briefly looked down at Karian.

Bea noticed the Heaven Stone warriors were back in position, in a circle formation around the glade. Not one of them bore the Sindria mark. Why? *And where is Chance?* she wondered.

Once all of the Sidhe had entered the rings of flame, the Sindria spoke in their own tongue to The Heaven Stone, who proceeded to carry the bodies of the dead into the largest of the portals. Bea's eyes welled as she listened to the chiming, melodic voices of the Sindria elementals. The same sound that she had heard on her visual meditation to Calageata, the little piece of heaven that Chance had shown her. It filled her whole being with an incredible sense of loss, knowing that even though she loved them both, a choice had to be made.

The Heaven Stone and the Sindria lowered their heads in Bea's direction, and then retreated to the rings. The hovering blue flames that had given light to the glade started to rise up and disappear in the early morning sky. Bea watched the last of the Sindria speak with one remaining Heaven Stone, outside a ring. The dark figure turned and began to approach her, and without seeing his face, she knew it was Chance. Her whole body suddenly felt weak, deflating in strength as the Heaven Stone knelt down next to her. He slowly removed his hood, and placed his hand over hers. "He'll be alright."

Bea's eyes glistened as they Chance's. What was the point in telling him that she loved him, needed him, too? She was carrying Karian's child. The guilt and sickness churned over in the pit of her stomach, making her turn away.

He gently stroked her cheek, guiding her eyes back to his. "There's something I need to tell you…I couldn't speak freely of it before, but know I wanted to every day…*I love you,* Bethany."

Please, don't say anymore, she screamed in silence, *not now… not ever.*

He sat in silence, and she knew he was waiting, hoping that she would say the words, 'I love you' in return, but nothing came. His eyes welled, and he lowered his head as she slowly pulled her hand away. Bea felt an unbearable eruption of pain spread throughout her chest at the loss of his touch. *Please, give me the strength to let him go,* she pleaded to the turmoil inside her.

Chance reached out to touch her face, but as his hand was about to come into contact, he withdrew, clenching his hand into a ball. "I don't expect you to forgive me, but I..." He broke off, staring out into the glade. "*Know...*that I hold your hand in mine...*Remember?* Even when you are unable to see it."

Tears rolled down her cheeks. She couldn't speak, too angry at herself, for letting him see the inner despair eating away at her heart. Hearing him speak the words she'd longed to hear, caused every protective wall inside her body to shudder. *Don't break.*

"Keep your light bright." Chance's voice became faint as he began to make his way back to the last of the Sindria portals. Bea's fingers clenched at the long blades of grass beneath her hand, squeezing, pulling, until clumps become loose from the soil. The sound of the grass being ripped from its life force expressed the inner torture of her scream...*I will not break!*

Jenny's hand rested gently on Bea's, and she instantly released the grass, tightly gripping Jenny's hand, scared that if she let go, the voice inside would scream out to him.

The last of the Sindria glided over the glade to join them. Jenny bowed and moved aside, gently releasing Bea's hand, and as she did, the elemental took her place. Bea looked into the Sindria's eyes. The varying reflecting hues of blues and purples moved as drifting nebulas across a dark sky, brought alive by millions of sparkling stars. It was mesmeric and filled her with such a feeling of tranquillity that she almost forgot all of the turmoil within.

The Sindria smiled and then looked down at Karian, immediately breaking the spellbinding stare that had brought Bea a brief moment of peace. The Sindria reached out, touched the centre of Karian's chest, and the light of the star, faded, Bea's heart sank as it dimmed, until his eyes started to flicker beneath the lids. His eyes opened, widening at the sight of the elemental hovering over him. "I will wait by the ring, so that we may go home together. It is time, Prince Karian." The Sindria turned to Bea and placed her slender hand on her belly. "Do not fear the unknown Bethany, for every unknown has the potential to become a wonderful new beginning. There is always a raging storm before the brightest of days." She placed Karian's hand on Bea's and bowed, retreating as elegantly as she came.

Tears flowed freely down Bea's face as she looked over at Chance, and then back down at Karian. She gasped, "You're healing!" His wounds started to clear before her eyes. Karian struggled to get up. She tried to help him, but he shook his head, and forced himself up with sheer pride and determination. He rested his forehead gently on hers. "It matters not to me that you carry his child...I still love you. Nothing will ever change the feelings I have for you...We *will* meet again."

Bea's mouth shuddered with a silent sob as she ran her finger around his face, down his nose and over his lips. "It's your child that I carry, Kari." She felt his whole body shake at the words.

"But, Cynthia...she...she said the child was not mine." His voice trembled as he spoke.

She saw the fear of daring to believe. She took his hand, placing it on her belly and shook her head. "She lied." Tears glazed his blue eyes. His lips quivered, as his mouth suddenly met hers. They moved with a mix of apprehension and need. Everything began to fade away, everything, but him.

Kitty looked over her shoulder at Anathon, then back at Jenny. "Do something, Jen."

Although she heard the desperation in Kitty's voice, and could feel Chance's pain, there was nothing that she could do. "I can't interfere, it's their Vororbla."

Kitty kept her voice low. "But she's carrying Anathon's child, too."

"Yes, but everything has a time and place Kitty."

"How can Bea make a choice if she doesn't know the whole truth? I would hardly call that balance?"

Jenny sighed, and glanced over at the Sindria. "I told you, there is so much more that you can't see or even begin to understand. I'm sorry, but I won't interfere."

Chance stood outside the last portal, struggling with every atom in his body to keep his feet planted on the ground. He wanted to run and rip Karian's head from his shoulders. He stepped forward, but the Sindria glided in front of him, and rested her hand on his chest. He tried to step around her, but froze as a white light emanated from the Sindria's palm, creating an aura around him. "This light…is within us all. Now is not your time to shine, Anathon, but know that true love is *timeless*."

He looked into her eyes and, by doing so, his anger

dissipated. "Why was I sent here?" He struggled to comprehend his purpose. "What is the point of all this pain?"

"Who do you see in the glade, Anathon? Open yourself to the training. See through the light and the image it casts."

He took a deep breath and forced himself to look over at the woman he loved embraced by another. He had to fight every ounce of crushing pain, churning inside him. It was hard to focus on using his inner power over such anguish, but with the energy of the Sindria pumping through him, everything became clearer. As he focused, it was not Bea's image of light in the glade, but Alithia's. His heart permitted him to breathe its deepest breath...one of relief.

The Sindria slowly removed her hand from his chest and he saw only Bea again, and looked away.

"Trust the self, not the mind. She will need you sooner than you think."

"How?" He turned to the Sindria confused. "He has won."

The Sindria shook her head. "He has seen *Bea's* Vororbla."

"I don't understand...how?"

The Sindria took his hand in hers, and gently placed her fingertips on his. "Like this."

On her touch, he saw a hazy vision of two figures lying on a carpet of purple flowers, but as he reached out, the image disappeared, and before he could ask if what he saw was the past or the future, the Sindria glided away. She stood waiting by the last ring as it began to spark with blue flickers of light. The soft chime of her voice echoed through the clearing. "It is time, Anathon of The Heaven Stone." She then beckoned Karian to join her.

Karian kissed Bea's ear and whispered. "Come home…Come home with me."

Tears filled her eyes, as they met with Chance's, beyond Karian. She lowered her stare as he stepped into the ring, and never saw the flames engulf him, but heard his cry of parting. "Keep your light, Bethany." She closed her eyes to hide the effect that the sound had on her.

"I know that you are still running…just let go, for us, for our child." Karian placed his hands on her belly. "*Please,* come home. I will never walk away…*Ever.*"

She opened her eyes, believing his promise. The words resonated with her more than he knew. His love had never faltered, even after Alithia's death. She knew that he would always fight for her and the baby, but how could she leave without saying goodbye to Liza. Many thoughts passed through her mind until she saw the Sindria nod once in Kitty's direction. "Yes!" She beamed, jumping in the air. "I'm going home, Jen!"

Jenny smiled as Kitty skipped her way. "I still have things to do here. Take care of yourself, okay?"

Bea pulled away from Karian, and ran over to Kitty. "I'll miss you so much, my Seelie friend."

"You should come with me." Kitty grinned. "Imagine the fun we'll have."

"Remember what I told you about looking up at the stars. Neither one of us is ever too far from home." Jenny reminded.

The three women stood in a brief embrace savouring their friendship in silent goodbyes.

The Sindria's soft voice reminded Kitty that it was time to leave.

Karian joined them and kissed Jenny's hand. "Take care of yourself, Seelie Deisi."

"You too...*Unseelie*. You had best go. It's getting light."

Kitty was the first to enter the ring, everyone could see the wide grin on her face, which sat so perfectly, almost ear to ear. The flames rose and within minutes, Kitty had gone.

Karian tilted his head paying respect to the Sindria, and then placed one foot in the ring. He paused, turned and extended his hand inviting Bea in. "*Please*...let me be a father to our child...*I beg you.*"

The sparks of the portal became more frequent and she felt torn. Her hands subconsciously went to her belly as his plea echoed in her mind. She saw the old fears return in Karian's eyes and she a felt terrible guilt tug at her heart. She didn't know what to do and looked back at Jenny, who shrugged, and shooed her to enter. Bea took a deep breath before accepting his outreached hand.

Bea stared back out into her world from the circular portal, everything outside had slowed down. Her heart started to race as sparks outside the ring turned violet. She suddenly became encapsulated by a nervous excitement. The fine hair all over her body began to stand on end as a new strength, a new empowerment began to fill every part of her – clarity. She had permitted herself to finally let go of her fears, and in letting go, she realised what she had forgotten. It became clearer with each new spark combining around her. In all this time she needed to love herself, learn to trust, believe in her choices. To not feel guilty about leaving the past behind, and to embrace each opportunity that came her way. Maybe the presence of the Sindria, their soothing, magical presence, had helped her recognise and release the fears she'd carried within for so long. The type of fear that lurks behind each excuse, I can't, I shouldn't, was replaced with *I can* and *I will*. Bea's fears of rejection had led her to believe that she was not worthy of love, and in turn caused her to hide from life, rather than experience it. The pain and the joy she now realised were only growth.

She felt Karian's arms lovingly wrap around her. He could not see the tears welling in her eyes. Through the glistening droplets, she looked out into her world, Earth, which appeared more beautiful than ever now that she was free of her fears. It seemed that with every cloud that was clearing, it was actually her fogginess dispersing. Her eyes drifted to the leaves on the trees, moving much slower than nature intended, and on looking up at the sky, she saw a bird in flight, yet, its wings hardly moved. Bea became mesmerized, until she heard what sounded like a thousand bees, buzzing. Karian tenderly kissed her temple, and held her tighter as the blue sparks of the portal began to turn into spinning rings of white and blue light around them. Everything had become a whirling, whizzing blur, and in the surrounding strangeness, she heard a whisper by her ear. "I love you." Karian nestled his face to her neck. "You're finally coming home."

It took all of Bea's newly found strength to enable her to pull away. She shook her head. "I'm sorry, Karian, I'm not Alithia…" Bea saw his face fill with shock and despair as she broke away, jumping from the ring, and before he had time to react; the blue flames of the portal rose and engulfed him.

Bea placed her hands over her belly, closed her eyes, and softly whispered, "This is our new beginning."

~ *The End* ~

Tracey-anne lives in south London with her family. With a background in charity work, she loves the diversity of working in a big city, but enjoys her work as a mixed media artist. Certified to teach, her world is filled with various forms of creativity. Her qualifications include Specialized Paint Techniques and Surface Design. Tracey-anne has exhibited art dolls in a Canadian gallery and has been published in various US magazines.

Her active imagination, mixed with a love of folklore and the old mysteries, inspired her to write a fictional story revolving around love and karma, blending reality with fantasy. Her novel *'A Carpet of Purple Flowers'* is synchronicity of a debut writer's mind with an artistic heart.

Urbane Publications is dedicated to
developing new author voices, and publishing
fiction and non-fiction that challenges, thrills and
fascinates.
From page-turning novels to innovative
reference books, our goal is to publish what
YOU want to read.

Find out more at
urbanepublications.com